An Annie Ogden Mystery

BY FREDERICK LEE BROOKE

Copyright (c) 2012 by Frederick Lee Brooke
www.frederickleebrooke.com
All rights reserved.
ISBN: 0615469493
ISBN-13: 9780615469492

This book is a work of fiction. The names, characters, places and incidents are products of the author's imagination or have been used fictitiously and are not to be construed as real. Any resemblance to actual persons, living or dead, or actual organizations, is entirely coincidental.

All rights reserved. No part of this book may be copied, re-transmitted or reproduced in any manner without express written consent of the author.

for Maria Luisa

*and in memoriam
David Foster Wallace*

Contents

1. End of a dream — 1
2. Lost GPS — 13
3. Family loyalty — 23
4. Mirages — 29
5. Hunting — 37
6. Betrayal — 45
7. Misunderstanding — 55
8. Collection — 59
9. Pickup — 63
10. Trigger — 75
11. Your mother — 85
12. Ginger — 95
13. Used phones — 99
14. Dante — 107
15. Ten dozen roses — 111
16. Indiana run — 121
17. Night visions — 135
18. Ten miles out — 139
19. Ancient creature — 143
20. Doing Max Vinyl — 145
21. New job — 149
22. Briefs — 161
23. Totaled — 169
24. Thinkpad — 187
25. Lance — 193
26. TRS Without I — 203
27. Olson — 219
28. Car Collection — 225
29. Furey — 231
30. Home Invasion — 245
31. Bonfire — 257
32. Witness — 265
33. Dork — 281

34. Broken Heart	283
35. Natural Causes	293
36. Tent	297
37. Ancient Rhythms	311
38. Forest Ranger	315
39. Offer	323
40. War	327
41. Server Room	333
42. C	339
43. Lawyers	343
44. Handcuff	347
45. Conestoga Carving	355
46. Seven Years	363
47. Sisters	371
48. Abacus	387
49. Bounced	391
50. Prairie Fire	399
51. Sexy	405
52. Timothy	415
53. Wet Drop	437
54. Barge Fight	439
55. Car Heaven	449
56. Shoreview	453

END OF A DREAM

On that Monday in early June, when it all started, Max Vinyl cashed in three million dollars and then let the girl of his dreams slip away, in that order, all in the space of thirty minutes. Though it was now just past ten in the morning, the humid North Suburban air was already uncomfortably warm. They had forecast a heat wave for this week, and there wasn't a cloud in the sky as he came back in from the parking lot, his loafers crunching on the gravel. He had gone out to watch her drive away, not believing it was happening, not believing Tris Berrymore could be taking off, not believing she had just said the things that still rang in his ears.

Not that he was some kind of dreamer. Dreamers didn't get far in business. Still, looking back, he would have forfeited the whole three million if only Tris had stayed. Like most troubles it wasn't that simple. You couldn't just trade off one for the other. Plus the trouble didn't end with her leaving. Her leaving was just the start of it. But he only realized that later, with the water up to his chest and the lights in his eyes and some giant creature from the deep bearing down on him, just under the surface of the water . . .

The problems had started in the late morning. The Koreans had left. Now Manny Rodriguez, his general manager, sat across from him. Rodriguez had cornered him in reception and demanded a meeting in Max's office. Christ, they should be out on the packing room floor uncorking champagne with the staff, but Rodriguez had something on his chest, something that couldn't wait.

"We're sitting in there dicking around with the Koreans. You know what *she* was doing?" Rodriguez's eyes flashed. He was always irritated about something. He had red streaks across his cheeks, as if he had been clawing at himself.

Max Vinyl would normally be unmoved by these signs of emotional upset in one of his managers, but Rodriguez was talking about Tris Berrymore. He felt the juices churning in his stomach. "What?"

"She made a file on her PC. And you know what it shows? She's comparing the number of containers going to the Koreans with the number going to recycling."

"Shit."

"You can say that again."

"But why?"

"Fucking tree-hugger, Max. I tried to tell you a hundred times. You never should've made me hire that one. Well, I caught her red-handed. I took the matter into my own hands."

A minute ago, striding into his office, he had thrown open the door, still giddy from his three-million-dollar payday. Now the lightheaded feeling was draining out of him like the last water going out of a tub. "Wait a minute, Manny, hold on. What do you mean you took it into your own hands?"

"I canned her. What else would you do? Next thing you know she'll be on the phone to the *Tribune*."

Max stood up. His chair rolled back and banged into the wall. He felt the heat rising in his neck. His breathing was audible. But he locked his gaze on the general manager's eyes and stuck out a finger for emphasis. "I got news for you. You don't fire Tris. Now go straight back and talk to her."

Rodriguez bounced to his feet. "She'll ruin us, Max. I can see it now. That's what the bitch came here for. Well, I'm not letting it happen. She's packing up her stuff. I've got security standing over her."

"I don't believe this. First we land the Koreans. They come here with their helicopter, their limos, their armed bodyguards. They walk in here like they own the place. They do own it, now, at least a part of it. They're forking over for twenty percent of this company, Manny. Do you understand that? Three million bucks. We took it to the next level. And you fire Tris."

"It's precisely *because* of the deal that we have to do it. Do you want to risk having the Koreans see some *environmental* story in the newspaper? You think they wouldn't find out about something like that? You're totally underestimating this threat."

"Since when did Tris become an environmentalist, anyway?"

"She joined the World Wildlife Fund at age twelve, Max. I did some checking."

He was so angry he couldn't see straight. He sank back into his chair, whipsawed between the highs and the lows. The problem was that Rodriguez was probably right. If the wrong information got out, maybe into the hands of some environmentalist journalist, it could be painted in a negative light, which would reflect badly on the company. Newspapers loved exposés like that; it was practically all they ever printed. Once something was printed it was out there, and then you couldn't do a damn thing about it.

Just when he had landed his glorious three-million-dollar payday, practically in the same minute. How strange was that? What good was a jackpot if you didn't have Tris Berrymore to celebrate with? The deal was signed. Song Young Park was on his way back to Korea to give the green light to transfer the money. Time to celebrate. And yet here stood Manny Rodriguez, messing with his mind.

"There must be another way. What in Christ can I do without a receptionist?"

"Don't be a jackass."

"I won't be called a jackass, Manny. Not by a Mexican, not by anyone else."

"Then don't be so damned desperate. Think of the deal. She's rough around the edges. Stop mixing business and pleasure. It's too risky. Look at me, Max, I stick my neck out like this, you know I'm doing you a favor. By the way, I'm from Costa Rica."

"You call this a favor?" He realized he was sputtering. He didn't care if the man was from North Michigan Avenue. There came a time for asserting your damned authority. What would Song Young Park do in this situation? He would kick some ass, that's what he would do. Song had people running right and left everywhere he went. *There* was a man who could run a business. When they had finally first met, seven months ago, having increased their cooperation steadily over the last four years, Song had shown him a photo to demonstrate how nobody screwed with him.

The picture showed Song on a beach somewhere, shirtless, tracks of dirt-caked sweat running down his chest, his bare hands in a death grip around the neck of a wild pig. He held the pig up to the sky like a trophy, his biceps bulging while the pig's bristly hairs brushed against his fingers, its body hanging limp, its white eyes blank in death. The sun was setting over palm trees in the background. One hour ago Song had stepped out of the chopper carrying nothing himself, people holding doors ahead of him, people watching his back behind him. He only had to make a slight movement of his finger and an aide would run up with a briefcase, a laptop, a phone. Song had his people in line. Sure as shit no one messed with *his* woman.

Max leaned on one elbow as the full impact hit him. Tris was packing her things while he sat here arguing with Rodriguez. In a few minutes she would be gone. When were they seeing each other -- tonight? No, tonight she was busy. It was tomorrow night. Was that off now, too?

His mind clouded. Caught red-handed, Tris was out on her ass. On the very day that the Koreans signed! Rodriguez sat in front of him, keeping him here, keeping him from talking to Tris before she left. Stalling him. Hell, Rodriguez was the one who should get the boot. But it would be foolish to make a snap decision on firing the general manager. The Koreans wouldn't ask questions if a receptionist was canned. The general manager yes.

"I'm going to talk to her. I've got to see what in Christ is with this file."

"Let it go, Max. We'll find one that isn't a goddamned tree-hugger." Rodriguez stuck his chin out. His chin always jutted when he thought he deserved more respect. He wanted to get Tris out the door before Max had a chance to see her. Well, it wasn't going to happen like that.

"Move on that."

Max sank back in his leather chair and waited. With this file business, you could forgive and forget. Turn the thing around. If they didn't see each other at work, they could spend *every* night together, instead of every other night or every third night. Tris would be hard to replace. Christ, that was just it. She *couldn't* be replaced.

How Ginger would laugh to see him like this, imagining everything worse than it probably was. Well, he wouldn't give her the chance, would he? Ginger belonged to the past. Because the future was spelled T-r-i-s. The future had become so much clearer suddenly, with the signing. The way he had had to suck up to the Koreans during the ceremony – Song had even wanted to hold his hand – and what had that been that they were chanting, a prayer? All that Korean gibberish . . . chanting things in Korean that no one could understand . . . men in suits frigging holding *hands* in the conference room. Truly, the only way to forget those cheesy rituals was with a night of mind-blowing, high-octane carnal pleasure . . .

He sat up straighter in his chair, trying to focus on something lighter. Like that three-million-dollar bank transfer that was only three or four days away . . . what a man could do with that much wealth, Christ! Dinner at the Olympic Club any night of the week – although of course it wouldn't be much fun *alone*. He could buy the cream-colored Bentley with the red leather interior in the framed photo hanging on his wall, something he'd been dreaming of. But then who could he go touring with? The brilliance of his entrepreneurial victory kept fading to the same unpleasant image in his mind – the image of himself *sans* Tris.

She had driven his cars. He adored nothing more than being chauffeured around in one of his own classic automobiles by Tris Berrymore. The 1963 silver e-type Jaguar. The 1967 yellow T-top Corvette. His white 1959 T-Bird with the portholes.

There was something so sexy about the way her strawberry blond hair curled around the cheap plastic stem of the telephone headset. The way she sat on the edge of her chair, shoulders back, smiling into the screen. Did this mean an end to those romps on his bedroom carpet late at night, in front of the cathedral windows with Lake Michigan in the background?

A knock on the door. In she came, white skirt hugging her hips, sandals cradling the feet that had sweetly massaged his neck. The turquoise peasant blouse highlighted her tiny waist. She practically disappeared in your arms when you hugged -- though she certainly didn't look to be in the mood for hugging now -- and he glanced at the neckline that dipped so interestingly and drew the eye so irresistibly to that point just in the center, where a tiny turquoise bow was sewn to the hem. On this hot, humid day she looked . . . *well ventilated*. Her eyes were an electric green, just like the color of the lake when there was a storm coming, and the sky would be filled with black clouds, but a shaft of sunlight would find a gap in the clouds and light up the water, almost so it looked backlit. That small, straight nose, those freckles sprinkled across the bridge of her nose . . . but now he couldn't help noticing how her chin pointed, her jaw set in a way he hadn't seen before.

"Well, so tomorrow night still OK?"

Her eyes widened. "I got fired. Didn't Manny tell you?"

He tried to make his face show pain. He took her pain and tried to make it his own, with his expression. Maybe a flash of manly desperation came from his eyes, but also sympathy. He waited for some acknowledgement, some softening, but nothing came. Something told him she wasn't buying it.

He changed approaches, dismissed half a year's employment with a wave of his hand. Speaking now as owner and president of TSR Inc., he said, "Sure, I got that. But about tomorrow night. What I'm asking. We said seven-thirty. Still on, aren't we?" Seated across from beautiful women, his words sometimes glommed together. Amazing that it still happened with Tris after so long together.

"Max, I'm gone. It's over. That means both my job and . . . well, whatever shit was going on between you and me."

Her answer caught him by surprise. The finality of it. The decisiveness. And the nonchalance. It hadn't mattered to her. This he was *not* prepared for. In fact he couldn't believe what he was hearing. Yet there could be no misinterpreting her words.

I'm gone. It's over.

The words echoed in his mind like cars crashing into each other. Those words simply did not belong in this discussion, in *any* discussion. The noise in his mind grew loud and drowned out everything else, the rattling of the air conditioner, the sound of Tris's breathing, the sound of a fan whirring somewhere deep inside his computer -- instead this crashing, roaring sound. Like his Mercedes Gullwing two weeks ago, that horrible sound of metal bending and breaking, only now many more cars, whole lines of cars smashing into opposing lines. A catastrophic image. Explosions . . . balls of fire . . . thunder and noise . . . but then it came again, steady and quiet, as if filtered through this noise.

I'm gone. It's over.

His own voice came through the noise, as well. He heard himself saying that she couldn't possibly be serious.

"Yes, Max."

"But I don't get it. Just like that?"

"It was going nowhere."

"But it was. We were getting serious. I was thinking about . . . you know, I was sort of thinking of asking if you would want to . . . you know, *stay* together."

For Chrissake, this wasn't the moment to pop the question. He had once promised himself not to do that again without a lot of advance planning and thought, and here he had almost gone and done it now.

"No, Max."

She wasn't budging. "Because of what happened? Hell, that doesn't mean anything. Maybe it'll be better like this."

She laughed. "The answer is no."

He searched her electric green eyes. *That cold laugh.* Christ, didn't she have feelings? How could she sit there laughing? "You act like you're happy about it. Like you couldn't care less."

"I just got screamed at within an inch of my sanity. I got accused of stuff I didn't even do, all right? You know how that feels? I'm a little numb."

"Yeah, what in Christ is with this . . . this *file*?"

She took a deep breath, then let it out. He noticed she had a paper in her hand, something she had idly picked up from his desktop. The paper was shaking in her hand. It looked pretty funny. In fact it would've been comical to see Tris so nervous if she hadn't been in the midst of driving a stake through his heart. "Well, things don't really add up around here, do they?"

"What are you talking about?"

"All the old worthless gear. Some of it goes to Korea in containers."

"All of it goes to Korea."

"Bullshit. By my calculations no more than a third goes to Korea. Hardly any goes into recycling. I joined this company because you said you were recycling. What about the rest?"

"What calculations?" The idea made him feel hot and itchy. But he saw her trembling. She was nervous and scared. She wasn't sure of what she was talking about. But it was all too clear Rodriguez had been right. The whole thing made him furious. "What in Christ have you been calculating?"

"Too bad he deleted the file before I could show it to you." The paper floated to the carpet and she stood up.

"You'd better be happy he deleted it. Whatever it was."

There she went again, burning him with those eyes. Like somehow she was furious with *him*. When he thought back to all the evenings they had spent together, all the weekends, all the fine Sunday afternoon tours in his cars, there hadn't been a single moment like this. Never a fight, scarcely even a disagreement. A little strange, thinking back, but there it was: they got along. Like they were made for each other.

Yet look at her now, green eyes like lasers that could burn through walls. If she had never been mad at him till this moment, how could he suddenly be such a monster? Until yesterday they had been in high gear together. In a car, you couldn't shift straight from fourth gear into reverse. How could this even be happening?

Maybe if he bought her a ring . . . like a kind of engagement ring . . . or if he told her about his three million dollar payday . . . would that bring a change of heart? He had to tell her. He tried to think how he could work it into the conversation.

Remember that night at the Skinny Whip, all those Koreans?

Then again, this wasn't the moment. The way she fixed him with those eyes, never letting go; Rodriguez must've slapped her around. Better just to wait and see, see if she could cool down and be her old self again. It certainly didn't look good. Rodriguez's words came back: *Goddamned tree-hugger.*

"Then those other computers that come in, Max, like brand new ones," Tris went on. "They disappear. They don't get on the website. They're not in inventory. I want to know what happens to those machines."

"Christ, what is this garbage?"

"You're not going to listen, are you?"

"I am listening."

"No, Max, you don't listen. It's like it goes in one ear and out the other. You think I don't know what happens when people don't pay you? People who cause trouble?" She kept staring. When she looked at him like that he felt himself squirming, even though he sat rigid on the edge of his chair. "Everybody knows. It's one reason I'm going. I've got my eye on you. Don't try any shit on me, Max, I'm warning you."

"You've lost me now." She couldn't possibly know what she was talking about. What in Christ had she gotten her nose into?

"Go to hell, Max."

He made his face go innocent, puckered his lips, the little Cupid smile. It covered up a sinking, burning feeling of catastrophe. Had Tris just said what he thought she said? Was this the same girl who had made him so happy for the last six months? Who so athletically banged her pelvis against him eighty or ninety times only three nights ago, leaving him a sore but also a happy man? With her he became a legend between the sheets, a sex king, a stud. Tris made it happen. She brought that out in him. With Tris, sex could go on for *hours*. And then it stayed in your mind for days afterwards.

Was he truly losing this?

"What did you say?" It came out a whisper. His insides hurt so much at the thought of her voice saying: *I'm gone, it's over.* The ache reached deep into his breast. His throat had gone tight. He could barely squeeze words out.

"You heard me. I've got my eye on you. Just don't try anything."

"Where does all this . . . *poison* come from? I was thinking how much I'm going to miss you. I still can't believe this is happening."

She laughed. "You'll manage." She jumped out of her chair like a track star coming out of the blocks. In her hurry to leave, one sandal caught on the carpet. Her foot was bare. In that moment when the sandal was off, and left behind, one step behind, he imagined the feeling of the threads of the carpet worming in luxuriously between her bare toes. He had nosed into those lovely spaces between her bare toes just recently himself, and he had tongued them quite thoroughly. She had laughed, he had laughed, they had been wet and silly and sexy together, they had wrestled and kissed and tossed around on the bed, and finally she had let him lick her into a state of pure, noisy ecstasy, right where she belonged. Where she still had been happy with him -- well, and *happy* wasn't even quite the word, was it?

She stopped now, aimed her foot into the left-behind sandal, arched her back, wriggled it back onto those delectable bare toes. The door clicked shut behind her.

He felt a huge, echoing loss, a hollowness inside him, a quickly expanding black hole of sadness. All those happy, carefree moments they had spent together . . . like how she would watch TV on the couch with a glass of wine, but just one glass. Like him, she hated ruining her evening with booze. Some girls got too loose once a bottle was open. Passed-out girls revolted him; it was as if you had a dead body on your couch. The situation got worse when they woke up.

Tris Berrymore was the opposite of that. Earthy and natural and sexy all at once, her lack of inhibition had opened his eyes. With her your fantasies became reality. On summer nights she would pad around the house in pyjama shorts and a button-down pyjama top that she didn't bother to button. Some men might find her breasts a trifle on the small side; to his eye they were sublime. She hadn't worked as a stripper for nothing. She went around barefoot. She ate no meat. When she slept she hardly made noise at all, like a hibernating animal.

The day had started off so damned terrific. A three-million-dollar payday didn't land on your desk every day. In fact, he had never before experienced anything quite like it. But that huge rush had been cruelly replaced by the feeling of being adrift, out of control. Alone. *Single*. And the whole thing had happened so suddenly. Amazing to think a day that started off so beautifully could turn so incredibly rotten.

Lost GPS

At that same moment on Monday morning, Ike Mullin sat behind the wheel of his 1984 Lincoln heading north at seventy miles an hour on I-94, the Edens Expressway. It wasn't the two margaritas in his gut that were making him sweat; the problem was the A/C in the Lincoln was on the fritz. He realized now, with the first heat wave of the year, he'd never gotten around to it last summer. He kept one eye on traffic while fiddling with the electric window control, a little up, a little down, trying to find a balance between a refreshing breeze and getting blown right out of the car.

He blinkered his way into the right lane. Anything to get out of the chaos of the middle lanes. At least in the far right lane people only barged in from the left. A sudden double honk blared out of his blind spot.

What the . . .?

The big brown Lincoln rocked left and right as he swerved back into his lane, its suspension system trying to recover from his jerk of the wheel at high speed. For an instant he thought he had lost it. He had a vision of flying off the road and landing nose-down in the cattails by the side of the road. But the Lincoln righted itself, saved by forward momentum and a new set of radial tires.

"Damnation!"

A burgundy Corvette blew by on the right, high beams flashing. Tinted windows hid the bastard's face. Sweat beaded up on Ike's forehead. Too shaken by the near miss to think of any other choice words, he grunted, "Oughta run their ass off the road!"

"Drive much?" said Tranny, once he'd quit laughing. Tranny was Vietnamese by birth. They had met in jail.

"Idiot shouldn't be passin' on the right."

"Anything goes on the 'spressway, man."

"You woulda laid off that fourth margarita, you'd be driving," Ike said. He'd stopped at two himself, pacing himself through the morning. Alcohol turned Tranny's skin a frightening shade of red, even if it never seemed to make him drunk. Just one sip, and he looked like a bomb set to explode. Ike normally wouldn't let him drive then, but not so much because he worried about accidents. He simply felt a duty to keep his partner out of the way of law enforcement. Which meant Ike wound up driving most of the time.

"You got the GPS, right?" Tranny asked now, changing the subject, patting his pockets. For a second Ike thought his partner might be playing one of his usual tricks. He glanced away from the traffic ahead. Tranny was checking his shirt pockets, then the pants, front and back.

"Please tell me you're shittin' me."

"No, man. I ain't got it. I checked under the seat and all. You think maybe you left it somewhere?"

"You saying *I* left it somewhere?"

"All I know is I ain't got it."

Ike kept calm. *Eyes on the road.*

"I thought you had it, man."

"Don't give me that pussy excuse. You're in charge of the GPS. If you wouldn't have had to show it to that waitress, you'd have kept it in your pocket where it belongs. Why'd you have to show to her, anyway?"

"That's it," Tranny shouted. "We left it in that scummy restaurant!"

"Not we, asshole," Ike corrected.

If they had to go back to Max Vinyl minus the GPS, he definitely wasn't standing for this we bullshit. Without further discussion he angled off the highway, up an exit ramp. A minute later they were speeding back in the other direction again, heading for Chicago.

Tranny groaned. "I never even got to show it to her. She was always runnin' off. Place wasn't even busy. You think she was avoiding me, man?"

"We're going straight back and get it."

"What if it ain't there anymore?"

"It'll be there."

"Yeah, but I mean, what if it ain't?"

Ike's foot touched the accelerator, partly out of irritation, partly because some feeling inside told him Tranny might be right. There was no time to waste. The boss would go postal if they lost his GPS. There was no telling what he would do. Ike preferred not to think about it. Plus there was all that information Lance had put on the GPS a couple weeks ago.

"Tranny boy, lemme tell you something. In life there ain't no point in asking, 'what if?' It just gets everybody uptight about shit that might not even be worth worrying over. Half the time things turn out ok, and then you worried for no reason at all. Either it's gonna be there or it ain't, and we're gonna find out real soon."

The GPS was an expensive model that calculated positions even out in the middle of Lake Michigan, not just on roads like most GPSs. They used it for their trip out on the lake every other night. Otherwise how would you ever find the right spot?

The boss didn't have to know about the work Lance had given them. He wasn't going and checking what they put on the GPS.

A half hour later they stood on the outdoor terrace of the Falling Domino restaurant. Ike scanned the faces of the early lunch crowd. He headed straight for the table where they had drunk their margaritas. The man at the table, seeing them coming, put his enchilada down and sat up straighter in his chair. Ike noted with respect the heavy muscle in the guy's arms and chest.

"We had this table before. You find anything?"

The man held his eye for a long moment, as if waiting to see if Ike was done speaking. "Nada," he said.

Ike led Tranny inside, toward the hostess stand. "The guy ain't lying," he said. "In this joint they don't seat you till the table's cleaned up and set. So he couldn't have taken it." His eye was drawn elsewhere. Two hostesses, long, spindly legs like frigging flamingos, stood chatting at the entrance.

He slapped one hand down, hard, on the wooden hostess stand. The sound echoed as if the stand was hollow. The whole dining room went quiet. The two girls stared with their bambi eyes. "Listen up," he said. "We left something on our table when we was here."

The one hostess had big round brown eyes and long, thick eyelashes. Her blond eyebrows were so delicate they seemed to blend right into her skin. Her lip gloss glittered when she talked.

"Do you want to tell me what it was?" She had a high, squeaky voice.

"Yeah, a GPS," Tranny said.

"'Bout yay big," Ike said. He saw her eyes flick upward. She would be checking out his eyebrow. At her age she probably hadn't seen too many men with a number 14 steel lag bolt perforating the skin of their eyebrow.

"We've got our lost and found right here." The hostess picked up the lamp on the stand to illuminate the contents of the drawer. He stuck his hand in and rummaged among the phones, glasses cases, wallets, paperback books, slips of paper with phone numbers. But in all this mess no GPS. "Are you sure you left it here?" she asked in that squeaky voice. "Not someplace else?"

"Someplace else for sure," Tranny said.

"He means we left it *here* for sure," Ike said.

"That's what I said," Tranny said.

The hostess looked from Tranny to him, then she stared again for a long time at his pierced eyebrow. "Doesn't that . . . kind of weigh you down?"

Ike started working the outer wing nut. It always caught a little on the lock washer, though he sprayed it weekly with WD-40. When you turned the nuts on their threads, the skin around his eyebrow stretched and twisted. To an innocent girl like this it looked as though if you weren't careful, you might just peel off a chunk of your face.

She couldn't take her eyes off it. "Gag me."

"Marry me, I'd put my ring up here," he said.

She took a step back. The other hostess had already retreated to the wall.

"You keep staring, you gonna get cross eyes," Tranny said.

Ike scanned the dining room, his gaze following waitresses going through the kitchen door at the back. "Come on, man. Waitress bitch musta swiped it. Let's go find her."

"Anything left behind would be here in our lost and found," said the hostess. Ike pulled Tranny away. They weren't getting anywhere here. The hostess turned to some other people. "How many in your party?"

Waitresses stepped out of the way, giving him room. A good eyebrow-piercing got people's attention, all right. Some people jingled change in their pocket. He had his bolt loaded with nuts and washers. When he walked in a certain jaunty way, they made a pleasing sound: *chink-a-chink*.

The heat of the kitchen slammed into your face like an invisible wall of heat. It had to be twenty degrees hotter in here. Waitresses picked up plates that waited under heat lamps. The food on the plates looked like it was held together with glue. Waitresses, busboys and cooks shouted at each other while dashing in different directions.

"You gonna know her when you see her?"

"Ain't seen her yet," Tranny said.

"Who're you looking for?" A girl that looked like a skeleton in white shirt and black trousers stood off to one side, wiping trays with a rag. She had shiny black hair in a short haircut. Her thin arms, neck and bony face didn't look normal. Probably one of those girls that starved themselves on purpose. He personally liked a little more meat on the bones.

"This waitress," Ike said. "We left something on the table about an hour ago."

"On the terrace?" asked the waitress. "What'd she look like?"

"Really hot, you know?" Tranny said.

Ike elbowed him. "Little taller than you, maybe. Sort of a ponytail, but not long, like. Tall and skinny. Real pretty smile."

"Alison Paine," the waitress said. "Breakfast shift today. She got off at eleven."

"Can I be of assistance?" A round-faced black man carrying a tray heaped with dirty dishes joined them.

"Yeah. Where do we find Alison Paine?" Ike said. The busboy flashed a dirty look at the black-haired waitress. He was steamed about them knowing Alison Paine's name. So they were on the right track. Ike spoke louder. "She took something that belongs to us."

The busboy shifted his tray. "You must be the guys with the phone. She showed it to me when I bussed the table. Garmin, something like that."

"Yeah, that's us," Ike said. He moved a step closer so that his chest was even with the tray balanced on the busboy's fingers.

"Went straight into the lost and found. Watched her put it there myself. Less than an hour ago."

The busboy couldn't even look him in the eye. Bad liars put Ike in a rage. He had beat up a ton of liars in prison.

With his open hand he heaved upward suddenly at one edge of the tray. He put all his strength into it. The weight of it surprised him as everything went flying. Forks, spoons, steak knives, wine glasses, beer steins, food-caked plates and a giant iced-tea pitcher launched into the air in all directions. Some of those glasses were still half full. Two or three stacks of dirty plates had been piled on that tray. Those plates, now headed for the floor, would never make another trip through the dishwasher.

The busboy yelped like a kicked dog.

"What the hell you do that for?"

Glass and china started to hit the red quarry tile, shattering with an ear-splitting noise, one plate after another. It was enough to rupture your eardrums. He remembered once, back in prison, a machine gun spraying bullets in a steel-walled room. That had sounded a lot like this.

Then waitresses screaming, covering their eyes, tripping and falling down as they ran away . . . glass shards, splintering china, ice cubes and drops of iced tea ricocheting off the walls, stainless steel tables, and their clothes . . . and the busboy twisting and turning in an effort to save something, anything, but the load a total loss . . .

Ike uncoiled and drove his fist into the liar's solar plexus. The busboy sank to his knees, doubled over, gasping and wheezing for breath.

"Ain't acceptable to lie to myself and Tranny, see?" he said.

People had to know, shit like that had consequences. Ike lined up a kick, setting his sights on the man's balls. But the tray was all tangled up in the busboy's legs. His kick would just get deflected by the tray. The angles played out in his head, and he decided to let it go.

Time slowed down. He had time to see something flying through the shimmering air coming straight his way. Something brown, something with steam. *Boiling hot coffee.* He saw the steam wafting off the flying coffee.

His eyes followed the twisting cloud of coffee back to the pot. The outstretched hand of the Puerto Rican cook that held the pot, the contorted expression on the cook's face – he had time to see all these things, yet still not enough time to move his feet and get out of the way.

Boiling coffee splashed across his chest, neck and arms. It burned on his skin like hell itself. He heard a roaring and a bellowing and realized it was his own voice. He sank to his knees, feeling broken glass digging into his kneecaps, but alive only to the fiery pain in his chest and arms. The boiling coffee soaked his shirt. Now it was the shirt burning him, blistering his arms and his chest and his collarbone. He stripped off the scalding t-shirt. It hurt so much he knew layers of skin were peeling off with the shirt.

The cook had snuck around from behind somewhere. He crouched in front of them now, like some sort of street-fighter, coffeepot in his left hand, steam pouring off the dry glass, his right hand waving a ten-inch butcher knife.

"You gonna be sorry," Ike shouted, standing up again now. His arms had gone strangely cold. He feinted left, all instinct now, shirtless, big white belly swinging with him. He saw Tranny off to his right, dodging and feinting as well.

With a sudden manic movement the cook smashed the coffeepot on the side of a metal table. Glass crunched underfoot. The cook now brandished a plastic coffeepot handle with jagged glass edges sticking out. That thing would *fillet* you. It looked more lethal than the butcher knife in his other hand.

"Take him on that side," Ike yelled. But Tranny couldn't sneak around behind the cook any better than he could.

"Fat fuckers outta my restaurant! Royal, call de cops!" The cook pointed at the wall phone with his coffeepot weapon, backing up another step. He had room to maneuver. The busboy crab-walked out of the fight zone. The cook brandished that knife like he *wanted* to use it. Little scraps of meat still clung to the blade, raw pork or chicken. With that glass-studded handle in one hand and the big knife in the other, the cook held both of them back singlehandedly. Macho bastard had no fear. He didn't even break a sweat under that runty moustache.

The busboy had the phone at his ear.

"We got two men in the kitchen threatening the staff with a knife," he said. He named the restaurant and gave the street address. This was Rush Street. It wouldn't take long for the cops to show up.

Ike backed toward the door. "We don't find our GPS, we'll be back for your asses."

"You ever come back, we gonna cut off your dicks an throw you sons a bitches inna freezer," yelled the Puerto Rican.

Ike kicked an unbroken wine glass against the wall, where it exploded and added to the mess. Waitresses and busboys cowered against the far wall, covering their eyes with their hands. Looking at them, you'd think it was a bank robbery, with guns and shooting. Ike straight-armed the door and emerged in the coolness of the dining room.

"You ever hear anything that crazy?"

"How's he gonna fit a grown man in a freezer?" Tranny asked.

"That's what I want to know."

"'Specially one the size a you."

"Shut up, Tranny boy. You hadn't left the GPS here, we wouldn't have had this problem in the first place."

"Wait a minute, I know," Tranny said. They were passing through the bar area, headed for the hostess stand and the exit. All eyes were on Ike's bare belly. "Chop him in pieces. Shove 'em in there one at a time."

"He wanted to cut us up with that knife a his, that's sure."

"Like to see him try."

Ike caught the eye of the hostess on the way out.

Chink-a-chink.

She stared back. This babe wanted him. She didn't mind a tiny beer belly. He flexed his biceps going by.

Family loyalty

Max Vinyl wondered how his Uncle Gordon could possibly go on working.

The old man sank into the chair slowly. His yellowed white hair hung across his brow at an odd angle, as if he had chopped it himself, which he probably had. He clipped coupons and paid in pennies, counting them out one by one with maddening slowness, driving store clerks crazy. The lines around his eyes, and then around his mouth, formed a series of deep triangles. The lines deepened with any expression of his face, but most of the time he seemed to be grimacing in pain. His shoulders hung at a strange slope, beset by arthritis. His hands were spotted and his fingers didn't straighten.

He wore a trench coat in this heat, and an old cotton sweater underneath. Max's eye fixed on an unidentifiable stain on the collar of the sweater. Gordon's circulation was weak. Even the lousy air conditioning here at TSR made him feel cold.

"Sure are getting bigger all the time, Max."

"Not really. Hauling more stuff, but prices dropping. Too much damn competition. Four years ago I got 50 cents a pound. Now it's down to 30 cents. Driving the price down all the time. I've got to keep an eye on costs, otherwise I'm toast."

"You'll do all right."

"Hell of a way to make a living. If I didn't have you, I don't know what I'd do."

"You're good to your old uncle. You scratch my back, I scratch yours."

"How is Aunt Greta? Any news?"

Max handed across his desk first, as always, the unmarked manila envelope. It contained two thousand dollars in twenties. Two thousand every Monday. One hundred thousand a year. They had been doing it for three years, now. Uncle Gordon had no use for hundreds and fifties; they would just draw unwanted attention. His uncle had a look inside, then closed it up again. "Personally, I think it's hopeless. But she keeps coming back from wherever it is she goes to, you know. They wait on her hand and foot over there. Medicare doesn't cover it all. Costs me an arm and a leg. That's where this comes in."

"I know."

"When are you coming to see her? You could get lucky. For you she'd open her eyes. If she knew about your support, she'd be mighty grateful."

"Christ, Gordon. If that's what it takes to give her some quality of life, not to mention . . . you know, a shot at some kind of recovery. Hell, it's what money's for, isn't it?"

They'd had the same conversation a hundred times. He knew the money was a gift from Heaven for Gordon. It meant Greta not having to live in some Medicaid home that smelled of urine, where even the buttons off your shirt got stolen by the shift workers, and where the doctors were glad to get the hell out as quick as possible. The place where Greta had lived these last years was full of people whose face would light up just at the sight of you, people who honestly cared for her, people who had gotten to know her before she finally sank into this sleep. Even before the three-million-dollar payday, long before, he had never held back with the money for her care.

But the passing thought of his windfall brought back in a rush the painful memory of Tris's voice: *I'm gone. It's over.* The memory of her cold eyes jolted him like a convulsion.

"You okay, Max?" Uncle Gordon's eyes were alert now. They were horribly red-rimmed and shiny. Max wished he could get his uncle to drink less, but on the other hand how could you get any man to change? Aunt Greta's illness didn't make it any easier. "You look like you saw a demon," his uncle said.

"We're on the outs." Max couldn't look him in the eye.

"Tris? Don't tell me."

He nodded. "Looks like it might be over."

"What? Such a nice girl. Where is she, anyway? When I walked in, no one was there. Finally Manny came and let me in."

"Manny caught her nosing around in something. Canned her without even asking me."

"That bad? So now she's mad at you?"

"I've never seen her so mad, tell you the truth." He swallowed the rest of what he was going to say. It hurt to talk about it. Then again, it felt good to have someone listening. For a long while Tris had been his listener. Now he was spilling the beans to old Uncle Gordon. He heard himself groan.

"Listen, Max," Gordon went on. "When a girl is mad, you got to back off. I'm just telling you. You probably know it better than me. Things like this don't change from one generation to the next. Give her some time. Could be it was some kind of misunderstanding."

"I don't think so."

"Give it some time, believe me. That girl loves you just as much as you love her. Something's wrong here."

"I thought so too, but the more I think about it . . ." He didn't finish the sentence. He was thinking back to that calamitous event of two weeks ago. Something he hadn't attached any special significance to until just this moment.

They'd been heading south on the tollway, Tris at the wheel of his 1957 Mercedes 280 SL Gullwing coupe. The doors opened upward, like the wings of a seagull. Tris had become distracted by a spider as it dropped down in front of her face. His antique cars stayed parked in the barn for months at a time without being dusted. It was natural that a few bugs and spiders got in there. The silver Gullwing, current insured value more than three hundred thousand dollars, had been one of the highlights in his seventeen-car collection. Suddenly the spider, dropping down from the visor, had disappeared down her shirt.

This had happened just as they downshifted into the toll plaza. Reducing speed. On the final approach to the tollbooth, the spider had scuttled ticklishly right into her cleavage. Screaming, she had jerked the wheel and gone out of her lane. Before Max could react, she had plowed the front end of the Gullwing into a concrete barrier. They couldn't have been going more than ten miles an hour, but that solid concrete had pushed back. The Gullwing front end had crumpled with a horrible accordioning of metal. Why hadn't he reached over and grabbed the wheel? How could he have just sat and watched it happen?

Then, as if that weren't disaster enough, impact from behind. A tailgaiting Ford pickup had mashed the rear end. The driver had apologized. Said he had taken his eyes off them to count the coins in his hand.

It had all happened as if in slow motion, yet so fast there had been no chance of avoiding it. He and Tris had walked away from the wreckage. The Gullwing had gone to the junk heap. All because of a spider.

She had made up for it with her kisses that night.

Could she have *planned* an accident like that?

The idea had never occurred to him. But after this morning, it suddenly seemed thinkable.

When he had described the accident in detail, Gordon shook his head. "Impossible, Max. No one could orchestrate something like that on the tollway, even if they were crazy enough to try."

After all the things Tris had said, he wasn't so sure.

Max next got out a thick gray envelope made from 100% recycled paper with the company logo on it. This envelope was filled with the forms that Gordon would file at the Greater Lake County Environmental Agency. The forms contained proof that computer gear had been broken up into its component pieces, sorted by material and class of hazard, and disposed of in ways that were environmentally acceptable.

It was what people expected. It was good for business. It was also completely phony, the papers prepared by Rodriguez every week at some point between Friday afternoon and Monday morning. The software generated reports on all the equipment that came in. He would then fill out the forms manually, using the numbers from incomings – 30 screens here, 50 PCs there. This way there was at least a halfway legitimate paper trail on what was being recycled. But the truth was that in more than seven years of doing business no one had ever come to inspect the premises or ask questions or follow the paper trail. No one had even called. They relied on self-regulation. Which meant all this was a waste of everybody's time. And in any event there existed no laws regulating the disposal of computer waste in the State of Illinois. Just a set of vague recommendations from the EPA that were never enforced, and would carry no penalties even if they were.

The environmental certificate hung in the reception area, blown up to poster size. It certified under the seal of Lake County that TSR Inc. continually re-evaluated to make sure that they were using best practices in the disposal of computer waste.

"Question, Uncle Gordon. Would a change of ownership alter the way we work together?"

The old man's eyes clouded over again. It wasn't clear if he was thinking about some old memory, considering the question, or just reacting to some new pain in his shoulder. After a minute Gordon said, "Could do so. Between us there's a certain trust. If I've got to sit down with some fellow I don't even know, and meanwhile you're long gone . . ." He didn't finish the sentence. He sat perfectly still, Max knew, because his neck was so stiff that even turning his head was painful.

"Don't worry. That's a long way off, if it ever comes. Thing is, I've managed to sell twenty percent of the company. Just signed the papers this morning. Means I'm holding on to eighty percent. Not leaving anytime soon."

"Oh. Well, I guess it's ok, then."

Uncle Gordon looked relieved. His lips were bluish, as if they weren't getting enough blood circulating to them.

MIRAGES

Annie Ogden let her body sway with the light side-to-side rocking of the boat. Five miles out, with the sun already below the horizon, the Chicago skyline looked like something she'd seen in a postcard on the other side of the world. The Sears Tower off to the left and the John Hancock Building up north framed a random jumble of building-block skyscrapers. Triangles, rectangles, some higher, some squatter, each building pointed to the sky in its own signature way, the only sort of mountains this monumentally flat city had to offer.

The vaguely fishy smell of the water and the sound of the light swells lapping against the side of the boat lulled her into a state of welcome calm. At the end of a sweaty Monday, cool breezes on her face felt good.

"Earth to Annie," her sister said.

Could it be that only three months ago she had still been strapping on body armor just to go outside? Or was she dreaming now? Were this watery view and this brimming lake just cruel mirages after her years in a desert country? Her mind played back the tape of her long trip home, first to Rhine-Main Air Base in Germany, from there to Atlanta Hartsfield, and finally back to O'Hare, the endless flights, the sleep loss, the bureaucracy. No, it was all so real. She was home.

"Right here. I'm here."

"The hell you are," Todd said. "Look, I know we didn't catch a salmon. Hell, it isn't even a fish. But I didn't expect you to start crying over it."

Todd was always going for laughs. Why he tried so hard she would never understand. True, the tears were flowing more often these days. They came with no warning, like a real storm in the desert. Happened to a lot of returning vets, she'd been told, crying and depression and panic attacks. She knew it was okay.

"They don't put you in a padded cell for this. For a few minor leakages," she said. Still, just knowing she was clinically okay didn't make her feel any better. Who could say? They might have misdiagnosed her.

Her brain was running ahead of her, and Todd and Alison were looking at her funny. She decided to stop trying to explain things that couldn't be explained, and produced a meaningless little giggle, in deference to his efforts.

"Oh, I get it," Todd said. "You're crying because you're, like, happy?" He looked out across the water toward the city. "Personally I find it pathetic. You're trolling for salmon, right? And you think you've finally got one on the line, like you've hooked the last living sockeye salmon in the southern end of Lake Michigan, and what've you got? Somebody's lousy printer cable covered with algae. Disgusting!"

"Do they ever catch any fish?" asked Alison.

"I hear they've started melting down the fish for their metal content," Todd said.

"This view alone is worth the price." Annie tried to make him feel better. He didn't have to take responsibility for her mood. She hugged her shoulders, suddenly shivering in the evening lake breeze. Most passengers stood along the rail gazing at the skyline, a glass of wine in one hand, pointing out buildings. She led her sister and Todd inside, where only a few people sat. They drank coffee and looked out the window.

"So you're really going to stay out in those woods?" Todd asked, obviously making conversation. Alison was content to study the skyline, maybe listening, maybe off in her own world. "Aren't there a lot of kooks running around in there?"

"Like to see someone provoke me."

Todd looked anxious. "Be serious. You and your jogging. Rapists go out to that forest just to pick off joggers. It's like a sport for them."

She lived in a narrow strip of forest of white oak, birch and sugar maple, through which a slow-moving section of the Des Plaines River ran, all this just two miles from O'Hare Airport. When she had come out for her run this morning she had gone straight down to the riverbank, wondering what all the splashing was about. Just off the opposite bank, maybe fifty feet away, in a little cove where a tree trunk lay half-submerged, a pair of mallard ducks batted the water with their wings, dodging in and out, half running, half flying, all for the amusement of the brown-feathered female floating at a safe distance a few feet away. Just then a jumbo jet thundered in over the treetops, flaps fully extended, on point for runway 28 and drowning out all other sounds. The plane was so low you could read markings like *no step* on the side of the engines. If the ducks could ignore it, she could too.

She considered telling her sister's husband about the ducks. But then they would probably look at her strangely again. In a quiet voice she said, "If that's the case, we should take it back from the rapists."

"You're home now, Annie. End of insurgency."

"And we sure are happy you got home in one piece, kid." There was something warm in Alison's eyes. If Todd hadn't sat there slouching between them, they might have hugged.

"Don't you think there might be a few running around the city, too?" she asked. "As if that's any safer."

"At least in the city someone might hear the screaming."

She fixed her gaze on the skyline again, unconvinced. What did he know about ambushes? Down in the alleys between Chicago's skyscrapers, someone somewhere was probably getting mugged at this moment. Well, with his work for the newspaper he probably knew more about city crime than most people. But he didn't know what he was talking about when it came to the forest preserve. She doubted he had ever even set foot there before three months ago.

More importantly, there were quite a few things he didn't know about her.

She loved Alison and Todd, her husband, but small doses were best. They argued so much it was almost like they fed on arguments. As girls growing up they had fought their share. Sibling rivalry. Arguing and fighting and belittling each other – those were things all kids did. You didn't expect to see so much of it in married people.

She had visited with them every week or two since coming home, sometimes just with them, sometimes in restaurants, twice at her cabin in the woods. When Alison had invited her on the salmon fishing tour on Lake Michigan, it had sounded like the perfect alternative to sitting around in some air-conditioned dining room.

"I like the forest," Annie said, answering his question with a sugar-coated version of the truth. "Guess I'll stay for a while if nobody throws me out."

"Or till the first airplane falls out of the sky and obliterates you. We're waiting for another invitation, you know. Just so we can have the pleasure of declining."

"Speak for yourself, bonehead. I'll come," Alison said. "Assuming I can find the place again."

Todd was digging in the pocket of his windbreaker. "Oh yeah, that reminds me, some bozo left this at the restaurant today. Alison brought it home for my collection. Thought it was a phone."

Annie studied the buttons. "It's a GPS, not a phone."

"I know. That's what made me think of it, when Al said she might not find your place. She's probably the only person left in Chicago who doesn't know what a GPS is."

"Maybe she thought you'd want one for your collection."

"No really, she didn't know."

"Well, excuse me for not being some drooling techno-geek, like you two," Alison said. "It so happens I could talk the pants off you both when it comes to Giacometti or Paul Klee. Fat chance of getting you interested in that."

Annie switched on the GPS. Blue numbers lit up the digital display. "Let's see what this baby remembers. Looks like a special model. There's about ten positions scattered all around the city." She scrolled down a list of addresses. "I don't really see a pattern. One position way out in the lake. That's weird."

"What is?"

She studied the distance between the tour boat and Navy Pier. They were five minutes from the dock. Maybe the GPS was simply showing their present position. But it wasn't; she was looking at memory. "It's farther out than where we are now, about ten miles out. And maybe twenty miles north of here."

"That doesn't make any sense," Todd said.

"Why not?" Alison said.

"What's ten miles out in the lake? Nothing at all."

"You don't know that. Maybe it's a good fishing spot."

Todd smirked. "You wouldn't catch anything ten miles out, either. This lake is one giant watery wasteland. Probably no fish for fifty miles in every direction."

"Fifty miles to the west would land you in a cornfield," Alison said. "I guess only you would imagine there might be fish *there*."

"Mind if I hold on to this?" Annie asked.

"Be my guest," Alison said. "Just keep your eyes open for a fat dude with blond hair and a bolt in his eyebrow, and a shorter Asian guy that looks like he got crossed with a gorilla. They beat the living daylights out of one of the busboys when they came back for the GPS. They're annoyed with me, to say the least."

Annie felt the blood rushing to her head at the thought of Alison getting attacked. "What were they like? Did you serve them?"

"They drank a ton of margaritas before eleven a.m., that's all. We didn't exchange phone numbers."

"But they do have your name," Todd said.

"Drop dead, will you?"

"How did they get your name? Jesus," Annie said.

"The busboy, of course," Todd said. "Deserved what he got, don't you think?"

"Why would they beat someone up over a GPS?" Annie asked. They all stared at the device in her hand with its blue numbers.

Alison looked as if she were about to cry. "All I know is, they think I stole it and they're definitely capable of getting rough. My friend from the Domino called. He thought they were going to kill him."

Annie stood up, then sat down again, a charge of nervous energy shooting through her legs. "I don't like these guys. I don't like them one bit."

They were docking. A dock worker in a sailor suit took the rope thrown by one of the boat employees and wound it around a huge bollard while the engines churned in reverse. Then everyone stood up.

"I wouldn't worry about it," Todd said.

"You *wouldn't* worry," Alison said. "That's so typical."

"Come on, you guys," Annie said. "I'll drive you home." She followed them down the gangplank and onto dry land. Her stomach ached. This wasn't the coffee. She realized suddenly it came from fear for Alison. She felt the adrenaline pouring into her system. Those thugs would find her, if they had any brains. It had to be important if they were beating people up in public places. Alison didn't have a clue how to defend herself.

She decided not to share her thoughts. You could always be wrong. No sense giving them even more to bicker about, all the way home. That ache in her stomach was a signal she'd learned to trust. Her hand inside her windbreaker pocket closed around the GPS.

Hunting

Ike Mullin and Tran Phan Ng were pointed south on Michigan Avenue, the Lincoln idled at a red light next to the old stone Water Tower. Crowds of people filled the crosswalk in front of them, even though the light had changed to green. Ike let up on the brake, inching forward into the mass of bodies, and leaned on the horn. He kept up forward motion. The bumper came inches from human knees. People leaped to one side or the other, made a bow wave in front of the car, out into the middle of Michigan Avenue. They shook their fists and twisted their faces into ugly shapes as if *he* was at fault.

Tranny yelled out his window, "Can't you morons see we got a red light, here? You wanna get killed or something?"

"Tell 'em, partner. Try and tell 'em we got a *green* light, though."

"That's what I said, man."

Twenty minutes later they parked in front of a house at 4748 South Halsted. It was a narrow, wooden, two-story house that smelled like it had been freshly painted, white with green shutters. Ike grabbed hold of the metal railing as they climbed the stairs onto the porch.

After prison, the thing he hated most in the world was *stairs*. All stairs. Everywhere you went you had to climb stairs. His heart would give out one of these days, and he knew it would happen on a flight of stairs, very possibly in the apartment he and Tranny shared, which could only be reached by going up three flights.

Ike was still panting from the stairs when the door opened. A man wearing jeans but no shirt or shoes stood in the door. The setting sun glinted off his dark brown skin. He flipped a pair of sunglasses down over his eyes.

"Help you boys?"

"We left our GPS at a restaurant downtown," Ike said. "Our waitress was Alison Paine. So we thought . . ."

The man laughed. "Alison Paine is my grandma, boys. She's seventy-nine. I'd say her waitressing days are over, if she ever did have any. You take it real easy now." He closed the door in their face.

"Hey, wait a minute," Ike said loudly. He hadn't climbed these damn stairs for nothing. They hadn't gotten a word in edgewise with this wiseguy. But no matter how long he stared at it, this door wasn't going to open again.

"Cocksucker."

"Yeah. Whaddya think – Should I bust in? I didn't like the way he laughed in our face."

Tranny shook his head. "Ain't worth your trouble. Where's the next place?"

"Something tells me he ain't lying."

"Wrong fucking skin color, man, in case you're so blind," Tranny said.

"What do you mean? It don't matter what color *his* skin is."

"He's black, man. You dense or something?"

"So what if he's black? Maybe that white bitch is his girlfriend. Maybe she's taking her clothes off in his bedroom right now."

"You deaf or something? He said it was his grandma."

"So you just believe him?"

"The point is, if it really is his Grandma, she's got to be black too. Or at least *half* black, right? So it can't be *our* Alison Paine. Now you get it?"

Tranny punched him lightly on the arm as they walked back down the steps. Ike grunted and let it go. Discussions like this had tended to set him off a couple of years ago, when he'd first started working with Tranny. They'd gotten into some real shit-kickers. Then he'd realized they usually came down to a difference of opinion over the meaning of a word or two. Now he knew enough to let it go.

Tranny had enough difficulty nailing down the right word as it was. Sometimes he had a weird way of saying the opposite of what he meant to say, like there was a screw loose in his brain. If he told you to turn left, you had to stop and second-guess and make sure he didn't mean right. There'd probably been something toxic in Tranny's childhood that fucked up his brain permanantly, like maybe paint chips he'd eaten off walls or something.

If you talked with a little respect, Tranny would do anything you asked. He would change a flat on the expressway with trucks barrelling past, just two feet from his head. He would pry up cast-iron manhole covers from the street, rip out a toilet with his bare hands, or drag two hundred feet of copper wire out of a wall – whatever needed doing. With those Asian eyes he was usually the first to throw punches. They made a good team.

The next few addresses were on the North Side. Hours later, past midnight, they stood in front of an old brick apartment building, four stories, a little patch of grass out in front. Every window in the house was dark. Working people, here. This Alison Paine occupied 3L, according to the directory. Ike put his finger on the button. He heard the buzzing in her apartment from down here. The day had been hot, and now it was a muggy night. She must have the window open. Half a minute passed and nothing happened. He pressed the button again, and this time held it down. The buzzing came from a screen three floors above them on the left.

"Hey, asshole," came a man's voice. It came from that same dark screen up on the third floor. Ike couldn't see the guy, just a dark screen. "The hour is late. We're sleeping up here. Go away and come back tomorrow."

"I ain't asleep," Ike said. "And I ain't *gonna* sleep till I get my GPS back that Alison Paine stole." He punched the button again for emphasis. Buzz, buzz, buzz. Tranny grinned. A light went on over to the right, up on the top floor.

"Now we getting somewhere," Tranny said.

"What are you talking about?" asked the man behind the screen.

"My friggin' GPS," Ike said. "Alison Paine stole my GPS from the restaurant. I need it. And I ain't coming back tomorrow." In a lower voice, but loud enough so the man behind the screen would be sure to hear, Ike said, "See about that lock there, Tranny. We're going up and talk to this fucker."

"I'll call the police, Todd," said a woman's voice from the apartment up on the right, top floor.

"Good idea, Mrs. Murphy," said the man behind the screen. "Tell them home invasion in progress. Stick around," the man went on. "Home invasions, the cops usually come in two or three cars, guns out, safety off. But you guys look like you've been there before. I figure you've got about ninety seconds to get out of here without taking a chance on handcuffs and a few nights in the Cook County lockup. You better hope I don't get your plate number."

Ike saw Tranny getting a tool out of his kit. Tranny would have that door open in thirty seconds. But if someone really was calling the police, the only option was retreat.

Somewhere in the distance a siren echoed out of the orange sky. How he hated that sound. It practically made his knees go to jelly. It brought him back to the Indiana State Prison in Michigan City, Indiana, and its forty-foot walls. Nowadays, they built new prisons that cost a billion dollars, but nobody messed with forty-foot walls anymore. That was how you knew the prison was more than one hundred years old, built in the days when the state still did hangings and lynchings and all sorts of primitive shit. Those high walls were all that remained. It was bad enough without hangings. You might as well try and escape from Hell itself.

There was no telling whether that squad car had their name on it. It couldn't possibly have gone that fast between when the woman called and a car was dispatched. But why take a chance? Even if it wasn't the one with their number, going up and getting in the door and busting the jaw of this idiot to get their GPS back definitely was going to take way too long.

"Come on, Tranny."

"What about the GPS?"

"Later. Cops, man." He led his partner back out toward the street.

"We can't leave without our GPS."

"I know. But I ain't screwing around with the cops."

"Twice in one day we're running from the cops, man. There ain't even any cops."

They got in the Lincoln. Ike started the engine. "You're telling me. And all we're trying to do is get our GPS back that she stole from us. It ain't right at all. Let's go get some beers."

"At least we know it's her."

"What do you mean?"

"Way that guy acted. Wouldn't you say?"

Ike thought about the man behind the screen. He too had suddenly been sure this was the right address. But what was it that had made it all so clear? He tried to remember what the bastard said. Then it hit him. It was what he *hadn't* said. The dude had gone all nice and quiet when he accused Alison Paine of stealing the GPS out of the restaurant. Like he didn't have a good answer. He didn't have a story cooked up. *Bingo*. He knew all about it. That was when the other lady had offered to call the police.

"You're right, Tranny boy. Our GPS is in there. Buy me a beer and I'll tell you how we're gonna get it back."

* * *

"This scares the hell out of me. How did those low-lifes find out where I live? They come here in the middle of the night ready to break down the door. They're sure to come back. If they don't come back here, they'll come to the Domino and make trouble there. What could be so special about this GPS?"

"How much do they go for?"

"How should I know?"

"You're the one who took it."

He heard her sigh. Had he said something wrong? What now?

There was something vaguely exciting about whispering in the dark, with the window open. Between the stuffy, sweaty air in this bedroom and the electric argument he'd just had with a total stranger out the window in the middle of the night, Todd doubted sleep would come any time soon. No sign of the police. Probably Mrs. Murphy hadn't called them in the first place.

"So, did you notice anything special about these bruisers?" he asked in a voice so low only Alison could hear.

"Put away a lot of margarita mix. Big tippers."

"How big?"

"Twenty."

"On?"

"Fifty." She waited for a comment, but it didn't come. "Tell me you're not jealous."

"Why would I be jealous? I'm happy if you make good money. Actually I was thinking about Annie."

"Why?"

"I hope they don't find out she's got the GPS. She didn't have anything to do with it."

"What're you worried about Annie for? I'm the one that's in danger. They think I have it. Where can I go that's safe? If

I stay here, they'll find me here. If I go to the restaurant they'll find me there."

"At least there're a lot of people at the restaurant. What're you worried about, anyway? How are they going to know anything? If they confront you, just tell them you put it in the lost and found, period. Anyone else could've stolen it. There's no reason why it should have to be you. Stick to your story."

Not long after, he heard her breathing turn regular, and he knew she was sleeping. How could she drop off so quickly if she was so frightened? He wished sleep would come so easily to him. For him the air buzzed with current. For all he knew, they were waiting in the bushes outside. They sure had sounded dumb and crazy enough to come back.

Mrs. Murphy's light went dark.

Well, the joke would be on them, since the GPS wasn't here anymore. He envisioned the headline: *North Side Couple Slain Over Stolen GPS* . . . and the dumb part was the killers wouldn't even find it. Maybe it would've been smarter to tell them Alison didn't have it anymore. Well, but then he would have implicated her. And they might have forced him to tell who did have it. Why had Annie wanted to hold on to it, anyway?

Annie had changed during those years in Iraq. She didn't used to be this . . . *assertive*. She used to be so shy and introverted. She was the one who would sit at the table for an hour without saying anything, just listening. You felt sorry for her. Now look at her. Well, four years in the army would do that to you. He remembered how surprised they had been when Annie had enlisted. They had laughed to think of Annie in boot camp, some drill sergeant yelling because her buttons weren't shiny enough.

Fifty push-ups, private!

Alison's body, stretched out beside him under the thin sheet, filled with long steady regular breaths, then emptied again, like a bagpipe without music, filled, then emptied. Filled. Emptied. Her dark hair spread out on the pillow around her head. The one sister dark, with brown eyes, the other white-blond with blue eyes.

And then, after Annie's second tour, when she had come home, how she had been so heartbroken because her boyfriend over there, another soldier, had been killed. Michael. He remembered seeing her then. Her boyfriend dead. Something about a prison. That's right, she had gone to Joliet to visit the dead guy's friend. Why had she wanted to visit that guy in prison?

And then how she had gone back over, back for a third tour. Not many soldiers did that. Not many women soldiers. Must've had a death wish, that dead boyfriend and all. Was that possible? Annie Ogden? Nah, not Annie. And so anyway, she had finally made it back. Home for good, now. Quit the military for good, she said.

Alison's sister, Annie Ogden.

Annie Ogden . . .

BETRAYAL

This white sand of Waikiki, thought Alden Sterling, had to be one of the seven wonders of the world. The wide flat beach, and beyond it the ocean, the Pacific Ocean, stretched to the horizon to a blurring point at which the line of the water met the line of the early morning sky. To a Midwesterner from Sycamore, Illinois, this view had a curative power that seemed magical.

He had come out onto the balcony for breakfast. He admired his son, Trip, curled in the chair waiting for him. Instead of drinking in this wondrous view in order to store it away in his memory for all the days of his life, Trip Sterling, aged twelve, merely turned another page in his comic book. Donald Duck with those three duck detectives, Huey, Duey and Louie.

Two waiters, after wheeling in their forty-dollar breakfast on a wooden cart covered in white linen, had just left the room with a five dollar tip (which they could split between them as they saw fit). Silver chafing dishes with scrambled eggs and bacon. A basket with toast in napkins. Juice in a crystal pitcher; coffee in a silver coffeepot. The platter of fruit laden with pineapple, melons, mangos – standard fare here in Hawaii, but still it dazzled him. This cart would easily feed six. But it was just Trip and himself, here, on the last day of their one-week Hawaiian vacation.

Alden unfolded a napkin and gazed over his son's head at the waves crashing on the beach six stories below. Not many sunbathers out yet, mainly joggers and walkers. A couple of kids wandered around collecting shells.

"If you want to bring home shells, today's your last chance," he said. "We fly back tonight."

"Probably just buy some in the gift shop," Trip said.

"Why pay money when you can just go and pick them up off the beach?"

Trip didn't look up from his comic book. That, too, he had bought at the gift shop. Alden wondered if he hadn't been too generous with his vacation stake. He had given his son one hundred dollars on the plane to Hawaii, figuring it would go for bubble gum, a t-shirt, music CDs, maybe a present for his mother. He'd guessed Trip would want to save half the money. But he hadn't put restrictions on it. No sense giving a kid spending money if you were going to forbid him from spending it. The whole idea was to teach him to spend wisely. All he had said was, not one penny more. It seemed like plenty for a twelve-year-old.

The twenty-seven comic books had cost close to seventy dollars, by Alden's reckoning. The *Sports Illustrated* swimsuit issue from four months ago was full of women in tiny bikinis. More than seven dollars Trip had shelled out for that. Why pay for a magazine when the beach was thronged every day with real boobs and bikinis?

Fathers understood their sons up to a certain point, but beyond that lay a vast unfamiliar ground. Beyond that point, they might as well come from different families, different cultures, different continents. After twelve years of fatherhood Alden knew this. Still, after a week of such treatment you started asking yourself if it had really been worth the expense.

"What would you like to do on your last day in Hawaii?"

"Pool." His son's focus on the comic book never wavered.

"Don't you want to go and do something?"

"Pool, Dad."

For a kid who couldn't stop reading about daring adventures in comic books, Trip was surprisingly phlegmatic.

He had dragged his son to a luau. With half a day of persuading he had managed to get him to the wild animal park. Another day they had been forced to cut short the helicopter tour which would have given them bird's-eye views of volcano craters and deserted beaches when Trip started throwing up over downtown Honolulu. They had ducked under a waterfall, seen natives prance barefoot across hot coals, watched dancers juggle flaming batons. Every time they got back from one of these excursions, Trip wanted only to sit around the hotel pool with his music player, a stack of comic books, and a glass of 7-Up with a maraschino cherry in it. Generally he was too lazy even for a swim.

All week the excursions had been Trip's choices – or what Alden thought a boy must like. The whole week Alden had been waiting for a chance to go on the one excursion he would find interesting.

"This morning I've got a cool surprise for you."

"What surprise?"

"Don't look so suspicious. It's cool." He fingered the brochure peeking out of the front pocket of his Bermuda shorts to make sure it was still there.

"What is it?"

"If I told you, it wouldn't be a surprise anymore."

"What about lunch?"

"I'll give you a hint. It involves getting on a boat. We'll have lunch out there."

Trip groaned.

It seemed absurd to be talking about lunch while still pigging out on breakfast. But planning meals, Alden knew, was one of the primary challenges on vacation. You had your meals to plan, your excursions to book, your itinerary to check.

It was amazing how a man's normally huge capacity to get things done could shrink to fit this limited number of tasks while on vacation. You turned into this sluggish lout that had trouble focusing on the most elementary problems. Eight hours went by, and what did you have to show for it? One excursion checked off the list, one lunch, one bottle of sunblock purchased, maybe two postcards written, one to C., the other a general greeting to the team, back at the office. Whereas at home you would be meeting with clients, looking up complex points of tax strategy, haggling with tax authorities, consulting with lawyers, writing reports, and dealing with the ever-shifting needs of nineteen employees. Here in your hotel room, you spent your whole day trying to win arguments against a twelve-year-old.

"I don't want to go on a boat," Trip said.

"Just a short ride," Alden said. "The boat part lasts fifteen minutes."

An actual smile then, and eye contact, if only for an instant. Well, that was settled. But it was certain to be a long afternoon after the excursion, and then a long flight. Maybe Alden should patronize the gift shop, too, and pick up a book for himself. Figure three hours reading by the pool in the late afternoon, plus another six hours while travelling tonight, including two hours in the gate at the airport. Deduct a couple of hours of possible sleep during the night flight back to Chicago. Still enough time to read something – a good thriller to keep him from going up the wall.

Trip was not exactly King Conversation.

They arrived at the Visitor Center before ten o'clock and received numbered tickets. A National Park volunteer confirmed that their tour would start in exactly two hours, and recommended the audio guide.

"We'll take one of those," Alden said, thinking they could share it. But Trip snatched the headphones right out of his hand

and hooked the sender to his belt, flashing a highly annoyed expression.

"A boring old war memorial. Some way to spend our last day in Hawaii."

"Let's go back outside and look at that anchor," Alden said. But Trip was already listening at high volume to the audio tour. Alden could hear the voice through the headphones; Trip had maxed out the volume so that he wouldn't have to listen to his dad.

Alden went back outside to admire the anchor himself. The tour was free, he had read. Four thousand visitors per day, seven days a week, one and a half million visitors per year. Because it was free, all the tickets every day were usually gone by noon.

The anchor towered over him, all 19,695 pounds of it, polished black cast iron. To think the U.S.S. Arizona had carried three of these massive anchors, weighing ten tons each. Now the boat rested on the floor of Pearl Harbor, where it had sunk on December 7, 1941, only a few minutes after being hit by Japanese bombs, taking more than a thousand sailors to the bottom with it.

The Visitor Center was onshore, and they made you wait here for an hour or two studying the exhibits before you were ferried out to the actual memorial. Alden stood in front of a wall-sized aerial photo of the war memorial: a modern white structure that floated above the massive sunken superstructure of the Arizona. That was where they were going. The Navy launch could only take 150 people at a time over there, two miles across the harbor.

The memorial floats in the water above the Arizona without actually touching it, he read. Like a shrine. The Arizona had been a sitting duck in Pearl Harbor that morning, one of nine big ships on Battleship Row when the Japanese attacked. Eight o'clock in the morning. The men all freshly shaved, breakfast over, performing their morning duties.

The planes had come in from the North, had buzzed the entire island without any defensive action taken. The radar station at Opana Point on the north side of the island had picked them up but thought they must be American planes flying in from the carrier Enterprise, or else B-17s arriving from the mainland, and had not radioed any warning. The Japanese had achieved total surprise.

He remembered the discussion back in high school history class. His history teacher had left them speechless by claiming President Roosevelt had *purposely* allowed the attack. By not tracking the advancing Japanese aircraft carriers north of the islands, by blocking the early warnings, he had ensured that the American sailors would have bombs raining on them without warning. Roosevelt needed a shock to roust the country out of its stubborn isolationism, to get Congress to declare war and come to the aid of the British; Pearl Harbor had forged a spirit of unity all over the country overnight. *But at what hellish cost!* Mr. Scanlon's face had gone purple in his fury. *The betrayal!* All those sailors lost that morning in Pearl Harbor . . . they were on Roosevelt's conscience.

Alden's parents had been so revolted his father had called up the principal to complain. And he hadn't been the only one. Mr. Scanlon, the history teacher, had been suspended for two weeks. What president would knowingly throw away the lives of American men? The school board did not take kindly to a teacher making such accusations.

Was it really so inconceivable? Alden asked himself now, looking out across the blue water, feeling the tropical breeze on his brow. By age forty-one you had lived half of your life. When you had firsthand experience of people's betrayals over half your life, Roosevelt's gambit suddenly didn't look so outlandish. Roosevelt had been under serious pressure from Churchill. With German bombs raining on London, he'd felt a duty to aid Britain and save the continent from falling under the yoke of evil. When one evil was greater than another, a man had to choose the lesser evil. Germany had to be repulsed at any cost, but the British war machine was too weak on its own, too damaged. Without help from America, England would have fallen to Hitler. Roosevelt's aims had been achieved.

Later, in the snack bar, while waiting for their tour to begin, it happened. Trip started to talk. His audio tour had finished, leaving him bored and hungry. Trip only had to have a plate of French fries in front of him, and his blood sugar revived.

"Dad, could we talk about what's going to happen when we go back home?"

Alden instantly paid attention, fingered his moustache, murmured something affirmative.

"Like with Mom and everything? I just wanted you to know that this vacation has been really fantastic and everything, but I'm not coming to live with you. So you can just get that idea out of your mind, because I know that's what you were hoping for."

"Oh? How did you know that?"

"It's so obvious, Dad. But you can forget about it. I'm not coming to live with you."

"Your mother and I both want what's best for you, Trip. It's just that sometimes we don't agree about what that is."

"I know, I know. But what you don't get is that I have a say in it, too. I get to decide who I live with. At least partly I do. You know what I mean. It's not just you that decides it, or Mom. I can say what I want. And I want to go on living with Mom."

Alden took a deep breath. The words of a twelve-year-old could hurt more than anything you ever imagined. So breezily spoken, they pierced his heart like long knives. He didn't look away. Trip gazed out at the aquamarine ocean. In his son's face Alden saw the high cheekbones and the almond eyes of his wife, Deborah, the former high school cheerleader, the former Homecoming Queen, the future ex-Mrs. Alden Sterling.

"I get you," he heard himself saying. "You want to live with your mother, not with me."

As soon as he'd said it, a twinge of doubt. Hadn't that been unfair? One long blade going back in the other direction, easily piercing the boy's tender heart. You didn't do that to a kid. But it had the intended effect.

"It's not that I don't *want* to live with you, Dad."

He'd promised himself not to stir up guilt in his son. But he was only human, too, wasn't he? A man with his strong moral compass had precious few tools at his disposal.

Trip was saying, "It's not a question of wanting. It's just that with your work and all it wouldn't make *sense*."

Change in argument. You couldn't expect a twelve-year-old to reason like a practiced debater. And you had to remember that any son's greatest inner need was to make his father proud. Trip was no different. Pulled in two directions, having won his battle already, he was now working to help his Dad save face.

Alden hesitated about wading back in. Another rule he had was to give Trip the last word whenever he could. A pang of guilt here and there might be unavoidable. But he wasn't going to railroad him. And he wasn't going to badmouth Deborah, either. That was one thing they had agreed on – though there had been times recently when he wondered if she was keeping up her end of the deal. With her it was always the alcohol that was to blame. Wine always gave her an out.

"Actually, I thought we had figured out a way with the schedule," he contradicted as gently as he could. Between Trip's soccer practice and school, their schedules meshed perfectly. He could get home half an hour before Trip without breaking a sweat, and leave later in the morning. He was the owner of his company. Meetings could be rescheduled. He could be on call at work in case Trip injured himself or came home sick. The argument that he could not be around for Trip didn't hold water. Judge Hernandez had been the first to agree.

"It's not just my schedule, and you know it," Trip said. "Mom knows all the stuff I like to eat. She knows my medicines. She helps me with my homework. She knows my friends. She knows when to help me and when to leave me alone."

Alden listened patiently, waiting for his son to mention something that he would have to agree with. His mind went into list-mode: food, medicines, homework, friends. He nodded amiably. "That makes sense. You've been living with her all this time. She knows those things better currently."

"Oh, Dad, give up already with your 'currently'."

He smiled. Giving up was of course not an option. But to go into the reasons why it was not an option would force him to speak ill of her in a way that he would never do, with his son. And not just because he had promised it to her. Because it was what kids deserved from their parents. A lot of them failed at it. He wasn't going to fail.

"Well, you know I'll always be your Dad." It was all he could say without dragging out the argument further, which would have been pointless. Trip took it as acceptance.

"Attaway, Dad. I knew you'd see it my way." Trip got up from his chair, stripped off the headphones, and walked away to get more ketchup.

Misunderstanding

"You lost the GPS? You numb-nuts are telling me my GPS is out there somewhere in the possession of Christ knows who?"

Max Vinyl glared first at one, then the other. They had both found a spot on the floor to stare at. They did not dare look him in the eye. He left them standing. Ike Mullin and his ugly, half-infected pierced eyebrow – what was that, anyway, a bolt? People all over TSR, Inc. were doing work, meeting targets, producing revenue. These two foul-smelling ex-cons dared to come in here, stinking up his office, and tell him some line of bull about losing his five-hundred-dollar GPS.

"First you lose my GPS." It was close to shouting. "Then you miss your one o'clock shift last night. Where in Christ were you knuckleheads?"

"Looking for the GPS, boss."

"Thanks to you we've got a . . . an *overload* situation on the barge. You don't show up, you don't call, nothing. Do you have any idea of the problems you cause when the barge doesn't go out? They're filling up Dumpsters every day. I don't have six more Dumpsters. Even if I owned them I wouldn't have any place to put them. We've got to keep it moving. It's only Tuesday, and I've got shit piling up to the roof, thanks to you guys."

"We're real sorry," Ike said. "We thought we couldn't go out on the lake without the GPS anyway."

"Why not?"

Ike stared at the boss. "It tells us where to go. I mean, you know, where to stop."

"Ten miles is important, yes," Max said. Some EPA recommendation had said something about ten miles. "But I hope you're not stopping at the exact same spot every time. I told you that lots of times, Ike."

"At least we know who's got it. This waitress at a restaurant we were at, see."

"We know where she lives," added Tranny.

"You boys listen up." Max did not have any more time for this discussion. You talked this way to children. "Get that GPS back. I want it back tonight, and I want you here at one o'clock to make up for last night, and I want you here at one o'clock every night this week. You owe me. Now move on it!"

How was it that he still had to deal with low-level employees like these two? Did he have time for this? The Koreans would expect better management for the money they were paying. But now he had an additional worry. One lost bit of gadgetry couldn't be allowed to tie up the workflow of the whole company.

It struck him this was a training issue. Ultimately they didn't even need the GPS. The GPS merely ensured they went far enough out, on the one hand. On the other hand, they had to avoid veering too far to the south, in the direction of wealthy suburbs like Lake Forest or Highland Park. There would be a chance of some party-boat passing in the middle of the night and witnessing the work of TSR off their upper-crust beaches. Off Waukegan, ten miles to the north, the lake at two a.m. stretched out in infinite blackness, no boats, no lights and no witnesses anywhere for miles around.

Think of the Koreans. Song Young Park had more important things to do than keep a couple of tough guys in line. He was touring the U.S. and Canada at this moment buying up companies. Song probably wouldn't let himself be torn to pieces by the loss of a girlfriend, either. Max sank back into his chair.

How could he be losing control of things that were fundamentally so simple?

Later, stopping in the wrapping room on his morning walkaround, Max paused to watch a young woman with interesting short-cropped red hair. Interesting until your eyes registered the pin in her lower lip, the gum grinding in her teeth, the grudge in her frowning eyes. He liked the tank top that exposed her bony shoulders and arms. Couldn't be more than twenty-four, twenty-five.

She tore the address label at the perforation without wasting time reading it, laid it out on the work table beside the shrink-wrapped computer part, and took a pre-folded box from under the table. She wound bubble wrap around the part three times, taped it, and set it in the box. Her jaws worked in rhythm to the beat she was listening to. From a bin beside the table she took a baggie of jellybeans and dropped it in the box. She taped the box shut end-to-end, then crosswise, checked the corners, and stuck the address decal on the front.

Max Vinyl checked his Rolex. Sixty-five seconds. The woman plucked another item off the belt.

"What's your name?"

"Amy Kozlowski," she said, and pulled her earphones off. "What's yours?"

"Max Vinyl. Owner of the joint."

"I know."

"Anything you need over here? Anything we could be doing better?"

"Aside from the pay?"

He pointed to a blue banner hanging high on the wall. In huge white block letters was written MINIMUM WAGE PLUS 25% - TSR POLICY. "You don't like the policy?"

"You think it's something to be proud of?" She rolled her eyes. He resisted the urge to argue. Actually yes, he was proud. Many employees were college students, or dropouts. Why pay more than minimum? He could recruit just as well paying flat minimum. He only paid 25% above minimum for that slight goodwill advantage he imagined it got him. Obviously he hadn't won any points with Amy Kozlowski.

The Koreans would probably cut it right to minimum, first thing they would do. Maybe he should do it for them: lower the payroll, maximize profit, and raise the selling price when they raised their stake to forty percent in three years. *Idea!* He got out his organizer to take a note.

"Maybe we should get music in here." He motioned to her headphones.

"Then it would be your music," Amy Kozlowski said. She turned her back and put the buds back in her ears.

Well, same to you, he thought. Polish name, Kozlowski. Imagine coming home to this bitch. Well, someone else had to come home to Amy Kozlowski every night, not him. He had the pleasure of coming home to Tris Berrymore. At least he'd had that pleasure till yesterday.

He gazed around at the other workers at nearby stations. They all seemed to have their own music. People liked their freedoms; music was one freedom he was happy to leave them. There was a lot of dope being smoked on breaks. That didn't bother him either.

What bothered him was Tris walking out of his life. He couldn't get her out of his mind. His brain was so damned sluggish today. Every time he tried to focus he got interrupted by a message from somewhere in his frontal lobe: *I'm gone. It's over.*

Rodriguez claimed she'd been trying to engineer his downfall, bring down the company, but he hadn't produced any hard evidence. Had she really done anything, or had Rodriguez just screwed up her head? Maybe she'd only ended their relationship because of Rodriguez lowering the boom. Accusations like those could screw up anyone's head. That had to be it . . . didn't it?

He had to talk to her again.

Collection

"You sure caused us a lot of trouble," Ike Mullin said, back in the Lincoln. "You should thank me for sticking with your ass."

"I'd stick with my ass, too, if it was you. You know that."

"You mean you'd stick with my ass."

"That's what I said, stupid."

Ike waved it away. "Tell you what, man. If we can't get the GPS back from that bitch, we're gonna get ourselves a new one at the store."

"Hold on a minute. How much one a those things cost?"

"Who gives a fuck? I don't even know why I'm offering to pay half. I don't wanna get canned just because you go and leave the GPS in some restaurant. Plus we lost all those valuable locations from Lance."

Tranny gave a toss of his head. "I ain't paying for no new GPS for the boss, man. We already get stuck for all the gas we put in this car, all our meals on company time. When he starts paying some of those expenses, I'll think about replacing his GPS. Besides, a new one wouldn't have our special position."

"He just told us we don't have to go to the same position anymore. We just hafta make sure it's ten miles out."

"How we gonna know it's ten miles without the GPS?" Tranny asked.

"You got a point, there."

"Duh. Let's just find the fucker and problem solved, ok?"

Ike parked across the street from the brick apartment building where they had talked to that asshole through a window the night before. They stayed in the car just long enough to finish their coffee, watching the building. It was ten-thirty in the morning.

"You think they're at work?" Tranny asked.

"Only one way to find out."

To be on the safe side, Ike buzzed Alison Paine's apartment. Broad daylight, you didn't take chances. Meanwhile Tranny got the tools out of his kit and started on the lock. In twenty-five seconds they were in the lobby and headed up the stairs. On the third floor, left hand side, was a nameplate that said A.+T.P.

"Do the honors," Ike said.

A minute later they were in the apartment. Ike stopped short three steps inside the door, his eyes glued to an amazing sight. He had never seen anything like it in his life. All along the entire living room wall was shelving, and on these shelves were cell phones. Nothing but phones. The shelves went from the bay window at the front of the apartment clear to the kitchen door at the back. The shelves were attached to the wall. Four long shelves, the entire length of the room.

Tranny bumped into him from behind. "Hey man, outta my way."

"Lord almighty, take a look at that."

Tranny whistled. "What are they – phones?"

"Sure as hell looks like it."

Ike went closer. There were little labels stuck to each phone. Motorola 1991. Nokia 1999. Phone after phone after phone – there must have been two hundred phones.

"Look for the GPS," he said. "I'll check the left side. You check the right. It's got to be here somewhere."

"Man, do they need A.C. in this place," Tranny said, wiping his brow.

Ike swept the shelves with his eyes, searching. But he found only phones. No GPS anywhere.

They must've hidden it.

Tranny ran into the bedroom while Ike took the kitchen. He tore open the fridge, the freezer, pulled everything out and threw it on the floor, opened up Tupperware containers, ice cream, checked the spice cabinet, the cereal cabinet, the bag cabinet. All the drawers went crashing to the floor, forks, spoons and knives everywhere. The faster he went, the angrier he got. What the hell were they going to tell Lance? Why did Tranny have to leave the GPS in that damned restaurant?

They met back in the living room. He handed Tranny a couple of big shopping bags he had found.

"Here's what we're gonna do. Get all these phones and dump them in the bags. You take that side, I'll take this side."

"I never seen so many goddamn phones."

Two minutes later they were back in the Lincoln with Tranny at the wheel. On the floor of the back seat stood four shopping bags filled with cell phones.

Pickup

"'Sterling Accounting Services'," said Brainard Combs. He compared the sign on the wall with the words printed on the ticket in his hand. The computer system at TSR had generated the ticket. They had a pickup at this Sterling place.

"We there?" asked Tom Fuentes, who was driving the truck.

"Turn in that driveway there. That'll probably take us around back." With his mobile he called the contact number on the ticket. "Can I speak to Mr. Olson?"

A dude in a suit and tie stood at the delivery entrance when they arrived in the back. He held the back door open. He had a large shaved head, and in his other hand he held a quart container of milk.

Brainard stood off to one side, frowning, while Tom backed the truck right up to the door.

"That wouldn't be *whole* milk," he said.

"Local product," Olson said. "Comes from a dairy about five miles outside of town."

"Drinking your way to an early death, buddy. Just choose the no-fat. You get all the protein with zero fat."

"And zero taste."

Brainard stared as the bald dude took a big swig. Had he once been this arrogant, at this kid's age? At that age you thought you would live forever.

"Let me show you what we've got," Olson said once Tom had climbed down from the truck. Olson led them down a hall and unlocked a door on the left. You couldn't have gone five feet into this room, it was so stuffed. Computers piled on top of other computers three, four, five high. Big heavy screens that looked like TVs from the 1970s, printers, laptops, keyboards – junk piled almost to the ceiling in the entire room. They would practically have to tunnel in, as was often the case.

"How many people you got working here?"

"Us? Oh, just nineteen of us at Sterling Accounting," said Olson. "But see we went around and collected from all the tenants in this complex and also the one next door."

Brainard shook his head, marvelling at the pile. "Hope you charged 'em something."

"I'm not an accountant for nothing," Olson said. "Now we weighed all this stuff as it came in. That's how you charge, right? Thirty cents a pound?"

"Righto."

"We came up with four thousand, four hundred and ninety-six pounds."

"We'll talk about that later when we've weighed it," Brainard said, walking away. He didn't allow this Olson fellow to go on talking. It was a bad sign when a customer told you the poundage right off the bat. Not to mention being a whole milk drinker. In any case, no point discussing it before he had his own number.

Tom was already back with the forklift and the first cage. They formed a two-man assembly line. Brainard would pull a PC or a monitor from the pile and hand it back to his partner. Tom would take two steps backward, into the hall, and set it in the cage. Brainard would meanwhile be picking up the next item from the pile. He liked the exercise. After over an hour in the truck, it felt good to be using his arms, his shoulders, his back. This old junk wasn't heavy. They warmed up quickly. He liked the sheen of sweat on his upper body under the thin tank top. A day out on recovery beat a week's worth of trips to the gym.

He stood a quarter inch under six feet but weighed two hundred and forty pounds. How much of that might be fat was a topic that occupied his mind a fair amount of the time. A big man could go to seed so easily, especially after rounding forty. Watch what you eat, get plenty of exercise, keep a positive outlook. Those lessons had not come easily. He had rules. Once a man had rules, all he had to do was stick to them. No bread. No salad dressing. No alcohol. He ate hamburgers without the bread. He ate dry salads. He drank water or juice. With these three restrictions, he could eat as much as he wanted and still stay trim and fit, as long as he exercised. Since his work gave him plenty of exercise, he had no trouble keeping fit.

They filled up cage after cage. The steel-mesh cages stood six feet high, six feet deep and 30 inches wide. They had lockable wheels. They could be hoisted with the forklift and placed in the truck in a way that optimized the use of the space. This size truck carried twenty-four cages plus the forklift.

Brainard's mind wandered as he burrowed through the junk, lifting out one piece at a time and handing it to Tom Fuentes. Back to the ax. Back to the days when he had been a skinny runt of a kid, down in Kentucky. The auto graveyard overflowed with old Datsuns, old Chevies, old Fords lined up as far as the eye could see, parked in the tall grass in Uncle Von's bottom land, their final parking place.

Their tool of choice had been an ax. One car after another. That old yellow Datsun . . . for some reason he had a memory of an old faded yellow Datsun. Must've been one of the first cars. Start with the windshield. Smash it with the ax, push it in with your boot till it fell in on the bucket seats, all harmless chunks of safety glass. Start chopping at the window molding, the roof supports, front, back, sides; work the roof free. Wade into the tall grass in between the Datsun and the Chevy Nova next to it, crawling with wood ticks – which you later removed from your skin, one by one, by holding a lighted match near – swing your ax, cleave those last bits of metal connecting the roof to the passenger compartment. Get under it with your arms, and . . . up and over. The roof landed in the high grass next to the car, on the other side. Uncle Von would drive up with his half-ton and they would load the Datsun roof onto it. Next came the fenders. The ax would cleave any bolt, any fastener, two or three swings max.

With the fenders hauled away in Uncle Von's truck, the Datsun was starting to look less like a car and more like a wrecking project. He went at the thick bolts that held the boxy interior attached to the chassis. Uncle Von came back for a third trip. The sweat would be pouring off him, just like now, only this was easy, clean work, hefting old computer monitors. Uncle Von would bring a cold can of Pabst around mid-morning. Later he would bring a bag of cold cooked chicken and a six-pack and they would eat lunch in his truck. The chicken tasted of metal shavings, motor oil, summer heat. The beer was pure Heaven. They'd drunk it like water in those days, two decades before he started monitoring his body mass index. Nowadays beer was taboo, being nutritionally worthless.

The ax had become an extension of his body, like a third arm. Like an arm with a blade at the end. He could swing it light or heavy, aim with his eyes closed. He'd sharpened it every morning on the whetstone at Uncle Von's farm. Later he'd kept the ax in the front seat beside him, driving around town. Nobody fucked with him then. In those days, boys fought with knives. Guns were for hunting, knives for fighting. Nobody dared take him on, not with that ax.

In prison his greatest deprivation had been the ax. But the image alone, the memory of it, had kept him sane. He'd spent his days in prison reliving the time when they had chopped up old cars. For armed robbery he'd done two years. He had stayed cool whenever a fight broke out in the shower or out playing hoop. He was the ax. No one fucked with him, almost as if he still had it in his hand.

Six months after getting out, a teenager in a 7-11 store in Berwyn had died of a bullet wound to the neck. The bullet had come from a gun in Brainard's hand. Second degree murder had stuck. So when he'd gone up to the federal pen in Marion, Illinois for twenty years during the permanent lockdown, he'd done some figuring. Now, he reasoned, he would either come out a different kind of man, or he would come out in a coffin.

It had taken years to transform himself. All the time he pumped iron in prison he tried to picture himself in a new way. No more ax. No more pure muscle with a brain attached. More like a brain that happened to be in control of a body. He kept up the regimen year after year, working on his chest, his legs, his abdominals, his neck. It was all you had in prison. Four walls, a cot, a toilet, the slimeball you had to share your cell with, the slime they gave you to eat . . . and your body. You could sculpt it, build it by degrees, day by day, marking the passage of time and making it into what you wanted at the same time.

Your body was an extension of your mind. It was the mind's work. The body was the ultimate expression of the power of the mind.

Slowly, and not without enormous mental effort, he had banished the ax from his mind's eye. For the ax represented the old Brainard, the man who couldn't keep himself out of jail. He'd repressed the fantasies and the memories. The weeks had turned to months and the months to years. He was *not* the ax any longer. With his mind, he made the ax fade and vanish until it no longer existed. The mind could do that little trick. Now he was the brain. That's why his Mammy had called him Brainard. A man could change his identity by a trick of the mind. That was what he had done.

By the time he got out, having served sixteen years, he had gray hair. A job had been lined up by his parole officer. A company called TSR, Inc. It stood for Tri-State Recovery. Something to do with recycling computers in the three-state area including Illinois, Indiana and Wisconsin. He liked the idea of recovery, sort of like guys recovering from spending half their life in prison. The general manager was from Costa Rica. Manny Rodriguez interviewed him in the front seat of a late-model Buick Cutlass.

"I'm not gonna commit any more crimes, so if that's what you're after you can let me off at the next exit."

"Suits us fine," Rodriguez said.

"What is it I'm supposed to do?"

"We need someone who can manage men who have been in prison."

That's when Brainard had learned about drivers carrying around thousands of dollars in cash. The first time he had heard about it, he had thought, *this can never work*. They were sent out across the state with a truck in two-man teams. They had to find the place for the pickup, deal with the people there, sometimes negotiate a little, sometimes use a little diplomacy. Then they had to drive back and deliver the load and the cash.

It sounded simple. But there were a lot of things that could go wrong. Giving an ex-con an empty truck, a forklift and a full tank of gas was madness. Trusting him with thousands in cash was pure lunacy. Somehow Max Vinyl pulled it off. Not once had anyone run off with a truck. Nowadays they knew Brainard was waiting at the other end. He was careful to drop names of the people he had been in the same prison with, people like Manuel Noriega and John Wayne Gacy, almost as if they had been friends. That kept the men in line.

Then there were Max Vinyl's odd jobs. The kind where a different kind of pressure was needed. The kind that made the victim wonder if he was just having an extra bad day. Brainard wouldn't think of slashing your tires, like the Mafia. Max wanted something more subtle, and also something more deniable, yet something that would convince the person that paying what they owed was their best option after all.

Say the guy would come out of the movie with his date. It would be after midnight. The parking lot down at the mall emptied quickly at that hour. They would reach the car. "Oh, shit," the guy would say. Flat tire. Simple as that. Not slashed, just flat. It could've been something he ran over, or maybe the tire was just worn out. He would spend the next half hour changing the flat, or waiting for the Triple A to arrive, while his woman stood around in her nice clothes. A major inconvenience. And then it would happen again three days later. Same car, different tire. It would happen over and over again until the guy finally got it.

Deniability was as important to Brainard as it was to the boss. Only a person with shit for brains got sent up a third time. Only someone with a death wish went to prison over the age of forty. Prison was no place for a man whose hair was graying at the temples, even if he could still bench three-twenty. He was not going back to prison, period.

So the tire jobs were careful, discreet, and untraceable. The viruses on a person's home computer were something everyone assumed just came off the internet – even when it happened five nights in a row, even when it didn't help to buy a completely new computer.

No one got killed. No one even got a clear message. But once he started working on them, he didn't stop till they had paid. The boss always seemed to have someone who refused to pay their bill. It was always an unpaid bill. When the boss told him the bill had been paid, the person's bad luck stopped as suddenly as it had begun. The best part of this work was that he was working in secret and reporting directly to the boss. Nobody had ever connected him with the accidents that happened.

After an hour of work, the storeroom was empty and the truck was full. Tom checked the tie-offs that held the cages in place in the truck while Brainard phoned Olson at Sterling

Accounting. A couple minutes later Olson showed up. His bald scalp shone in the sun.

"You guys work fast," he said.

"Your scale must be broken," Brainard said. "We weighed all your junk and we came up with five thousand, six hundred and twenty pounds."

The accountant puckered up as if he had bitten into a lemon. For a minute he said nothing. Then he said, "That's thirteen percent more."

"See how fast the kid worked that out, Tom? Sure is quick with numbers."

"What are you insinuating?" Olson said.

"I'm just asking myself how you came up with an exact figure like that so quickly, you know?"

"We weighed it. I'm asking myself how you came up with so much more weight."

Brainard ignored him. "I've got a paper here that I'm supposed to sign," he said. "I sign it. I give it to you. It releases your company from liability connected with the disposal of this computer equipment. Transfers the liability to us, see? If we can't agree about the poundage, I can't sign the form. That means you're liable if any issues come up."

"Well, it's simple. No signature, no cash," said Olson. He turned and looked out across the highway. "I've got one thousand, four hundred and seventy dollars right here. Cash for you, based on four thousand, nine hundred pounds. We weighed it carefully. It was a lot of work. I honestly don't know how it could suddenly weigh more." He held out a wad of bills.

"Seven hundred and twenty pounds difference," Brainard said. "Maybe one of your people in the complex brought over eight or ten PCs a week later, didn't get counted? Maybe something didn't get weighed, like when you weren't here?"

Tom Fuentes stood listening. Tom was new on the job. Brainard was showing him the ropes. Tomorrow Tom would be out on his own with another, less experienced partner. In a few weeks Tom might be asked to train new recruits himself. But Olson didn't want any part of it.

"I collected the cash myself based on the weight. This room was locked. There is no way we could be off by seven hundred pounds," Olson said.

"See, Tom," Brainard said. "Mr. Olson is trying to cheat our asses out of more than two hundred dollars."

"That's not true," said Olson. "I'd like to have a look at your scale, if you don't mind. One computer. We could weigh one machine on your scale, and then we weigh it on mine. Could be it's a problem with the setting. I'm sure we can get to the bottom of this."

"So what we do, Tom, is we hold on to the liability release. It's real simple. Without this paper his lousy company is liable for any environmental claim that gets traced back to this load. I'm sure somewhere in that truckload someone forgot to wipe the hard disk. The authorities'll trace it straight back to them. Those kind of claims get very expensive."

"OK," said Tom.

"We lose a little time, this way," Brainard went on. "But we got another pickup in the area anyway, don't we? So we just go dump all this shit in a ravine somewhere nearby here where the acid'll be sure to start leaking out after a few weeks, and then we go do our next pickup."

"Hold on a minute," said Olson. The kid's face seemed to have gone a little pale. Brainard had never once failed to collect, using this threat.

"I'm not gonna argue with you, Mr. Olson," Brainard said, backing up and heading for the truck. "Haven't got the time."

"Wait . . . it's all right," Olson said. "We need that paper. If I have to, I guess I can probably . . . come up with it." Olson pulled another roll of bills out of his wallet. "So that makes two hundred and forty dollars more. I don't agree with your poundage, but you fellas leave me no choice."

"That's more like it, Mr. Olson." Brainard signed the paper and handed it over. "By the way. You want to answer me a question?"

"Shoot."

"That shaved head a yours. You're what, twenty-eight? Thirty? Why in the world so many young guys like you want to shave it all off like that?"

Olson stood up straighter and dug his hands in his pants pockets. He looked for a minute as if he wasn't going to answer. Then he said, "I think you should know that we're going to think long and hard before we ever call your company again."

Brainard nodded. "You didn't answer the question."

"I'm seriously considering reporting you to the Better Business Bureau," Olson said.

They drove away, Tom at the wheel. Brainard counted the money once more, then stuffed the cash in his pocket and filled out the form he would need to hand in back at TSR. Drivers were expected to pad the poundage, but never by more than fifteen percent. You didn't want some security guard coming out and making you re-weigh everything at gunpoint.

Once they were back on the highway he said, "You believe that dude back there? Is there such a thing as a Better Business Bureau?"

"Hell no," Tom said. "He's about as fulla shit as they come, you ask me."

* * *

Bob Olson stood for a full minute, watching the big TSR truck circle the rear lot and finally exit by the west driveway. Swindled in broad daylight. There hadn't been a damn thing he could do. The job had cost two hundred and forty dollars more than it should have.

He walked back in out of the heat and sat down across from his secretary, Marge Waters. When he explained what had happened she said, "Alden would never make a stink about that. You got a receipt, didn't you?"

"It's not what Alden thinks. It's the principle that kills me. They come in here, we have a solid deal, and they're cheating from the word go. Like it's part of their game plan."

"Haven't you got enough to do, Bob? So we ended up paying, what, thirty-two cents a pound instead of thirty? Look at the bright side. The storage room is cleaned out. All that gear is going to be recycled. The job is done, and just in time for Alden's return."

He had worked at Sterling Accounting Services for eight years and never had such an experience. "If all our suppliers cheated us like that, where would we be? We don't cheat our customers. They expect honest dealing, and they trust us. That trust is what brings us more business, year after year. Even the IRS trusts us, because they know we're so frigging honest."

"It's the right way to be," Marge said. "Just don't expect all of God's creatures to sing the same tune."

She was right, but still it bothered him. The image of those men cheating him out of two hundred and forty dollars stayed with him like an unresolved problem. It niggled at him at some subconscious level all through the day as he supervised work on tax returns for first extension filers (June 15 was right around the corner), dictated letters and outlined new projects for three different office assistants. Swindled right out in the back parking lot. The feeling nagged at his consciousness as he walked home from work at seven p.m., and he was aware of it while he ate his dinner, alone. It was even there, somewhere in the back of his mind, while he watched a one-hour nature program before bed on cable TV on the life cycle of puffins.

Puffins were a hardy black and white sea bird that lived on rocky coasts in the North Pacific and the North Atlantic, pretty much all over the world, in fact.

By the time he went to bed he had finally forgotten about it. He had not known that male and female puffins stayed together for years.

TRIGGER

Even now, an hour after getting home, Todd Paine could not believe the sight of those empty shelves. He felt as if he had never seen the shelves before, they looked so strange and dusty and bare. So the phones were history. The whole collection, every last one. He had seen it the moment he walked in. Then he had found the mess on the kitchen floor.

Annie and Alison had arrived after urgent calls from him. Annie had the GPS. The three of them sat in the living room, Alison hyperventilating while Annie held her tight.

"You were right, Al," he said. "Those guys came back. They broke in here. When they didn't find their GPS, they stole my phones."

"What if I had been here? That's all I can think. They would've beat me up, too. Maybe worse."

"You're right," Annie said. "It's lucky you weren't here."

"I can't believe my collection is gone. Just like that."

"Who cares about your collection? Those sleazebags were in our apartment. Look at the kitchen. I feel so violated. What about my safety?"

"All they wanted was the GPS."

"I can't stay here anymore," Alison said. Her voice had jumped an octave. "I can't sleep here another night."

"They won't come back again. What would they come back for?" Todd said.

"I don't care. I can't stay here."

"Where the hell are you planning to go?"

"What's the note say?" asked Annie.

"They want a meeting. They want to trade the GPS for my phones."

"Call the police," Annie said.

Alison shook her head. "They're going to say I stole it. I'll get fired. I like working at the Domino. You're not calling the police."

"So you actually want to do what they say? You really think I'm going to get my phones back?"

"How should I know?" asked Alison. "If they get their GPS back, I won't have to worry about those guys anymore. That's all they want."

While Todd cleaned up the mess, Annie took her sister for a walk around the block. Exercise and fresh air would calm her down. She stopped crying as soon as they got out of the house. By the time they reached the end of the block, she seemed to be breathing normally again.

"Alison, remember that guy? When we were little, in the forest?"

"I was just thinking about him. As long as I live I will never forget him." After a minute of walking in silence she added, "Although I've tried. Believe me."

Annie had seen her share of brutality in the military. To see it here at home revolted her. To have her sister be the object of it made her feel like stomping on somebody's face. She had turned in her weapons, but she still had her hands, her feet, her boots. She knew what to do with dudes like these. Her stomach turned over to think of them having gotten so close to Alison.

She took them in her car. They were both so quarrelsome she wouldn't have trusted them in city traffic.

It was pretty clear they were dealing with crazy, stupid criminals, here. She heightened her alertness, as if on patrol again. Telling herself to stay focused, she took in people she saw walking on the sidewalk on Belmont: the tall, thin, white-haired man with a telephone at his ear; two women in Ray-Bans pushing strollers. She locked onto them in perfect focus. She registered a sparrow pecking at a branch, the quivering leaves around it, the bright blue sky beyond the tree. Turning south on Clark, she drove as slowly as traffic allowed, tuning out the bickering from the back seat.

The note said Alison should sit alone in the McDonald's at Clark and Division. By three-thirty, half an hour before the meeting time, Alison sat at her table with a Coke and the GPS in plain view next to it. Todd sat six tables away under an electric guitar that supposedly had been picked by Jimi Hendrix. He was doing some work on his laptop. He had his cell phone on the table in front of him, and a chocolate shake.

Annie waited in her car with her own phone ready, and kept an eye on the people going in. She couldn't say why, but doing surveillance in downtown Chicago gave her a major buzz. She watched the parade of people going into McDonald's: teen-agers with rolls of fat that stretched their t-shirts in the arms and the tummy; out-of-shape Moms that waddled like penguins; old folks who limped in, favoring a knee that supported fifty pounds too much; men who looked like they had their shirt stretched over an exercise ball.

What a difference to the people she'd last kept under sur-veillance. They ate well in Iraq, but sparingly. Potatoes, rice, dates, meat, pistachios, honey, yogurt . . . she'd had some unforgettable meals in the local restaurants. But over there it was different – they didn't stuff themselves just because they were lonely or depressed or stressed out. She felt that energy she had felt back in the war zone coming back to her now, just to be looking for someone, just to be doing what she was trained for once again.

At quarter to four her phone vibrated.

"Brown Lincoln, west entrance," Todd said.

"Got 'em." Annie had the binoculars up. Big heavy dude, blond crewcut. Pierced eyebrow – God, what *was* that? Shorter Asian male in the passenger seat. They parked and got out. "Hang up, Todd. Make yourself invisible. Don't look directly at them."

The men went into the dining room, spotted Alison, and walked up to her table. From her car Annie watched through the binoculars. She kept one hand on the door handle, ready to sprint in and lend muscle. The men stayed standing, talked a minute with Alison. The blond one with the pierced eyebrow stood with his face to her. Some sort of enormous bolt, she saw now, with a bunch of washers and nuts on the end. All at once the Asian one grabbed the GPS off the table. She saw his mouth working, angry words. The men walked back out again without even a look back at Alison, still talking to each other, not looking around the parking lot, not suspecting a thing, and got in their car.

She phoned Todd.

"They're leaving. What's your status in there?"

"Alison's fine," he said. "Bawling her eyes out, but fine. She'll be OK. She handed over the GPS."

Annie wasn't sure how well Todd was able to judge the state Alison was in. She had just been in the presence of the two guys who had beat up her friend, who had stood outside her house in the middle of the night threatening to break in, and who had in fact broken in this morning and torn the place apart. Maybe that recurring thought, *What if I had been there?* was a thing only the two sisters could relate to.

"What about your phones? They didn't have anything with them." Annie started her engine, keeping an eye on the brown Lincoln now passing directly in front of her.

"Said they were going to ditch them in deep water," Todd said. "In the lake. Said we deserved it."

She started her car and pulled out of the lot. The brown Lincoln turned right and headed north on Clark. She let a car go by, stepped on it, then laid off the gas. No sense in getting pulled over just because she was irritated.

"No way are they going to do that," she said. "They're just trying to make you crazy. How much are they worth, anyway?" Talking calmed her down. The Lincoln had settled into traffic three cars ahead of her.

"I don't know," said Todd. "Some are pretty rare. Most are just worthless old chunks of plastic."

"I'm following them."

"What?"

"Tailing their asses. See if I can find anything out. See where they go."

"Haven't you got anything better to do, Annie? Hey, come back here. How are we going to get home? Aren't you going to drive us home?"

"Walk'll do you good." She ended the call.

The brown Lincoln turned east on Belmont. It was a sparkling sunny day. She kept the window open and her Oakleys down, letting the breeze blow on her face. At Sheridan Road they turned north. The road twisted and turned. Most of it was slow going, stop sign after stop sign. Sometimes she glimpsed an emerald flash between two buildings, then she would come around a bend and the entire Lake Michigan vista would open out before her, broad as the ocean. The watery, fishy smell blowing through the open windows invigorated her. It blew away the anxiety and depression that had been following her around. She belonged here. She was meant to be doing this. It was so simple keeping three or four cars between her and the brown Lincoln. They didn't give any sign of knowing she was there.

Something about the two men she was following took her back to another place, another time. The way they had treated Alison, the way they looked.

Michael had joined the army to get out of prison. He had spent less than a year in jail, but he had told her lots of stories, and he had made friends with other soldiers who had done time.

"What did you do?" she had asked, not sure she really wanted to know.

"Stealing cars. Nothing else to do in Buffalo. Siphoned a little gas, got caught doing that, too."

"Cars? Multiple cars?"

"Hell, Annie, kind of dull just stealing one. Generally we had classy models on our list, you know? Lexus, Cadillac, Audi, BMW. They would be shipped out to some other place within like minutes of us bringing them in. Resold in California or Texas or somewhere, I don't know."

"Like a car ring."

"Pretty speedy, aren't you?"

"Leave me alone. I never slept with a car thief."

"Would you still have joined the army if you had known they were going to hook you up with riff-raff like me?"

"Why, is it contagious?"

Michael was serious again. "My friend Oliver stole cars. I learned from him."

"Where is he now?"

"Where do you think? He's in jail. Probably made a smarter choice than me, too."

"Why do you say that?"

"They say you come out of here with skills, leadership and all that. But that's if you come out. Alive, I mean."

She saw his dark eyes again now. Michael's eyes so dark, such a rich dark brown they were almost liquid black, his hair cropped almost to a shave like everyone else's, his high Latino cheekbones, that beautiful big monument of a nose. It hurt to have that full-screen image on again in her brain. She shut it out, staring at the sparkling water off to her right, the sailboat half a mile offshore.

Joliet, Illinois. Back from her second tour. Suited up in desert camouflage to get her nerve up. She, Annie Ogden, low on courage ... but yes, for once, yes.

Here to see Oliver Greenwood, please.

The bag of sugar cookies, x-rayed but not opened. *Sure ma'am, no problem.* Then he was there, sitting across from her. Bulletproof glass between them, thick as steel plate. And Oliver Greenwood about as different from Michael as two men could be: the dirty-blond hair, the cold eyes, the scars around the eyes and the bridge of his nose, the nose that had been broken badly, the scars on the fingers laced together on the table on front of him. She pictured those fingers twisting the arms or slapping the faces or pulling the hair of innocent people – girls, old folks – for small amounts of money. Those eyes must have seen people cringing in fear at what he was about to do to them. And then he had done it. Otherwise why would he be in prison?

"So you knew Michael?" Oliver said.

She nodded. "He talked about you. Talked a lot about you."

Oliver Greenwood's face loosened. You couldn't call it a smile. "We did a lot of shit."

"He considered you his best friend. He would've wanted me to tell you that."

The man on the other side of the glass sat mute. He didn't blink. She held his gaze. Finally he said, "How did my friend die?"

She told him what they had told her. A firefight in some village, snipers shooting when they went in to pick up the pieces after a roadside bombing. He had been shot while evacuating a wounded soldier. Shoot the helpers.

"One fucked-up war," Oliver Greenwood said. "At least he had you. Guess he was happy when he bought it."

"I wanted to give you the news in person," she said. "For Michael. In a way he loved you, too."

Oliver Greenwood stared much too long. Well, what else did he have to look at? She supposed time itself had a different meaning for people in prison. Maybe it was normal for them to let a minute go by between each question and each answer. A minute that felt like an hour.

Time was the one thing people in jail had too much of. The inmates would do anything to make time pass more quickly. Everyone on the outside moaned about wanting to slow things down. You were a slave to the clock, each person caught in her own personal ratrace, sleeping too little every night for years, stressing to the point of a breakdown. Not to mention dying young. Time was the thing Michael had run out of, much too soon.

At last, just when she thought he wasn't ever going to answer, Oliver Greenwood said, "Thank you for that."

The meeting had ended after ten minutes.

Almost without considering any alternatives she had gone back for a third tour.

What had she been looking for, exactly, revenge? On some unknown assassin? To join Michael, wherever he was? Or for some kind of weird validation of his death? Eighteen months ago she had known what it was that made her go back. Now that it was over forever, that chapter in her life, that knowledge too was lost. She couldn't dredge it out of her memory. She couldn't reconstruct it. She only knew she hadn't found any answers. She also hadn't found him.

Michael's body had gone back to upstate New York. Retrieving any tangible impression of him now was about as easy as reversing the direction of time. She saw him in dreams and fantasies, but she would never again lose herself in the look of those eyes, or feel her nose touching his nose when they kissed, or feel the earth shake when they made love. The third tour in Iraq hadn't brought her one atom closer to any of those things.

Still, it hadn't been a mistake to go back. She knew it hadn't.

The brown Lincoln cruised on a quarter mile ahead. To the east of the highway she saw stands of forest and wetland, on the other side of which could only lie Lake Michigan. They had been heading due north for thirty minutes. They passed a sign that said Waukegan, city limits and a population of 90'000 and some. She hung back when she that up ahead, at a stop sign, the men were turning right, toward the lake.

When she turned at the same stop sign fifteen seconds later, she found herself at the top of a hill. Directly ahead stood a high traffic barrier and flashing orange arrows right and left. The road forked. Off to her left she spotted the brown Lincoln heading north a quarter mile away. No other cars were anywhere near. She slowed and surveyed the scene that opened up in front of her as she approached the flashing arrows.

Down below, at least a hundred feet down, lay a large cluttered industrial zone, and beyond it the open lake. She saw what looked like a cement works with silos, warehouses, a concrete breakwater, a small public park with a boat launch, and some railroad tracks running parallel to a north-south road. There was an island or a spit of land out in the water, on which there was another huge industrial site, with barges and boats moored alongside, and a channel running between it and the land. A sailboat motored up the channel headed for the open lake.

She watched the Lincoln through her binoculars as it drove away to the north. The left fork was a long ramp that led down into this industrial zone. If they hadn't seen her by now they had to be pretty dim. Or they didn't care. Well, she didn't care, either. At the bottom of the ramp, maybe half a mile away now, the Lincoln beetled north along the train tracks another three hundred yards before turning right, toward the lake. Beyond the railroad crossing it entered a driveway that had chain link fences rising on both sides, then across a wide asphalt area where both cars and boats up on trailers were parked.

With her binoculars she studied the massive blue warehouse that loomed over the parking area. From this vantage point it appeared to be situated directly on the channel, but the Lincoln disappeared between the blue warehouse and the channel. Where in the world were they taking Todd's phones? There must be a strip of land back there, and a road. She got back in her car and drove after them.

A minute later she was crossing the tracks and entering the fenced parking area herself. The blue warehouse looked like a boat hangar for very big boats, or maybe a place where they built boats. She found the narrow strip of road that ran between the warehouse and the channel. Two hundred yards farther on, at the other end of the blue warehouse, she found herself in a gravel parking lot. Forty or fifty cars were parked here in neat rows.

She immediately spied the brown Lincoln at one end. The two men, each carrying heavy shopping bags that she guessed had Todd's phones in them, were just nudging open a screen door. She kept the car rolling, heading toward them, her tires chewing gravel and making a lot of noise. With ten lines of cars between her and them, they didn't even turn to look.

The black structure they went into was a low-ceilinged annex attached to the massive blue warehouse behind it. There was a sign attached to the black siding. She came around the phalanx of parked cars and pulled close enough to read it. Under the big block letters TSR she read *Tri-State Recovery, Inc*. A buzz went through her again at the sight of it, just because she had the audacity to be here, doing this. The sign made it real. A real company. They were receiving stolen property. Those two tough guys could come tearing out at any minute, demanding to know what she was up to. Only the door stayed closed and they didn't come out.

She took her foot off the brake and headed back out. The phones were here. Call it a day.

Your mother

"Dad, would you please reveal to me what we're doing here?"

They stood in the white steel floating bridge memorial of the U.S.S. Arizona, the Pacific Ocean breeze blowing steadily through the open windows, dozens of tourists standing to their left and right, in front of them and behind them. Ocean of *peace*, he thought. At the far end of the memorial, out here on the water, was a marble slab on which the names of all the dead were engraved. Over a thousand men were entombed in the ship that rested on the ocean floor directly beneath their feet.

"Think what that must've been like," Alden said. "To have the ship burning and men yelling. Then suddenly the whole thing is sinking."

Trip wandered away, his face a mask of extreme annoyance. Alden let him go. Had he been so annoyed with everything and everyone when he was twelve? He didn't remember. His parents of course hadn't had the same thorny problems he and Deborah had. He stared down through the opening in the steel floor into the water. His eyes followed the dark wavy outline of the U.S.S. Arizona, only a few feet below the surface. A watery tomb. They had tried to make this place peaceful, with the wind blowing through, the blue sky above, everything open, and the steel memorial structure carefully suspended above the Arizona, never actually touching it. But after a while you realized the place was haunted. Men down there whose lives had been cut short unfairly, with no warning, in all probability betrayed by a president. How could it be anything but haunted?

He looked down into the murky water, searching under the surface, and he saw scenes from twenty-five years ago.

She was the girl every boy in the whole high school desired. With her fair hair and her blue almond eyes, Deborah Snyder had always made boys turn and stare. Studying her face, you saw her eyes had that slight slant, and then those dimples she had when she smiled. The dimples would deepen and she would let out that laugh that revealed all. She *liked* you. She liked what you had said. You were important to her. She was interested in you. She liked being with you. All this was contained in her laugh. He had observed it countless times between Deborah and her friends.

"You're Alden, right?" she had said once, in math class.

It was the first time she had ever spoken directly to him, though he had been manager of the football team for two years. Normally she never even turned around. Certainly she had never actually looked at him, and to have her speak directly to him, saying his name, proving she knew he existed – well, that had just been pure bliss.

Think fast.

"Born and baptized," he said.

She reached something across to him, a small white envelope. "This has to get to Troy after school today. You'll see him at practice, right?"

"Sure, yeah." He put the envelope in his pocket.

"Thanks, Alden."

He had stored away that golden smile. For years afterwards he had nourished himself with it. Many times he had seen Deborah Snyder's smile beamed at others. This one had been for him alone.

Without the slightest hesitation he had steamed open the envelope at a janitor's sink in the athletic complex, where the water came out illegally hot. Troy Iverson was the quarterback. Big muscles, good looks, a strong arm for throwing passes with a perfect spiral – the dream partner for the beautiful, honor-society cheerleader, Deborah Sterling. But instead of the love note he expected he found only a baggie with three joints in it. Marijuana. One sniff told him it was the real stuff.

Carefully he glued the envelope back together. This put him in a tricky position. If he didn't deliver the envelope, it would look like he had stolen the dope. If he gave it back to Deborah she would think he was the biggest loser who ever walked the planet. If he got caught with it himself, he could be arrested by Officer Leahy, the town policeman who patrolled the school. There was only one option. He had to deliver the envelope as she had asked him to do.

Everybody knew Troy and Deborah were going steady. Even Alden's mother knew it, from grocery store gossip. You saw them walking hand-in-hand down Main Street, or making out in the movie theatre. The football scores were front-page news every Wednesday, when the paper came out. Sometimes a picture of Troy would grace the page, helmet in hand, hair matted to his scalp, the two-finger V for victory held high. Troy and Deborah had gone to the junior prom. It was a foregone conclusion that Deborah would be elected Homecoming Queen and that she and Troy would get married.

That very day, Officer Leahy had done a surprise search of the lockers of all the football players. In one locker he had found a marijuana pipe with traces of weed in it, in another a baggie with 50 grams of Columbian and two hundred dollars in cash. In a third he discovered a small white envelope with telltale bulges that greatly interested Hoover, his German Shepard. Troy Iverson had to open the envelope in front of the whole team. When he saw what it contained, Coach walked away without a word. Troy Iverson had tears running down his cheeks as Officer Leahy took him and the other two boys away.

Alden Sterling knew how to keep his head down. It was common practice for boys to pick each others' locks, steal from each other, plant things. No one even bothered to question Alden. Troy and the other boys were kicked off the team. The shock reverberated through the town for years afterwards.

"I was tired of him being king of the heap all the time. He didn't deserve it," Deborah told him much later, after they were married, once when they were reminiscing about the day when Troy and two others had gotten busted.

"You were tired of it? But you were his Queen."

"You thought it was a coincidence?"

"Too many things happened that day for it to be a coincidence."

Deborah nodded. "Anonymous tip."

"From you?"

"Not me. It must've been Nora. Old Moral Nora." Nora had also been a cheerleader on the squad – the only one who refused to drink and smoke. Nobody paid any attention to her, because she had such high standards. She made the other cheerleaders appear slutty. Only Nora could come close to Deborah's intelligence, so there was a rivalry. One hint would have been enough to send Nora straight to Officer Leahy with a tip.

"You ruined his life on purpose?"

"What makes you say ruined? Look at him now, managing his Daddy's car dealership. He's a rich man, Alden. All because he worked hard in college and went on to business school. Getting kicked off the team was the best thing that ever happened to him. But I didn't do it to save his life, either, any more than I wanted to ruin his life."

Then it dawned on him. "If you wanted to break up with him, why didn't you just tell him straight?"

She went pale. Then she surprised him, speaking so softly he had to lean forward to hear it. "What makes you think I wanted to break up? You always think you've got everything figured out, Alden. Doesn't it ever occur to you that sometimes there might just be a possibility you haven't thought of? Suppose I told you I did it because I wanted more of him to myself? I didn't imagine for a million years it would be the end of him and me."

Years later though it was, he didn't know whether to feel happy or sad knowing that Deborah had once lost at love. You gazed at her from afar, and you had this idea that nothing could ever go wrong in a charmed life like that. Beautiful, smart, popular, her name on everyone's lips, Homecoming Queen . . . what man could resist? She could have had any man she wanted.

"Dad, they're calling us." Trip was pulling on his arm. "We're supposed to get back on the boat."

"I'll follow you. Lead the way."

The Sterlings, father and son, moved down a gangway across open water with one hundred and fifty other tourists and boarded the Navy launch. Another tourist-filled launch idled noisily a hundred yards off.

"You said we would eat here," Trip accused.

"We can eat when we get back."

"There wasn't even a restaurant on that stupid memorial."

"Trip."

"Well, it's true."

"People died a terrible death there. Their bodies are still right down there in that water, in their final resting place. Do you think it's respectful to call it stupid?"

Trip merely looked away.

Alden stared out to sea, looking for other boats, maybe a passing aircraft carrier or a submarine breaking the surface. But there was just an ordinary collection of big yachts and sailboats, nothing he could point out to Trip without earning another sneer. The launch headed slowly into the breeze, aiming for shore.

The town hadn't known him the way it knew Troy Iverson. People were glad to buy a car from Troy Iverson. They wanted to give Iverson their money. But with a little advertising in the local newspaper and a little word-of-mouth through his parents and other contacts Alden had picked up enough clients in the first twelve months to pay the bills.

"What's Alden doing these days?" would come the question in the grocery checkout line. His mother was only too happy to spread the word.

"He was in Chicago for the last few years, you know, one of the big firms. He just didn't like the city life. He's home now, started up his own firm."

"Oh, he did?"

"Right down on Main Street, you know. They do tax returns, company work, all the stuff accountants usually do."

His mother's friend would report the news at home during a lull in the dinner conversation. If her husband happened to be listening at that moment, and if he happened to be dissatisfied with his present accountant, or had a new project, or had a special question and needed expert advice, or wanted a second opinion, or any number of other possible scenarios, Alden would get a call.

"Heard you're in business for yourself, now, Alden."

People admired that. He began to get the feeling people were happy to see a man like Alden Sterling make money, too, not just the star quarterbacks of this world.

The rest was just hard work.

Within two years he had two secretaries to pay, plus two other accountants. Gray-haired Molloy, hired away from a competing firm in town, inspired confidence when they did presentations at companies with older management.

"Deborah Snyder wants to interview you for an article in the *Courier*," Alden's secretary had said one day. "This afternoon okay, or do you want me to tell her tomorrow?"

His heart practically stopped at the mention of her name. Then it started to race.

"Interview me?"

"She said they're doing a series on local small business owners."

The interview had taken place that afternoon. Otherwise, he reasoned, he would have lost eight hours of sleep in anticipation of it. All those old feelings from his high school days flooded his brain again when she walked in. Those crisp Saturday mornings in November when the cheerleaders sprinted out onto the field in their red pleated miniskirts. Those hot feelings of longing when she would put her head back and laugh at something. He shook her hand now, looked into those smiling almond eyes. She laughed that laugh. She hadn't really changed at all.

"Good to see you again, Alden. Still got that beautiful thick moustache, I see."

"Beautiful? My moustache?" He had never thought of his moustache as beautiful. It wouldn't have occurred to him. He kept it thick and bushy. A man could wear a moustache. It was part of being a man.

"Such a perfect moustache. I really like the way it looks on you."

"Well, I guess you're not planning to write about my moustache in the newspaper."

"Why not?"

He was horrified. Then she smiled, and he understood that she was just teasing.

"Mind if I record?" She placed a miniature tape recorder on the desk.

He didn't mind.

"Otherwise I can just make up random things, and put that in the paper." There came that smile again. She pressed the record button. "I came prepared with questions. But if we get off the track, that's okay too. What I want to do is give people an idea who you are as a small business owner, what makes entrepreneurs tick, that kind of thing. Sound okay?"

"Just one thing, Deborah. About how long will this go?"

"Oh, I think forty minutes or so should be enough. Would a half hour be better?"

He had cancelled everything for the rest of the afternoon. He would have agreed to spend the rest of the week with her. But he said, "I don't want to bore anyone. I can't imagine what you're going to write."

"Just leave that to me. I got a degree in journalism, you know." She looked down at her notes and, without looking at him, started speaking again. "I'm with Alden Sterling of Sterling Accounting Services. So, Alden, how long have you been in business for yourself?"

She looked him straight in the eye. If only, he thought. *If only . . .*

"We'll be celebrating two years next month."

"And what gave you the idea to start your own business?"

He told her his story then. How he had started off at the Big Eight firm in Chicago, working on the sixteenth floor in one building, living on the eleventh floor in another, then in his second year moving up to the twenty-ninth floor.

"My office was on the twenty-ninth floor. My boss was on twenty-eight, and the canteen where we had lunch was on twenty-six. Some people get used to orienting themselves vertically. I grew up – you know, we grew up out here in the cornfields. For me, the best kind of elevator is a grain elevator. I didn't feel at home there. I couldn't tell down from up, even after five years in Chicago."

"Are you saying you're afraid of heights?"

"Not exactly afraid. I mean, I can stand on the observation deck at the Sears Tower and I don't get nervous or anything. I just never got used to working in skyscrapers, let alone making my home in one."

"What about the people in the city? Are they different from the people back home?"

He thought for a minute. You didn't want every gory detail showing up in the newspaper, where your mother and all her friends would read it. "I think fundamentally people are the same everywhere, don't you?" She smiled but didn't say anything. "In the city maybe it's that people try to pack more into their lives than we do here, so they're always short of time. Here we have more time. I mean, you know, we have time for other people, time for a conversation, even without an appointment. I think that's a difference."

"But you must've met some interesting people, living there for five years."

He had the feeling she was fishing for information about girlfriends. Well, let her fish. She wasn't going to get far.

"I made some good friends at the firm, sure. You go to parties, you meet people. One thing I never got too interested in was sports. People are really into the sports teams in Chicago. The Cubs, the White Sox, the Blackhawks, the Bulls, the Bears . . . I might watch a game once or twice a year, but as a subject of conversation, well, you lose me. So some people found me a little boring, there. I guess maybe I was lonely sometimes."

He was talking to Deborah Snyder now, opening his heart to her, come what may. He hardly noticed when she changed the tape.

"I'm still asking myself how a person could take a secure position – you were a partner, right? – at a presumably good salary and chuck it all out the window and take the risk of starting off on your own."

Soberly he explained. What looked like risk to other people only seemed so because they did not see the business landscape as he did. In Chicago there might be an accounting firm in every skyscraper, but here at home there were only two or three small firms in the whole town. At the big city firm he had learned the most modern accounting practices. Modern practices would help people do their work more efficiently and make more money. There was no risk in bringing these things back home. There weren't enough accountants here. He had never been afraid of hard work. He reminded her of how he had worked as manager on the football team back in high school.

"And my last question," Deborah Snyder said. More than two hours had passed. She was out of tapes. "Your ultimate ambition?"

"That's easy. I'd like to have dinner with you." The question had surprised him. His answer came from the heart. He hadn't prepared it. He almost couldn't believe he had uttered such a crude come-on to Deborah Snyder.

She stuck out her hand. "Tomorrow?"

"Tomorrow. Pick you up at seven?"

It was the first time he had seen her blush. Something had happened during that talk. A new connection had formed between them, something magical, chemical. He was as rock-solid sure of that as he'd been when he'd decided to open his own firm.

Ginger

The answering machine clicked on. Ginger's voice in a can. Max Vinyl decided to go ahead and leave a message. "Hi Babe, it's me. I guess you're probably off in the islands with your boyfriend of the hour, or whatever, but . . ."

"Max, I'm here, I'm right here. Don't hang up. You are four months in *arrears*. You know that, don't you?"

"You do love that word."

"I just wish I didn't have to use it."

"You don't need the money."

"What do you know about my needs, Max? Hah! That's a good one. You set me up for that, didn't you? Pay up, or I'll serve for triple damages."

"In your dreams, Baby." As if it were even possible. Triple damages, Christ. Ginger had a weakness for exaggeration. *Ask Furey about triple damages.* "What I wanted to tell you. I'm going to write you a check next week. Four back payments plus July and August in advance."

"Six months all at once? Your ship must've come in. What's going on, Max? You want Mommy to come and take your temperature?"

"Very funny. For your information, I just sold a twenty percent stake."

Why was he telling her this? To show he was good for the alimony money? To buy time? Whatever the reason, his news had an effect. Her tone changed instantaneously. The admiration in her voice dosed him with pure satisfaction.

"You sold a share of the company? Well, well, to whom?"

"Oh, no you don't. It's been a very delicate negotiation. I'm not at liberty to say. At least not till the money gets here."

"Probably Waste Incorporated, one of those giant companies. They've got the bucks. They're always looking for new ways to fleece the public."

"We're not exactly in the garbage business, here."

"I should've made sure I got a piece of the action myself. Goodness, what was I thinking?"

"I know what you were thinking. You thought I was small potatoes. It wouldn't have dawned on you in a thousand years to bet on me. Even if you'd had any money, that is."

"What a cruel thing to say, Max."

"Anyway, you came out all right, with the settlement and all. By the way how's your engagement? Have you set a date?"

"What engagement? Why would I get married again, after what you put me through? I'm not even sure I have a boyfriend at the moment. Do you know something I don't? What on earth are you talking about?"

"Thought I heard through the grapevine, you know, you were engaged." If Ginger ever did do him the favor of remarrying, he would be off the hook on alimony payments.

She laughed. "So how much does a twenty percent stake in TSR go for these days?"

"Wouldn't you like to know."

"I'll find out anyway, so you might as well tell me."

He knew she was right. She had friends in the company. Anyway, telling her about his accomplishments felt good. If a man couldn't beat his breast once in a while, what in Christ was it all for? It wasn't as if Ginger could ever squeeze more out of him, just because her ex-husband was going to be richer by a few zeros. The divorce agreement was almost two years old.

"Three mill, including the option."

He heard the quick involuntary intake of breath. "Three million dollars!" He relished the genuine surprise in her voice, the way the word *million* rolled off her tongue. "Three million for twenty percent? Max, you've been working hard up there. Congratulations."

"Thanks, Babe."

"How in the world did they come up with a valuation like that, I wonder?"

"For one thing, I came up with it. For another, they did what's called *due diligence*. That means they went through my books with a frigging magnifying glass. It just so happens the company has doubled in size two years in a row."

"I had no idea."

"You knew I won entrepreneur of the year last year, didn't you?"

"I totally missed that, Max. You mean in the the State of Illinois?"

"Well, Lake County."

"Congratulations. Where was I?"

"It was in the paper. Very good P.R. for us. I love articles in the paper. We get an absolute flood of new business afterwards." He felt his face glowing. The money was going to be a welcome reward for his work. At least that.

"I'll say, Max. By the way, what's this option all about?"

"Well, you know, these things are always fluid."

"You mean you're going to sell out entirely?"

"They want to increase the stake to forty percent in a couple years' time, so I gave them the option."

"You *gave* it to them?"

"It's included in the three million."

"That sounds more like the Max I know," Ginger said. "Like for example one million for twenty percent of the shares and two million for the option to buy more."

"Hah, hah."

"Seriously, Max, I'll bet it was a long, hard negotiation. Those big companies are known for their tricky lawyers. You must be absolutely drained."

"Actually it was . . ." He caught himself just in time. He wasn't about to tell her about the Koreans, and he certainly wasn't going to reveal that a key meeting had taken place at a club called The Skinny Whip. Without full background, she was liable to misinterpret details like that. "Well, yeah, it took up a lot of my time. But I figure on the whole it was worth the effort."

"Of course it was, Max."

"Baby, I'll bring that check over if you like."

"OK, but do me a favor and call before you come. I wouldn't want you to get all the way here and find out I'm entertaining."

Used phones

It was 4:45 when they pulled in to the TSR warehouse lot. Tranny jumped out of the car hefting two shopping bags filled with heavy old phones in one hand and cradling the recovered GPS in the other like a baby in swaddling cloth. Ike followed him in, lugging the rest of the phones.

"We gotta see the boss," Ike said in a loud voice. No one was at the reception desk. He looked for a bell to press. He heard a door in the inner sanctum click.

Max Vinyl was suddenly standing there in the doorway. "What in Christ is all that shit?"

Ike lowered the bags gently to the floor, going easy on his back, rising again slowly. Tranny held out the GPS like an offering. "Look boss, we got it back, no problem."

"Damn straight," Max Vinyl said. "Otherwise you two would be history. I'm giving serious thought to letting you go, anyway. You're on probation, here. I repeat, Ike, what is in those shopping bags?"

"Two hunnerd mobile phones from a collection. Our gift to you. We're thinking you can get a hunnerd apiece on account of the collector value. Then if you wanted to give us a little piece of the action, well, we wouldn't have any objection, would we now, Tranny boy?"

Max turned one over in his hand. On the front it said Motorola 1000. It looked like one of those mobile radio sets you saw in old army movies, the kind they used for calling in the artillery. A relic from the 1980s, he guessed. A glance in the bag showed a number of other early beauts – Nokia, Sony, Ericsson.

"A collection? Whose collection? How did you get them?"

"We figured you could sell 'em on the website," said Ike.

"So they're stolen. Give me credit for that little assumption?"

"Well, she stole our GPS," Tranny said.

"Oh, very bright. You steal a collection of phones from the girl that steals our GPS. Then you want me to sell the stolen property on our website. Don't you see what a dumb-ass idea that is? Do you guys want to go straight back to jail, or what? How do you think that would reflect on this company? Get them out of here!" He kicked one of the bags for emphasis.

What could Rodriguez be thinking to employ losers like this? What would Song Young Park say if he knew that the company kept screw-ups like these on the payroll?

"Get them off my property. I have never seen them. I am never going to see them again. First my GPS, now stolen goods. You guys are on very thin ice. Is that clear?"

His eyes fell on the thick bolt poking through the disgusting web-like hole in Ike's eyebrow, wing nuts and washers screwed on the threaded end, the whole thing clinking and clanking whenever Ike moved. What a stain on the company image!

Get rid of these guys.

On the other hand, who else was going to do the barge run in the middle of the night? He needed two men for that job. Not just anyone would be up for that work. They had been so dependable until now.

"Yeah, boss," Ike said, walking backwards.

"And furthermore you will be here tonight at one o'clock sharp for the shift that you missed yesterday. Stone cold sober, ready to go. That's if you want to keep your TSR paycheck. Now move on it."

They carried the four shopping bags back to the car. Ike made the wheels throw gravel getting out of the parking lot.

"The man walks from a twenty dollar birthday present," Tranny said. "Can you believe that shit?"

"Twenty *thousand* dollars," Ike said.

"That's what I said, man. And not only that. You see how disrespectful he was? I call that fucking disrespectful."

"I don't get it, either," Ike said. Something was wrong with the boss. He definitely wasn't himself today. He had never yelled at them like this before. And just when they had recovered the GPS. To say no to a valuable haul like these phones was weird. To yell at them for even suggesting it.

"Hey, you passed Denny's. I thought you said it was dinnertime. I'm so hungry I could eat a double portion, man. Where the hell're you going?"

"We're gonna be rich," Ike said. He had overshot their ordinary dinner place. "Plus we gotta work late. We're gonna have ourselves a fancy dinner tonight."

"No way. Olive Garden?" Tranny asked.

"You got it."

"Yes!" Tranny set up for a high five, but Ike was fiddling with the outer wing nut on his eyebrow bolt. Sometimes when he was lost in thought trying to figure out a problem, he would unscrew the outer nut a couple of turns, then screw it in again, just to stretch his skin a little.

Their misfortune had actually turned into a lucky break. If Tranny hadn't lost the GPS, they never would've stumbled onto this treasure trove of phones. They were going to make a small fortune, here. Once they were seated in the restaurant they ordered a big dinner and a pitcher of frosty beer.

"I guess the boss is nervous on account of the phones being stolen," Ike said.

"That's what he said, all right. Hell, she ain't gonna report it. She started it when she stole our GPS. If she goes to the cops she's gonna have to explain about that little detail," Tranny said.

"I know that. You know that. The boss don't know it. Anyways the phones belong to that stud, not the waitress. But he ain't gonna want to get his woman in trouble." Ike spread his arms wide to absolve them. "The way I figure it, we're clear. The money is ours."

"All we gotta do now is find someone to unload the fuckers on," Tranny said.

"That's all right. Lance gives ten dollars for any phone, no questions asked."

"Ten dollars! That ain't what these babies are worth. These are collector items. We can get a hundred apiece. Or at least fifty."

"Who're you going to sell 'em to for that kinda money, the Getty Museum?" Ike said. He dipped into his soup. It was deliciously thick, like a bowl of melted cheese. He tested to see if the spoon would stand up on its own. It sank slowly, settling after a few seconds without a sound against the side of the bowl.

"I got an aunt in Chinatown that buys phones. Least she used to. Last time I saw her was before I went in, you know. She used to have quite a racket – phones, radios, TVs, whatever. She works out of a restaurant that's owned by, like, a cousin or somebody. We could try her."

"How much she pay?"

"Don't remember. It's been a long time. But if that don't work we could put 'em on eBay and sell 'em one by one."

"Too much damn work," Ike said.

"Yeah, but then we'd get more money."

"Plus that asshole could look on eBay and report us."

"Man, you say no to everything. You got any idea how you sound? You sound like an old lady worried about this, worried about that. I get tired of always having to come up with the ideas, and you just say no to everything. How about you try saying no for a change and I get to have some ideas?"

"You mean I should come up with the ideas, and you get to say no?"

"That's what I said, stupid. Don't try and turn things around that I say. I don't go correcting you all the time, asshole."

He let it go. Why be cruel in the middle of a nice dinner?

"I'm just saying I'd rather have the money up front, even if it ends up being less."

"Even if it ends up being less," Tranny said sarcastically. "Like the difference between three thousand and twenty thousand. I don't know about you, man. I'm ready to bust my ass a little for that kinda money."

* * *

"Well, what did she say?" Todd asked. Alison had just hung up.

"They drove way up north somewhere, halfway to Wisconsin. She thinks somewhere near the funny GPS location. The one out in the lake."

"And then?"

"Then she got tired and went home."

"And my collection?" He read the look on her face. "So it's gone. I'm never going to see my phones again."

"Have you even considered running their license plate with your friends over at the department? Do I have to think of everything? At least you'd have their name and address."

He exhaled again once she had left the room.

Ten years ago he had bought a box of old junky phones at a garage sale. He had thought they might be worth something one day. And they probably would be worth something in about fifty years.

More than that, when you spread them out on the table and took a closer look, you began to be struck by the differences. The older phones were so much bigger and clunkier. How the displays had changed, the keypads, the designs. In the early days there had only been one color choice, black.

Then in the late 1990s other colors had arrived on the scene. He had started picking up old models nobody wanted anymore on Maxwell Street, at garage sales, at pawn shops. No doubt many were stolen. Never had he paid more than three or four dollars for a phone.

Cataloguing them, he had gotten into it, sorting them by manufacturer, then by year. That's when the passion had taken hold of him. He had put up the shelves himself. One whole shelf had been devoted to Motorola. Another to Nokia.

Most of the phones no longer actually worked. He hadn't bothered to try to get them working. What in the world would you do with two hundred ringing phones? What a horrifying thought. Silent, inert, even a little dusty, they had existed purely for contemplation and study, like tagged specimens in a museum.

Looking at those empty shelves now gave him an aching, hollowed-out feeling. It was a bit like a food craving, like a really strong case of the munchies. Only he knew this craving couldn't be satisfied so easily, and also wouldn't go away, not for a long time. There was no making up for all those years of collecting, cataloguing, sorting, cradling them in his hands, admiring them at odd moments, even just knowing they were always there. Because he knew the phones would never be found. He felt it.

"If only you hadn't decided to keep that stupid goddamn GPS," he said. "I collect phones, remember? Not GPSs."

"How could I have known it would turn out like this?"

"Actually, I'm surprised that stealing comes so easily to you." He felt a flash of irritation. He decided to let his anger come out for once rather than repressing it, as he usually did.

"How is it stealing if they forgot it on the table?"

"Because you brought it home even though it didn't belong to you. Most people would define that as stealing, Al."

Her knee bumped the table when she stood up. Tea slopped on the table, and after a few seconds the puddle ran over the side and onto the floor. Her face had gone red. "It's a little late for you to go on the high horse. You didn't exactly refuse it. You knew what I did. You didn't exactly make me bring it back to the Domino."

"I told you I didn't want it. Besides, when did it become my job to teach you right from wrong?" But even as he said it, he thought it sounded a bit lame.

"You're just upset because of your collection. Who wouldn't be? Personally, I think you should try a little harder to get it back."

"How do you want me to do that?"

"They got their GPS back. They promised to give your phones back. I think you should hold them to it."

"You're crazy. Or maybe you want me killed."

"You're the one who's rolling over and playing dead. If it were me I would get out and do something. A deal's a deal. We kept our end of the deal. They should keep theirs."

"Yeah, because they're obviously such honest, law-abiding citizens."

"You want to know what I think?"

He didn't like the way she was looking at him. "What?"

"I think deep down you're secretly glad they're gone. It's like they were getting to be a burden for you. Every collection becomes a burden to the collector. Your burden is gone. You're sitting around doing nothing because you're relieved. By the way, if you're really going to make no effort to recover them, you could take down these godawful shelves so we can have a normal living room like other people."

Was she taking revenge for his comment from before? It hadn't sat well when he called her a thief. Now, as she harangued him with her logic, he studied the way her upper lip curled up a little on the right side. He had definitely never seen that curling lip before they were married. He wondered how he could have missed it – or was it just something that was developing with age?

"You know, Al, you couldn't be more mistaken. You want to know what it feels like? It feels like a part of me, a piece of me, is gone. I didn't actually realize how important those phones were to me. It actually hurts. It feels like there's this hole in me now. Where the hole is, it aches like a son of a bitch."

"How poetic. Your talent is so lost on that crap newspaper. All this aching and weeping about lost phones, and yet here you are expending zero effort to get them back. Explain it to me, Todd. I don't get it."

"What do you expect me to do when I have to work all day? What am I supposed to do in the first place? Besides, we've got Annie out looking for them."

"Yeah, at least Annie seems to know what to do."

"What's that supposed to mean?" The flash of irritation came back again.

"Oh, never mind."

Dante

The present barely fit through the door. Luther made a big show of holding it up with one brawny arm, though it must have weighed fifty pounds, judging from the rippling of the muscles in his right arm and chest. Even his toe muscles seemed to be flexing in his sandals. Tris held the door open. Luther had to turn sideways and hold the present high up out in front of him, it was so big and bulky.

Covered with red- and yellow-striped paper and wrapped in clothesline, one loop of which he used as a handle, the package ended up in the middle of her living room floor. They sank down together on the carpet.

"It's not even my birthday. What's going on?"

"Open it up. It's for the start of your new life."

"I can't imagine what could be so big. Is it a TV?"

A sound came from inside the package. It sounded very much like a bark. Like the sound a dog would make.

"One TV is way more than enough," Luther said.

"Did I hear what I thought I heard?"

She started tearing the paper, peeling it back from the hard box underneath. She felt as if something inside her was tearing along with it. It was just like Luther to surprise her with a huge present for no reason at all. She only needed to tear away one tiny window of paper to see there was an animal inside. First came its shiny black nose, wet and sniffing, moving, taking her in greedily. The next strip that fell away allowed a first meeting of their eyes. A puppy . . . but he was so little! He looked so . . . *tiny* inside his enormous plastic carrier.

"Luther, he's beautiful! How did you ever get the idea?"

Then Luther was helping, and in a few seconds they had all the paper off. The puppy whimpered. It wagged its tail so hard it kept falling down. It licked its chops and yelped to get her attention. When she finally got the latch open, the puppy wriggled out, did a little dance a few feet away from them, and peed on the carpet.

"No, not there. You can't pee there," she said. She was on her feet and scooping up the puppy, but it was already finished peeing. It wriggled out of her grasp and ran across the room to the hallway, where it stopped and looked back, whipping back and forth with its tail.

"Playful little guy."

"He's a miracle. An absolute miracle."

"I thought you might like a puppy. But he needs to be trained, you know. Problem is I don't have time to train him."

"I can do it."

She pictured herself talking to the puppy, praising it, giving it treats. What in the world did you feed a German Shepherd puppy? And how often? How in the world did you train them?

"Do people do this themselves or . . . like, is there a doggie school you take them to?"

"Start reading."

Luther pulled a sheaf of papers out of his back pocket, where they had been sticking out the whole time. She had wondered what those papers were when he came in the door. Over the course of the next hour, reading a page here and page there in between playing with the puppy and playing with Luther, she became an expert on training puppies.

"We're going to do it at my brother's beach house," she announced. "I'm sick of Waukegan. I want to go down there now. Tonight. We can take him for walks on the dunes. He can do his house-training there. My brother isn't coming back till

August. We can stay there for a couple of months if we want, and get him all trained up."

"Couple of months should be enough." Luther's fingers scratched between the puppy's ears as it lay in her lap. "What're you going to call him?"

She had been thinking about this as she read the training instructions. It was just one of the things she had been thinking about.

"Dante."

"Why Dante?"

"I've been reading Dante. He covered just about every sort of human weakness, you know. It's a good name for a male."

The dog was on its feet again, now, on her lap, licking her face. *Go ahead, pee on me.* She didn't care. The puppy was covered with yellowish fluff that made it look like stuffed. Here and there were black hairs in among the yellow. Over and over she picked him up and set him on his back, then tickled his tummy while he struggled to stand up. She could have sworn her puppy was laughing just as much as she was.

All at once, a familiar sound rumbled in from outside the house, making the windows vibrate. Even with the curtain closed, she knew a car had pulled into the driveway, and from the throaty sound of that engine she knew exactly which car. With a sinking feeling she asked herself, do I know anyone else in Waukegan with a BMW? Do I know anyone else *anywhere* with a BMW? What the hell was he doing here?

"Quick, put the chain on." She pointed at the front door. Luther got up and went to the door. What could be going through Max's head? Their date for tonight? But she had cancelled it. He had asked about it. She had completely nixed it. But a glance at her watch told her that must be it. Somehow Max must have convinced himself that it was still on, like a peacock blinded by its own tail. "How could I be so incredibly stupid?"

"Let it go," Luther said.

"I mean, like, in the first place. How could I have fallen for him?"

"You're obsessed," Luther said from the door. "You thought you'd bagged Mr. Environment himself."

She listened to him, rapt, despising herself. To think she had made love to Max so many times; to think she had loved him. She wanted to scream. *Channel this*, she thought. *Make him the object of it. Not yourself. He deserves this, not you.*

She heard the car door slam, that solid, BMW door-closing noise that Max worshipped. A moment later came the doorbell. Then, just as she was trying to decide whether to go to the door or not, the sound of the key in the lock. Good grief, he still had his key. What in Heaven's name gave him the idea that he could use it, the day after he had fired her? Only Max Vinyl would have an answer for that one. Luther's expression formed a big question mark. Grimly she drew a finger across her throat.

The door opened, but only a little way, stopped by the chain. Luther's broad back blocked her view of the rest.

"Tris, it's me," Max called.

At the moment she heard his voice, she had Dante's fuzzy ears in her hands. Still trembling from the sheer force of her momentary spell of self-loathing, she shook her head to say *no, no*, and rubbed noses with the puppy, to show Dante she didn't mean him. Dante was confused. When his tongue came out and slobbered over her nose and mouth, tickling her wetly, with the sounds of a struggle at the front door growing louder, she giggled. Some men never would learn.

TEN DOZEN ROSES

When he left work, Max Vinyl's BMW 735i was waiting outside in the gravel parking lot. At this time of day he had mixed feelings sometimes. Part of him would rather stay at work and go on tracking the numbers that added up to success of TSR, Inc. It was a 24-hour business, like a market that never closed, so there were statistics a man could follow all night long, till he keeled over.

On the other hand, if Tris Berrymore were waiting for him on the living room couch in a v-neck t-shirt, that by itself had enough gravitational pull to get him out of the office at five o'clock.

Only tonight she wasn't going to be waiting. Not at five. Not at six. Not at seven. Manny Rodriguez had seen to that yesterday when he'd fired her. She hadn't called to set things straight. All day Max had waited for that call. Anything would have done. But no, all contact with Tris had been broken for more than thirty hours.

The steering wheel felt good in his grip as he opened it up on the short stretch of highway after leaving the company. Cows, barns, telephone poles flashed by. He brought it back down to legal speed to enter the ninth largest city in the state of Illinois, Waukegan, turned right at the first light and pulled into a gas station.

In the mini-mart, while paying for the gas, his eye fell on a large plastic bucket next to the counter with bunches of roses in it. Ten dollars a bunch. Red roses, yellow ones, white, pink, orange.

"Seventy-five in cash for ten bunches?" he asked. The pimples on the clerk's face and neck were so thick they looked like a rash. Poor kid was straight off the boat from India, dark skin, long eyelashes like a girl's. So they got acne just like American kids. The Indian kid looked at the flowers Max was pointing at, then back at Max.

"Ten dollars a bunch," the kid said, his voice breaking.

"This isn't a math test," Max said. "I'm making an offer. In two days these flowers won't be worth diddly. I'm offering to take half the stock off your hands."

The kid dug in his pocket. Out came a phone. He mumbled something that sounded like "manager."

This was one of the things that set Max Vinyl apart from the crowd. Never, ever pay the asking price. Below the asking price, there is always room to run. Sometimes lots of room. And who would know it better? The king of bidding and asking prices, the emperor of arbitrage – making money off small differences between the price here versus the price there, or the price today versus the price tomorrow. Who had the market cornered in this little neck of the woods for pre-owned computer parts? Max Vinyl did!

That was what Tris had so admired, too. How he transformed simple negotiations into killer deals. She had watched him trade up for the BMW, a negotiating high-wire act right up there with the big ones. She had seen him talk his way out of speeding tickets, when by all rights he should have had his license torn up into tiny pieces.

"My boss said to take your offer," said the kid.

"I thought he would," Max Vinyl said. He watched the kid wrap up the ten bunches on the counter.

After all the ups and downs of these two days, he craved the sight of her face. What if it was all a misunderstanding? What if Manny had screwed things up with her on purpose, and Tris was *afraid* to call? Could be she was embarrassed. Maybe at TSR she hadn't felt able to speak openly to him . . . something like that. How her face would light up at the sight of the flowers. She was a sucker for roses. He would make a path of rose petals to her bed.

He parked in her driveway and checked his Rolex: half past seven on the dot. She would marvel at the sheer size of the bouquet. Wrestling it out of the passenger seat, he climbed out of the car and went up to the door. It was just for show that he rang the doorbell. When you had your own key, you didn't have to ring. He slid the key in and clicked open the lock, full of expectation. Just wait till she saw these roses!

The door opened but stopped after a few inches, stuck on something. The chain. She had the little chain on. Never once had he seen her put the chain on. He didn't even know this door had a chain.

"Tris, it's me." He looked through the gap and tried to see into the living room, but with this chain stopping it he couldn't see around the corner of the doorway into the living room.

Another face suddenly popped into view in the crack, inches from his own. Not Tris, but a man's face. Stubble on his chin, long black hair in a thick ponytail, blue eyes, hot breath.

"Tri-i-is, it's me-e-e," echoed the man in a deep nasal twang, like a Southern accent, an ugly, mocking impersonation of Max's voice. Flecks of *gray* in that ponytail. The man stared back at him through the gap between the door and the doorframe, a smirk creasing his face.

Who was this ape? Max felt the sweat on his lip, but an evening breeze suddenly blew cold against his skin. A man stood inside Tris's door, inside her house, with the chain on the door, insulting him. So this was what it was coming to. The bouquet went heavy in his hand. This bouquet had to weigh twenty pounds. One hundred and twenty roses. The sweat from his hand was soaking the wrapping paper covering the ends of the stems.

"Who the fuck are you?"

He stuck his foot in the base of the door, and just in time. An instant later, with a grunt, Tris's ape-friend with the gray ponytail threw his whole weight against it. He was built like a football lineman, for Chrissake. The top half of the door bent and slapped against the metal doorframe under the man's weight. It would have slammed shut had Max's foot not been wedged in between the bottom of the door and the threshold.

It put an awful pressure on the side of his foot to hold it there. The man was either very strong, very heavy, or both. The pressure against the side of his foot sent urgent pain signals to his brain. Sweat ran down Max's forehead and from there down his neck. More sweat ran out of his armpits and soaked his shirt. But the perspiration emergency was the least of his problems. Who was this maniac? Some sort of rapist or murderer? More likely the new boyfriend. Or an old boyfriend.

She's rough around the edges.

Maybe Rodriguez was right. There was no telling how many boyfriends Tris had had. It could be just some bouncer she knew from the Skinny Whip. He pushed back on the door, wishing he could just put down the bouquet.

"They didn't teach you manners, did they?" said the man. That smirk again. Half his mouth curled down while the other half curled up. The man shifted position and flipped his ponytail, and just in that moment, behind him, Max caught a glimpse of a white t-shirt passing. It had gone by in a split second. *Tris.* It could only be her.

"Tris, call off this geriatric hunk!" he shouted.

A bark reached his ears, muffled. Since when did Tris have a dog?

"Time for assholes to take a flying leap," the man said.

Max had all of his weight committed to blocking the door open. His whole upper body was having little effect despite his wedged foot, which was rapidly going numb. His foot was still stuck between the bottom of the door and the threshold. His heart was racing like a Cadillac at 7000 rpms. He was redlining, ready to throw a piston, growing dizzy. When the pressure let up momentarily, he must have relaxed for a split-second.

The spray caught him full in the eyes. Something wet and cold on his skin. Then a horrible stinging filled his eyeballs and exploded across his brainpan. His eyes shut tight in a reflex reaction. He could not have opened them again to save his life. Ten thousand blood vessels in each eye, each one of them swelling up uncontrollably and within two seconds blowing apart. A wave of shocking, searing pain flooded his nasal passages and left him blind and sputtering. A reddish curtain appeared before his eyes, then blackness. He fell backwards from the door. He lost his strength and balance simultaneously and felt himself falling.

Breathe.

He couldn't breathe. He had to have air. He sucked air, blinded, unhearing, unaware of any other sensation except the roaring, stinging, burning in his eyes and nasal passages, scarcely even feeling his body as it crashed to the pavement. He fought for each breath, wondering if this was the end. Or would this bring on the heart attack he was surely due for?

Some time later, it could have been seconds, it could have been minutes, he lay on his stomach on the pavement, blind to the world, touching his face, the burning areas. They felt wet. With the tip of one finger he felt his fluttering eyelashes, just to locate his eyes. To his amazement, he noted that they were open. His eyes were open, yet he saw nothing. Blinking but not seeing. The world completely dark.

Black as night, but a terrible rushing and whistling noise blew through his brain like a high dangerous wind. He felt the hard ground under him, the sandpapery pavement under his chin, and a stinging at his arms. He wrestled himself up on his elbows, aware of his own blinking, fighting against the rushing noise, trying not to panic at the pointlessness of it. These stinging sensations all across his arms were nothing compared to the burning, aching, gouging pain in his eyeballs.

Just as he was starting to wonder if he had been blinded permanently, the first blurred images in shades of gray, then blotches of pink, red and yellow started coming in. Some sort of pepper spray, probably. Tris packed pepper spray, he knew that. That she should squirt it into his eyes, as if he were a *rapist*, one of those monsters with violent animal urges they couldn't control, now that was something new. That was plain *wrong*.

Pink and yellow blurs resolved into flowers. Some roses that lay crushed under him, the petals just inches from his eyes. This stinging all over his arms. He was bleeding. He struggled to his knees, everything blurry, his aching, stinging eyes filling with water as fast as he could blink it away, and tried to focus on the damage to his arms. They seemed to be covered with blood, the blood running from cuts and puncture wounds. The blood all over his arms was shocking enough, but his eyes stung like Christ. In the dirt to the right of the porch, one pink rose stood straight up in the dirt, where it had been driven when he fell, like things blown about in a tornado.

Another rose was stuck to the side of his face. He pulled at it and realized it had been hanging from the side of his face by a thorn embedded in his skin. He spat and stood up, then turned to look behind him. Tris's door was closed tight now.

"Son of a bitch," he said. Talking to himself now, his arms bleeding, blood dripping from a dozen wounds in his face and arms. His eyes ached and throbbed and stung all at the same time. Most of the roses still lay in a clump on the sidewalk, where they must have cushioned his fall. Roses lay scattered across the walk. Bargain-priced fucking roses. Those punctures ached like a sonofagun. The stinging in his eyes didn't just blink away. They felt like they were full of sand. He stumbled down the walk, losing blood with every step.

That last glimpse of white t-shirt passing behind the attacker – it had been Tris, he knew it. She had given pepper spray to that brute. Or she had sprayed him herself.

She had done this to him.

He lined up like a place-kicker and launched the rest of the bouquet, hard, into her front door. The bouquet came apart on impact with his loafer. Some flowers sailed up to the ceiling of her porch, others landed in the hedges. The rest were catapulted with full force against the door. He hoped the paint was at least a little scratched. In the end sixty or seventy roses lay scattered at her doorstep and plenty of red blood was smeared across the front of the house. His blood. Someone should make her clean it up. While she was scrubbing his blood off the walls she could maybe for a moment stop and think about her outrageous treatment of him.

This day had actually gotten worse, just when he'd thought there was a decent chance of saving it. So much for one last look at her face. So much for clearing up misunderstandings.

He drove down the street slowly, trying to pull himself together. A drink of water would have gone down fine. His head clanged like a bell, the pain in his eyes like the clapper banging against the inner walls of his head. His eyes stung and his face and arms burned. He felt weak and banged up. He had lost blood back there. He must have gone down hard.

Still bleeding, he drove gingerly two blocks, then turned around in a driveway and doubled back. At the beginning of Tris's block, six houses down from her place, there was a huge family-sized camper parked on the street, must've been twenty feet long. He snuck into a parking space behind it, so that he still had a partial view of her front porch and driveway, then speed-dialed her number.

"Hello, this is Tris."

"This is Max. What's left of me, anyway. Christ, was that necessary?"

"Were you born stupid? Or is it just happening more lately? I told you it's over."

"What did I do to deserve pepper spray?"

"Breaking in to my house."

"What breaking in? I had my key."

"You should have given it back. You had no right."

"You expect me to think of everything? When we catch you trying to sabotage the company like that?"

"What exactly were you hoping to accomplish?"

"I thought there might've been a misunderstanding."

"In your dreams."

"Yeah, I guess I was still dreaming, till you did that job on my eyes."

"I had a feeling you were going to have trouble with this."

"I'm a human being, Tris. We had something wonderful between us."

"Your opinion. What would I have done if I hadn't had Luther here to protect me?"

"Who is this Luther? How can it be over so suddenly?"

"Are you blind, Max? You only see what you want to see. It was over weeks ago. Months ago."

"But I've only *known* you for six months."

"Give me that." It was the man's voice now. The man spoke slowly, putting childlike emphasis on every syllable. "Forget . . . Tris . . . now. Forget you knew her. Throw that key in the lake. Cold shower time. I catch you stalking her, I'll twist up your sorry balls with my bare hand like a goddamn twisty."

Reflexively Max gulped. He needed water. "You listen, hotshot. I'm not scared of some musclebound country grandpa." His own voice came across something like a croak.

A tinny laugh came through the phone. "Cut your losses, Max. Vamos. Ciao."

"Wait!"

But the line was dead. He punched redial, then mashed disconnect. What was the point? Rodriguez had fired Tris, giving her the perfect excuse. Now she had attacked him with pepper spray and loosed this security prick on him. She was angry. Christ only knew what had set her off. She was tying him up in knots. No one had ever hurt him like this.

Fifteen minutes later, a car pulled in to the parking space behind him and cut the lights. It was getting along toward dusk. Max stared at his phone, waiting for it to vibrate. When it did, he pressed the button to connect.

"You see the blue house up there, six houses up on the right?" He pointed without looking back over his shoulder. "Stay watching till they come out. Get someone to come and back you up. Don't go up against them alone. Also got a dog in there. Ike and Tranny, maybe. Report back in the morning. Move on that."

INDIANA RUN

Max Vinyl should have driven away after this short call. When the big BMW stayed put, Brainard got out of his own car to investigate. He couldn't carry out instructions he didn't understand. He found Max in a curled-up ball on the reclined front seat of his BMW, almost in the fetal position. The boss had blood on his face and arms, his skin raw and bleeding. The cuts looked superficial, but his face and his arms were a real mess. He stared out of glassy eyes, red as blood. The boss was in shock.

"Boss, pull yourself together. Sit up, now."

It jolted him to see Max Vinyl like that. Always clean-shaven, his hair in perfect order, styled with some high-priced, fine-smelling hair wax, the boss now looked like he'd been worked over. Which was pretty much what had happened, as Brainard pieced the story together from Max Vinyl's stuttering over the next few minutes.

He ran back to his car for a bottle of Powerade. He kept a case on the back seat. This restored electrolytes to the boss's system. A man in his girlfriend's house had apparently attacked him with pepper spray, unprovoked. This man and Tris were still in the house. Standing beside the boss's BMW, Brainard took a long appraising look at the blue structure up the street.

"You want me to get her out of there?" he asked. "Like a rescue?"

Max was sitting up now, one hand gripping the wheel, the other clutching the plastic bottle. He didn't look good. Blood dripped from six or eight cuts on his cheeks and forehead. Some of those punctures might be deeper than he'd thought. His skin was chalky, his eyes the color of blood. He looked ghoulish. Max shook his head. It came out so soft, Brainard had to lean in close to hear.

"Didn't tell you. Got fired yesterday."

"Fired?"

Max could only nod once, his eyes shut tight. Brainard thought about it. When people quit, the boss sometimes asked him to go and mess them around for a few weeks. But this was the boss's girlfriend. Fired. No wonder he hadn't been informed. He wouldn't have wanted Brainard to mess with his girlfriend.

"So who's the guy?" he asked. "Why does he go after my boss? What am I up against?"

He helped him drink the rest of his Powerade. Max tightened his grip on the wheel. "Bitch *made* him attack me. Could even be she did it herself, I don't know."

Brainard felt his throat tighten. The thought of another employee hurting the boss had that effect on him. It hurt just to think of it. A man who had offered opportunity to so many when they got out of prison. A good man. Some things you just didn't do. To think some bitch could reduce the boss of TSR Inc. to this state made something flare in him. With this attack the girl was playing hardball. To observe him now, sitting there shaking his head, sad and morose, hardly able to speak, like some person whose brain had been scrambled, made Brainard feel sick inside. No one fucked with Max Vinyl like this. That was why the boss called him. That was why he was number three on the boss's speed dial, right after Rodriguez and Tris.

"You sure about this, boss?" The whole thing would be completely incredible if he weren't observing the damage with his own eyes.

The boss had his hand on the key. The rumble of the BMW's engine made the pavement vibrate underfoot. "Don't try it alone. Guy in there, big as an ox. Stronger than you, even. Call Ike. See what you can find out."

He backed off from the car. "You gonna make it home, boss? You sure? You put some cream on those cuts."

Afterward Brainard sat in his car to call Ike, keeping an eye on the blue house. Then he just waited for a while as the light in the summer sky began to fade once and for all, this night. A wimpy guy like the boss wouldn't put up much of a struggle, but still he was probably right. Better to wait for help. Especially with a dog. Dogs were bad news. He had gone up against his share. The only two options with dogs were poison and bullets, and he had neither along with him tonight. With three of them they could circle the house, bash in the dog's skull with a tire iron, and overpower any person who made the mistake of crossing them.

When Ike arrived with his partner Tranny, he briefed them. They sat and waited in Ike's car, an old Lincoln, Brainard in the back seat. The two men reeked of cigarettes, deep-fried food and beer, as if they had just come from a tavern. It didn't matter. If they had driven here, they were fit for a fight.

"Here's the plan," Brainard said. "Soon as it gets a little darker, maybe about half an hour from now, we go in. We conk the bastard on the head. Then we have a good talking-to with Tris."

"What if she calls the cops?" Ike asked.

"We could cut the phone line," Tranny offered.

"Too risky in a place like this. Neighbors watching. Better if we just get right in, do our business, and get out again, one or two minutes."

"So, you're saying we grab her, take her for a ride?"

"Probably the best bet," Brainard said.

"Probably ain't got a land line anyway. Most people just got a cell phone these days," Tranny said.

"What makes you think she ain't got a land line?" Ike asked.

"I just meant everybody's got a cell phone. You can't cut the line of a cell phone. There ain't any line to cut."

"He just said we ain't gonna cut the line. It's too risky."

"There ain't no line to cut if she ain't got a land line."

"It's too risky, even if she did."

"Stop repeating what I said."

"You're the one repeating the hell outta things."

"Hey, boys, look at that." Brainard pointed at the blue house. The garage door was going up. They all watched in silence as a little red car backed out. Up to now, it could've just been an empty house; in that car had to be a person. It backed slowly down the drive and into the street. The garage door closed. Ike fingered the key in the ignition.

"What now?"

"Follow them," Brainard said. "That's Tris's car all right. I want to know if they're both in the car."

"Can't see," Tranny said. "They're too damn far away. Go closer, Ike."

"No," Brainard said. "Stay on them, but make sure they don't see you."

"Yes, sir," Ike said.

Brainard heard the sarcasm in Ike's voice. He let it go. The sight of the boss in that state had rattled him. Good thing the others hadn't witnessed it. For them this was business as usual, just another job. For him it had become something out of the ordinary, something personal. Max Vinyl simply did not get beat up. Nobody did a thing like that to the boss. He didn't like it one bit. If Tris was really behind it, well, she was going to pay.

"Mitsubishi, ain't it?"

"You got that right, Tranny boy."

"You guys know Tris got canned?" They were getting on Route 94 headed south, the little red car floating in traffic ten cars ahead.

"News to me," Ike said.

"Me, too."

"Never saw her much," Ike said. "We mostly work nights, you know."

"Including tonight," Tranny said. "We better not be late, either."

"What time you guys have to be back?" Brainard asked. Though this special job had to be more important than their normal work.

"One o'clock sharp," Ike said. "Down at the dock."

"Otherwise he's gonna fire our asses, just like hers," Tranny said. "Man, he must be in some kinda firing mood."

"You got that right," Ike said.

Brainard checked his watch. Not even nine, almost full dark. The little red Mitsubishi taillights bounced around in the traffic up ahead. Where were they headed? No doubt someplace in the city.

"What the hell you guys have to do at one in the morning down at the dock?" Brainard asked to pass the time.

"Barge duty," Ike said.

"Three times a week," Tranny said. "Sometimes four. Hey, man, want a beer?" He handed a Coors tall boy into the back seat.

"Don't be stupid," Brainard said. "You're in a moving vehicle. No open containers in here."

"This ain't a container."

"A can is too a container," Ike said.

Tranny drained a quarter of the can into his mouth. "You should stop fucking correcting me all the time, Ike."

"I told you not to drink in the car," Brainard said in an even voice.

"Man, I don't care if you ain't thirsty, but I wish you would stop trying to tell me what to do." Tranny was just licking an excess drop from his lips when he felt something hard close against his teeth. What happened next went lightning fast. The wound-up handkerchief snaked through the space between

Tranny's upper and lower rows of teeth like a bowstring in a groove. Brainard tied it off tight to the metal stem of the headrest. Tranny raised his brawny right arm to try and claw it off – while carefully holding aloft the beer in his left hand – but Brainard had tied it so tight he couldn't get his fingers under it. Tranny couldn't move his head because of the straightjacket on his mouth. He was pinned in his seat.

"Thon of a bitch!" Take thith off!"

Brainard grabbed the windmilling right arm and yanked it around behind the seat.

"Don't make me break this, dickless," he said calmly. "Put the beer on the floor between your feet, so it doesn't spill in Ike's car. Make it so no cops notice. Like that, yes."

"Let him go, man," Ike said. "He didn't do nothing."

"You keep your eye on that Mitsubishi," Brainard said.

"I'm gonna lose 'em if you guys keep distracting me with that fighting. I thought we was all on the same side."

"You're right. That's why I was so surprised when Tranny here disobeyed my order."

"Wha' fuckin' order?" Tranny yelled.

"I told you what to do, and I even told you why. It's against the law to have an open container of alcohol in a car. Everybody knows that. Something this stupid could put all three of us back in prison. I do not want to end up in prison again because of a stupid fuck like you."

"I don't believe this bullshit. Let go of my arm, man. That hurts like hell."

"I got more where that came from if you don't behave."

After letting go of Tranny's arm, Brainard scooted backwards, out of reach of a knife, just in case. But Tranny only rubbed his sore upper arm with his left hand. The beer can stayed on the floor. Tranny's head stayed lashed to the headrest.

"We're on a mission for the boss, here, right? Like commandoes. Whether we feel like it or not. That car we're following has his girlfriend in it and some guy who attacked the boss.

Maybe he's holding a gun on her right now. Or maybe she's pulling a fast one on the boss. Either way, we're gonna find out."

"I'm just saying," Ike said, "who made you the guy that gives the orders, here?"

"Yeah, man. You ain't driving. You ain't even in the front seat."

"It's not about where you're sitting in the car. Max Vinyl asked me to take care of this situation with your help. I report to him tomorrow. That makes me team leader. Now he's counting on us to come through for him. Is that a problem for you guys?"

"I got a big problem with that."

"Well, I've got a problem with going back to prison. You want to get pulled over by the cops for drinking beer in a car? Is that what you want?"

"No, man."

"A team needs a leader, and the leader is not the one that fucks up the mission with stupid shit like imbibing in the car. The leader is the one that has to report to the boss on the success of the mission. You want to have that responsibility, Ike?" He listened to himself ranting. It felt good to rant a little after that image of the boss with his red eyes and all messed-up and bleeding.

"Not really, no, actually."

"So is it OK with you two guys if I am the leader of this group, for tonight?"

"I can live with that," Ike said.

Tranny grumbled something that was not, technically speaking, any recognizable word, but which Brainard took to mean he gave in.

The red Mitsubishi led them South on Lake Shore Drive through the heart of the city. They stayed with the traffic, which was heavy enough not to be noticed but light enough to allow them to keep the Mitsubishi in view.

Once they were south of the city and getting on the Dan Ryan Expressway in the direction of Indiana, Ike said, "Untie him now. He learnt his lesson."

"That true, fuckhead?"

"Yeeeeth," said Tranny. He sounded plenty irritated, but at least it was the right answer.

Brainard untied the knot.

"We got some old cell phones, in case you know anybody that's interested in that kinda thing," Ike said.

"What kind of cell phones?"

"Take your pick. Motorola. Nokia. Samsung. We got every kind of phone."

"I could use a new phone. Don't want an old phone, thanks." He kept one eye on the red Mitsubishi and another on Tranny. But he wasn't moving now. Just rubbing his chin and his cheeks, where the handkerchief had dug into them. "Stolen, are they?"

"Not exactly," Ike said.

"We traded for 'em," Tranny said.

"Traded for what? How many phones're we talking about?"

"'Bout two hunnerd, all in all," Ike said.

"Hey look. They're getting off at the Gary exit. Ike, you know what to do."

A pair of minivans cruised up ahead between them and the red Mitsubishi, giving them good cover. Once off the highway, they turned onto a road that took them north, toward the lake. They drove through what looked like farmland or vacant land of some kind. It was dark and deserted. Ike kept the Lincoln a quarter mile back of the Mitsubishi. They all watched it turn off to the right, way up ahead.

A few miles up that road, in a small town, the car parked ahead of them at the side of the road in front of a row of houses. Cars were parked all up and down both sides of the road. The houses were set back at least a hundred feet. Ike slowed way down as they got closer, but he kept going, so as not to attract attention.

"There's two of them, right?"

All three of them peered into the dark. Two figures were walking up the driveway as Ike drove by.

"He got a gun on her?"

"I didn't see no gun."

"I can't see a thing in this light," Ike said. He pulled into a driveway half a mile down the road, turned around and drove back.

"I was starting to see double from staring so hard," Tranny said.

"Park the car," Brainard ordered. "Don't lose them now."

Ike parked a few cars down from the Mitsubishi and killed the lights. They stared at the house Tris and the man had walked up to. Brainard saw an old wooden house, three stories tall, set way back from the road, the windows all dark. No lights on in any of the neighbors' houses, either. This whole section of the street was dark. He sat there, waiting for a light to go on, any light, anywhere.

"You think the big guy lives in that house?"

"They're in there right now. Why else would they park right out front?" Tranny said.

"Why don't I see no lights if they're in there?"

"They could be sitting in the dark looking out. Like if they knew they was followed."

"Yeah, sitting in there with a shotgun," Ike said.

"The boss thinks they're probably together in this," Brainard said.

"You mean she helped him attack the boss?"

"That's what I aim to ask."

"It was too easy following him all the way down here, you ask me," Ike said.

"Bullshit," Brainard said. "He knew he was being followed, he wouldn't have brought us straight here, would he?"

"You got a point there," Ike said.

"What we're going to do," Brainard said, "is get out of the car and go around and have a look out back. You two guys go around the left and meet me in the back. Let's see if we can see any sign of life."

"What makes you so sure he ain't gonna shoot outta one of them windows when he sees us walking around in the dark?"

"What kind of chickenshit you made from, Ike? He ain't got any reason to shoot anyone. Just tell him you came to read the electric meter, anybody asks."

They separated according to Brainard's plan. He walked slowly around the house on the right, moving through the dark on the balls of his feet. The yard was hard-packed dirt, little patches of grass and weeds here and there. The property looked vacant. It had the feel of being not just empty, but as if it had been empty for the last ten years. The night air was hot and muggy, but he felt totally calm. He felt the gnats bouncing off his cheeks and ignored them as he moved into the back yard. They didn't bite; for some reason they just liked human sweat.

His eyes moved over the ground in the back, looking for reflected light. But no light came from the back of the house, either. Small trees dotted the back of the property, like young elms or birches. Movement caught his eye at the far side of the yard, toward the back. Tranny and Ike slunk along a dark hedge like the sloppy amateur burglars that they were. They met up at the rear of the property in the shadow of a low hedge.

"You wouldn't really think anyone was in there," Brainard said.

"But they are," Tranny said. "Cause we seen them goin' in."

Brainard looked around. The hedge back here was a scraggly thing, the height of his waist, breaks in several places. Beyond the hedge lay another yard, another row of dark houses and backyards. Those houses would be facing onto a parallel street. It could just be that they had cut through here to that other street. Not even ten o'clock at night, and not a light on in the whole neighborhood. It seemed a little spooky.

"What if they cut through this yard to get to that yard over there, and out the other side?"

"Why would they wanna do a thing like that?"

"Maybe they did see they were being followed. Come on." He led Tranny and Ike back around to the front of the house. They headed for the car. Ike walked faster than usual.

"What're you so nervous about?" Tranny said. "That guy ain't even here."

"Who said I'm nervous? I ain't nervous."

"You're practically runnin'. I'd call that nervous."

"I am not runnin'."

"Hey, did one of you guys leave the trunk open?" Brainard stopped and pointed. The trunk of the Lincoln stood open.

"Hell no," Ike said, and stared, astonished. They crowded around to inspect the trunk. It was empty, just as it had been before. Ike slammed it shut.

"It ever pop open by itself?" Brainard asked.

"No sir," Ike said. "This baby was opened. You believe that shit?"

"This car's falling apart," Tranny said. "Whaddya expect with a twenty-year-old car?"

"This car is in mint condition," Ike said.

"The brakes are loose, the fuel gauge is broken, the AC don't work. Now we find out the trunk opens when you're not looking. Get a new car, man."

Brainard was turning, looking all around. In the dark he could see little. The only light came from the Lincoln. Light and noise. The sound of the two men with their chatter distracted him from thinking just as the light kept his eyes from seeing in the dark. He made a decision.

"You boys go on back home now. I'll take over from here. You got a shift to work at one o'clock anyway, right? You don't wanna be late this time."

"How the hell're you gonna get back?" Ike asked.

"I'll be driving that sexy little Mitsubishi."

Ike's eyes widened. "You serious, man?"

"Go on, get outta here," Brainard said. "We may have lost them, but they're gonna lose their car. I'll see you around." The other two got back in the Lincoln and started the engine.

Brainard's mind was working a mile a minute as the other two drove away. Tris and her companion obviously had seen they were being followed. Once the men had gotten out of their car and gone away, they must have circled back and searched the Lincoln. That trunk could not be a coincidence.

The only question was, why leave it open? Because they had surprised them when they came back? More likely to leave a calling card. They wanted him to know they weren't going to be fucked with. They had a dog. The Mitsubishi still sat there in its parking space a few cars up the road. Which meant they could just still be here, watching him. But that was unlikely. A dog would have made noise, giving them away.

He waved at the other men as they drove away, then walked back toward the Mitsubishi. He stepped into the street and leaned to look in the driver's side window. No one in the car. Satisfied he was alone, he fished out of his hip pocket a kit with some special tools. With a stiff wire that fit in between the upper lip of the window and the rubber molding, he unlocked the door from the inside. Once he had lowered himself into the driver's seat, another tool enabled him to pry off the cowling at the base of the steering column. A few seconds later, the motor was running. Half a tank of gas. He flipped on the lights, locked the doors, and pulled into the empty street, making a U-turn and heading back in the direction of the highway.

What kind of game was this fellow playing, screwing with the boss's girlfriend? A dangerous game. Max Vinyl wouldn't take this lying down. With this open-trunk business they had thumbed their nose at him. Well, they wouldn't be too thrilled when they came looking for the Mitsubishi.

"Come and get me," Brainard said, and checked the rear-view mirror. But in this lonely place, as far as he could see, he ruled the Indiana night.

NIGHT VISIONS

A silver Honda had followed the brown Lincoln from the address in Waukegan all the way to Indiana. Annie Ogden was parked halfway up the block from the Lincoln, other side of the street.

Out came the night vision glasses. It was after ten and darkness had chased away the last streaks of light on the western horizon. These night eyes picked up all ambient light – moonlight from the crescent moon reflecting off vehicles, for example. She saw the tall blond driver with his gigantic stomach and eyebrow bolt. Next to him rode the muscular Asian. A third man in the back seat did most of the talking. She pressed a button on her phone.

"This is Todd."

"Guess where I am."

"Annie? Where?"

"Your phones have become part of an interstate crime. Indiana."

"Are you off your rocker? If I had known you were going to take it this far I would have refused to get their address for you." Todd had used a contact at the Chicago Police Department to run the license on the Lincoln. Her phone had rung while she was having a bite at a restaurant right in Waukegan. She had decided to go and watch the house.

"Here I thought you'd be happy."

"Those guys are dangerous, Annie. Like, you know, I can just see the headline: *Chicago Woman Murdered in Northern Indiana Phone Caper.* Do it now."

She had never known Todd was such a pansy. She didn't know which he was more afraid of, her getting hurt, or what Alison would think. Well, she wasn't about to let these thugs terrorize Alison. "Let me worry about that," she said. "By the way, is Alison around? Can I speak to her?"

"She's back at the Domino, working the dinner shift. If she sees them, she's going to tell the manager and get out of sight. Annie, you get home now. You don't belong in Indiana, doing whatever you're doing."

"Just when I'm starting to have fun." She saw movement up ahead. The men were getting out of the Lincoln. She lowered her voice. "Got to go, Todd."

She cut the line and watched the men through her night vision goggles. The Asian one walked bowlegged. A lot of weightlifters in the Army walked like that. The third one had short gray hair, a black t-shirt and a very trim waist. He too had massive biceps. Compared to the others, he looked like ex-military. The men were walking up to the dark house they had parked in front of. Only they didn't go to the door. The two phone thieves went around to the left, and the one from the back seat, the one with gray hair, went around to the right.

When they had gone around behind the house and she couldn't see them anymore, she got out of her car. It was a short fifty-yard jog to the brown Lincoln. With her night vision goggles she swept the interior of the car – nothing but a few beer can empties. No phones. That left the trunk. She stared in the direction of the house where the men had disappeared. No movement. They were gone.

The Lincoln was an old model. She felt around under the rim of the trunk lid until her fingers found the hasp that held it shut. She checked her fanny pack to see if she had anything she could use on that hasp. With a small screwdriver she worked at it until she felt it bending. All at once the trunk popped open. A small bulb lit the inside of the trunk. The light hurt her eyes. She pulled off the goggles. No phones. Aside from the spare tire and a folded-up blanket, the trunk was empty.

She heard men's voices. Half a second later she knew it was the three men coming back already. She stayed rooted to her spot behind the car, trying to decide what to do. There was no way to run back to her car without them seeing her. If she closed the trunk now, they would hear it. They would also see her. If she left it open, they would know she had been here. The voices were getting louder. She was out of time. The open trunk lid hid her from their view, but only for the next two or three seconds. Keeping low, she ran away down the street along the line of parked cars. After the sixth car she dodged in between two cars. From here she heard their voices clearly.

"Hey, did one of you guys leave the trunk open?"

"Hell no."

The trunk slammed shut.

"It ever pop open by itself?"

"No sir. This baby was opened. You believe that shit?"

Six cars away, all went suddenly quiet. Now they would be listening and looking around. The pavement felt warm and smooth against her cheek. It smelled of motor oil. Or maybe that was the smell of the Chevy Suburban she lay under, out of sight, at least for the moment. She waited to see their legs as they trotted by, looking under all the cars, or hear their voices approaching. But these were not professional killers with Uzis, merely small time burglars. They didn't come looking.

Instead, low voices, the sound of car doors slamming. Slam, slam. There should have been three doors, but she had only heard two. Was one man staying behind? She heard the big engine of the Lincoln start. The wheels squeaked as they turned on the asphalt, then it eased out of the spot and drove away.

She lay perfectly still, breathing in exhaust on the humid night air, and listening. A seagull cried in the distance. Then the sound of a car approaching. The car passed in a roar of whistling wind. Then silence again. Just when she thought she might have been mistaken, she heard another sound. The sound of leather on pavement. Then a second step and a third, slow and deliberate, definitely human.

So the third man *had* stayed behind. The steps halted before she could tell if they were getting closer or farther away. For a minute there was no sound at all. Then the sound of a car door opening. A minute later another car engine starting. A tingle of relief went through her. The car drove away in the same direction the Lincoln had gone. She didn't move, didn't take the chance of looking, didn't move a muscle as he drove by. Her blond hair was reflective enough in a situation like this; her white face would catch his eye like a spotlight, if he happened to look at just the wrong moment.

It could only have been the third man. She waited another full ten minutes under the Suburban, her cheek resting on the warm smooth asphalt. She hadn't found the phones, but at least she had kept tabs on the two bastards who had stolen them. She felt radiantly alive and satisfied with her day's work, even if the only sounds now were the birds and the lake breeze and the night insects.

TEN MILES OUT

The barge was ninety-five feet long, longer than a city bus, and twenty-five feet wide. It had six cargo bays that went down four feet below the waterline. Along one side of the deck ran a track with a small crane attached. The crane made it possible to pick up something heavy, swing it around, and set it in any of the cargo bays. The standard load was an industrial-sized Dumpster, twenty feet long, eight feet wide and eight feet deep. The Dumpsters were loaded onto this barge under cover of the boathouse.

When Ike and Tranny arrived, the barge was fully loaded and low in the water, so you could just read the name painted in white cursive letters above the waterline: Lake Mule. The six Dumpsters were piled high with old or broken PC housings, monitors, printers and keyboards, old power cords, old plugs and switches of yesterday's technology, disk drives for floppy disks or 3-1/2 inch disks never used anymore, half-gutted motherboards, stripped of any components that still worked or had value, with broken lead and solder lines, heaped upon broken keyboards, spent toner cartridges, scratched printer drums, shattered flatscreens.

This was the stuff that could not be resold on the website, not even marked down to ninety-nine cents. The clunky old monitors were the size of old TVs from the 1970s. They weighed thirty pounds. They sank like concrete. The Dumpsters were piled to overflowing after three days without a barge run.

Ike stood next to Tranny together in the little pilot house on the barge, waiting for the motor to warm up on choke. He opened a can of Milwaukee's Best.

"Dumb question, but you got the GPS?"

"Check."

"What that damn GPS ain't been through," Ike said. He eased in the choke, going slow so the engine wouldn't die, ready to yank it out again. The engine coughed once but roared into life again. He put a hand on the gearshift. "And us, too, because of it."

"Don't start on that," Tranny said. "You want I should untie?"

An hour later, having finished off a sixpack between them, they arrived at the GPS point. With the crane, the Dumpsters could be lifted out of the compartment and swiveled out over the water. Then, by means of a third chain attached to one end of the Dumpster and a winch on the crane, it could be tilted up slowly. When it reached a certain angle of incline, with a great deafening grinding and scraping that made your hair stand on end, the entire load slid out of the Dumpster and dropped into the coffee-colored water. Flatscreens, monitors, PCs, keyboards, printers and printer cables – they hardly made a splash. In twenty minutes all the computer trash had disappeared into the water, and the empty Dumpsters were back in their bays. The men turned the barge around and headed back in.

"We got about eighty feet of water under us," Ike said after a while. "Just think how much water that is."

"Helluva lot of water," Tranny agreed. "Specially when you think it's ten miles back to shore."

"Boggles the mind."

"You realize we ain't never once seen a single other boat out here?"

"We never do," Ike said.

"You know what I thought?" Tranny asked. "Now the fish can surf. Get it, surf? Because of all that internet gear we throwed 'em."

"So funny I forgot to laugh. More like the poor bastards are getting bonked on the head when it falls down through the water. Or else going radioactive because of the chemicals in the computers."

"Chemicals?"

"Yeah, you know. All that mercury and shit in the screens."

"Hey, man, what's gotten into you?" Tranny squinted at him with those Vietnam eyes. "This lake is big enough for a few loads of clean old garbage. It's not like we're putting dirty diapers in the water."

"Diapers is nothing," Ike said. "Biodegradable paper and baby shit. Fish would gobble that sort of thing right up."

"Don't make me puke, man."

"Seriously, Tranny, Max Vinyl is dumping shit that's gonna poison this water for the next five hundred years." Ike started another beer and was careful to put his last empty into a garbage bag they kept in the pilot cabin.

"Five hundred years, my ass," Tranny said.

"Think about your children. Your children's children. And that would only be the next sixty years."

Tranny whistled and tossed his empty over the side. "Man, you better cut down on your drinking. You becoming what they call delusional. I ain't even *got* any kids."

Ancient creature

The water moved the sand. The wind pushed the water, and the water pushed the sand against the land, under the water. It had been so before she lived, and before the ones before her lived, and before them, and on and on going back for as long as her kind had existed.

Old as the Civil War, she cruised along the bottom scooping up crayfish, snails, tiny freshwater crabs in her maw. Looking into her eye was like staring down a dinosaur. Unlike most fish, she had no scales. She needed little effort to move through the water, an instinctive, peristaltic action in the muscles running the length of her eight-foot hulk propelling her in search of food. Now sweet, now acrid, the water could taste of a thousand different things. In spring she tasted the mud of the spring runoff, the brooks and streams and rivers filled with the melted snow of winter flowing faster and emptying into the lake. Summer brought fires to the land, and the smoke and ash that fell with the rain into the rivers that choked up with it but still ran through their meanders into the lake made the water taste of smoke.

She had tasted the blood of her million cousins when they were slaughtered as pests, the bony plates on their scaleless bodies continually tearing the nets of the fishermen to shreds. Men had stacked their bodies onshore like cordwood to rot in the sun. Here, where she cruised just now, the water tasted of that silver metal, mercury. It sank to the bottom heavier than stones and lay beneath the surface to be absorbed in the flesh of critters that she ate, to be stored in their flesh, and when she devoured them to be stored in her flesh, in her eggs, her roe. Her offspring carried the curse of the mercury and the other chemicals that built up on the bottom, where she fed. It could not be otherwise.

But her generations were long, and her line was old, older than most other animals on the planet. Her forbears in other lakes, not this lake, for this was a young lake, had dodged the crashing footfalls of giants when they roamed the swamps and rivers three hundred million years before. Her forbears had survived the dangers and the poisons of their time – the volcanic ash that made the lakes and rivers a toxic mush, or the meteor that descended like a fire from the sky and landed in water far away and made the world dark for years afterwards – her forbears had survived the curses, and the curse in her flesh was mixed with the curses of all ages past. She too would survive them.

DOING MAX VINYL

Wednesday dawned cool and breezy in Northern Indiana. Tris Berrymore knew it wouldn't stay this way. It would grow beastly by noon. She dug her toes into the cold grainy sand of the Indiana Dunes. She loved this moment of the day on the beach, the sun still barely hidden below the horizon but ready to come in view at any moment in a first brilliant fiery red line, and a ghostly mist rising from the sleepy cove. As the sun rose higher in the sky, towards midday and into the afternoon, you wouldn't be able to move, nor even *think* without breaking a sweat. But at this hour the air was cool and sane and a thing of beauty.

She wasn't going to work today. Not today, not tomorrow, and not the day after that, either.

The first thought that had come to mind, even before opening her eyes, was that she now owned a puppy. The thought of Dante waiting had propelled her out of bed. His whole little body had quivered with pleasure to see her awake and stooping down to his level. They had left the house dressed as they were – she in panties and a t-shirt that came down to her knees, he in his funny yellow fur.

Dante took four bounding steps for every one of hers. Every sort of beach smell tantalized his three-month-old nose and made him crazy with joy: dead fish, old driftwood, damp sand. He ran along beside her and ahead of her, pointing his nose into the wind, checking to see if she was still following. He peed once; as part of the training she was keeping a record.

They headed back to the beach cottage, where she started the coffee machine. An old Mr. Coffee left by her brother. Everything dated from years and years ago, when he had left for the job in Sao Paolo – the coffee machine, the dirty yellow couch in the living room, the old small Sony TV. Now he came back just once a year for two weeks in August with his family.

She wanted Luther to wake to the smell of fresh coffee. First she put puppy chow in a bowl for Dante, and a bowl of water next to it. Then she laid out breakfast things on the counter: juice, bread, eggs. When she heard the shower down the hall, she put on water for the eggs and toast in the toaster, without putting it down. Then she took Dante out for another short romp.

You had to take a puppy out often to let him get used to holding it. His bladder would grow as he grew, but you also had to train his mind. All so much easier than training a man. She took him to a corner of the yard, where the pine trees started, and waited there while he pranced around. When Dante finally squirted, she praised him over and over and rubbed behind his ears.

Later she sat at the breakfast table with Luther.

"Happy now?" he asked.

She watched him tap a crooked line around the egg with his knife. Then he slid the knife in and pried off the top. He salted the egg, then ate it out of the shell with a tiny egg spoon.

"I feel like a new person. Thank you so much for this idea."

The puppy lay in his carrier, three feet from their table, nose on his front paws, tummy swollen full of puppy chow. He raised his head expectantly every time she looked at him. She would give his digestive tract another twenty minutes, then take him out again.

"If you don't stop thanking me, I could get ugly."

"Just not in front of the dog."

"Seriously, Tris, could we talk?"

"What?"

"I thought maybe you could bury it now. He got the message last night. Today is going to hammer it in a little more."

She smiled at the thought. "Going to have a rough day, isn't he?"

"And so then I'd say we might just be finished doing Max Vinyl. What about you?"

"Finished? Max? If he were *dead*, well then I guess it might possibly be finished."

"Don't talk like that, Tris. It scares me. It sounds like you mean it."

She didn't answer right away. She loved it when he didn't shave for a day or two. That gray stubble, the gray in his ponytail, the blue eyes, the complicated muscle in his shoulders and chest and arms – because just when you thought you had Luther buttonholed, then you found out the package contained even more than you imagined. He had sold his software company to one of the biggies and was independently wealthy; he had made music videos for MTV; he had spent three years of his life travelling through various countries in Africa, sometimes working, sometimes just touring; and he spoke a language called Yoruba and another one called Swahili, only he called it Key-Swahili.

"Does a man like that *deserve* to live? Surely that is the question," she said.

"You feel personally wronged, I give you that. He's a scourge to the planet. Fine, but what about the next scourge you find out about? And the next one after that? Max Vinyl can't be the only environmental bad guy in the Chicago area, right? He's probably not even the worst one."

"He's not stupid, you know. Just the opposite."

"Neither are you. So tip off the police. Let them take care of him."

"We've talked about this. That's part of the problem. There is no law. They could catch him red-handed and they still wouldn't arrest him."

"That's another reason to lay off Max. He's such a small insignificant part of the problem. The system is the real problem. Focus on getting the laws tightened up, if you want to make a difference. Make a video. What I'm concerned about is this pumpkin right here." Luther touched the top of her head with his index finger. "Whatever's going on in there in the way of what you're planning, there might be laws against that. I don't want to see you, or us, on the wrong side of those."

"Stop trying to make me into someone I'm not. Do you think I can just turn my principles on and off with some little switch?"

She felt a swelling in her chest. She wanted to shout out what she believed, she was that sure of it. Luther's frustration was comical. He stared at her, visibly struggling to think of a way to get her to see his point.

"I just think you go too far," he said quietly. "I'm not going to lose you twice."

Luther stood up while his laptop made its turning on noises. When he pulled her into his arms, she smelled his sleep smell and his man smell. He was a big man. Sort of like hugging a giant – you didn't really want to stop, not for anything. After a minute Dante yipped.

New Job

Blinking, flashing images filled the screen on Annie Ogden's computer. It reminded her of the phosphorus tracers they used to light up the battle scene. Strobing pictures of computers, PCs, laptops, printers, scanners, flat screens, old-fashioned monitors – the company recycled old computer equipment.

Tri State Recovery, Incorporated.

The website made the company seem bigger and more sophisticated than the gravel parking lot and humble screen door in the side of a container she had seen yesterday. You could order used computer parts or a refurbished computer, and have these delivered to your house. Companies could call up TSR and ask to have their old equipment picked up and hauled away. The really old stuff was recycled.

A line in red boldface type under "current news" caught her eye.

Receptionist sought for full-time work. E-mail applications only.

Now here was a chance. The phones had gone in that door. Maybe they recycled phones as well as computers. The brown Lincoln had driven straight there and the men acted as if they belonged. The idea of applying for a job sent a tingle of pleasure down her spine. Here was a way to find those men and confront them.

She spent thirty minutes updating her resume to fit the receptionist job, hesitating only when she had to put down her address. She couldn't very well let them know she had taken over an abandoned forest preserve cabin on the flight path to O'Hare. She wrote: "Staying with friends on the North Shore," and clicked the send button.

She lay on the floor and did two hundred and forty crunches. In the military she had learned that staying in shape cleared your mind. When she opened the door, the sunshine flooded in like a spotlight on her bed, her table, her clean-swept floor.

Home. My existence.

She locked the door and hiked through the forest to her car. It felt good to reduce your existence to an illegal cabin in the woods in the middle of greater Chicagoland. It felt like freedom. And if she wanted to spend the day recovering stolen phones, no one could stop her from doing that, either. Even if the phones were beyond her reach, it would be worthwhile figuring out a way to make sure those thugs didn't bother Alison anymore.

Just before nine o'clock she pulled into the gravel parking lot of TSR in Waukegan for the second time in fifteen hours. If the brown Lincoln was here, she didn't see it. Standing in the hot sun in front of the TSR sign, reading the words Tri State Recovery Inc., she asked herself, *is this crazy?* Well, she wasn't asking Todd and Alison. She wasn't asking her mother. Michael wasn't around anymore to ask.

Who cares what anyone thinks.

A bell chimed somewhere within when she walked in the door. She stood in a reception area with a desk at the rear wall, doors on either side, and a glass display case to her right. It held laptops, flatscreens, keyboards and other computer parts on glass shelves. Thirty dollars for a laptop. Ten for a flatscreen. The equipment looked old and battered, but you couldn't beat the prices. How did they do that?

One of the doors burst open and a man came out. Male Hispanic, aged forty.

"Hey, can I help you?"

"I applied for the receptionist job," she said. "Thought I'd stop by and make sure you got my mail."

The way he stared at her, either the khaki shorts and sleeveless blouse must be inappropriate, or she had come at a bad moment. He put out his hand. "Manny Rodriguez, general manager. Recognized you from the picture. We don't get many applications with photos."

She shook his hand, careful not to overdo the pressure. "Annie Ogden. Is the position still available?"

"Answer me one question," Rodriguez said. "What the hell do you want with a low-end job in a scruffy place like this?"

The confrontational sort, she thought. In the army she had met her fair share. First they watched how you dealt with flak. The rest came later.

She sighed. This wasn't going to be all play-acting. "I did three tours, Mr. Rodriguez. Had enough of mangled bodies. Now I've been back a few months, too much sitting around. Looking for a way to get started again, pretty much."

"But why us? Why should we be so lucky?"

She shrugged. "I saw your website. It's cool what you're doing for the environment. You know, recycling and all that."

He nodded. Was this a job interview, right here in the reception area?

"Attack helicopters, helicopter pilot, that right? Little hard to picture, you know, pint-sized lady like you at the controls. Like 'Apocalypse Now', right?"

"In Viet Nam they flew Hueys, Mr. Rodriguez. Different generation of bird."

He dismissed her with a wave. "Forget helicopters. Bottom line, you don't fit in."

"How can you tell if you haven't even seen me work?"

He frowned. "Too damned smart. Too well-educated. No challenge for you here."

"Excuse me, but I do get irritated when people make assumptions about me."

"I'm paid to make assumptions."

"Why not give me a chance? Then you could just check it off your list. I bet you've got a mega-long list of things to do."

Rodriguez looked away at something in the distance, as if this was about the dumbest reasoning he had heard in a long time. So dumb he didn't have an answer.

"I could start right now."

He gave a kind of snort. She held his gaze and said nothing. Finally he echoed, "You want to start this morning."

"You need a receptionist. I'm right here. You've got everything to gain and nothing to lose."

By the blank look on his face, she realized she had surprised him. Being the general manager, he wouldn't like surprises. For a minute he just stood there. Then he said, "So, what about boyfriends? You got a boyfriend?"

It was her turn to be surprised. Rodriguez wore a button-down shirt and tie, but the buttons of his collar were unbuttoned. The tips of the collar curled up like little delta wings, as if no one was ironing his things. Looked like he probably didn't have anyone checking how he looked when he went out of the house in the morning. How badly did this clown think she wanted the job, anyway?

Focus on the stolen phones.

"That's personal."

"I've got my reasons."

"Suppose you tell me your reasons. Then I'll decide if I want to answer."

"Fair enough. One of our people keeps hitting on the receptionist. I need someone that knows how to say no. Bad for business, this kind of shit."

Rodriguez had gone red in the face. She decided to go along with him, even if he was way out of line. She was here to find pierced thugs and stolen phones, not straighten out this Rodriguez fellow or whoever was harassing the receptionist.

"Picture it this way. Anybody steps over the line, I aim for the balls. Army training, and all that."

Rodriguez nodded. He seemed closer to being convinced. "Be a hell of a lot easier if you were ugly," he said. "Not much we can do about that, is there? I'll get you started, see how it goes. We can print out a contract after a few days if you're still here."

It seemed as though he had embarrassed himself into giving her the job. He showed her the phone console and walked her through how to answer, how to cut off, how to transfer calls. An organizational chart showed the names of different managers and their extensions. By ten o'clock she was trying on a headset.

"You're logged on as Tris," Rodriguez said. "We'll leave it like that till I can get you set up with your own profile, just so you can work."

"Who's Tris?"

"Sat in that seat till day before yesterday."

"Left suddenly?"

"You could say," Rodriguez said. Annie dropped the subject. It obviously had to do with this harassment situation. *The phones*, she thought. Find the men with the brown Lincoln. The rest didn't interest her.

"I bet there's a lot of demand for second-hand computers."

"That's what we do," Rodriguez said. "We're out there every day in the whole three-state area picking up old gear. Illinois, Wisconsin, Indiana. Bring it all back here."

"Then what happens?"

He ticked off the options on three fingers. "Refurbish, recycle, export. The things we refurbish are sold on our website, lots of times for a dollar or two. Some incredible deals on the website. Lots of little garage outfits get all their supplies for custom-built PCs from us. For fifty or sixty bucks they get everything they need. Takes them a few hours to put it all together, test it, get it working right. Then they re-sell for three or four hundred dollars. We support their business. Kind of like a clearinghouse."

"That's me, here at reception?"

Rodriguez clicked his tongue. "Not at all. You're just transferring calls. First you got recovery – that's the guys who are going out collecting the old gear. They call in if they've got a problem with a pickup. Or sometimes the companies call in where they're supposed to do a pickup, ask where they are. Sometimes customers call to complain about a delivery. This number here's not even on the website. They shouldn't be calling with complaints and delivery problems. There's a toll number for that, and we've got a 24-hour answering service doing nothing but helping people out."

He showed her a screen on her computer that showed all the trucks out on recovery today. She could see where each truck was headed, its estimated time of arrival there, and the names of the two-man team in each truck. The routes of the trucks on the coming days were also programmed in, and the capacity of each truck.

"Why are these trucks down here at the bottom not on the chart?" She pointed to a bank of ten or twelve colored tabs that represented idled trucks. There were twenty trucks in all and only eight or nine were actually running.

"Staff shortage there too," answered Rodriguez.

He showed her the database with all the employees of TSR and their internal and cell numbers, and a floor plan of TSR. He opened and closed the drawers in her desk showing where paper and supplies were kept, how to feed faxes into the fax machine, and how the coffee machine worked.

"So, what do you think, ready for your first call?"

"Sure."

"OK. Press there."

She put on the headset and pressed a lighted button. "Good morning, TSR, how may I help you?"

"Young lady, do you realize I have been on hold for the last eighteen minutes?" asked an older man.

"My apologies for the delay, sir," Annie said. "How can I be of service?"

"I ordered an AMD 356 Athlon chip," said the man. "Now it arrived, but see this is a 256. It's not what I ordered. There's a mother of a difference between the 256 and the 356, know what I mean?"

"If I understood you correctly, sir, you were shipped the wrong item. To rectify that error, you have to call the service line listed on our website." She read off the number. "There is a service charge of ninety cents a minute for that call. But they can help you quickly and efficiently. Good bye, sir." She pressed the button to cut off the call. The light on the other button was still on, meaning another call waiting, so she pressed it again.

She managed sixteen calls in the next hour before the light finally went off. No one left on the line. Every single caller had had a complaint. These people had found out the landline number of TSR in the hope of saving ninety cents a minute. Instead they ended up being on hold for ten or fifteen minutes, only to be referred back to the service line. They yelled at her. Either they talked a mile a minute, or they sounded drunk and slow-witted.

They called her shocking names, like the one who had called her "one frigid bitch." That hurt. Where did the guy get off, calling her *frigid*? You put your head down when you heard the whistle of an incoming rocket. These calls might not take your head off in reality, but that was how they made you feel.

She hadn't noticed when Rodriguez went away. She stared at the screen, wondering if there was anything to learn by having access to someone else's computer profile. She clicked on the e-mail program and scanned the names of the senders of all the unopened mails. The names meant nothing to her. She couldn't even tell if the mails were business-related or just friends of this person named Tris.

She was about to open one of these mails when the door to Rodriguez's office burst open. He marched straight over, eyes narrowed, wrinkles bunched on his forehead, chin sticking out like a pit bull.

"What do you think you're doing?" he demanded, his eyes on her screen. On the screen was the list of emails to Tris. Either they had a video camera somewhere, or Rodriguez had a very keen sixth sense.

She kept cool. "I handled the calls that were stacked up, and there's a bunch of unanswered mails. I was just getting started. I don't know if they're company business, or personal, or what."

"Let me look," Rodriguez said. He waved for her to stand up. "I'm going to log out of here anyway and test your new profile. By the way, another question. You're the first applicant I ever hired who didn't even *ask* about the pay. You mind explaining that?"

She had actually wondered about the pay after hanging up on the caller who had called her that vile name. She had her answer ready.

"I didn't want to put you off. I doubt you can match the U.S. Army pay scale, including combat pay supplements, and I wouldn't expect you to. Just put me down for whatever you consider fair."

"I thought maybe we'd found ourselves a volunteer."

"Now, that really would take the fun out of it." She tried her best to look charming.

Rodriguez seemed to accept her story. After all, she had proved herself by answering calls for a solid hour. He said, "Take a break. Right through there to the canteen. Meet some of the other staff."

She went through a door and found herself in a very large warehouse room filled with assembly line machinery, workstations, people standing all around the room with computer parts on tables in front of them and tools in their hands. They glanced at her and kept working. A big blue banner twenty feet long hung from the rafters in the ceiling. On it was written in white block letters: WE PAY MINIMUM WAGE PLUS 25%!

The canteen was at the other end of the big room, through a door. She noted vending machines, a drinking fountain, a bowl of fresh fruit. She took a peach and watched a man lean over to get a can out of a machine. He glanced back before disappearing through a door on the other side. Through the door, before it closed, she caught a glimpse of the outside. She followed. A dose of sunshine would do her good.

In the shade of the warehouse she found two women and two men. Two were smoking. They held their drinks and stared at her through their sunglasses.

"I'm Annie. New receptionist," she said.

"What? Where's Tris?" asked a woman with short red hair. She had her headphones down around her neck, her face twisted in surprise.

"Left on Monday. They didn't tell me what happened."

"Amy," the woman said. They shook. "This is Roberto."

"Hey." A man reached out a long bony arm. She shook his hand. "Lucky if they tell you anything around here," he said.

"Murray. How you doing?" A man with a ponytail, not as tall as Roberto, shook her hand next.

"We're in testing," Roberto said. "Me and Murray."

"Speak for yourself," Murray said.

"Take the PCs apart, remove anything usable, put stuff on the tester, shit like that."

"Like, only yesterday, Tris was here," Amy said. She ran a hand through her short red hair. "Or was that Monday? Yesterday I had the day off. I don't believe this. Like from one day to the next. How could she be gone? You guys hear anything?"

"It is weird," Roberto said. "Especially when you consider that her and Max are shacking up."

Amy tapped her cigarette. "Is that confirmed?"

"They were all over each other in the Olive Garden in Waukegan a week ago," said a woman with blond shoulder-length hair. Black barrettes in the front held it back from her forehead, and a white bow sat on top of her head. The 1950s white dress with black polka dots had *flea market* written all over it.

"I was there with my mom. Happened to be a couple of tables away. Luckily Mr. Vinyl doesn't know me. He pawed her all through dinner. Tris saw me, she knows who I am, but she didn't care. My Mom and I were like, grow *up* already. Oh yeah, I would say that's confirmed, all right." She stuck out her hand. "Kathleen. Nice to meet you. Just because we're freaked out about Tris doesn't mean we're against you."

"They must've had a fight," said Amy. "Such a slimy bastard. I don't know what she saw in him anyway."

"Maybe they decided to end the working relationship," Kathleen said. "Would that ever get old, if you were seeing each other privately."

"I just would've thought she'd say something," Amy said.

"I saw a notice on the website, applied for the job, and came down," Annie said.

"And they hired you, just like that?"

"That phone rings nonstop," Annie said.

"I'll bet it rings like a motherfucker."

"Roberto, watch your language when you're around nice girls," Amy said.

"I do."

Amy took a swing at his head with her empty Coke bottle. It was a glass bottle. She didn't miss by much.

"You're mental, Amy."

"Better to be like me than to be a complete and utter *wuss*," she said.

Back in reception, Annie found a second man talking with Rodriguez. The white shirt might have looked good with the pastel blue suit if he didn't have it open three buttons, showing lots of curly black chest hair. With those bloodshot eyes he looked seriously hung over. When he smiled he flashed a gap between his front teeth. It caught your eye. A heavy dose of gel made his hair look lacquered. His face was all scratched up, with several light scratches and one or two deeper ones, in addition to some puncture wounds with very fresh scabs.

"Max Vinyl, owner of the company," he said, sticking out his hand. "You're the new receptionist."

She shook his hand. "Thanks for the chance."

"Thank Manny. Good to have an army vet on the team. What did they have you doing over there?"

"Shooting bad guys. Learning to fly choppers."

He smiled, she thought, a little too warmly, as if he liked to show off that gap in his front teeth. He looked meaningfully at Rodriguez. "That's relevant work experience."

"Conflict management," Rodriguez said. He sounded defensive.

"We don't have conflicts."

"Only when we least expect them."

"Looks like you had a conflict with a cat," Annie said, changing the subject. The managers were disagreeing in front of her, but she was used to this in men. There was a certain kind of man that had to pick fights with other men as soon as a woman was present, even a woman they had never met before. Most men seemed right at home playing that game.

"Me? I don't even have a . . ." Max Vinyl realized what she was looking at. He laughed. "Oh, that. Close encounter with my ex-wife's rosebushes."

Focus, Annie.

One of these men might have seen the phones that had come right in this door the night before.

"Excuse me, but I do have a question." The two men looked at her. "I was just thinking. My Dad's got this box full of old cell phones. Do we refurbish old phones, too?"

"What in the world gave you that idea?" asked Rodriguez.

"One of the calls before, they were asking . . ." She hesitated, thinking about the hidden camera. Could they catch her in a lie? "I mean, this guy's English was really fractured. I thought he was asking about a cell phone he had ordered but it hadn't been delivered yet. I gave him the toll number like all the rest. Seemed a little strange."

"Probably confused our website with another one," Rodriguez said. "You won't find a single phone on ours. We don't do phones."

The two men disappeared into the office.

We don't do phones.

Why had those half-brains brought Todd's phones all the way here last night? Maybe Rodriguez was lying. Except his answer had seemed natural and spontaneous. The body language of the other guy had confirmed it.

Yet the phones had come in here. She had seen it with her own eyes.

BRIEFS

The thick express envelope fought against Max Vinyl's fingers. The waybill had Tris's name on it. It was covered with plastic that his letter opener couldn't cut through. It didn't want to be opened. Why did they make these things so hard to open? It didn't help that he was trembling uncontrollably, like a man with a palsy.

Was this her apology, at last? After last night's vicious attack, he certainly had an explanation coming.

He took a pair of scissors to one end of the envelope. Peeking inside, he saw it contained some sort of material. He tugged at one corner. Were these . . . briefs? Bits of colored material all bunched together spilled out onto the desk. It was like they were cut up . . . could these be *his* briefs? Could he have cut into them when he opened the envelope? He unfolded a pair of navy blue Calvin Kleins.

At the very sight, something heavy sank in his gut. There was no accident. The crotch had been scissored out carefully from each pair of briefs, seven in all, leaving a gaping hole in the part that normally cradled his own personal crown jewels. Seven iterations of sick, man-loathing madness, seven 100% cotton reminders of the same insidious message: *no more sweet pussy for you, asshole.*

He dumped the rest of the contents on his desk. The jumble of material and threads and pieces reminded him of one time when he had upset his Aunt Greta's sewing basket. When he laid them all out on his desk, it became clear that all the briefs were cut up in the same bizarre manner. It was like Tris had done a job on his manhood.

An envelope lay buried in the mess, a small pink envelope, not sealed. So there was a letter. Out of habit he sniffed. Her perfume. He inhaled deeply, savoring the memory. Passion, by Chanel. Unbelievable, he thought. *The stuff we did. The trips we took. The restaurants. The sex. And now this, and completely without warning!* What in the world had he done to deserve this? He unfolded the note.

Dear Max
I actually thought I liked you. Then I realized what a world-class prick you are, what a fraud the recycling is. My mistake. You left some briefs in my place so I'm returning them to you. My therapy consisted of some virtual surgery through your briefs; my therapist said it only had value if I sent them to you. Maybe you can still wear them . . . like with one of those iron-on patches or something? Don't come looking for me because I have Luther here. You met Luther. He takes my protection seriously. By the way, my car was stolen and I was wondering did you have something to do with it? If so, please return it to my place in Waukegan. Otherwise I will get even more irritated.
I hope you will find peace in your life (without me),
Tris

Sick! Sick is what it was. That they should have a disagreement, that she should get herself fired for cause, even that she should break up with him – those kind of things happened in life. Grant her that. But what kind of woman sent an express envelope with your briefs all sliced to ribbons? Only a sick woman would even conceive such a thing.

He recoiled at the thought that he had rolled around in bed with such a disturbed person. He looked at his hands, holding the note, and saw they were trembling. He buried the note in his lap. His hands were shaking and he couldn't stop them.

If only we could start over again!

But no, a girl who was capable of taking your underwear and cutting it up into pieces could do real damage. Somewhere you had to draw the line.

There had been no warning . . . that was what he couldn't get over. How could anyone have known it would turn out like this? This was the girl who, two days ago, had sat right here in this office in her turquoise blouse and white miniskirt. Even then she had still been his. With this little stunt she showed she was well and truly gone.

A knock came on the door, startling him. His hands were shaking so much he had trouble stuffing the note in his breast pocket. His heart was pounding so hard it felt like it would fly right out of his chest. He must've drunk too much coffee. Yet his mouth had gone dry as dust. His hands trembled as if they had a mind of their own.

His ex-wife, Ginger, strode into the room before he could hide the briefs. She carried a gooey-looking chocolate cake on a platter. She set it down on his desk next to the colorful pile of cotton material, which he scooped up in one motion and stuffed in a drawer.

"I baked it myself, Max, to celebrate your success. The new girl out there, she let me in because I told her it was a surprise. What in the world are you doing with underwear all over your desk? I hope those are clean."

"Long story." He came around the desk and planted a kiss on her cheek. She wore a white sundress with spaghetti straps, a pink straw hat, and Dolce Gabbana sunglasses perched on the brim. Her toenails were decorated with an orange-red base and some sort of silver and gold designs with black highlights. That toenail job looked expensive. Ginger rather forcefully turned it into a full hug. Her breasts pressed against his front like big balloons, not unpleasantly. He was glad he had taken off his jacket earlier. He forced himself to calm down again, after the shock of the mutilated briefs. Ordinary conversation helped. "Cool anklet," he said. "Is that new?"

"Goodness Max, what happened to your face? Those look nasty. I hope you disinfected them properly."

"Of course," he said. "You can't be too careful with cat scratches. What about your ankle bracelet?"

"It's a charm bracelet." She placed her right foot up on the chair so he could examine the charms more closely. The hem of her sundress rode interestingly up her thigh. Her calf was thoroughly tanned, the muscle tone superb. "I'm collecting charms on the theme of elephants."

"Oh, why elephants?"

"I like elephants. You know that, Max. Or did I start with elephants after . . . ?" She thought about it. "Doesn't matter. Just buy me elephant charms if you run across any. Max, I have to know about those briefs. Those were *your* briefs, weren't they?"

"Baby, we are no longer married. If I have to improvise sometimes when it comes to laundry, that's my business. So butt out." His semblance of calm was deserting him. Those mutilated briefs just could not be happening. He felt himself growing more irritated by the second. He felt unable to tolerate visitors right now, especially Ginger. But if he kicked her out he would have to give an explanation. Sometimes under pressure you just had to bear down. *Bear down*, for Chrissake. Only this was just such a different species of pressure: Pepper spray attacks? Mangled briefs stuffed in an envelope? And now Ginger sticking her nose into the story about the briefs.

How much of this could a man endure?

"All right, all right. Aren't you going to have a piece of cake?" She sank a knife into the swirls of chocolate frosting. A giant green plastic dollar sign graced the top. He stared at the cleavage she offered while she bent to cut him a piece.

"The settlement doesn't bump up just because I've hit paydirt. I hope that isn't what you were thinking."

"Goodness, Max. The thought didn't cross my mind. Though Ricardo might have something to say about it. You did say next week on that check, didn't you?"

"Yes."

"Can't a girl just be nice once in a while? Honestly. What happened to your eyes? They're so red. Did you open them underwater or something?"

Another knock came. Manny Rodriguez and Brainard Combs filed into the office. Max was glad to divert attention from himself for a few moments. He sank into the massaging leather of his chair while Ginger handed out slices of cake. Just when he was starting to relax again, Rodriguez raised in the air on the end of one finger something he had found . . . and Max felt his stomach turning. A red piece of fabric, a crotch *cut-out* from one of the briefs. It must have fallen on the floor when he stuffed the rest of the briefs in the drawer.

"What is that?" Ginger asked.

Rodriguez studied it, holding it by the tips of his fingers as if it smelled bad. The white piping around the fly made it clear which part of the briefs he was displaying. "Is this what I think it is?" he asked.

"That depends what you think it is."

"Max, let's don't go there. I told you she was trouble."

"Who?" demanded Ginger.

"None of your damn business, Baby."

"That's a fine way to thank me." Ginger stood up. "What're you so jittery for, Max, anyway? Honestly, he's not himself today."

Max chose to ignore her. "Manny, I've got to get with Brainard for a few minutes. Can I catch you later?"

Rodriguez stood up. He didn't look happy. "I've got about twenty items to report on, too," he said, and stormed out.

"Congratulations again on selling the company," Ginger called from the doorway.

"Small part of the company," he called after. Christ only knew what people would be saying, Ginger and her big mouth. The door closed behind her.

He was alone with Brainard. Brainard hadn't touched the cake on the paper napkin in front of him. He didn't eat sugary things like cake, Max remembered.

"OK, so what happened. Where do we stand?"

"Like I told you on the phone," Brainard said, "we lost them. We couldn't find them after they got out of their car. So, what I did is I hot-wired the car and drove it back."

"The Mitsubishi?"

Brainard nodded. Tris's note confirmed.

"Now, let's think. Assume she's reported it. Christ, you were lucky last night. Whoever drives it now gets pulled over."

"Fold," Brainard said, palms up in surrender.

"Where's the car?"

Brainard blinking rapidly. "The garage at my condo."

"Inside? Out of the way?"

"Nobody's gonna see it in there."

Max thought for a second. "Don't take it out anymore for anything. Last thing we need is you getting picked up. Let's get rid of it. Bring one of the big trucks over there, load it on, bring it back here. That car goes out on the barge tonight. I want that filmed, and the clip in my email by tomorrow morning."

"Got it," Brainard said.

"That's the first thing. Now the second thing. This would be for tonight maybe. You see this?" He pulled something out of the drawer. Brainard took a long unbelieving look at the red briefs Max held up, the crotch sheared out. "You saw what she did to me last night. That was yesterday. Today this crap. I don't know where all this is coming from. I want you to find her. Send a message. An unmistakable message. You know, in your special way."

"You're sure, boss? I mean, this is *Tris*."

Meaning: *Do you really want me to harass the woman you were screwing till the day before yesterday?*

In the other man's face Max saw disbelief. "Move on that."

Brainard leaned one elbow on the table. "Only problem is, I ain't going to find her, boss. They took us on a wild goose chase last night, clear to Indiana."

"Indiana? Right outside Gary? Little place, near the beach?"

Brainard lit up. "I don't know about the beach, but outside Gary, yeah. They got out of the car and walked away. We stayed back so they wouldn't see us. After a while we tried to find them, but they were gone."

"Her brother's beach house. That's where you'll find her." He drew a detailed map from memory. He knew how to draw good maps, complete with with roads, landmarks, mileage. That went with being a car collector. So many tours, and several weekends of nonstop sex at her brother's beach house, too. "You'll figure out what to do."

Brainard tapped his temple. "Use my imagination."

No sooner had Brainard left the room, the new receptionist buzzed him, the short blond army vet.

"I have a Mr. Park on the phone," she said.

"Top priority when he calls. Put him through." He waited for the line to open. "This is Max. Hello, Song."

"Ah, hello Max. Just wanted you to know, it's probably going to be Saturday when we come through again. You name the time. Okay for you?"

"Make it Saturday, ten o'clock."

"My board wants more details on your logistics. Bar code system. Maybe I take a few pictures. You can prepare specifications? Might make sense for us to migrate to the same systems at our Korean plants, use same bar code concept so your system flows into our system. We check it out. Okay for you?"

"I'll have the specs on Saturday, no problem at all, Song. See you then."

"Okay, Max."

He hung up and breathed a sigh of relief. Marrying logistics systems would be a gigantic project, just gigantic, but it would bind them together even more closely. It could only increase the value of TSR in the eyes of the Koreans. Imagine if Tris had managed to get some article on the *Tribune* and scared off the Koreans. Just when they were all signed on and the money about to be transferred. That he would not have forgiven and forgotten. That would've meant war, had she succeeded. As it was, the Koreans were making very positive sounds.

Just as long as Song didn't make him go to the Skinny Whip again. Or for Chrissake *Korea*, he thought with a shudder. If anyone had to go to Korea, it was damn well going to be Rodriguez.

TOTALED

"You're old enough for me to speak frankly," Alden Sterling said. "I want you to reconsider."

"Stop boring me, Dad. No can do."

"How do you know before you try it?"

What he really wanted to ask was, *How in the world could you choose her over me?*

"You're getting on my nerves."

They were sitting on the plane. Trip of course had the window, the one who ignored the views. Alden felt the air conditioning blowing on his tan, his tan starting to shed, like a snakeskin. He wondered what folks back home would say about his tan. One thing about this tan was it had turned his moustache white. An optical illusion, but also a bit shocking. With his usual Midwestern pallor, borne of far too much time in fluourescent light, the moustache normally looked gray, normal, vital. Suddenly he looked ten years older.

"Wine, Dad?" Trip asked when dinner came. He made big eyes. "You do know it has a more intense effect at this altitude, don't you?"

"In honor of your mother." Alden raised the little airplane-sized wineglass and took a micro-sip.

Trip wagged a finger. "Don't go there. Mom's not here to defend herself."

Alden's eyebrows shot up, the picture of innocence. He steered the focus back to himself. "So you thought I was some sort of teetotaller?"

"You are kind of weird, Dad. You have to admit it."

At that moment Alden was almost knocked over with a gush of feeling, for what he saw in Trip's grin was in fact Deborah grinning . . . but on the other hand maybe it was just the alcohol from that first sip of wine reaching his brain.

Thirteen, fourteen years ago . . . his first date with Deborah Sterling. Not used to wine, Alden had stopped after half a glass, his head already spinning. He hated that feeling, especially since he was trying to memorize every word she said, every expression on her face.

"I didn't choose journalism because I wanted to be the next war correspondent for CNN, running from one war zone to the next," Deborah had said.

"You wanted to make sure the public is informed, the search for truth and all that."

"Something much more practical. In a town like this, journalism is a good profession for moms raising kids."

"How many kids are you planning to have?"

"Not less than one, not more than four."

"That narrows it down."

"Have to find Mr. Right."

"That shouldn't be too difficult. Not for you."

The smile vanished and she put her glass down hard. The frown on her face made his heart skip a beat. "What's that supposed to mean?"

"Nothing. Just that you're so popular and all."

She leaned forward. "Alden, forget high school. Do you live in a time capsule? We're not in high school anymore. That wasn't real life back then anyway. That was just all of us kids muddling through their childhood, each one in her own unique way."

That was oddly disingenuous, coming from the girl who had been crowned Homecoming Queen; the girl who had always known the answer in math, even without studying; the girl everyone adored. The kids she had hung around with, the football players and the cheerleaders, had all surfed through their childhood, like surfers riding the waves in Hawaii. They made it look so easy, coasting all the way in. Her crowd had had it just as easy.

During football games he would stand on the sidelines, clipboard under his arm, the whole game picturing himself in bed with Deborah Snyder – those red cheeks, the pleated miniskirt, the tight sweater, the neat white tennis shoes as the cheerleaders ran in from the football field, their hair bouncing on their shoulders.

He would be enjoying this fantasy, there on the sidelines while the game went on, and if by chance he turned around for some reason his eye would fall on Cary Williams, sitting up in the stands, and next to her that stepfather. There was always something greasy about Cary Williams. Her hair needed washing. Her skin seemed waxy, as if she didn't get outside much. Her teeth were crooked because her parents didn't have enough money for braces. Everyone knew how poor they were. And in his mind's eye he would suddenly see, instead of him and Deborah Snyder, Cary Williams and her stepfather having sex. That was the rumor that went around school. Maybe Cary's mother would be listening at the door, or even in the room with them, leering at them . . .

"What ever became of that Cary Williams?" he asked. "You know, that one . . .?"

"Still there in that old house, would you believe? Living with *him*."

"Terrible."

"He should be thrown in jail. And her mom alongside him. You'll never convince me she hasn't known all along what goes on."

Alden detested paying for restaurant meals. He couldn't help adding up the cost of all the ingredients in the food on his plate. He couldn't keep from analyzing the prices on the menu.

So after their fourth date in a restaurant he invited her to his apartment for a home-cooked meal. She arrived with a bunch of tulips and a bottle of icy white wine. Which was good, because he hadn't thought to buy wine.

"You have to drink this one cold," Deborah said. He was learning to like wine better. It tasted like Deborah's kisses. Her kisses tasted fruity, and, as it turned out, she gave them as freely as her smile, whether in his living room in front of the TV, in a restaurant, or in the car when he drove her home.

He hadn't wanted to make love yet, not that night. But once it happened he never wanted to go back, either. The fantasy of making love to Deborah Snyder had resided in his brain for more than fifteen years by the time it happened. He had come to love the fantasy just as you would love a person, fully reconciled to the fact that it would never become reality. Thus that hesitation, maybe. Although he had known other girls, the fantasy of him and Deborah had never been far away. It was a part of him. And somehow the fantasy images melded with images of Deborah in the flesh, this night, her skin touching his, neither of them eighteen anymore, but so much the better. The fantasy became reality in the most wonderful and unforgettable way, with cheerleader images in his mind even as her body strained against his body, her skin moving against his skin, taking him into her as far as he could go, moving against him and moving with him until finally she came, with a shuddering that he felt and that made tears come to his eyes.

Despite her denials, Deborah was as popular as she had ever been. Every Friday and Saturday night they went to parties. She agonized over which invitations to accept, with two and sometimes three invitations for the same evening. Alden preferred dinner parties to cocktail parties, because you spent most of the evening planted at a table with one person on either side. You had time to get to know people in a natural way. Silences were acceptable.

At cocktail parties, where you spent most of the time standing around, the dynamic shifted constantly as people moved around. Conversations never got very deep at cocktail parties. People who could tell a joke or a funny story did best. Those skills were useful at the dinner table, too, but they were essential at cocktail parties. Generally he just stood around listening at cocktail parties, not saying a thing. Nobody expected an accountant to liven up the conversation.

Still, any kind of party was good for business. When new clients contacted Sterling Accounting, he usually found out that he had seen them socially. Naturally it was partly because of Deborah that people were so open to him, both while they were dating, even more so after they married. Everyone still craved Deborah Snyder's attention, even fifteen years out of high school.

The men were all drinkers, first a cocktail or two, then, after moving into the dining room, glass after glass of wine with dinner. The men drank to get drunk. The women had one glass of wine during cocktails and another during dinner, or just one all evening, and constantly made jokes about what it did to them.

"One sip is all it takes..."

He must have heard it a thousand times. Funny, he could have said the same about himself. The women stayed sober so they could drive their husbands home and put them to bed.

To be honest, those women were all a bit shallow and silly. Deborah, on the other hand, was such a skilled talker she instantly brought energy into any conversation. As a journalist, she had a natural curiosity about people, events, and ideas, and she knew how to use questions to make people talk. What always interested her most was the opinion of the person she was talking to at that moment.

The thing that bothered him was that she drank like a man.

"What can I say? I have a high tolerance for alcohol. I don't feel it like others do," she said one night when he asked her about the quantity she had drunk. They were in the car.

They had left a party. Alden held the wheel tight in his hands, trying to blunder his way home through a blinding snowstorm. "It must be in my genes," she went on. You don't see me rolling around the floor or making a fool out of myself like some of those men. I'm half the size of some of those guys. I can drink them under the table."

Her personal policy dictated no drinking during the week – only Fridays and Saturdays and only in the evenings, together with other people. She went at it with a vengeance. She enjoyed life to the fullest then.

"I'm not counting glasses. I'm not a bookkeeper," she said.

He smiled at the slur. "You wouldn't make a cake with twice as much sugar as the recipe called for, would you?"

"What's a cake recipe got to do with enjoying a few drinks with my friends? I don't get it, Alden."

"We have a household budget, too. You wouldn't want us spending twenty percent more than we earn, would you?"

"Alden, you're not listening. Don't try to take me and put everything into neat columns that all add up perfectly, the good parts and the bad parts."

"I'm not."

"I'm not a balance sheet."

"I never said you were. You're making that up. I just meant . . ."

"You just don't like alcohol. That's fine. I accept that. But I happen to like it. I like the taste of it, and it doesn't affect me, so I think you should stop nagging me about it."

The headlights swept the snowy road ahead of them. The silence lay heavy over them, like the combined weight of all the snowflakes hitting the windshield at that moment, and the ones falling after them through the air. The snowflakes were so big and heavy they stuck to the glass. The windshield wipers could not whisk them away fast enough. He imagined ten pounds of snowflakes covering the windshield each minute, six hundred pounds in an hour; in a short time, if they were to stop and if the snow kept falling, the car could be buried under tons of it. He looked across at her in the light of his headlights reflecting off the snow, and he saw why she had gone quiet. Deborah was asleep. Or was she just avoiding further discussion? The snow fell even more thickly on the windshield. A flash of dark blue or gray on the road, just to the right of the car, and . . . *thump*. The car continued along on a slick layer of snow like a hydrofoil on water. He couldn't have stopped if he'd wanted to.

He took his foot off the gas and stopped a short way up the road. No other cars approached from either direction. Had he hit something? He *had* hit something. Out of the dark window he craned. Snow was caked on the windows. The windshield wipers couldn't sweep it away fast enough. There were no headlights anywhere in either direction. Deborah stirred.

"Why'd we stop? What's going on?"

He gunned the engine. The wheels spun in the snow. At last they grabbed. The car slid into motion and his hands gripped the wheel. The bottom had dropped right out of his stomach. Stone cold sober now – what he had drunk? One glass? Two glasses, all evening? The certainty of that thump, the uncertainty about what it had been. An animal? A person, God forbid?

Four days later the headline blared across the front of the weekly *Courier*, front page news. The certainty of it. The knowledge that it had been him.

Local Man Hit by Car, Killed

Longtime Sycamore resident Charles L. Williams was killed Saturday in an apparent hit-and-run accident while walking on Plainfield Road during a snowstorm. "He shouldn't have been walking on that road in those conditions. There isn't even a sidewalk on that stretch of the road," said Police Chief Larry Matthews. The police estimate the accident must have occurred at around eleven p.m. Saturday night. A motorist saw the body in the roadway and alerted authorities.

Williams, 65, was known to take walks at all hours of the night. His stepdaughter, Cary, 30, who lives in the same house, was quoted by police: "I tried to get him not to go out in that weather." Williams was widowed two years ago.

Authorities speculate the driver may not have been aware of the collision with Williams, due to the weather conditions and low visibility Saturday night. A memorial service for Charles Williams is planned for this Friday.

Someone touched him on the shoulder. Had he been dozing? The flight attendant put a tray of breakfast down. In the seat next to him Trip was already forking a bite of omelette into his mouth. In a few minutes Trip would be begging the flight attendant for a second meal. In two hours they would land in Chicago. Slowly Alden unwrapped the silverware, ice cold in his hand.

How ironic it was that his accident . . . his only accident . . . had ended fatally. Whereas a guardian angel had always watched over Deborah.

The first car Deborah totaled had been the Chevy Cavalier. She had swerved to avoid a deer in the road, had gone into a ditch, bending the chassis permanently, and ended up wrapped around an ancient fieldstone wall. It was the kind of wall made by their ancestors in the early eighteen-hundreds, back when Illinois was first settled. The wall had stood. The car looked like a giant troll had picked it up and hurled it through the air in a fit of anger. The air bag had inflated around Deborah for one-twentieth of a second. It had done its work perfectly. Her right thumb had slammed against the gearshift. The broken thumb had been her only injury.

The call had come in to his office nearly two hours after the first police car arrived on the scene of the accident, as he learned from the police report. He had found her at the hospital, her thumb in a splint, ready to be driven home. Four-thirty in the afternoon.

"She's had a shock," said Dr. Pete Allers, the emergency room doctor who checked her out. They had gone to high school together with Pete. "I gave her something to calm her down. We checked for brain trauma, Alden. Nothing. She's a lucky girl."

"I'm a lucky girl," Deborah said from her wheelchair. "Thanks, Pete."

"Can you walk, darling?" Alden asked. He would have carried her. She stood right up and took his arm.

"Walk. Dance. Whatever you like."

He looked at Pete. The doctor was checking something on his clipboard. "What did you say you gave her?"

"Nothing to worry about, Alden. Take her home, fix her some dinner. She'll be fine in the morning. That thumb'll be sore."

He hadn't even realized she was drunk. With hindsight he realized Pete Allers must have known it but had chosen to say nothing. Even though, hours after the accident, she was still swaying on her feet. Didn't he think that was his job? If it wasn't the doctor's job to point out a problem like that, whose job was it?

The next time it had happened, she had smashed up the Volvo D8 wagon. The car was less than a year old. She was six months pregnant with Trip.

Once again a call after lunch, this time Officer Reed Hunt from the Sycamore Police Department. Hunt was at the scene, down on Route 64. It was July. They should have been on vacation, up in Wisconsin, but Deborah hadn't felt well enough for the three-hour drive, so they'd canceled.

The driver of the UPS truck stated that the Volvo crossed the centerline when they were just abreast of one another. He had been making deliveries in Sycamore for ten years and recognized Deborah at the wheel. He had noticed the car weaving as it approached, but because it was two in the afternoon had thought nothing of it.

The rear of the Volvo had caught the rear bumper of the UPS truck as they passed each other. The UPS truck had spun out. The Volvo had rolled all the way over and ended up on its wheels tight up against the guard rail. The Volvo looked like it had been through a meat grinder. The car doors were sealed shut. The fire department had to cut the top off the Volvo to get Deborah out. It was another twenty minutes before they had her on a stretcher, intubated, and in the ambulance.

"All this big noisy fuss for yours truly," she said when she saw him. He sat beside her in the ambulance, on the way to the hospital. Her breath reeked of wine. This time he smelled it.

"How do you feel? Does it hurt anywhere?"

"Not a bit. Look, I can wiggle my fingers and toes."

"Have you told these guys?" He motioned to the two emergency medical technicians who were monitoring her vital signs.

"Told them what?"

He turned to the nearest EMT. "You've got another passenger in this car."

"We got a fetus?" asked the EMT. He rolled his eyes and whipped out a stethoscope. "You shouldn't be drinking in the first place, honey. Let's have a listen, see how your baby's doing." He guided the stethoscope around her abdomen till he found a good place. He checked his watch. "They'll do a full examination at ER. Far as I can tell, your baby didn't even notice a break in the action." The other EMT radioed ahead to say that the patient was pregnant.

"Of course he didn't," Deborah said. "He's safe and sound. That's why I drive a Volvo. I'm *his* Volvo."

"Nobody's going to drive that Volvo again," Alden said.

The conversation continued at home two days later, when she came home from the hospital. The baby had stayed where he belonged. They'd been damned lucky. Alden took his vacation days and stayed home and cooked hot breakfasts and dinners. He poured out all the wine in the whole house.

"After the baby is born, we go back to eating and drinking whatever we want. Now we were given another chance, Deborah. We're going to avoid alcohol for the next three months, agreed?"

"Speak for yourself, Alden. Number one, since when do you lay down the law here? Number two, the problem was not the drinking, it was the driving."

"Yes, it's getting a bit expensive with the cars, now that you mention it."

"There you go again, counting everything up."

"I was just going to say, Deborah, I don't give a damn about the cars. What I care about is you. How many times can we be so lucky?"

"Do you think I'm trying to wreck our cars on purpose?"

"Why do you keep changing the subject? You're not a bad driver, and you're not illogical. Except when you're defending your drinking. You can't drink and drive, Deborah."

"Don't tell me what to do, Alden. I'm fine. The baby's fine."

"For me it's like . . . like a cry for help."

"I don't want your help, Alden. Down boy, down. Go home."

"For your information, I am home. This is my home. You are my wife, and I love you. You happen to be the love of my life."

"You happen to be the *nag* of my life."

The words still rang in his head, so many years later. Over and over they had had these discussions, for years. She had been right about the baby. Their boy, Trip, had been born in the fortieth week, on schedule down to the day, probably down to the hour, eight pounds, two ounces, with a good set of lungs and a high APGAR score.

In Deborah's third car wreck, Trip, age two years and three months, had been protected by his car seat. This time Deborah had suffered a collapsed lung and a broken arm. The police had told him the entire accident scene, like so many others they saw, had smelled strongly of wine.

Yet Deborah wasn't cited. From the policemen to the EMTs to the doctors in the emergency room, every last man in town seemed to have idolized her during high school years. Nobody had the guts to put that first black mark on her record. Alden felt alone. Would they rather see her dead? Wasn't there a single person in the world who could help him set her on a different path?

One day he had had run home from the office at eleven in the morning to get a file he had forgotten. He needed it for a meeting after lunch. He parked in the driveway rather than waiting for the garage door to rumble open, just to save time. He let himself in the front door. He had just closed the front door behind him when a police officer strode into the living room from the kitchen.

"Reed," Alden said, shocked to find the policeman in his living room.

"Morning Alden."

"Is . . . is something wrong? Deborah . . .?"

"Burglaries in the neighborhood. We're having a look at window latches, back door security, things like that. You home for lunch?"

Something seemed strange . . . yes, that was it. Where was Deborah? He was standing in his own living room talking to Reed Hunt. While they stood talking, what was she doing? "Why no, I . . . uh, forgot a file and came home to get it."

At this moment Deborah came out of the kitchen. "Hi, honey. Forget something? You could've called. I could've brought it to you."

He didn't answer, merely went past them and into the kitchen. His mind was in a whirl. From there into the hall and up the stairs. His office was up there. He grabbed the file from his desk. In his mind tumbled a frenzy of images – Deborah, Reed Hunt, the smell of wine, the sound of a siren. An unnamed instinct drove him. He pushed open the door to their bedroom. Everything clean and neat. Trip's room he didn't check. Trip was at daycare today so that Deborah could work.

In the guest room he found the bedspread pulled away, the covers messed around. He took two steps into the room, imprinting the scene on his mind. He didn't want to forget a single detail. Although the window was open, the smell of sweat and sex lay heavy in the air. His saliva ran acid. He clenched his fists. Those messed-around covers, the image of their bodies intertwined . . . in the guest bed. In his house. At eleven in the morning. While he sat in his office working. He backed out of the guest room, not touching a single surface, leaving the door ajar.

When he went downstairs, Reed Hunt was gone.

"I was just on my way out to pick up Trip at daycare."

"I thought you were working this morning."

"I was. I mean, I did. I interviewed the mayor." She looked at him. "Did you find your file?"

"Maybe I should come home at this hour more often. At night . . . you know, we're both always kind of tired."

"Whatever, Alden."

She jingled her keys and went out through the door to the garage.

Back at work, he had dragged himself through the tasks of that endless day. That night, he had hesitated when it was time to go home. If she was going to have an affair, he would have to pull himself together and react. Other men, he knew, went to the whorehouse up Route 64. They went to bars and got drunk. They went and watched striptease. They went to somebody's apartment. They gambled. None of those things held the slightest attraction for him.

Where in the world could a man in his situation go?

At home he found candles lit on the table, and no sign of wine anywhere.

"Chicken Kiev with rice," Deborah said. "Your favorite."

Trip was in bed. Alden sat with leaden feet while Deborah chatted about her afternoon. She had proposed a new series for the *Courier* about the Fire Department: how it was set up, all the fire-fighting equipment they had and its history, and a special focus on the men and women who risked their lives every day. He ate without appetite. In his mind's eye he saw images of her having sex with Reed Hunt in the guest bedroom.

If you're fucking the policemen, why not the firemen, too?

"Deborah, I've been wondering," he said at one point when the conversation flagged. "Reed Hunt here this morning and all. I saw the bed all messed up in the guest room. Is there anything you wanted to tell me?"

"Alden, what're you trying to say?" She sipped her iced tea.

"Come off it. Anyone could see you two were fooling around up there."

She looked him in the eye without saying a thing, the color rising in her face like boiling water going up a pipe. Suddenly she reached across the table and socked him in the ear with one balled-up fist. He didn't move. Then she was hitting him with both fists. He raised one arm to protect his eyes. He let her fists rain down on him till she tired.

"You are evil! You are evil for even thinking such a thing."

"Maybe I am," he said. "God knows I didn't want to think it. I didn't want to have this problem."

"You're the problem."

"Okay so tell me, Deborah. I'm listening to you now. How am I the problem? Help me understand, damn it!"

But she couldn't go on. She couldn't tell him. They stayed there hugging and sobbing, both of them still in their chairs. But the conversation had not gone on.

You're the problem.

That night he had wondered, as he often had wondered before, whether this had been a breakthrough. Or had it just been something to say in that moment that seemed to make sense, as if it would sound logical and plausible, and that alone had been sufficient to make her say it? Was he really the problem? She was capable of saying things that had no meaning, when you analyzed the words. Things that weren't logical. She said things that sounded good, words that went together, but when you tried to figure out how the words corresponded to reality, it became clear that they were just empty clichés.

You're the problem.

On the advice of a friend he pampered her with everything he could think of in the weeks that followed. He brought flowers and presents. He didn't nag her about drinking and driving. He asked her opinions about problems at work. He took her and Trip on weekends to Milwaukee and St. Louis, where they went through museums with Trip in tow. He encouraged her to go somewhere with her girlfriend, Denise, who liked to travel. The two women spent a week in New York. Six months later they went to Los Angeles for a week, while he stayed home with Trip.

Yet there were other affairs that he knew about and some, he felt sure, that he didn't know about. She would never admit to them, and would never discuss their problems any more than to say that she had low self-esteem, as if that were the answer to everything. Maybe that was as deep as it went. But knowing all about it still didn't excuse her cheating on him.

A private detective shot the photos at a Super-8 Motel outside of town. The man in the photos was unknown to him. The woman was the woman he knew best in the world. Yet he did not know her well enough to know how to fulfil her.

If there had just been one or two other men, and if the pattern had stopped, he thought, he would have found a way to put it behind him. But it seemed to go on and on, and she changed from one lover to another, as if she were looking for something she would never find, trying to satisfy a need that could never be satisfied. The problem, he realized, was far more serious than some flaw in himself, or some quantifiable adjustment needed in their marriage.

With his bushy moustache and his iron self-discipline and his penchant for adding things up he was far too plain vanilla for beautiful, sparkling Deborah Snyder. That much he had always known, though in the early years she had led him to think otherwise. But that was only part of it. None of those other guys she went to bed with was good enough for her, either. There was some terrible flaw in her psyche, wherever it may have come from, that caused her to want to hurt herself. She could not stop hurting herself. His love and support could never be enough.

One day, he thought with a pang of fear, the flaw in Deborah could carry over into her relationship with their son. What if Trip could never be good enough for her? Would she have an uncontrollable need to hurt him, too? And what if Trip turned out to be like her, to have in him this same self-destructive flaw? What if he was picking that up from her?

By this time Trip was ten years old and had started adolescence. He talked back, used foul words, wore his clothes inside out to look like the other kids. His grades were sinking. His teachers used words like "disturbed" and "distracted" in their report-card comments.

Alden chose a Friday afternoon to bring up the subject that had been on his mind for a long time. Trip would be at soccer practice for at least another hour. They were in the kitchen. Deborah had just come home from the grocery store and was putting food away.

"Deborah, how do you see our marriage going on from here?"

"What now?"

"Some things I could learn to live with, even though they put you and our son at risk," he said. "Like your drinking and driving."

"There he goes again."

"Other things I have a harder time with."

"Other things. Do I look like a mind-reader, Alden?"

"I'm talking about other men. You have this need for companionship with other men that I will never understand. Let me finish, Deborah." She was yelling something. He waited till she stopped. He pulled a photo out of his breast pocket and laid it on the counter. It showed her in the Super-8 motel room, topless, underwear on. She was sitting on the bed, face to the ceiling, eyes closed. The other man stood leaning over her, a dark head of hair but not his face visible. He was naked, his penis half-erect. "I have more photos," he said. "More than I ever would have wanted."

"You dirty sneaking filthy rat," she said. It was a low, gravelly voice he had never heard before. "I should've known you'd be capable of spying on me like a low-down scum."

He said nothing. What was the point in discussing what he had done if she wasn't willing to discuss what she had done?

"I think a divorce would be the best thing for Trip, don't you?"

"Are you crazy? I knew you were going to say that."

"With your behavior, Deborah, it's like you're begging me to leave you. Well, I give up. You win."

"How could it be the best thing for Trip not to have a father around?"

"Oh, you misunderstood, Deborah. Do you think I want Trip growing up in a house with the example you're setting, with these strangers?"

"What are you saying?"

"Trip is going to live with me."

This was the most obvious thing in the world. Over the last two years he had thought about it over and over again, a thousand times. No rational person could possibly see it any other way. Deborah was a drinker and had put her own son in danger. Repeatedly. She was carrying on with other men – multiple partners. This was documented.

You didn't build a house on quicksand. You didn't leave a loaded gun on the table for children to play with. It was every bit as obvious as those things. When a mother had the kind of problems Deborah had, the father got custody.

For a long moment she stared. The anger seemed to leave her face. Then she walked out of the kitchen, turned in the doorway and looked back. He followed. She walked halfway across the living room, stood in one spot, held her right arm straight out and pointed at the front door.

"Get out."

"I'll pack a suitcase, if you don't mind."

"You can forget your dirty plan, Alden."

"We'll see about that."

He walked into the kitchen and up the stairs. In fifteen minutes he was back down again with his big suitcase. She hadn't moved from that spot in the living room. He walked past her, wheeling the suitcase. He went out through the door to the garage, loaded his suitcase in the car, and backed out of the driveway.

He had to focus on Trip now. He would cut back at work, if needed. His son's welfare was the most important thing. Any judge would see it that way. Trip could visit his mother any time he wished. The town was small. There wouldn't be rancor.

By the next night he had found a furnished apartment half a mile from the house and moved in. The following Monday, divorce papers were served on Deborah Snyder Sterling.

That had been two years ago. Trip was still living with Deborah and they still were not divorced.

The justice. Where was the justice?

Thinkpad

"I'm calling to report a whopper of a fuckup, the ramifications of which cannot even begin to be fathomed," the caller said.

Annie Ogden had started hanging up on people who used this kind of language. In this case, something about the deliberateness of the caller's voice made her hesitate. Her finger hovered above disconnect.

The man went on, "I need to speak to your manager, your scheduler, your chief of operations, or whoever would know where a certain piece of equipment ended up. My world is crashing before my eyes."

"Suppose you tell me, in a nutshell, what the problem is, so that I have some idea who to transfer you to," Annie said. Either it was some sixteen year old on acid, or it was the real thing, someone with an honest-to-goodness problem. At least it wasn't another one of those creeps who had received a wrong item.

"TSR, your boys, came and picked up a truckful of our gear yesterday, see?" the man said. "And I'm not even going to bother you with the fact that they overcharged me. My real problem is that one of my colleagues here at the office thought it would be so funny to put my boss's laptop in the pile of stuff for recycling. You know, kind of stashed under other stuff?"

"Uh-oh," Annie said.

"We're talking IBM Thinkpad city, here. Not more than maybe three months old, a four-thousand-dollar laptop crammed with every imaginable application the boss might've needed, plus, of course . . ."

"Which company did you say you are calling from?"

"Sterling Accounting Services. Name's Bob Olson. My boss is Mr. Alden Sterling. He got back this morning from a week in Hawaii. He just about lost it completely when he walked in, and no laptop."

"I've got a question for you." Annie ignored the light on her console that meant other calls were stacking up. She was looking at the list of pickups from yesterday. Sterling . . . ten o'clock, there it was. "What makes you so sure your boss's laptop was on the pile that we picked up?"

"First of all, because it's not here on his desk where it should be. And then, you know, he comes out of his office this morning yelling and shouting and all purple in the face like I've never seen him before. He's grabbing people left and right by the scruff of the neck. Like he's completely lost it. And then McCoy, he's about to wet himself because the boss has just turned to look at him, McCoy, he says, 'Talk to Olson. He was in charge of getting rid of all the computer equipment. Probably made a mistake and put your laptop down there with the old stuff.'"

"Oh, my God," Annie said.

"For real," Olson said. "All this twenty minutes ago. Not a pretty sight. Well, Mr. Sterling is no idiot. He knows I would not take his *personal* laptop out of his office, unplug the power cord, unplug the connection to the router, you know, all that stuff, and then bring it down to storage to be hauled away. We didn't take *any* machines out of *any* offices for this project. Just all the old stuff that's been in storage for years. So McCoy was out on his ass within sixty seconds. Because anyone could see that what was really happening here is McCoy tried to set me up so that I would get fired. The scumbag. Give Mr. Sterling credit for seeing through that. But then he turns to me, he says, 'Go find it, Olson. Call up that outfit. Get my laptop back.' I've never seen him like that. Like, not just angry . . . more like *desperate*. And he sent me packing. Can you imagine? I've got work to do. I'm in the middle of some big projects, all of which he knows about, and he sends me home. He was like, 'Drop your projects. This is your project.' I'm not allowed back in the door till I get that laptop back."

"Jesus," Annie said. "I'm going to look into this. There must be something we can do. Give me a number where I can reach you." She took down his cell.

"I'm coming down there today," Olson said. "I want to take that Thinkpad with me. Think you can find it?"

"I will," Annie said. "But listen. Don't come till I call you. It won't . . ."

"Be there in two hours," Olson said, and hung up.

She strode through the door into triage, and from there into testing. She looked around at the many stations. At last she spotted Roberto, the tall bony man she had met on break earlier.

"Hey," she said.

He pulled off his headphones. "What's up, Annie?"

"Got a problem." She explained about the like-new Thinkpad.

"Probably around here someplace." Roberto scanned the other worktables around him. "We get a fair number of Thinkpads in. Hey, Murray!"

Murray, two tables away, pulled off his headphones and came over. "Yo."

"Score any Thinkpads, last couple of days?"

"Two or three, I think."

"You should smoke less of that funky weed, man. Takes the edge off the memory chip in your *cabeza*."

"Takes the edge off having to look at your ugly face," Murray said.

"Guys," Annie said. "The dude needs his laptop. Any chance of finding it? Where could it be?"

"Only way he's gonna get it back is if he buys it off the website," Roberto said.

"By then it's gonna be wiped clean," Murray said. "He wouldn't even recognize it."

"All the files?"

Roberto nodded. "People usually erase their own files and shit. We're not interested in that anyway. We're looking for any working software, applications, operating system, also the hardware of course. Our job is to figure out what works and what doesn't, tag it, and off it goes for resale."

"Get the machines apart, get the motherboard, the graphics card, the game card, whatever's in there," Murray echoed. "Liver. Kidneys. Blood, guts . . ."

"Half of that shit gets shipped to Korea, anyway."

"You seen that barge they've got?"

Roberto nodded.

Annie surveyed the setup around her. An assembly line snaked around the vast room passing at least forty or fifty workstations. At each workstation stood a worker with a computer and other testing equipment, tools, and a big tabletop. PCs, laptops, printers and other equipment rolled past continually until a worker snagged something to work on. When a worker put something back on the line it was tagged with a bar-coded decal. At the far end of the room two workers were taking tagged items off the main assembly line and placing them on another line that snaked through an opening into another room.

"So it would've come through here," she said. "And one of you guys would've picked it up off the line . . . what would you do if you got a nice new one like that, anyway? You wouldn't start tearing that apart, would you?"

"Nah, we never get new stuff down this line, Annie-Cakes. All we get is the junky shit, like old antique PCs that won't boot, screens that won't light. If you can get it to boot at all, it's so goddamn slow you'd have time to write a letter to your mother before the first application would open."

"He's right. We usually never even see the new shit," Murray said.

"Want us to ask around for you?" Roberto asked.

"We could ask around," Murray said.

"Only because you're so ace," Roberto said.

"Man, we fight for that shit." Murray picked up a wrench.

"Guys, I've got to get back to my desk or I'm toast. I'm coming back in an hour. I want that Thinkpad."

They gawked at her as she turned. From their silence she assumed they were still staring as she walked away. Well, that was what boys did. Her butt was not exactly her best feature. It didn't seem to matter that she ran every morning and did her crunches; since being back, she had flabbed up some.

LANCE

Inside it was incredibly dark for a sunny June morning. So dark, Ike felt practically like a blind man, standing in the hallway. All the windows must be covered up or blacked out or something.

Well, Lance wouldn't want anyone peeking in the windows in this place.

"Right in here," said the girl who had let them in. They followed, each man carrying two heavy shopping bags. The room they found themselves in was a living room with couches, a bar and a big mirror covering the whole wall behind it. The man they had come to see sat on a black leather couch in the middle of the room, facing the door they had come in. He had dark sunglasses but you could tell from the cheekbones, the blond hair, the accent, that he was Eastern European. His fingers held a shot glass with whiskey in it. On the red couch at right angles was a hot African-American girl in a bikini top and baggy Hawaiian shorts. She had a copy of *Rolling Stone* open on her leg, one foot on the floor and the other up on the couch, her legs spread wide. Ike tried to catch the girl's eye, but she didn't look up from the magazine, not even once.

"You got my copper? You guys work fast."

"Hey, Lance," Ike said. "We're working on the copper. We checked the locations you put on the GPS and we're making our plans. This here's about a special side deal. We wanted to give you first crack."

"Looks like you put on some weight since three weeks ago. You want a beer?"

"No thanks," Ike said.

"Sure," Tranny said. The girl on the couch got up without looking at them, went behind the bar, and brought back a bottle of beer.

"What we got today, we got phones," Ike said.

"They work?"

Ike looked down at the bag between his feet. He hadn't thought to *try* any of the phones. "Sure, man. Why wouldn't they work?"

"Show me," Lance said.

Ike rummaged in the bag. The phones on top were the oldest sons of bitches, phones like bricks, probably dating back to the 1970s. He dug down and pulled out a smaller phone, a Motorola. It looked kind of old, too, but at least it came from the modern era.

"Let's see here, I guess you gotta press this." He waited. Nothing lighted up. No little shake. Nothing.

"Give it here," Lance said.

Ike handed it over. Lance tried the button. When nothing happened, he pulled the back cover off. He made a face and dropped the phone like a hot potato. The phone hit the hardwood floor and broke into three or four pieces. "That is foul."

"What?" Ike stepped forward and picked up the pieces. "Probably just a little battery gunk is all."

"What you trying to sell me old broken shit for?" Lance asked. He held the shot glass high in the air as if he thought germs from the leaked battery might spring through the air into his drink.

"This here is a phone *collection*," Ike said, switching gears. Maybe some of the phones worked, but he had no way of knowing which. It would not be wise to choose another phone at random and hope it worked, only to have the same thing happen. "Like I told you on the phone, a collection. Historical value in these babies."

"Who wants a collection of old broken phones?" Lance asked. "I can't sell shit like that. No market for it. People want a phone that works."

"Collector's items, worth double the money," Ike said.

"You should've told me they don't work, save yourself the trouble."

"I did tell you. I told you a *collection*, remember?"

"Collection meaning a lot of phones, two hundred phones. You dissing my English now, man? I speak better English than you fuckbrains. I don't need this shit. Outta my house, you gonna diss my English. Now." Lance slammed the shot glass down on the coffee table, then rose to his feet.

"Sorry, Lance. No, man, I didn't mean it like that."

"Take it easy, man," Tranny said.

"Don't come back again. You guys fucking losers."

"We're gonna call you, we get holda that copper," Ike said.

"Don't bother."

When they were outside the door again, in the blinding sunlight, Tranny said, "That guy was steamed, man."

"He thought I said his English was bad."

"Nothing wrong with his English, you ask me."

"I know, man. That's just some idea he got in his mind."

"But his English was fine, really was."

"Anyway, that's not what's got me worried. What if he's right about the phones? I never thought about whether they work or not. Who's gonna want these old phones if they don't work?"

"I thought you said we shouldn't go around saying 'what if'."

"Hell, Tranny, this ain't the time to start an argument."

"I'm just saying, you're always correcting me and all. Why can't I say something if you screw up? Besides, it was a lot of work getting those phones. I ain't giving up. Now we're gonna go see my aunt."

"I want five thousand minimum, we agree on that?" Ike asked.

"What's that make per phone?"

"Well, you got two hundred phones, that makes forty a phone."

"Twenty-five."

"Twenty-five what?"

"Five thousand for two hundred phones would make twenty-five per phone, not forty. Forty would be eight thousand. You said forty."

"Whatever. Stop jerking me around with your math problems."

Tranny shook his head. "Anyway, we ain't taking less than a hundred per phone. Then we get twenty thousand bucks, ten thousand each. I want a new car."

"You're dreaming," Ike said. But he let it go. Who knows, maybe Tranny was right. He wouldn't say no to a new car. That trunk popping open had scared him. What if your trunk popped open at seventy mph on the highway? All your stuff blowing out all over the roadway. You'd have the police swarming around you, and that was all she wrote.

They drove around for a while, Tranny hunting for an address. At last he pulled up in front of a Vietnamese Restaurant in the ground floor of a corner building. The sign in the window said, *Sorry we're closed*. It was eleven in the morning. Tranny knocked persistently, but even the old person sweeping inside ignored them.

"I think that one don't hear so good," Tranny explained. He punched a number on his cell phone.

A minute later the door opened and another woman bowed them through the empty dining room into the kitchen, where a number of Asian people were running around between stoves, refrigerators and cooking tables. At the back of the kitchen was a stairway. Ike eyed the long flight of stairs with disgust. The woman had already reached the first landing up above him, Tranny right at her heels.

"You coming, man?" Tranny said.

Take your time.

He labored up to the first landing, then stopped to rest. Damned phones were heavy. With these damned bags he couldn't even put one hand on the railing, help himself up. No point getting to the top and keeling over with a heart attack. *Then the price you get for these damned phones really wouldn't matter anymore.*

"Ike, you ok down there?" came Tranny's voice from somewhere far above.

He climbed the rest of the way to the second floor, breathing hard now. Always more stairs, everywhere stairs. Even more than a new car, he needed a new apartment with an elevator. He stopped mid-stair and looked up. He had bumped into Tranny.

"What the . . .?"

"Gimme those bags, man. I'll help ya."

Ike pulled himself up the rest of the way, hauling himself up by the railing, letting his arms and shoulders do the work. At the top he felt light-headed, a little dizzy. Those had been steep stairs. His heart was pounding. He had a stabbing cramp in his stomach. Still panting like a water buffalo, unable to talk, he motioned to Tranny for the bags. They walked in together, each hauling two bags.

The door was open. They entered an apartment filled with sunshine. In a sort of sitting room they found Tranny's aunt sitting behind a big wooden desk.

"Don't come any closer," she barked in a low, scratchy voice. It could have just as easily been a little old man's voice. Her face had about a thousand wrinkles. "You out of prison already?" she asked Tranny.

She could have been the mother of the woman who had pointed them up the stairs, or even her grandmother. She breathed heavily, as if she had asthma. Ike wondered if she too had just come up the stairs. Her hair was black, clearly dyed, but her skin was as wrinkled as an old apple he had once left in the sun for a month. Wrinkles branching into other wrinkles on top of other systems of wrinkles. She wore a bright orange dress that puffed out around the shoulders and completely hid her arms, even in this heat. Ike couldn't see her hands. She probably had tiny little Vietnamese hands.

"Why they let you out?" she went on. "You got thirteen years no parole, I remember right."

"Come on, Auntie Lee. They say no parole, but they never mean it. I got out after seven years and seven months, good behavior. Got a good job soon as I got out. Me and Ike here, we work together. We work for the same company."

"What's the name of this company?"

"TSR Incorporated. Tri-State Recovery. Like recycling old computers and shit."

"Nasdaq?" the old woman asked. "Big board?"

The two men looked at each other. "Not boards, Auntie. Computers."

"Never mind. You wanna sell me phones. You need money, why you not ask for money? I give you money so you no have to steal phones."

"We didn't steal the phones, Auntie. I learned my lesson and changed my ways, see. Ike and me, we're in business together."

"Bullshit," the old woman said. At that moment she raised a pistol out of the sleeve of her orange dress. Before Ike could make a move, she shot the bag clean out of his grasp. The thought that went through his mind was: *The old bitch does have hands.* The bullet slammed through the phones in the bag. The bag came apart. The phones scattered all over the floor. The smell of burning plastic rose from the pile at his feet. It happened in a split second. Ike was left holding the paper handle of the bag, phones spinning in place on the parquet floor in front of him. "You no lie to me, Tran Phan Ng!"

Ike noticed she pronounced his name Tran Phan *Mmm*. He had always said *nag*.

"I'm not lying, Auntie. Put your gun away. We got 'em fair and square, in a trade."

She levelled a finger at Ike. "You meet my nephew in prison. He told me. What crime did you do?"

"Now don't let's go into ancient history," Ike said, still breathing hard. "That won't get us anywhere. We'll just take our phones and . . ."

With no further warning she shot the other bag out of his hand. The sound rang in his ears in the little room. The smell of burnt powder and melting plastic made his stomach queasy. Now he stood in front of her empty-handed, loose phones spinning everywhere on the polished wooden floor around him. He felt a wave of nausea coming. First those stairs, and now being shot at. What did you say to calm down an old, trigger-happy Vietnamese woman?

"Stop shooting, Auntie," Tranny said.

"I wanna know who my nephew hanging round with. I want the truth. Either you tell me what you did, young man, or I blow your balls off." She aimed the pistol square between Ike's legs. Smoke was still rising from the barrel. "Maybe we serve them inna soup today."

"Shit, no," Ike said. "I'm gonna tell you. Tranny here knows all about it. We're talking bank robbery, ma'am. I used to rob banks."

"How many banks you rob?"

He was about to say, "One too many," but decided this was no time for a wisecrack. "I was planning to rob all the banks in Indianapolis. I was up to the H's when I got caught. Hoosier State Bank, something like that."

"So they were waiting for you?"

He nodded. "Guess I wouldn't necessarily do it in alphabetical order next time."

"Ever shoot a man?"

"Plugged a guard once."

"He dead? You aim good?"

"He went down, but I think he survived."

"You think?"

"Guess I'd still be in jail, otherwise."

The old woman nodded, but kept the gun levelled at his scrotum. "This terrible thing in your eyebrow. You fall on your face in a hardware store? I never seen such a big, ugly piercing like this."

Tranny started laughing. "He got pierced like that so people wouldn't stare at his fat tummy."

Ike felt his face going hot. "That's not true. Where the hell you get that idea?"

"It's the truth, man. Nothing to be 'shamed about. Just admit it."

"You lay off talking 'bout my tummy. That ain't nobody's business. Not even yours, Tranny."

"Hush you two, lemme tell you something," the woman said. She laid the gun down on her desk. Ike began to relax a little. Looked like he'd passed the test. "You Tran Phan *Mmm*'s friend, you gonna watch out for him, hear? His momma's dead, his daddy's dead. I'm only close relative he got, only one care about him. I don't go around with him every day, watching over him. You gotta do that for me. You gonna help me, understand?"

Ike swelled up with pride. No need to lie about this one. "Yes ma'am, I'll help you. I don't mind. Cause Tranny and me, we're partners."

Tranny nodded. "It's true, Auntie. Ike and me, we stick together. Ever since we got out of the hospital."

"You mean since we got outta prison, man."

"Duh, that's what I said."

The old woman's face darkened. "Anything happen to Tran Phan *Mmm*, I hold you responsible. I find out where you live. I come and shoot you with my gun, clear?"

"Yes ma'am," Ike said.

"Now, I got more bags right here." The old woman pulled some sturdy looking canvas tote bags out of a drawer in her desk and handed them across. "I really don't want those phones. But if you can't find anyone else take 'em off your hands, I give you ten dollars cash each phone, no questions asked. Fair enough?"

"Yes, Auntie."

"Yes ma'am."

Ike led the way out and down the stairs, bags in hand, still coughing from his exertions, and back out onto the sidewalk. No sooner had she closed the door on them, the woman in the restaurant turned the sign around so that it said, *Yes, we're open*.

They got in the car and drove away in glum silence. It damn well wasn't going to be so easy to get rid of these phones. First Lance had thrown them out. Then the old Vietnamese lady had shot at him. Finally she had offered him charity, just for taking care of Tranny, which he was doing anyway.

Tranny interrupted his thoughts. "I dunno about you, man. I'm sure glad I don't have to eat their soup."

TRS Without I

When it happened, Annie Ogden was staring at her screen, trying to understand how they assigned certain trucks to certain routes. Suddenly right on her screen the green rectangles that represented trucks all acquired thick white outlines. Then the trucks themselves turned white and became blank white shapes. Two seconds later, the white shapes and the entire gray background grid vanished entirely. All that was left was a solid blue screen.

The computer had crashed. She had seen this sort of thing before.

What came next she had never seen before. Slowly, one after another, four words in plain white type appeared on the blue background.

Tris. TRS. Without. I.

The cryptic message stayed on her screen and could not be clicked away. She touched her mouse. No cursor, nothing. Nothing at all worked.

Rodriguez burst out of his office.

"Denial of service!" he shouted on the run, his door banging against the wall.

Whatever that meant.

He crossed through reception in three steps and disappeared into triage. She heard Rodriguez shouting orders before the door closed.

On her computer nothing reacted even now, neither the mouse, nor the buttons on the keyboard. Oh, well – she held the power button down for a few seconds, keeping one eye on the screen. The hammer approach, Michael used to say. When all else fails, power off. The screen with its strange message held for a few seconds, which was normal for a frozen machine. Then it switched off and the screen went blank.

In the distance she heard yelling. It was coming from the warehouse rooms, probably Rodriguez. She pressed the power button once more. Only the blue screen came on. Still frozen. No message this time.

She ignored the incoming calls, took off her headset, and walked into triage, and from there into testing. Over on the other side she spotted Roberto again.

"What's going on? I had some weird stuff on my screen. Now my computer's dead."

"Lemme guess, something about Tris," Roberto said.

"Yeah, that was a good one," Murray said.

"Why'd she leave this job? What can you guys tell me about her?"

"I don't know, but my guess would be she's getting her revenge on old Max today," Murray said.

"You probably did it yourself, you old bomb-thrower," Roberto said, punching Murray on the arm. Murray looked seriously offended and ready to fight. But they were interrupted by Rodriguez race-walking through the crowd.

"You," he said, grabbing Murray's arm, then Roberto's, "and you. They need you down in the server room. Here's your chance to show your stuff. You," he steered Annie back toward reception. "Come back up front with me."

"Sorry I left my desk, Mr. Rodriguez. My computer's down."

"Everything's down. I need you back on the phones with the system down."

"It freaked me out, that message."

"What message?"

"Something about Tris. You didn't see it?"

Rodriguez laughed, but it was a thin, forced laugh, not like he really thought something was funny. "What a ditz. We're TSR, not TRS. Looks like that tree-hugging bimbo's dyslexic on top of all the rest." He disappeared into his office.

Tree-hugging bimbo?

Annie had just got her headset back on when the little bell over the front door chimed. A man in a brown suit with a shaved head stood there, squinting at her. He had on a white shirt in this heat, and a green silk tie with what looked like a pattern of birds across it.

"This is one hell of a place to locate." He walked up to the desk and put out a hand to shake. "Bob Olson from Sterling Accounting. I called earlier. Come to get my boss's Thinkpad back."

* * *

At that same moment, in a different room, Max Vinyl stood with Manny Rodriguez and watched the geeks hunched over their screens, checking logfiles, rewriting protocols, re-configuring firewalls and backup systems. The whole thing looked like a game to see which one of twenty programmers could type the fastest. On his time!

"What in Christ are they all doing?" he demanded.

"The DMZ was breached," Rodriguez said. "You know, the demilitarized zone? Max, tell me you remember this concept." Manny went on talking to him, talking *at* him, his jaw moving, his tongue wagging, his teeth grinding as he described servers, networks, viruses. Max had a short attention span when it came to the technical side of things. A *very* short attention span.

Especially when the whole network was down. Especially on a day when he had received an express envelope containing his own mutilated briefs and a note from a deranged lover.

"All this takes nanoseconds," Rodriguez was saying. "No viruses and worms can get across the barrier into the critical files of the company."

"If the system is so failsafe, why in Christ is our entire network down?"

"Sheer volume. Normally the system deals with a few dozen commands at any given moment. It could easily deal with hundreds or even thousands of different operations in a single second. But if that number runs into the millions, it takes the system down. The system chokes on the volume. We had over twenty million inquiries in the space of one and a half seconds. Twenty *million*, Max. Like twenty million spams. Classic denial-of-service attack."

"Spare me this detail. Why didn't you stop it? That's what I pay you for, isn't it?"

Rodriguez didn't look up from the ground. Two dozen programmers stared intently at their screens. At last, in a quiet voice, he said, "Max, don't be thick. We can talk in your office."

He followed his manager out of the server room. It gave him a sickening feeling to see scores of workers standing around, unable to work. Was that his heart that was burning in his chest? Or just a sympathetic pain impulse radiating down from his stinging eyes? You couldn't just tell ninety workers to go and sweep up or something. You couldn't send them home either, since they would be back online soon.

"How long till we're back up?"

"I'm getting status reports every fifteen minutes. Best guess is one to two hours."

"Did we lose data?"

Rodriguez shook his head. "Impossible. In the unlikely event that we did, it would be recoverable."

Back in Max's office, Rodriguez asked, "You want me to order pizzas for all these people?"

A glance at his face confirmed he was not joking. Max controlled his breathing. He didn't want to lose it right now. "Did you even finish high school? We're losing two hours of work from ninety people – that's one hundred and eighty man-hours – and you want me to spend money on a free lunch for this crowd on top of that?"

Rodriguez rolled his eyes. "Just an idea."

"You wanted to tell me something back there. You didn't want them to hear."

"Yes. What I didn't want to say in front of them was this attack was an inside job. The only way to set up a hole in the DMZ is from in here."

"Who then?"

"Tris."

"Tris?" He couldn't be hearing right.

Rodriguez didn't smile. He placed on the desk a piece of paper with a strange notation on it.

Tris. TRS. Without. I.

"What is that?"

"This was the last thing people saw on their screen when they powered off. Like a hacker signature. Everyone here saw it." Rodriguez picked up the scrap of paper and waved it at him. "She did this to you, Max."

"How could she? She's no goddamned programmer. Can't you get that through your thick skull?" Max realized he was yelling. He didn't care. Now he *had* lost control. He didn't yell often. But choosing to lose control was also a kind of control. At times like this Rodriguez shouldn't wave scraps of paper in front of his face as if he was retarded.

"I don't know how she did it. I'm just telling you it was her."

"Prove it, goddamn it." The fact was, anybody could have dreamed up a virus message that made it *look* like Tris had done it. Rodriguez himself, for instance.

"Why do you keep defending her? Why are we wasting time discussing this?"

"Because the system is down, and I expect you to get it going again. That's your job, isn't it? Well, for Chrissake, start moving on that."

Rodriguez stared at something on the desktop and sucked air through his teeth.

"Plan of action, Max. We've got to get through this. For the moment, we're cut off. No email. If the Koreans mailed you now, you wouldn't see it. We can't even check the website. She could've smoked that, too, for all we know."

"Christ, you're talking about a receptionist here."

Of course he knew, even as he said it, there was a remote possibility that Tris was somehow responsible. Considering the mutilated briefs, and the warped note she had written. Considering the pepper spray attack and that geriatric ape. Wednesday definitely was not turning out better than the previous two days. He didn't know *how* she could've done it, but if she was that angry . . . well, she would've had the motive. What was she so furious about, anyway? It didn't matter. He would give her something to be angry about. Goodbye Mitsubishi.

"Let's keep it short," Rodriguez said. "We've got to get out and lead the troops. But we have to coordinate."

"All you have to do is get the goddamn computers working again."

"'*All* I have to do,' he says. Max, you saw how many people are down there working to get the computers going again. Those guys know what they're doing."

"I'll believe it when I see it. If you're so sure it was an inside job, why can't you find out which computer it was done on?"

"We'll look at that later. Right now, I want to know who's on incomings. Where the hell is Brainard? His job is supervising incomings. Nobody told me he was out of the office today. I can't cover for him on incomings and also get the system up and running again at the same time. And all this time I'm losing ground on recruiting more drivers like you wanted."

Twenty trucks available, bought and paid for. Twenty trucks depreciating, every day of the week, and only an average of twelve trucks a day going out and recovering gear. The sores on his face were starting to ache. His skin felt hot. His eyes stung, and they were still bloodshot. He looked like a wreck.

"Obviously you have a time management problem. But I agree you'll have to deal with that later."

"If Brainard were here, doing his normal job, I wouldn't be worried about people stealing the cash that's coming in as we speak."

"Brainard is on special assignment today. Also probably tomorrow."

"Please have him torture and kill the person who hacked our system."

"Manny, for Chrissake, that may be the Mexican way of handling things. I can't have that kind of talk in here."

"I'm Costa Rican."

"South of the border. Christ, whatever."

"Nobody on incomings, Max."

People would be pocketing cash as trucks came in. Brainard's job was to make sure the cash went into the safe, and to supervise armored car pickups at the end of the day.

"I'll go," he said.

"Good. By the way, you really want to know the Mexican way?"

"Yeah."

"A Mexican would find some pathetic illiterate *gringo* to scrub his toilets while he lies in a hammock on the beach drinking rum and pineapple juice."

"Yeah, and when your stupid corrupt country runs out of money, we have to bail your lazy asses out."

"Right you are. And so, my broken-hearted Yankee friend, I ask you: who is the smarter one?"

They went back out. The new receptionist and a man in reception with a shaved head tried to get his attention, but Max walked by, ignoring them.

With no one on incomings, drivers would be stealing outright. Most of the recovery men were ex-cons plucked straight out of prison. Some of them, like Brainard, were truly reformed and determined to stay out of prison for the rest of their lives. Others were just one lousy decision away from landing in jail again, every moment of every day of their lives. Steal a car here, mug an old lady there, rob a liquor store, breaking and entering and stealing TVs and cash and jewelry – the wealth of experience in his team was impressive. That was why Brainard mainly worked as supervisor of incomings. Other ex-cons thought twice about screwing with Brainard.

Special assignment.

Max Vinyl stood on the loading dock staring at the noontime sky, contrails of planes crisscrossing overhead. The breeze coming in off the lake only a few hundred yards away felt good on his scratched cheeks. The cheeks of a wronged man. Who ever heard of a receptionist first attacking him with pepper spray, then sending him chopped up briefs in an express envelope, and finally bringing down the entire computer system with a lousy hacker attack? Where did this mean streak come from? This viciousness? These things didn't just hurt him, they hurt all the employees, they hurt all the customers. Apart from all else, it made no sense.

There could only be one answer. Rodriguez was mistaken. The briefs, that was one thing. The act of a sick, misguided lover. Something he had said, she must have taken it all wrong. Now it was over. OK, he could accept that. But this computer attack was way beyond her abilities, besides being out of proportion to whatever she might think he had done.

"Incoming," said the loading dock chief, Maurice. Normally he would be watching his computer screen. The locations of the trucks were tracked by the software, down to a few feet away. For cash-management reasons, they tried to avoid having two trucks come in at the same time. With the computer system down, Maurice had been on the phone with the driver. A minute later, the truck rounded the corner into the loading dock area. It backed into the loading dock. Maurice flipped his cigarette onto the concrete and pulled on his gloves.

"Pretty freaky, that bit about Tris on the computer. She find another job?" Maurice said.

"Guess I'd be the last to know."

"She told me she was quitting, but she didn't say when. Didn't know it would come so soon. She didn't even say goodbye."

For a second Max thought he hadn't heard right. The loading dock manager stood there stroking his chin whiskers, apparently totally serious. "Wait a minute, she told you she was quitting? She got her ass *fired*. When the hell did she tell you she was quitting?"

The truck was inching back into the loading dock, the annoying reverse-gear *beep, beep, beep* distracting the hell out of him. At last the beeping stopped. The rear door was lowering down onto the steel-reinforced concrete lip of the dock. Maurice walked away and got on his forklift.

"Couple weeks ago, must've been," he called over his shoulder.

"What'd she say?" Max shouted.

Maurice drove right onto the truck with the forklift and got his fork under the first cage, then backed out again, slow and steady, and drove over to the scale. In the floor of the loading dock was a scale that went up to three tons. The digital readout said 1142. The weights of the forklift and the cage were automatically deducted. Maurice entered the reading into his handheld, which it seemed was not affected by the computer hack, then drove back over to the truck. Meanwhile a second forklift driver brought the cage from the scale over to the opposite end of the loading dock area, where the cages were opened and emptied and the gear loaded onto the assembly line belt. Max Vinyl entered the reading into his pocket organizer for cross-referencing while Maurice went to get the second cage.

The driver and his partner smoked a cigarette in the parking area while Maurice drove in and out of the truck with his forklift.

Quitting . . . well, that was news to him.

Lately, whenever he wanted to have sex, Tris had always been engrossed in a book. He would sit waiting for her, patiently waiting for her to take the hint, while she went on reading and reading and reading.

"What're you reading?" he had asked one night a few weeks before.

"Just this novel."

"What's it about?"

She put the book down. Her legs were hidden under the covers. Two of his big white eiderdown pillows supported her back. He sat at the foot of the bed watching her, his back up against the footboard. He liked the way her pyjama top hung open, exposing skin right down to her navel. His own chest and washboard abs were equally exposed. All he had on was a pair of Calvin Klein briefs.

Ginger had always been hot, too, in her own flopsy large-breasted way, but she had never gone around *unbuttoned*. Ginger going around unbuttoned would probably set off fire alarms in nearby buildings. Tris was more compact in build, every part of her body in perfect proportion, like a jungle woman. They were jungle people, ready to make jungle love, roaring and clawing at each other. But the thing about Tris, he had realized that night, she wasn't with him at all as long as she still had that goddamned book in her hand. What a waste of a perfectly good erection.

"You really want to know what it's about?"

"Yeah, I do."

Why had he been so irritated, anyway? Because Tris would prefer to read rather than slowly and gorgeously work up to a multiple orgasm with him? How could you put off sex to the last possible instant just to read a few more lousy pages? Brazilians were supposed to be nymphomaniacs. Tris had outed herself as a Midwestern goddamn bookworm. Sometimes he no longer even believed she was part-Brazilian.

"Well, it's about this boy who survives a shipwreck. He finds out he's not alone on this lifeboat. He thought he was alone. But it turns out there's this tiger on the lifeboat with him."

He struggled to follow. "As in, the animal?"

"Mm-hm."

He smirked. "What kind of a crazy plot is a tiger in a lifeboat? For me a good book has to be believable."

"You don't believe it? Even though it's a true story?"

Was she putting him on? He noticed the picture of a tiger superimposed on the cover of the book. Maybe it was a true story. But he said:

"First of all, what is a tiger doing on a ship? Secondly, how does this tiger get on the lifeboat? Please tell me you saw *Titanic*. You're talking about a big animal. How in Christ does this tiger just slip in between the ladies and the children getting on the lifeboats? Thirdly, this is totally obvious, how come this tiger doesn't just scarf the boy in one bite?"

"That is definitely one of the central questions of the book, yes. Why doesn't the tiger eat the boy?"

"And the answer?"

"I don't know. Maybe in the end he does. I'm only halfway through."

"What I want to know, how can a story like that hold your interest?" With the effort of this discussion, his erection had withered to nothing. Hopefully it would come back. At least he had her out of the book and in conversation. Halfway there, so to speak. He pressed on. "You have to admit it sounds like a fairy tale, all this stuff about tigers and boys and shipwrecks. What I want to know is, what's it got to do with your life?"

"He makes it so believable, Max. I feel like I'm right there. I guess it's just a thrill, like any other."

"Now you're talking. I got a big thrill waiting for you, right here."

"I know."

"Guess you couldn't miss it."

She made a face. "Let me finish my chapter. I'm sure I'll be much more relaxed."

He imitated a Buddhist trance so that she could finish her chapter and get relaxed. Page after lousy page. Turned out to be a mighty long chapter. For all he knew, she had gone right on to the next chapter.

What could possibly happen in a fairy tale like that, anyway? Tiger eats boy, end of story. Boy defeats tiger, boy rescued, big deal. Shark against tiger, out in the middle of the ocean – that might keep you tuned in for a few minutes. But you were still left with the basic situation of someone marooned in a lifeboat.

He hated movies about people who were marooned. Lost in the desert, they died of thirst. Running out of food while trekking to the pole, they froze to death if they weren't first devoured by polar bears. Lost in space, and all the fear and anxiety about machines breaking down, the oxygen supply running out . . . what could be more earth-shatteringly boring? He preferred movies with plenty of action and not too much talk – quick deadly shots fired from pistols held sideways, fighter jets doing evasive maneuvers and firing heat-seeking missiles, blood spurting from severed limbs.

"Funny seeing you at the loading dock, boss."

Max came out of his reverie. The driver and his partner were coming up the stairs onto the loading dock, the driver with a bunch of papers in his hand. The driver would also have the cash. The driver, whose name was Ron Howard, like the child actor and movie director, gave him a smart salute. *This Ron Howard had spent three years of his life in solitary at the maximum security penitentiary in Marion, Illinois. Who knows what he had thought about during three years in that hole all alone?*

"Hey, Ron. Any problems with the truck?"

"Running real good," Ron Howard said. "We was over in Rockford this morning. First a little bullshit law office, then a town library, if you can believe that shit."

"Filled 'er up pretty full, looks like." The last cage was being weighed now. He took his organizer over to the desk and waited.

"What've you got?" he asked when Maurice got back with his handheld.

Their numbers matched. At thirty cents a pound, the driver should have collected seven thousand eight hundred and forty dollars.

"You always that red in the face, or just when it's time to hand over the money?" Max asked. "Don't tell me you're short."

"No, sir," said Ron Howard. "Our scale on the truck ain't the same quality as this one here. Don't know what else it could be. We got eight thousand, three hundred and sixty."

"Collected?"

"Damn straight." Ron Howard had a thick wad of bills in his hand. They bent over the desk and he counted them out, making piles that added up to a thousand each. *Training.* Max Vinyl signed for the cash, then brought it without further small talk to the safe, which was inside the loading dock office.

"Check the setting on those scales, Ron," he said when he came out again. Most drivers would find a way to pocket the difference if the boss weren't standing right there. This time the company would keep the change.

All this cash was a weak link in the chain. The drivers had to go around with cash in their pockets, the cash had to be counted at the loading dock, then it had to be locked up in the safe. The armored car company had to come and get it every day or two. At the end of any given day the safe had between one hundred and two hundred thousand in cash in it. When you thought about it, they were vulnerable to attack out on the road – all those ex cons certainly had friends and acquaintances to whom they bragged. It was only a matter of time before one of the trucks got held up.

Once Ron and the other driver were gone, Max went back to Maurice. "You were saying, about Tris. I was just curious what she said to you about quitting."

Maurice lit a cigarette and took his time closing his lighter, stowing it back in his jeans pocket. He blew out a long rope of smoke. "She was always down here snooping around on her break, you know. She peeked through that door at the back and saw 'em loading up the barge a few times. I think she must've figured out where the stuff on the barge ends up. That was probably what pissed her off the most."

Something crossed his mind then, like a shadow. Something Maurice had said about *when* Tris had decided to leave. *Two weeks ago* . . . a horrifying thought. So she *must* have totaled the Gullwing on purpose. He replayed the accident in his mind. Running into the concrete barrier head-on, putting them in danger on the highway, the shocking destruction of his car . . . and all that business about a spider . . . had he actually *seen* a spider?

Maurice nodded. "I've been here four years. You wouldn't catch me going ten miles out on the lake, middle of the night. No way, man."

"We've got a damned good record. Whatever she got into her head, she's dead wrong about that. Nobody can say otherwise."

"Damn right."

"Maurice, page me when your next incoming gets here."

OLSON

"It's my first day on the job. At the moment it's a bit chaotic," Annie Ogden said. Too bad about this dude's laptop, but she had other things on her mind. For one thing, she hadn't answered the phone in over an hour. On the other hand, she had something in common with him. She was also here on a recovery mission. But she wasn't about to tell him that.

"You don't understand," Olson said. "My boss is not letting me back in without that Thinkpad. God knows what he's got on it. He's the head of an accounting firm, for Pete's sake! You know, tax records, social security numbers, IRS audits on private individuals, company balance sheets, negotiations with the IRS. I don't want to even think of what would happen if that PC fell into the wrong hands. You see? You've got to help me, Annie."

"What do you expect me to do? I can't even turn on my computer. We've been hacked, here. We've got a total system crash."

"Then nobody can work just now, right? So you have the time to help me find my Thinkpad. Tell me where to get started. I'll do the rest."

The door to triage opened and Rodriguez walked into reception. The open door offered a glimpse of the assembly line going by with computer gear on it. Olson darted through before it closed. Rodriguez hardly noticed.

"They're still working on it. What're people saying on the phones?"

"What do you mean?" She didn't want to tell him she hadn't taken a single phone call since the system went down. Although, in a way, no one could fault her for not keeping up in the midst of a crisis during her first day on the job. Rodriguez was way too busy to listen properly, anyway. He didn't break stride, heading for his office.

"We've got to know if the outside world has noticed that the system is down. Let me know, okay?"

"Ah, Mr. Rodriguez, a question."

"Yeah, who the hell was that guy?"

Annie explained about the Thinkpad mixup. "Chances are he'll never see it again," Rodriguez said when she had finished. "Keep him the hell out of there. Call security if he gives you trouble. We don't let people run around in there like that." His door closed before he finished speaking.

She rushed back into triage. Callers had been waiting this long, they could wait a little longer. Olson wasn't there. She found him in inventory, picking through laptops. After parts were tested and tagged for resale, they went on a belt headed for inventory, where, based on their bar code, they were automatically shelved by robots. When an order came in with the bar code information for that piece, the robot found it on the shelf and put it back on the line, this time headed for the packing room.

Olson was standing at one of those shelves, leaning all the way in, looking for Thinkpads. One of the shuttle robots was coming down along a track headed straight for him.

"Hey, look out!" she yelled.

He jumped back just before the robot went by. It continued down the track all the way to the far end of the huge room.

"That was close," Olson said.

"You're not allowed here, so get out. Now. For your own safety."

"That's nothing compared to what Mr. Sterling is going to do with me if I don't bring his laptop back. This place is full of laptops. It's got to be here somewhere." He turned around to go on with his search.

"I'm serious, you know. What do you think would have happened if that robot had crashed into you?"

She didn't get an answer. Olson stayed bent over the shelves, moving slowly down to the left, hunting for his boss's precious computer.

"They're going to send security if I can't get you out of this room."

His back was to her. He didn't acknowledge her. She was starting to feel provoked. She wondered how Rodriguez would feel about her using karate on this obtuse person. Conflict management, indeed.

"You called?" A thick-necked security guard had appeared out of nowhere. Looked like Rodriguez left nothing to chance. The security man and his partner went straight up behind Olson. The first one tapped him on the shoulder. Olson turned and, when he saw the uniform, tried to run. He ran straight into the stomach of the second security man, who bear-hugged him, pinning his arms against his sides, and hefted him straight up off the ground. The first security man slipped a thick rubber strap around him and cinched it tight, pinning his arms to his sides. In one movement the second one bent at the knees and balanced Olson over his shoulder in a fireman's carry. They looked like they had done this before.

"Let me go! Let me go!" A pair of sunglasses fell out of one of Olson's pockets in the struggle. The first security man bent and picked them up. He nodded to his partner, and the two of them headed for a side door without giving her another look. Olson kept yelling about Thinkpads, his boss, something about a lawyer.

The door they went through led to the outside. Something about the careful way the security man had picked up Olson's sunglasses gave her the feeling that they weren't going to actually hurt him. They were enforcing company policy. The guy was annoying. She was sorry to have given him the time of day.

As she turned to go back to reception Annie saw Roberto, Murray, and a dozen others walking into the room from a door at the back.

"Battle stations," Roberto said. "We're online."

"It works?"

"Piece of cake," Murray said.

"You guys'll never guess who showed up," Annie said.

"Wait a minute, don't tell me. Tris came back?" said Roberto. "After that hack, the boss'll be having her ass for breakfast."

"In a manner of speaking," Murray said.

Annie shook her head. "The guy with the missing Thinkpad."

"He came here?"

"He actually snuck in and was rooting around, looking for it."

"Ballsy," Roberto said, looking around.

"Security carried him out kicking and screaming." Annie pointed at the door. But by the time Roberto opened the door, the grassy area outside the warehouse was deserted.

"I guess they made him leave. His car must be around the front."

"We can't have all the townies coming in looking for lost Playstations," Murray said.

"He's got a legitimate problem. Isn't there any way you guys could make a little effort to track down a Thinkpad that came in yesterday? I mean, how hard can it be?" She had a feeling Olson would be right back in her face at the front desk if nobody did anything.

Murray and Roberto looked at each other. "How hard can it be?" Murray mocked. "We might just have other things we're supposed to be doing, you know what I mean? Like getting this rickety old system back online, childish stuff like that."

"Hey, look at that." Roberto pointed up at the blue banner hanging across the room just below the towering ceiling. He started laughing. The white letters on the blue banner spelled out:

Tris. TRS. Without. I.

"I'll be damned," Murray said. "That wasn't there this morning, was it? That's like where that banner about the salaries usually hangs."

"How would you even get up there?" Roberto marvelled.

"If the system is working again," Annie pressed on, "couldn't you just check the database and see if a Thinkpad came in yesterday? There must be some information about what happened to it."

"She's right, you know," Roberto said. He was booting his machine. When it came on, he punched a few buttons and stared at the screen. "Nope. Nothing here."

"Surprised?" asked Murray.

"Why? What happens to new stuff that comes in?" Annie asked.

Roberto shrugged. "We mostly never see it. Sort of like finding a golden ticket in a Wonka Chocolate bar. So rare, you're not really sure it exists. Well, hang on. Once or twice I flagged a new machine, everything working fine, everything brand new, you know, the latest operating system, full of real files and software. Oh yeah, now I remember. They came and got it on a cart and took it away somewhere."

"Who? Where would they take them?"

The two men looked at each other. "You are a pain in the ass, Annie," Roberto said. "I just told you, I don't know, *no lo se*."

"Yeah, but when I pushed you, you actually thought of something useful. This cart business, remember?"

"Don't mind him," Murray said. "Raised by mutants."

She walked away from them in exasperation. She had given herself an idea. There must be a way of finding the Thinkpad in the database of stuff coming in, or inventory, or something, or maybe even on the website for resale.

Car Collection

When Max Vinyl had access to his email again, one message got his attention. The reference line said **Max urgent gold mine call me ASAP**. Normally he deleted spams with reference lines like that, but this one came from his lawyer, Oscar Furey. Furey was a partner in the firm Furey and Smith in Chicago. Smith, Max Vinyl knew, had left the firm ten years ago. Oscar Furey had been quite happy to go on as a one-attorney shop with three part-time paralegals and about as many secretaries.

The lawyer wrote: "Max, this trove is going to keep us busy for weeks or even months, like the last one did. Must see you SAP. Please call SAP."

Max tapped a message back proposing five o'clock. Furey had sent him six mails in the last 24 hours. Furey wouldn't trouble him needlessly. Even on a day that was turning into one of the most horrible days in recent memory it would be stupid to put off seeing Oscar Furey any longer. Maybe Furey could help him turn this tide of bad luck.

Manny Rodriguez knocked and came in.

"Damage report," said Max.

"Still running tests. No data lost. Website unaffected. Downtime fifty-six minutes. During that time we had approximately three thousand dollars in sales off the website from a total of around two hundred orders."

"Average revenue is down."

"Wednesday phenomenon. Middle of the week, orders go up but revenue per order goes down. If we knew why."

"All this while the system was down." He whistled. "And half the trucks idle. Just think if we could get all the trucks running."

"Give me another two months," Manny said. "We'll have twenty trucks running."

"Gangbusters."

"Yeah. By the way, just so you know, there's a guy in a tent out back, behind the warehouse. Says we picked up his Thinkpad by mistake on a recovery. Says he needs it back."

"Police?"

"Overkill. He's not committing a crime. Besides, he's wearing a suit. Also, it's probably true."

"What's true?"

"We've probably got his Thinkpad. Poor slob wouldn't be here otherwise. I saw the machine. Couriered it down to Oscar when it came in, like always. Spanking new thing, full of files. What's our policy on new machines like that, anyway?"

Max thought of the emails from Oscar Furey, his meeting at five o'clock. Oscar's tone of urgency became clear. "Be serious, Manny. Finders keepers."

"Good. Well, I'll keep an eye on the tent guy."

"Move on that."

He hunkered in his office for the next two hours, mulling a plan for the evening. The last two evenings had been so indescribably rotten. Tonight he had two options, as far as he could see. He could go home, get one of his cars out of the barn, maybe the T-bird, and take a drive as the sun set. That left the rest of the evening. The second option involved dinner, companionship, maybe a little boink, too. But who? With Tris out of the picture, who in Christ could he brag to about the Korean deal?

Cars were his passion, probably the only thing in life more precious to him than business. He had often thought what a kick it would be to buy and sell cars for a living. The problem was, once you had a car in your collection, how could you ever sell it again? That would be the problem for him. It was not like computer parts. Nobody in the history of the world had ever fallen in love with a used DVD drive. He often spent Sunday afternoons, tired of the internet, thumbing through *Hemmings Motor News* with its classified ads fifty to a page sorted by manufacturer – Chevrolet, Ford, even defunct manufacturers like AMC and Studebaker. He could fritter away hours just reading the classifieds and admiring all the pictures of lovingly restored cars.

As a high school boy he had saved up enough to buy his first car, a 1972 Chevy Camaro, the car made famous on the TV show "Rockford Files". The Camaro had spent a few years up on blocks in his parents' front yard in Urbana, Illinois, while he was in college. Because by then he had owned his first Cadillac – a 1979 Fleetwood convertible. It had wide whitewall tires, fire-engine red paint and black leather in the interior.

Girls who got into that Cadillac with him already had mapped out a future for themselved complete with the two-story house with a white picket fence, two kids and a dog. Seeing you at the wheel of a car like that had been enough to make a girl horny. The best had always been, he thought now, on warm summer nights like this, with the top down and a beautiful girl beside you, and all the stars giving you just enough light, spending a couple of hours parked somewhere.

Of course, his first Corvette had made heads turn as well. "The cops'll pull you over even if you're under the speed limit," Uncle Gordon had said when he got it. The Vette wasn't even red. It was yellow, a two-seater with eight cylinders and a three-hundred-and-fifty horsepower V8 engine. Which meant pure adrenaline rush if you could open her up on some back road.

That yellow Corvette had been joined in later years by a 1964 T-top Corvette and a 1969 black Corvette convertible, each a classic in its own right. His favorites in the collection were the cliché cars: the 1959 Thunderbird with porthole windows, right out of "American Graffiti" with Wolfman Jack; the 1957 Mercedes Gullwing Coupe (totaled by Tris Berrymore); the orange 1968 BMW 2002 series, surprisingly roomy in the back seat; the 1957 Chevy Bel Air, two- tone, white and red, headroom for basketball players, front and back.

Every year he added another car to his collection. They now numbered seventeen. He kept them in a converted barn on his property on the lake, approximately one mile north of the TSR warehouse. He had added an annex to make more space once the collection had hit twelve cars. The annex was filling up now. The whole place was climate-controlled at sixty degrees Fahrenheit and 50% humidity. You couldn't subject all that old rubber and leather to the wild fluctuations between Chicago's dry sub-zero weather in the winter and hot, humid summers.

The cars were parked at diagonals on a painted concrete floor, the walls of the barn covered with luxurious mahogany paneling. An automatic sprinkling system would douse the collection with fresh lake water at the first hint of smoke. The entire place was alarmed with the latest Honeywell gadgetry, with motion and heat detectors that set off alarms at the security company and a head-splitting alarm in the barn.

The first time he had shown Tris around he had let her set off the alarm on purpose, so that she would know it existed and so she would grasp the impregnability of it. With a new girlfriend, you never know. Lately when they had gone into the barn together, he had let her choose which car she wanted to drive. She would make her choice, he would toss her the keys, and off they'd go.

After last night, Tris was no longer an option.

With a certain reluctance he picked up the phone and dialed a number that he had taken care to unlearn two years before.

"I was wondering, these scratches are really hurting. Would you mind terribly having a look with your disinfectant after all?"

"Max, I'd be delighted."

"Just because, you know, it's my face. I probably shouldn't take a chance."

"You did the right thing, Max. See you at seven."

The last thing he did before his five o'clock appointment was to call Brainard. "Any trouble?" he asked.

"We got it on the boat okay," Brainard said. "Barge was already loaded. We hadda take one Dumpster off to make room."

"Good. And the other thing I asked you to do?"

"I'm on it."

What I would give to be out there and see it with my own eyes.

He hadn't been out on the barge in a couple of years. Truth was, it freaked him out, all that blackness around you ten miles out, all that murky water. At the same time, in the safety of his living room, with the soft deep-pile shag rug massaging his bare toes, that vast dark nighttime emptiness outside his cathedral windows always filled him with an unquenchable animal lust.

Furey

In the employee directory on her computer, Annie studied pictures of Ike Mullin and Tran Phan Ng. They lived together at an address in Waukegan. She had already parked outside that house once, and followed them from there to another street in Waukegan and then to Indiana. Could the phones be there, at their house? They weren't here at TSR, and they weren't in the brown Lincoln. So they might be at that house. The question was, how could she get in and get them back? That was going to be a problem.

At four she went on break and headed for the canteen and outside. She found a bunch of workers standing around. They were all talking about the yellow tent set up in the grass fifty feet from the building.

"That wasn't there this morning," she said.

"Thinkpad Man," Roberto said. "He doesn't give up so easy."

"No way. Has anyone bothered to talk to him?"

"He's just sitting in there. He went and hid in the tent when he saw us."

She walked over to the tent. The flap was zippered shut. "Hey, you in there? It's Annie."

She heard a rustling, then the zipper opening. Olson stuck his head out. "Present and accounted for."

"Is that supposed to be some kind of a pun? Do you always go camping next to dingy warehouses?" He crawled out and stood, brushing off his brown suit. The tie was gone, his shirt open at the neck. He tossed his suitcoat in the tent. The others wandered over.

"I keep this tent in the trunk of my car. Most weekends I go to campgrounds out on the Kishwaukee River, near where I live. Have you ever heard of the Kish?"

"They're not going to let you stay here," Annie said.

"I'll take my chances," Olson said. "Hi everybody. Name's Bob. I don't know if Annie told you why I'm here."

"Something about a Thinkpad?" Roberto said.

Olson nodded. "It belonged to my boss. It wasn't supposed to be taken away with the old stuff. I'm hoping you all can help me. I've got days left to live if I don't bring it back."

"What's so special about it?" Murray asked. "Thinkpad's a crappy design, you get right down to it."

"It's not the computer itself, it's what's on it. It's got all my boss's files and email and everything on it."

"Doubt you'll ever see it again," Roberto said. "Probably already re-sold and in the hands of some very satisfied customer."

"In twenty-four hours?"

"We work fast."

"What about the website?" said someone.

"I checked," Annie said. "There's Thinkpads for sale, but none that're in new condition, or anything like that."

"I'll pay a reward," Olson said. He opened his wallet and riffled through the bills, showing several hundreds. "Five hundred in cash to the person who gets my Thinkpad back with all the files intact."

Someone whistled.

"Guy's loaded," someone else said.

"Best place to look would be Max Vinyl's office, you ask me," Roberto said. Murray nodded. Roberto looked at Annie. "You're probably the only one with a chance of getting in there."

"I can get in, no problem. I might need one of you covering my butt."

"I volunteer for that shit," Murray said. He stepped around behind her, pretending to examine her ass. She ignored him.

"Shut up, dweeb," Roberto said. "Let's find that Thinkpad. We can share the reward. So Bob, you're not really going to spend the night here, I hope."

"Not my first choice. Depends on how things go, I guess."

His tent stood thirty feet from the long blue warehouse. This little sunburnt strip of lawn led from the edge of the parking lot at the front, Annie saw, clear to the channel at the other end, with boats tied up in the water. A kind of no-man's land.

"You got any food in there?" she asked.

"Salami. Potato chips. Iced tea. Just stuff I threw in the car. Anyone hungry?"

"I'd kill for chocolate chip cookies," Roberto said.

"So, you just sit in there and nosh potato chips?" Amy asked. "That is so gross."

"Why?" Murray said. "What do *you* do with potato chips?"

"Shut up, reefer-face."

"Tell you the truth, I've been reading a bit," Olson said. "Before leaving I picked up a book on Lake Michigan. Christmas present from a couple of years ago. Since I saw on my map that this place was right on the lake. Did you know Lake Michigan is the fifth biggest lake in the world? Number two if you lump it together with Lake Huron, which hydrologists do. And did you know it's nine hundred twenty-five feet deep at its deepest point?"

"What the hell is a hydrologist?" Roberto said.

"Which is nowhere around here, by the way. Here off Illinois and southern Wisconsin the water's only eighty feet deep, clear out almost to the middle of the lake, where it gets a bit deeper. You've got to go farther north to encounter the real depths. And nearly one hundred different species of fish live in this lake, including salmon, trout, perch, carp, bluegill, alewife and sturgeon, all of which are probably going to be decimated by four species of Asian carp in the next ten years. By the way, did you know sturgeon can grow to eight feet and live one hundred and fifty years?"

"No animal lives that long," Murray said. "Anyway how can they measure it? They take a fish census every ten years or something? Don't believe all the ecology bullshit you read."

"Just telling you what the book says," Olson said. "I'll let you have it tomorrow."

They walked away as Olson went back in his tent.

"Dude's off the wall, you ask me," Roberto said.

"You can say that again," Annie said. "Like, fish and chips, you know?"

"Ha, ha," Roberto said.

Annie spent the next hour answering calls. Was she avoiding the problem of confronting those thugs? It wasn't for lack of courage, she decided. At least she was here, in the door. More than in the door. That had to count as a good start. Sooner or later they would show up again, and they were bound to walk right through this door. The question was, what was she going to say when they did?

At five o'clock the little bell chimed and the front door did open. A man in a suit with stylish rectangle glasses and an orange tie walked in. She checked the agenda and saw that Max Vinyl had a five o'clock appointment.

"You must be Mr. Furey," she said. The man nodded. "I'll tell him you're here."

Furey stood waiting in front of the reception desk. Under one arm he had a thin, well-worn leather attaché case. In the other hand he had a charcoal-colored laptop. Could that be a Thinkpad? It looked like the ones she had seen on the IBM website. Then again, laptops all looked pretty much the same. Before she could make another move, bloodshot Max Vinyl sauntered out of his office. The two men shook hands and disappeared again. All she heard was, "Jesus, Max, what happened to your face?"

She googled more Thinkpad pictures. Bingo. Every single one was charcoal gray. They didn't come in another color. She enlarged a few of the photos. Variations on a theme, but they all looked pretty similar. She looked up Furey in the company database. He was an external contact, not an employee, but all his information was there. Furey & Smith Attorneys at Law, an address in Chicago. A lawyer.

At five thirty-seven Max Vinyl and the lawyer came out. When they shook hands, Furey had to juggle the attaché case and the laptop. Annie hurried around from behind the reception desk.

"Let me help you with that, sir," she said. She eased the laptop out of his grasp. "Which way is your car?"

She saw the look go between the two men. Something told her this laptop was not just any old Thinkpad, it was the very machine Olson had come for.

"It's okay, Max," Oscar Furey said. "We'll talk in a day or two. You take care of those scratches."

"Right."

"This way, young lady. Don't drop my computer." They walked out into the sweltering late afternoon heat. His reference to the laptop gave her a chance to change her grip on it and, while doing so, take a better look. Her face went hot when she saw the IBM logo. It had to be the one. How many of these could be there be floating around TSR, these days? Olson would kill for this. But he was nowhere in sight. His tent was way around the other side of the warehouse. They reached Furey's car, a big black Hummer.

"I was wondering, were you, ah, by any chance heading downtown?" Annie asked. Anything to stay with the Thinkpad. She could come back for her car later. Her workday was over. Furey stood looking at her across the hood of the car. With his

Oakleys she couldn't see his eyes. Then again, he couldn't see hers, either.

"Sure, my office is in the city. You need a lift or something?"

"Would you mind?"

"Not a problem. I'm down by State and Oak, right downtown."

"I can get a bus from there."

"Hop in." Furey unlocked the doors, turned on the engine and cranked the air. She left the Thinkpad on her lap and fastened the shoulder belt while he backed out of the space. Being in a Hummer with him and his Oakleys brought on a strong wave of déja-vu, even if the Army models didn't have this cushy leather. Every GI in Iraq had a pair of Oakleys. You had to. The other side of the Earth was closer to the sun, something like that.

She put out her hand. "Annie Ogden."

"Oscar," he said, shaking. "Oscar Furey. Attorney. Work with Max on company stuff."

"Lawyer." She gave a little laugh. "We had more of you guys than soldiers in Iraq, seemed sometimes. You wouldn't believe."

He stared. "You were over there?"

She often got this reaction. People were curious to meet a soldier. People were even more curious about women who served. How was it over there? Was it really like what they showed on TV? How was it for women? She knew what people really wanted to know when she told them she had served three tours was, what kind of woman wants to be a soldier? What kind of woman would want to go back again and again? She didn't know the answer herself. Even if there *was* a type of woman who wanted to fight, was she that type?

"Just got back three months ago. Seems like yesterday."

He was looking her over. "Came back in one piece, looks like. Thank God," he added.

"Three tours, one Silver Star."

"No kidding!"

They were getting on the highway. Her thighs were sweating under the laptop, but she left it where it was. Maybe he would roll the Hummer. Maybe she could just walk away from the crash, taking the laptop with her. Hummers did roll, as she could bear witness, but it took a hell of a lot more firepower than they were going to run into on the tollway.

"I had no idea. What was it like over there?"

Her eyes took in a wide marsh by the side of the highway. What now? How in the world was she going to get this machine away from him? Talk to him, gain his confidence somehow.

"It's probably a lot like what you've read in the paper. You know, you're driving through some city on patrol, suddenly there's a flash of light, a bang. No time to duck or anything. No time to think. Suddenly you're lying on the ground and all around you it's, like, barbecued chicken. Only then you realize it's not chicken, it's people, it's your buddies lying there, burned flesh and protruding bone and bleeding."

"You've been through that?"

She nodded, waited a minute before answering. "Seen enough death to last me a lifetime. What always got me wasn't so much the sight as the smell."

She saw his grip tighten on the steering wheel. His eyes were hidden behind the shades, but she saw the blood coursing in his jugular vein.

"The smell?" he echoed.

"Burning meat, burning flesh. You know the stink of burning hair?"

Furey made a face. "Everyone knows that smell."

"You're lying in a ditch sort of half-conscious going, what the fuck? You know something just happened, but you don't know what. And then, next to you, you see one of your buddies, all torn up and bloody, blood pumping out of his wound with each heartbeat. And then all at once you realize there's a hand missing."

"A hand."

"His hand is gone. See, those IEDs, improvised explosive devices, what they do is they throw twisted bits of metal in all directions. Generally you've got armor that protects the chest, the gut, you know. But your arms and legs and especially your feet and your hands are always hanging out somewhere, holding on to something. Just waiting for one of those Iraqi ninja stars, you know?"

He drove a stretch without saying anything. She figured he was processing what she'd told him. She had taken quite a length of time to process it herself.

"You must've lost some good friends over there."

"I try not to think about the men and women I know who gave their lives."

"That can't be easy."

"They train you to accept it. That you might have to make the ultimate sacrifice. All of us were two-hundred-percent ready to die for our country."

"Not that you want to."

"Sure. Nobody wants to buy it. There's a big difference between being ready, like accepting the possibility, and *wanting* it."

"That's training for you," Furey said. "Training is one thing our military is damned good at."

She nodded. "On TV they make it sound so sterile. Four dead, a dozen wounded. The dead ones might've died quickly or they might've felt their share of pain. The wounded ones, well, you can bet your last dollar they've been through pure hell. We're not talking simple broken arms, here. You don't get a bit of that from TV."

"Just the statistics."

"Right, some numbers. They don't broadcast the screams of men and women going insane from the pain, or the fear of the pain, or the fear of dying, or the fear of living. Can you imagine waking up and realizing you've lost both of your legs?

One guy I knew, he was a marathoner, and he lost both legs. So now his body still craves marathoning. He gets these sensations of needing to get out and go running, like this terrible *itching* in his legs, even though his legs are totally gone. He's got to live with that now. See what I mean?"

"I do admire their courage," Furey said.

She gazed at a truck they were passing. She had seen so many examples of courage, she never knew where to start. "Anyone can throw himself on an exploding device to protect his buddies. A spontaneous moment of courage. Pow! You're in paradise. Your troubles are over. The survivors have it harder. The ones who have to learn how to live their life all over again with a new body, a new limb, physical therapy, psychotherapy, a new way of dealing with the world."

I am one of those. So what's my new way?

Her throat filled as if she was going to cry. *Not now,* she thought. *Not now . . .*

Furey steered the Hummer off Lake Shore Drive and into the residential neighborhoods of the Near North Side. As he navigated the streets of his home neighborhood, she was no closer to having a plan than she had been when she had gotten in in the car. The problem was, she had somehow ended up on a mission for Olson.

"I can drop you off anywhere you like, Annie. But in all honesty, you know what I would like to do?"

She looked at him. "What's that?"

"Buy you a drink."

"To thank me for risking my life? You don't have to."

"I know I don't have to. I want to do it. I'd be happy to. That is, if you've got time."

Trying to simulate indecisiveness, she checked her watch. "Ok, I'd like that, Oscar. You can tell me what you were up to while I was over there defending your ass."

He drove south on State Street along Lincoln Park. The condominium buildings got ritzier as they cruised south, till at last the street narrowed and they were in a tree-lined section. She saw doormen standing in all the doorways. Furey swung the Hummer into a driveway and rolled down his window. He slipped a bill to a valet who stood waiting, opened the door and got out. He came around and opened Annie's door.

"Bring that with us, could you?" He motioned to the Thinkpad. "I don't like leaving my computer in the car."

"Looks like a new model." She walked faster to keep up with him as he strode down the sidewalk. Though she was sure he had heard her, he didn't answer. Up ahead she saw the bright lights and neon of Rush Street. Did he expect her to sleep with him? She wasn't prepared to go that far for Olson's laptop. The idea of sleeping with a cretin like Furey wakened violent impulses. She had to keep her focus on the stolen phones, and all this was actually taking her *further* from them. Then again, she was probably holding the lost Thinkpad in her hands.

Furey led her into a steakhouse a few buildings down from where he had left the Hummer. The restaurant was in back, the bar out front. In the vast, dark bar, they sat on stools at the window looking out onto the street. He ordered a double whiskey sour.

"White wine spritzer," she said to the waiter. She turned to Furey. "So what were you doing while I was over there fighting the baddies?"

He laughed. "If you want to make me feel like a gutless liberal, go ahead. Guilty on all counts."

"I didn't mean that. I can deal with people who think the war is stupid, or whatever. I just meant you, Oscar Furey, the last four years, you know."

"I was right here in Chicago." He cradled his drink, then finished it off and caught the waiter's eye before continuing. "Hell, I'm a lawyer. Do you want to know what lawyers do? I've been at it for the last fifteen years, not just the last four."

"Fair enough. You like it?" They both stared out the window.

"I like it."

"Actually I've never really understood what lawyers do. You work with companies, I guess, since you're working with Mr. Vinyl."

"Yeah, mostly companies. Also divorce cases, estate cases. Bread-and-butter stuff."

"Why do companies need attorneys so much?"

Furey laughed. "I guess because people tend to sue each other. But seriously, everything starts and ends with contracts. My job is to write the contracts so that they're in conformance with the law. Whether it's people starting or ending their employment with the company, or sales contracts, whatever."

"I had my first day today. Mr. Rodriguez is doing my contract."

"Sure, he's general manager, and they've got him doing personnel. The contract he gives you will be based on a template I provided. It conforms to the applicable laws."

"Don't worry, I'm not the type to sue."

"I don't have to worry. I wrote the contract airtight."

"So that's your work."

"Well, not everything is so airtight. That's where it gets interesting." Furey emptied his drink and looked for the waiter. "Refills."

"You mean like when someone does sue?"

"Oh, I can't remember the last time that happened. But sometimes there are discussions, yes. It's a complex business. Max Vinyl has a brilliant entrepreneurial mind. I can't even keep up with him."

"I thought so, too. That's why I applied for the job."

"Oh? What brought your attention to TSR?"

She couldn't very well tell him she had followed Ike and Tranny there in pursuit of stolen phones. She improvised. "I'm into recycling. Over in Iraq I had a lot of time to think. I got to thinking that was one of the things we were fighting for, a nice, cleaned-up planet. Then I saw the TSR website. It's really cool what they're doing."

Furey nodded. "We can't have people dumping old computers in the normal trash. Better for the environment if they're recycled. The ground water's probably poisoned enough by the factories that make them."

"Guess we would all agree on that."

He nodded. Their eyes met. She couldn't sit still any longer. She had to call Olson.

"Oscar, where's the ladies room?"

He turned in his stool and pointed the way. In the ladies room, she punched Olson's number. Olson was ecstatic. He was headed for his car before ending the call.

"Keep in touch," he said. "I'm on my way."

She had begun to hatch a vague plan. She could buy Furey another drink when he finished this one. If she could keep him going, he would get sloppy. Maybe Olson would be able to lift the Thinkpad while walking by their spot at the window while she distracted Furey. How she would then get away was not yet clear. Maybe Furey would just look down, and the laptop would be gone. She could act surprised, play along.

When she came back into the bar, she was the one who was in for a shock. She stared across the crowded room at all the tables by the window, but Furey was gone. Other people were sitting there. For a few moments she couldn't believe her eyes. Then she spotted him at the door, excusing his way through knots of people who stood waiting. He was leaving. He had crossed the entire room, the laptop tucked under one arm. He must have already paid. He must have stood up as soon as she had gone to the ladies room. Between her and the entrance stretched a large, crowded space, probably fifty cocktail tables, people lounging in stuffed chairs, drinks in hand, legs stretched out, aisles blocked. Catching up with him before he left was out of the question. Furey made it out the door, and didn't even look back.

So it *was* the Thinkpad – now there really could be no question. Otherwise why would he take off? But what could have given her away? Had something tipped him off? She picked her way across the bar and got out sixty seconds behind him. Outside, she stood under the awning behind a giant potted palm and watched Furey's hunched form walk up the street to the building where he had parked. She watched till he went in.

Phone in hand, she crossed the street. From behind an enormous elm tree she kept an eye on the door to Furey's building. The lobby was deserted. He had gone up in one of the elevators.

"Bob, false alarm. I lost him. He walked out on me. He must've gotten a feeling something wasn't right. Where are you now?"

"Sitting by the side of the road on the tollway. Speeding ticket. Officer's taking his sweet time. I think he's playing a computer game in his car."

"Well, no use coming down here now. Sorry."

"Oh, yes there is. I'm coming, Annie. Wait there for me, all right?"

"What do you think you can accomplish here? He's gone inside."

"I'll be there in forty minutes. Just keep an eye on things till I get there. I can drive you back north and you can get your car. It's the least I can do, right?"

"You're nuts," she said. But she felt a little tingle in her stomach as she said it.

Home invasion

An hour later she sat with Olson in a different restaurant right across the street from Furey's building. Twenty dollars out of Olson's wallet had gotten them a table in the window with a perfect view of the entrance to the lawyer's building. The place was loud enough to make talking difficult. Olson drank Coke. His shaved scalp reflected pinpoints from halogen lights attached to a pipe above them.

"Let me get this straight. This lawyer brought the Thinkpad to TSR, had it with him during a meeting with the owner of TSR, then brought it back to the city with him?"

"Correct. He's got it in his condo."

"And you hitched a ride down here with him and cadged drinks off of him?"

She smiled.

"Girl, you've got balls."

"Pardon me, but I do not have balls."

"Figure of speech." Olson took another bite out of his bacon cheeseburger. He chewed slowly with his mouth closed. He looked at her through his big owlish accountant glasses, then looked back out the window, checking across the street. "The more I think about it, the more it makes sense to me."

"What makes sense?"

"Him being a lawyer."

"I don't get what you mean."

"Think about it. New Thinkpad comes in the door, full of documents and files and all. Somebody has a look at that stuff, makes a judgment. Somebody decides, let's check with the lawyer and see what we can do with all this stuff. The lawyer has a look at the files, calls a meeting with the boss to discuss it."

"Wow."

"Companies always call the lawyer first. That's a no-brainer."

"So, like, now I've got no brain?"

"That's not what I meant. You're a bit sensitive, aren't you?"

She realized she was flirting. What in the world had gotten into her? "Go on," she said.

"No really, I should thank you. You didn't have to jump into action like you did. Putting yourself in danger. What made you go and do it?"

"You'd be surprised." She stabbed another piece of chicken from her salad. She didn't feel like telling war stories again. Not twice in one day. "So how do you plan on getting your Thinkpad back, now that you know who's got it?"

"I had an idea on the way down. What if I bought another Thinkpad, exact same model?"

"You mean switch it?"

"Hell, yes."

"What's that going to cost? You're really giving me the impression money is no object for you."

"I think my boss would be good for it. Assuming I get his Thinkpad back. We could use another laptop in the office."

"Anyway, the question is when? And how?"

"Damned if I know. I guess knowing where he lives is a good start."

"You're going to be here all night, you know."

He shrugged. "It's here or my tent."

"You're crazy."

"Not crazy, desperate. If I don't . . ."

"I know, I know, your life as we know it comes to a crashing end if you don't get your precious laptop back."

Olson wrinkled his eyebrows. He took a bite out of his cheeseburger and didn't talk again till he had finished it. So she had hurt his feelings. She wasn't about to apologize. He had a habit of repeating himself.

"It's about more than just keeping my job," he said. "I've been there for eight years. But it's more than just how long I've been working there, too. I finished my degree in accounting and went straight to work for this firm as a junior associate. Junior associate at a firm like Sterling means distributing the mail, making coffee for people. Maybe you get to do a little real work, besides, but we're not talking masters of the universe, here."

She was about to ask if that was his goal in life, but she held her tongue.

"And then?"

"And then night school. Accountants go to night school. It's part of the master plan for accountancy. You work a normal killer workday, and then two or three nights a week plus Saturdays you go to school, for like two years. You take a lot of exams along the way, and at the end you take a humongous bear of an exam that a lot of people fail. And then you're a CPA. From that day on, as an accountant, you have rights."

"Excuse me?"

"Certified Public Accountant. It's like a license to practice. Without it you can't advise companies, sign off on their balance sheets, things like that."

"I see."

"So like six years ago, I'm halfway into this CPA night school program and Mr. Sterling offers to make me his personal assistant." He looked her in the eye.

"Wow, that's pretty significant."

"Damn right. He created the position for me. In those days he was still trying to do everything himself. I'm not talking about the stuff you give to the secretary, writing letters or sending invoices, you know? I'm talking about number crunching, running balances, deciding how to advise clients, writing reports that he used to write himself."

"And he gave you this level of responsibility before you even took your exam?"

"Exactly," Olson smiled. "Because he could see the potential in me. We communicate well. I don't . . . well, it sounds a bit conceited, but I don't make mistakes. With numbers I don't, anyway."

"I certainly hope not, if you're an accountant."

He laughed. "You think accountants don't make mistakes with numbers? Lordy, the doozies I've seen. Say, Annie, do you know where the word 'doozy' comes from."

"No idea."

"There was a car called the Duesenberg. It was so big and powerful and sensational when it was first produced, back in the 1930s, the word 'doozy' came to mean anything big and sensational."

"How did you know that? Did you read a book about cars, too?"

"All right, now you're making fun of me. Whatever. Actually, all I did the whole day was drive around. My brain is fried. First I drove from Sycamore to Waukegan. And believe me, just finding TSR I nearly lost my mind. Then I got thrown out by those two security guards. And now I get a call from you and I'm tearing down the highway and get pulled over for speeding."

"So how much is that ticket going to cost you?"

Olson stared at her a moment. "He goes on this trip to Hawaii, you know? A one-week vacation, just him and his son. Then he comes back, and *wham*. Here I am. In Chicago, with you, far from where I live, far from my own bed. I'm asking myself this whole time, what the hell am I doing here, you know?"

"Listen, I just had an idea."

"Tell me."

"This guy is a lawyer, right? Pillar of the community?"

"Yes to the first. The second does not automatically follow."

"Okay, but assume he has your boss's laptop."

"Get to the point, Annie."

"So tell your boss to give him a call. He calls him up and demands to have it back. The lawyer'll probably be so shocked he'll agree."

Olson looked at her. She could see him turning the idea over in his head. He looked away, got the attention of their waitress and signaled for the check. Then he said, "It won't work. It couldn't possibly work."

"Why not?"

"Well, this lawyer has obviously figured out who the owner of the laptop is. I mean, he only has to look at two or three documents in there, and he knows. You with me on that? So if he hasn't contacted Mr. Sterling of his own accord, then it's pretty clear that he has no intention of giving it back voluntarily."

"Yes, but if your boss called him? If he confronted him?"

"Saying what? First I would have to convince him that Furey has his laptop. This lawyer in downtown Chicago? Second, I have to convince him to call up this guy, a total stranger. Third, assuming Furey denies all knowledge of the Thinkpad, Mr. Sterling has to somehow get aggressive and confrontational with him. It's a bit much to ask, don't you think?"

"I thought he wanted his computer back. To me it seems like a no-brainer."

"Very funny," said Olson. "I just thought of another reason. Right now, Furey doesn't know we know he's got it. His defenses are down. Maybe we've got a chance of getting it back. If Mr. Sterling calls him up and gets confrontational, he's going to go into defensive mode. After your charade with him tonight, he would have to deduce that you were the one who tipped off Alden Sterling. We might never see it again."

She watched him pay the bill. His wallet bulged with cash. "Do all accountants carry this much money, or are you just loaded?"

"In my job I get pretty sick of money. That's actually where the camping comes in. I like taking nature photos. Birds, animals, flowers. Not professionally or anything, just for kicks. But right now is an exception. Technically, I'm out of a job. I feel a little less helpless when I'm flush. Maybe it's irrational. What's the difference if it's in my pocket or in my bank account? I don't know. But it might come in handy."

Olson had paid, and they were just getting up from their chairs when Oscar Furey walked out of the building across the street. Furey had changed out of his suit. Now he was dressed in Chinos and a blue oxford button-down shirt with sandals. He was rolling up one sleeve as he walked down the sidewalk. No laptop under his arm now.

"There he is." Annie pointed.

"That's the guy? You're sure?"

"Of course. I can't believe how lucky you are. Where could he be going at this hour?"

"Quick," Olson said. "Here's the plan. I'm going in. I'm going to try to get into his condo and snatch the laptop. You follow him. If it looks like he's headed back, you call me so I can get the hell out of there."

"How are you going to . . .?"

"Just go. Otherwise you're going to lose him. You're my early-warning system."

She hurried out after Furey and, after watching Bob cross the street, fixed on the sight of the lawyer in his light blue oxford shirt. To see her, he only had to turn, but he didn't turn. This dude had walked out on her two hours ago. He walked to the end of the block, looked right and left, and crossed, continuing south into the Rush Street crowd. The crowd was thicker in that next block. As he vanished into the crowd, she broke into a run.

She lost the cover of the big leafy trees, crossing the street from his residential block into the pedestrian zone that would be busy till the early morning hours. The crowd itself gave cover. It also covered him. She had lost him.

She stood in the glow of a giant brilliantly-lighted shop window, filled with cameras, computers and phones. She scanned the crowds to the south, looking for that light blue shirt. It was almost impossible separating out one person from another, with the night-time pandemonium of faces, arms, legs, bodies, shopping bags, gold chains and sunglasses that filled that small space in the half block ahead of her. She moved up to the edge of the shop window and peeked around the corner to the right. Something told her he must have gone that way. The crowds were thinner that way.

Her eyes swept the foreground first, the nearest ten yards, searching for that light blue shirt. Numerous people stood looking at the display in the electronics store window. Beyond them people walked away from her and towards her. She swept a larger perimeter with her eyes, thirty yards out, looking for light blue. At eighty or ninety yards she caught sight of the light blue shirt. She gauged body size, hair color, posture. It could be him. A light blue shirt just going into the Walgreens store. The timing would be about right, considering the distance from here to the Walgreens. That slight hunch, the sandals. It had to be Furey. Still looking all around as she went, in case he popped out of a different store entrance and surprised her, she walked toward the Walgreens entrance. Should she go in?

The last thing she wanted now was to bump into him. She'd better have her story ready. The front of the Walgreens was one big glass wall. She had a good view of the checkout lines. Her watch said five past eleven. Seven minutes had passed since Bob Olson had gone into Furey's building. She lingered outside, unsure what to do, and kept an eye on the checkout lines. Bob was crazy to try and steal the laptop. How did he think he was going to get into Furey's condo, anyway?

One minute later, through the plate glass window of the Walgreens she caught sight of Furey standing at the end of one of the lines, a sixpack of beer in his hand. Three or four people stood ahead of him in line. A beer run. All it was was a beer run. Jesus, with a sixpack of beer he would be heading straight home.

Instantly she backed off from the Walgreens, crossed the street, headed for a group of tourists that were blocking the sidewalk in front of a big bookstore. She heard strings of words in German, a language she had last heard while travelling through the Air Force base at Rhein-Main in Germany. She was able to make out that they were arguing about whether it would cost more to go to a movie in Water Tower Place or have a drink at one of the bars on Rush Street. From behind the German tour group, she had a decent view of the entrance of the Walgreens. Furey would never see her here among all these tourists, as long as she kept her head down. All these Germans were a head taller than she was anyway.

She opened her phone and punched Olson's number. Furey came out of the Walgreens, looked both ways, and started walking. She held the phone it to her ear, letting it ring over and over. A thin brown plastic bag weighed down by the beer dangled from Furey's fingers. Bob's phone went on ringing as Furey rounded the corner at the electronics store. *Son of a bitch, pick it up!* She hung up and started walking, keeping an eye on him. She tried the number again as Furey crossed the street, now in his own block. It seemed to take him half the time to get home that it had taken to get to the Walgreens. In sixty seconds Furey would enter the lobby of his building.

"Yes," Olson said, this time answering on the first ring.

"Wake-up call. He's coming."

"Where is he?"

"In ten seconds he'll be in the lobby downstairs."

"For Pete's sake, why didn't you call me before?"

"Are you in? Where are you?"

"In his bedroom. I can't find the Thinkpad."

"Get out now. He's standing in the lobby, waiting for the elevator."

"If you were him, where would you hide it?"

"Bob, get the hell out. He's getting in the elevator."

The call ended. Olson had cut her off. She crossed the street. There was nobody in the lobby of Furey's building. Olson was still upstairs. What if he confronted Furey? What if Furey had some sort of alarm that tipped him off to Olson's presence? The scenarios in her mind became more frantic with every step she took. She had to do something. Keeping one eye on the elevators, she went in, looked up Furey's name, and pressed the intercom button.

"Yes, who is it?"

She recognized Furey's nasal voice. Furey seemed calm enough. It wasn't the response of a person in the middle of a confrontation. That was something. But what was keeping Olson?

The line was still open. She heard nothing in the background. If she said anything, Furey would recognize her voice. She tried heavy breathing. In, out, in, out. She hadn't done anything like this since high school, crank calls on the phone with girlfriends.

"All right, scum, call it a night," Furey said. "Press that button again, and you can explain it to the cops."

The intercom went dead. She went back out and crossed the street to Olson's car, which was locked. She waited on the far side of it, peeking over the top at the building entrance. Now, either the police would show up, Furey would appear, or Olson would come back out.

A layer of sweat prickled her forehead. Her eyes fixed on the bank of elevators in Furey's lobby, waiting for that bald scalp to appear. She felt the adrenaline surge. With every muscle in her arms and legs and back and neck she yearned to see Olson's face appear. The realization surprised her. *You don't even know this guy. The little you do know about him . . . well he's a bit strange, isn't he?*

Olson stepped off the elevator, empty-handed, and strode out of the lobby. He crossed the street rapidly, unlocking the car with his remote while still ten feet off.

"Let's get the hell out of here."

He started the car and pulled out into traffic. Annie looked back over her shoulder, still expecting Furey to come sprinting out of the lobby. But the lobby was deserted. Olson didn't speak till they reached Division Street.

"I don't think I've ever been so scared in my whole life," he said. "I could hear the door being unlocked just as I was ending the call with you, see. I could hear him coming in."

"And you were where?"

"It's this big place, you know? Two bedrooms, kitchen, massive living room with thick carpeting, modern art, sculptures, mirrors. I couldn't cover the whole place. I looked everywhere I could think of."

"Maybe he's got a safe."

Olson nodded. "Possible, I guess. But would he put a laptop in it?"

"Did he see you? How did you get out? I was afraid you were going to confront him."

"I thought about it, but I decided it was too risky. Guys like that, you never know if they've got a gun. I don't want to die for this."

"I don't blame you."

"You saved my bacon, Annie. When you buzzed, he was on his way to the bathroom. He was ticked off at the interruption. It distracted him. So I'm hanging out in the bedroom, in the dark, not moving a muscle. Afterwards he practically *ran* to the bathroom. I think he really had to take a leak, simple as that, and you were keeping him from it with your heavy breathing. As soon I heard him lock the door, I grabbed my chance.

Wall-to-wall shag carpeting. I snuck across the room real quiet, and out the door. He probably never knew I was there."

They were at a red light. She looked at him, the way he was staring straight ahead out of the windshield. He must have been pretty freaked out, being in Furey's apartment with the lawyer only a few feet away from him. A good way to get shot, indeed, surprising someone in his own home, an *invitation* to get shot. Was that what Olson was thinking? He had been lucky to get out. Well, he'd been foolish to go in.

"So when you're not running around trying to find people's lost laptops, you go out camping?"

He tore himself away from whatever image he saw in the windshield. He met her eyes. "With the emphasis on photography. Not tents and campfires. Mostly birds, but if I see a flower or a moth or a beaver I'm going to get that, too. When it comes to nature shots, believe me, you never see the same thing twice."

A car behind them honked. The light was green. It took a few seconds before traffic moved.

Bonfire

He took his motorcycle for this job. He had spent all afternoon shopping, preparing and then meditating. The plan called for darkness. He parked on that same street where he had stolen the Mitsubishi. With the help of the boss's directions he had figured out how to walk to the beach cottage.

Five hours earlier he had consumed a protein-rich dinner of six boiled eggs, a quart of fat-free milk, and a half pound of fresh steamed broccoli. The eggs went down without salt, the broccoli without sauce. In the old days he had salted every bite and loaded his plate with sauces. But sauces were full of fat, and salt broke down the interior walls of your arteries. You altered your diet if you wanted to stay trim, getting older. His stomach was pleasantly empty now; there would be no burps or gas to give away his presence, should he find himself not completely alone at any point.

It was after ten as he walked through the dark yards and the hedges until he reached the dirt road that led to the beach cottage.

The moon was a sliver in the night sky, giving just enough light to see by. He had dressed entirely in black. He left the road two hundred yards before the cottage and threaded his way through the trees. The trees were spaced evenly, in rows. Some kind of orchard. A breeze came up. Then he smelled the apples. He moved slowly, making no noise, keeping an eye on the cottage and on the dark pickup truck parked in the driveway. At a distance of fifty yards from the cottage, out in the middle of the orchard, he stopped and waited.

The two-story cottage was completely dark. The front door faced the driveway, where the pickup was parked. On the south side, two windows on the ground floor and two upstairs. The roof sloped gently up to a point. Shingle roof, aluminum siding or wood, he couldn't tell. There would be plenty of wood in the structure. He checked his watch. Fifteen minutes had gone by since he stopped to watch. One of three possibilities occurred to him. Either they were in the house and already sleeping. Seemed a little early for that. Or they had a second car and were out, and could come home at any time. The third possibility, the one that worried him the most, was that they were out for a walk on the beach.

If they were out, he had to give himself plenty of time to get back under cover once they came back. He would hear them coming down the road. He approached the cottage slowly and stealthily, like a cat, keeping his own noise close to zero. He looked at the ground before placing each foot, taking care not to step on dead sticks that might snap noisily. He kept his breathing even. In between steps, he looked around three hundred and sixty degrees, checking for movement, changes, signs of life. He was totally alone here.

It was all far too careful. But you really could never be too careful, not if you wanted to avoid that third trip to jail. Tonight he was breaking his old vow. He was risking his neck, pure and simple. The sight of the boss in that messed-up state had rocked him into action, into taking the ultimate risk.

In his pack he had six small explosive packs, all rigged on one wire. He planted the first charge in a hole he found in the siding on the south side of the house. In with the mice and the beetles, he slid it in the hole far enough to make sure it wouldn't fall out if there were a little pull on the wire. The siding covered a plain wood frame, all highly combustible dried-out wood underneath. He taped the second charge to a windowsill. Through the window he saw a comfortable living room, a leather couch, two big stuffed armchairs, a thick rug, a bookshelf filled with books that covered most of one wall, and a fireplace. He stared in for a full two minutes before placing the charge. No lights, no noises, no people. And no dog.

The dog would have long since heard him or smelled him and started barking, if a dog had been here. He had half a pound of raw hamburger in his backpack, laced with fast-acting poison, in case the dog appeared. No dog probably meant no people. He would bet money there were no people in this house. The window would shatter and the fire would jump inside to curtains, rugs, furniture, papers.

No people would get hurt. Only property was being destroyed, here. This was important. This, too, was a line had had never been willing to cross, not since the kid had died in the 7-11 robbery twenty-three years before. Destroying property made a statement. You attack Max Vinyl with pepper spray, you're gonna hear back. Fair's fair.

He placed the other four charges at even intervals around the house, taping them in place or inserting them into natural crevices that would hold them. He took his time. He played out the wire slowly and silently, making sure there were no kinks, no irregularities of any kind to break the circuit.

On the north side of the house stood a row of pine trees. The lake could not be far beyond those trees. The pines sheltered the house from wind off the lake, he supposed, but there was still plenty of breeze to whip up a fire. As he worked he kept glancing over his shoulder, on guard against someone running out of the pines to attack him.

When he had placed the sixth and last charge, he went back around to the south side, inspecting his work. Satisfied, he moved slowly back out into the orchard, back to the spot from which he had watched earlier. Still no lights or movement of any kind in the house. His watch said 10:35. Let the bonfire begin.

He pressed a button on his controller. The charges exploded at the same instant, one big boom. He had programmed them well. The concussion pressed every organ in his chest cavity against every other. Each little ball of fire flared right up to the eaves before settling back in on itself. The first blast of heat reached him in a wave fifty yards out in the apples. With the cottage burning brightly, he zipped his pack, swung it around on his back, and started back the way he had come.

He hadn't taken two steps when the engine of the pickup roared to life. Then the truck lights flicked on.

Shit!

What in the world was with that truck? Was it possible someone had been sitting in there? How could someone have been sitting in that pickup the whole time? He had been here close to an hour.

The truck was moving down the dirt driveway now, driving away from the burning cottage, following him. He jogged through the orchard, keeping fifty yards of apple trees between him and the truck. Yes, the driver had to have seen him. Otherwise why would he be driving along the dirt driveway at the same speed he was jogging?

Up ahead was the main road, the road that led into Gary. It was a two-lane asphalt road that ended at the beach, half a mile to the north. He had to cross that road to get to the yards of those other houses, to the place where he could cut through and dash to his bike. The road was another two hundred yards ahead of him.

He stopped to think. What in the world had the person in that pickup truck been doing? Watching him? For almost an hour? Almost as if he knew what was going to happen. But how could anybody know, since he hadn't told anybody what he was going to do, or when? The boss of course knew he would cook something up. He alone knew Brainard planned to do something *here*. But what earthly reason could the boss have for setting him up?

The pickup stopped on the dirt road, its engine idling. A big powerful Ford F-150, he observed. Good acceleration on that model. Unconsciously, he stretched his leg muscles, getting ready. He carried no gun on principle. If you didn't carry, you couldn't shoot. If you couldn't shoot, people weren't going to die.

If the other guy had had a gun, he could have used it already. He would have had a pretty clear shot at Brainard's shape through the apple trees at fifty yards. So he meant to run him down when he got to the road, or maybe just head him off.

Behind him, the cottage burned noisily, crackling and popping as the flames devoured the structure. Surely he could get across the road either in front of the truck or behind it. The problem was they were going to see him. After all the trouble he had taken to avoid being identified, for the first time he was trapped. The thought kept coming back to him that he had been set up. But he couldn't deal with that now. He had to keep moving. Someone would see the flames and call the fire department. The police were probably on the way. Brainard started walking. The truck started moving again.

As he got closer to the road he quickened the pace, but saved his energy for the sprint across the road. He would have a fifty-yard headstart. The pickup would turn from the dirt road onto the asphalt fifty yards to his right. The truck would have to make a tight turn while accelerating. That tight turn might save him.

As he got closer to the asphalt road, the pickup speeded up on the dirt driveway. Now it was a race. He broke into a run. His feet in the motorcycle shoes propelled him over the uneven ground of the orchard. The pickup gunned it and took the corner with its engine screaming. Brainard hit the pavement at full speed, pumping his arms for more power. The driver of the pickup must have his foot to the floor, the way the truck was flying toward him. But the truck was still skidding sideways on the dirt and stones that covered the road surface, even as it leapt forward, its tires struggling to grab the pavement. That skidding would buy him a step, maybe two. He sprinted on the balls of his feet like a track star, cutting the air with his arms, ignoring the oncoming lights and noise of the truck.

Just get across!

He could feel it bearing down on him, a living thunder of light and noise and metal. They wanted to kill him. The truck was almost upon him.

On the other side of the road were six feet of emergency lane, then maybe ten feet of grass, then the first trees. The pickup was almost on top of him when his feet left the ground. He felt it rocketing towards him, prepared to kill him. The smell of its exhaust fumes burned in his nostrils. At the last moment he dove through the air, half expecting the grill of the truck to clip him in the ankles. He curled his head under to land in a roll. Without looking back, he was aware of the truck skidding to a stop in the loose gravel. He heard the desperate grinding and scraping of the locked tires sliding helplessly along the pavement. It would take three or four seconds for the truck to slow and stop. The acrid smell of burning rubber fused with the sweet smell of exhaust. He hit the hard grass rolling in a ball, like a floor vaulter, the truck behind him still sliding on the stones.

In one movement he was up on his feet again, tearing through the trees into the first yard. It was bad to run from a fire, very bad, but what choice did he have? He had been set up. It was the only possible explanation. The pickup driver had lain in wait. That was clear as anything. Try as he might, he could not think of anyone who would have been capable of doing it but one person, and that person was Max Vinyl. The question was why? *Why?* What had he done to deserve this betrayal? He ran till he got to the second yard, running in anger now, his face burning with shame, then walked fast to where his bike was parked. He burned with the feeling of having been doublecrossed, the feeling of having not seen it coming, the feeling of not knowing why.

Sweating like a pig, he turned the key and started the engine. Before driving off, he opened the storage compartment and got out the helmet that he rarely used. He was glad for something to mask his tears.

The sobs racked his body. How could he have been so blind? The boss wanted to kill him. Of course. Because then there would be no chance of him doing a plea bargain and turning in the boss with all that he knew. The boss had *sent* him to this place. He had even drawn him a map. Which meant it had been the boss behind the wheel of that pickup. Which was why there had been no people here in the first place. He must have known they wouldn't be here. Which was why he'd sat and waited all that time. It hardly seemed possible. There was no other explanation.

The engine's vibrations coursed through his muscles, calming him. No sign of the pickup now. The boss had tried to kill him. He headed back to Chicago, keeping to the limits, his mind going around and around in an endless tortured loop.

Witness

"Something tells me this isn't the first time you've made love in your truck," Tris said once they were unzipped.

"Guess I'd better take the fifth on that," Luther said, pulling her up onto his lap.

Dante lay on the floor, content to be with them and their smells. He had peed just before getting into the truck.

In Luther's embrace she felt safe. She had never been with a man who had bigger arms. But he was gentle and slow. He made love as if he had all the time in the world, as if he would have liked to go even more slowly than she wanted to go. Maybe it came from being older. He wouldn't say how old he was. She had the feeling there was a lot he hadn't told her.

They stayed hugging for a long time in his truck. The windows were cracked to let the air in, and with it came the song of the Indiana cicadas, the hoot owls and the whippoorwills. The night noises were like a symphony that never ended. It reminded her of her five days spent up in a redwood, years ago. Only here she could not fall down, all the way down, one hundred and eighty feet, to the forest floor. Here she was safe. Luther's even breathing, the movement of his thick chest against her chest, the feeling of being wrapped in his arms, lulled her into a peaceful state somewhere close to sleep, but not quite fully under. She could not have said how long they stayed like that, not moving, not even listening, just resting in each others' arms.

She had only managed five days. Six feet long and two feet wide, the platform was just big enough to lie down and sleep. You looked down from one hundred and eighty feet and, to tell the truth, though you couldn't even see the ground, you lost your nerve. Sheer terror had kept her awake. Even though she remained attached to the sling the entire time she was up there, she had never vanquished her fear of falling.

Being alone had not bothered her. The group had given her a two-way radio, and they used it to check on her supply situation. She supposed they were also checking on her mental state. Most of the time she kept the radio switched off. She read books. She listened to a voice in her head. When she read, the inner voice was the voices of the characters. When she was just thinking or dreaming, the inner voice was her own voice or it was other people who were talking to her. Often she heard her mother's voice, telling her about growing up in Brazil.

My thighs never bothered me back home. Nobody cares what you look like there. Black or brown or white, thin or heavy. Fat thighs, thin thighs. I never gave a thought to my thighs till I came to this country.

Back home meant Recife, at the family house where her mother had been born and raised, on the beach.

She had tried to use her inner voice to quell the panic.

You're not going to fall. How could you fall, hooked into this sling, with a main hook and a backup?

But it didn't work that way. Dozing off, the closest she ever came to sleep, in a hazy dream she saw herself unhooking the sling, some odd, anti-survival reflex making her do it. Her fingers would pull back the fasteners one by one. Her body would tumble off the platform. Then she would be falling. It was all in her imagination, but that sensation of falling would always jar her awake once more, just as she finally verged on sleep.

No, the voice had to come naturally. You couldn't just switch it on and off at will.

She peed from the platform, and her pee sprayed down, down through the canopy, all through the branches and the needles and the air. She watched the main stream break up into smaller, unconnected streams, these breaking up into drops, then the drops atomizing into droplets, and these into micro-droplets, and on and on. Some of the micro-droplets would evaporate in the time it took them to reach the ground. Others would strike a branch, or a leaf, or maybe stick to a feather in the wing of a bird flying around below her. She wondered if any of her pee ever actually reached the ground. Quite possibly not a single droplet had made it all the way down. That was how high up you were.

Redwood was valuable. It went for decks on which people cooked meat on a grill and entertained friends. They made expensive furniture out of redwood, and interior walls for saunas, and toilet seats for people in Santa Monica. It was exported to Japan for redwood-lined hot tubs.

You were yoked to the side of this tree, up here, this giant 1000-year-old phallus. Because of Tris Berrymore the white shirts told the chainsaw-toting men to wait. *Patience, boys. Can't stay up there forever.* But you knew there were other old-growth trees those men had their eye on. They redirected the crews all around Northern California to the places where her group was not present, and they took out the trees there. You couldn't camp in every tree. There were more redwoods in Northern California than there were people loony enough to try and sleep in them, on a platform high above the ground. Sooner or later, they would just cut the fucker out from under you anyway. Or they would drag you out of your sleeping bag by force, tie you up with rope, drop you by accident, *disappear* you . . .

On the fifth day, after sunup, she turned on the two-way and asked to come down.

There would have to be another way to save the redwoods.

In the next three years she went through five different jobs (and a few boyfriends), and left California. In Chicago she tried waitressing. Of all the jobs she had tried, this was the least damaging to the environment, though she did worry about the cooks pouring grease down the drain in the alley behind the restaurant.

You met people. The other waiters and waitresses, on the one hand, customers on the other. She had a policy of never dating a customer she had met only once. Only regulars had a chance with Tris Berrymore. Through conversations she got to know them a little.

"How's my friend, Tris?" asked a man who ended up being her lover. He knew how to tip. He always came in with friends, men and women, people he worked with. From the conversations she overheard she had trouble figuring out what he did. One evening they'd be talking about the latest movies. With another group he would be talking about Chicago politics the whole evening.

He always ordered wine. And two, three bottles, if the group was big. The tabs usually reached four hundred dollars or more. Nothing fazed this man. He tipped twenty percent.

He had broad shoulders, a big square chin, and a long, straight nose like a movie star. He was on the tall side and always wore a jacket but no tie, sometimes with a shirt, sometimes a turtleneck. What she loved most about him was his eyes, blue like the sky over Lake Michigan on a clear, crisp fall day. His blue eyes and the flecks of gray in his thick black ponytail would have made her nervous if he hadn't been so generous with his smiles. Lots of men looked right past her, even when ordering their food and drinks. This one looked *into* her, his eyes unlocking her, opening her up and taking her apart into her component pieces, right there in the restaurant: her soul, her heart, her mind, her sexuality. He was welcome to it. All of it. But she never imagined that her fantasy had the slightest shadow of a hope of becoming reality until one night he took her aside.

"I'm Luther Van Verst," he said. The rest of his group had gone outside. She shook his hand, wondering what was coming next.

"Tris Berrymore."

"Nice to know you, Tris Berrymore," Luther said. "I guess maybe you thought I came here so often because I like the food."

She shrugged. What did he want her to say to that? "We do get some good write-ups in the paper."

"Actually, I always came back because of you." His eyes crinkled half shut when he smiled. "Can I take you out one night this week? Let someone else wait on us? Who knows, might be we'd find something to talk about."

You might as well be asked out by George Clooney. Her calendar emptied instantly. She was working the next night, but the next two days after that she had lunch shifts. They met at another restaurant two blocks away. Within three weeks she had moved in with him. Two months after that she quit her waitress job.

"Don't quit," Luther said. "I'll work my schedule around yours."

"They pour their grease down the drain. The Chicago River is going to coagulate."

"Doesn't every restaurant do that?"

"My new baseline for restaurants."

"I guess those are the realities of the world."

"It should be outlawed."

He kissed her. Then he pulled her down on top of him on the couch and smoothed her hair back over her ears, over and over again, just like she liked it. It made her relax. And having those blue eyes gently unfastening the secrets of her soul. "So you've quit," he said. "What's next?"

Next had been a topless place called Skinny Whip on the Near North Side. One of the other waitresses moonlighted there. The money was good. The security was good. The owner made sure the girls were protected. And what could be more harmless to the environment than a bunch of drunken men watching women take off their clothes?

"You don't mind?" she had asked Luther.

"Of course I mind. I'm never going to see you at night, now. The hours are crap."

"The money is good."

"We both know it's not about the money."

"What's it about then, smarty pants?"

"You tell me."

"You don't like other men looking at my tits."

"I'd be lying if I said I did. But I'm not telling you you can't do it, either. I don't have to like it, do I?"

"Well, I'm doing it."

"I hope you find what you're looking for."

The Skinny Whip was usually half empty. It wasn't what you would call high class, with its beat-up old stage with two brass poles to lean on and wrap your legs around. The girls called them the north pole and south pole. The floor was sticky from spills by the late hours. It had to be scrubbed with an ammonia solution. Every night it smelled of ammonia until ten p.m., when the cigarettes and the cigars and the beer smells finally covered up the smell of the cleanser. The smoke hung in lazy whorls in lavender light, lavender changing to red, red to orange, orange to blue.

The job called for her to move sensuously around the pole, keeping one hand on it or just rubbing her hips against it. The music kept up a strong bass beat, now a fast tune, now a slow one. Another woman would be working the south pole, doing the same moves. They didn't rehearse much beforehand, yet still managed to stay in synch. The routine went on so long, twenty to thirty minutes, they had time to learn their moves right in front of the crowd.

The crowd kept ordering drinks. The drinks cost twice what they would cost in a normal bar. It didn't take much practice to keep one hand on the pole, and with the other slowly remove one piece of clothing after another. She was a farmer's daughter. Off came the apron. Off came the skirt. Off came the blouse. It went on and on, and the crowd could look from one farmer's daughter to the other, stripping in stereo.

They were easily satisfied, the men in these crowds. At ten o'clock she played a farmer's daughter, at eleven the dancers were nuns, at midnight meter maids, and the poles became parking meters. She looked them in the eye, the men sitting at the little tables, and got fabulous tips. She would find twenties and even fifties tucked in her g-string while the other girls found tens and fives. The other girls had warned never to look a customer in the eye. You didn't want to give them false hopes. But then you got lousy tips. Tips zoomed up when you looked like you meant it.

"We've got a new routine we've been working on," she said one day. They were lounging over brunch at Luther's. Two in the afternoon, and just on their second cup of coffee. "We dress up as flight attendants. We're like dancing around, and then these pilots come out and start undressing us. We get all irritated with them. We're like: 'Go back to the cockpit. Who's flying the plane?' You have to see it to believe it. It's incredibly hot."

"Yeah, I can imagine how it goes."

"What about tomorrow night?"

He shook his head. She waited for him to make a counterproposal. She waited until she realized he wasn't going to suggest another date.

"You don't want to see my performance. Something I've been working so hard on. Something artistic."

"Tris, this is pointless. Don't ask me to come and sit among all the other men, eating you up with their eyes. Why does that fascinate you?"

"Why does it turn you off? This is my body. It's just a body. But it so happens there's a real person in this body that's working on an artistic performance and wants you to come and appreciate it for once."

He had gone quiet then, like he always did when he wasn't going to give in, nothing more to say. She knew exotic dancing would never qualify as an art form for him. He put up with it the way you put up with a child that has a bad habit, like stealing or lying. He was just waiting for her to break this unpleasant habit. The realization that he was treating her like a child stung her. Anger had gotten a grip on her, and it hadn't let go.

It was a kind of stubbornness that made her leave him, or maybe a reaction to his stubbornness. He could've come and seen her *once*.

And yet she couldn't shake the feeling that the man she was leaving was the one good man out of all the men she had known. As if finding him had been too easy and she had been too lucky. Some things were too good to be true. Or maybe, even after all her speeches, somewhere inside her she was convinced that she didn't deserve him.

Three months after starting at the Skinny Whip she had moved out of Luther's. She hadn't wanted to leave. It was the last thing she wanted to do. She didn't know what it was that made her leave. She only knew she had to go.

One night there had been a group of Koreans. Bottle after bottle of expensive champagne went out to their table, plus bottles of Red Label. It was champagne with whiskey chasers or whiskey with champagne chasers, she didn't know which. They stuffed so much cash in her clothing she had had to enlist the help of Rupert from security. In the end she had netted three thousand, nine hundred dollars for a six-hour shift, and that was after paying out four hundred to Rupert. The Koreans held their liquor. Luckily they had drivers. For the local guys with them they had called cabs.

One guy had come back the next day to pick up his car. He had started apologizing to her.

"What for? It was no problem."

"I guess we were pretty boorish. I hope it wasn't . . . you weren't . . . "

They were standing out in the parking lot. She was just arriving, sunglasses still down, he just leaving. Behind the shades she could study his eyes without him noticing. Nice gray eyes. Big space between his front teeth. Normally she didn't talk to guys in the parking lot, but it was broad daylight. He didn't look like the type who would want to drag a girl into his car and hurt her.

"Believe me, I've seen worse. You know, groping types, guys with unrealistic ideas, like that."

"I can imagine. By the way, Max. Max Vinyl," the guy said. He produced a business card. Normally she didn't take business cards.

"Tris," she said.

"We're looking for a receptionist," Max said. She looked at his car, a big BMW, then at the business card. Tri-State Recovery, Inc., Max Vinyl, President and CEO. "Recycling business. Different kind of work from this, of course. Thought I'd mention it."

"Recycling?" she said.

A week later she had called him, and the day after that she had started work. Two weeks later she had rented a little house in Waukegan, near the company. She was glad to be away from Chicago, which now held painful memories. Independent, with her own place, Tris Berrymore now worked in a recycling company. The pile of money she had made stripping would cover the rent on her new house for a full year; the small salary she earned at TSR was plenty. She was helping make the world a better place.

The men drove around in trucks and loaded up old computers and other hardware that people didn't want anymore. They brought all this gear back to Waukegan, where computer jocks took it apart and tested it. The stuff that was still good was resold on the website. Some stuff was shipped off to Korea in containers, where it was re-sold there. The rest was recycled.

Or so they had claimed.

The workers driving the trucks were all ex-cons. The main recruiting seemed to take place at various jails around Illinois and Indiana. They were picked up at the prison gate upon release, some kind of prison-to-work program. The company got a subsidy for each worker hired, and a bonus for each one that stayed out of trouble for a year. They were no doubt happy to find any work at all. The recovery men with their bulging muscles and tattoos and thick necks might work hard, but they were readjusting to life on the outside and helping keep the earth clean.

When Max Vinyl had invited her to dinner one night after work, she had not been surprised. She had been expecting it. Max hadn't been subtle with the way he eyed her clothes and her body in those first days. He didn't act perverted or anything; he just caught her eye a lot and showed he liked her. And that gap between his front teeth. He grinned a lot, sometimes for no reason. She caught herself staring at that sexy gap.

So she wasn't surprised that he asked her out. What surprised her was that she said yes. He was the boss – that couldn't be a good idea, could it? Also she was rebounding from Luther. And, in a way, happy to be single. Or was it that she simply couldn't stand being alone? The truth was Max was kind of gorgeous, in a leisure-suit kind of way. She felt the pull of that unshakable confidence.

"How did you get the idea for this company?"

"Actually I get lots of ideas. But this one kept staring me in the face. People are constantly upgrading their computers, even more than their cars."

Or their women, she thought.

But she said, "Only you can't just throw an old PC in the garbage, because of all the poisons in it."

"Poisons?"

"What exactly do you call mercury, lead, cadmium, all those chemicals that are in electronic equipment?" Talking to the chief recycler, you would have thought they were speaking the same language.

"Anyway, old equipment takes up space. Nobody has space for the old stuff once they've got new machines. They just want to get rid of it, no hassle. They pay us to take away stuff that actually has resale value."

"It's brilliant."

Later, whenever she kissed him, the gap between his front teeth always got a very thorough examination by her tongue. But it was Max Vinyl's gray eyes that sent shivers down her spine. *Not good*, she thought. But what could you do? Don't stand in front of a speeding train.

"Let's talk about you," Max Vinyl said. "Where'd you get those freckles?"

"My Mom bought them at the baby store, I guess."

"You're pretty cute, you know."

"Is that why you hired me?"

A lighted candle stood on the table in between them. He reached across and moved it to one side.

"Tris, I admit I liked your moves up on the stage. I thought I would like to get to know you. I'm single, you know."

"Never married?"

"Once, sure. Didn't work out."

"So, never again, right?"

"Who knows? I'm not saying that. The problem wasn't marriage itself, the problem was the person."

"You mean her?"

"Maybe I was the problem."

"Half the problem."

"Maximum half."

"And you think it's a good idea dating your employees?"

"I try not to date them all at once."

He was way too glib, too full of slick answers, but at that moment she hadn't been listening to her instincts. He headed a *recycling* company. He was irresistible.

How could she have been so stupid? It boggled her mind to think she could have been taken in. It was so much more hideous than restaurants dumping their grease down city drains. It was almost laughable. You would laugh if you didn't first start to cry.

She opened her eyes. Some stirring of Luther's had brought her back to consciousness. When she opened her eyes, he was looking intently at something out the window of the pickup truck.

"Don't be afraid, Tris. There's someone out there." He stared over her shoulder, out the window on her side of the cab. She turned slowly. They were naked. Not that it mattered, but still. At first she didn't see anyone, staring into the dimness where Luther was looking. The sun had gone down at least an hour ago. Just the apple trees her grandfather had planted in the 1950s or the 1960s. Then a movement caught her eye. Something dark, yes. A human shape. A big shape.

"I see it."

"Get dressed but don't make any sudden movements. Don't make the truck move."

"You sure made the truck move before," she whispered. She got no answer.

They eased into their clothes. Dante stood at her feet, stretched, then sat, then stood again, looking at her expectantly, thinking she was going to take him out. She rubbed the fur behind his ears until his eyes drooped with pleasure.

The man was still in the orchard, but he was getting closer to the house. He moved closer to the house so slowly and deliberately she couldn't see him taking steps. She tried not to blink. He seemed to be moving each time she blinked. Then he was so close to the house that their view of him was blocked by the house itself. He had either gone right up to the side of the house, or around back.

"What do we do now?"

"I'm giving that some serious thought."

"Who could it be?"

"Who do you think it could be?"

"You think it's him?"

Luther shook his head. "Too big. You see those shoulders?"

"Well, what could he be doing back there? That's my brother's house. I don't want him there."

"Me neither."

"Are the truck doors locked?"

"Don't," he whispered. "Doesn't matter."

She had her own views on that, but she didn't touch the button. She realized he didn't want the noise.

"Luther?"

"Yeah?"

"My car wasn't there when you went back, was it?"

"Tris, would you forget about the car? There's no way of knowing if he stole it or someone else. Say goodbye to the car, like you said goodbye to him."

"There's a difference between my car and him. I loved that car."

He nodded. "It's a ratty feeling when someone steals something from you."

"If I find out he stole it . . ."

"Then you're going to let it go, Tris."

"No, I won't. Because you want to know why?"

"Why?"

"Of all things, he would understand from cars. You know, he's got his seventeen or whatever classic cars."

"You're right about that," Luther said. "Minus one Mercedes."

"All classics, like Jaguars and T-Birds and Corvettes. Worth a pile of change. But that's the interesting part about him and cars. He doesn't see them as money in another form. It's the one thing he doesn't constantly calculate the value of."

"You've been in there, right?"

"That barn where he keeps his cars? Sure, lots of times."

"Tell me about the security."

At that moment the dark figure appeared again in the orchard to their right, and they were quiet, watching him. He seemed to stop thirty or forty feet back from the house. For a long time he stood there, unmoving. Then, right before their eyes, the house exploded in a thunderclap that made the bones in her shoulders vibrate. Balls of fire rose in the air all around the house, lighting up the treetops to the north and east of the house. The fire lit up the interior of the truck, and it lit up Luther's staring eyes.

"No!" she screamed. Then she was sobbing.

"Stay in the car, Tris."

"Our cottage! All our stuff!" She was screaming and beating on his arm as he jammed the key into the ignition.

The engine rumbled into life and they started rolling. Dante yelped and jumped up in her lap, and she squeezed him in her arms. She saw Luther's eyes locked on the figure in the orchard. Luther took the truck back out along the lane, keeping even with the attacker, who was a hundred feet off to their left in the orchard, walking towards the road.

"This damn well changes things," Luther said.

"What am I going to tell my brother?"

"Forget your brother. Be glad you and I weren't in there."

She stared. He was right. Max had just tried to kill her. She had thought about leaving Dante in the house, too, while they went out for dinner and then, again, when they got back and decided to stay in the truck. She had come that close to losing Dante.

"What are you going to do?" she asked.

"I don't know," he said. He handed her his phone. "You'd better call the fire department. No, wait." He gunned the engine and the truck leapt forward. He took the turn without braking. They fishtailed on the asphalt, then the truck righted itself. The man in black was running across the road. For a fraction of a second she saw the man's face full in the truck's headlights.

"It's Brainard," she cried. "His name is Brainard something. He works at TSR. I knew it. I knew it!"

The man was easily going to make it. He ran in front of their lights like a spooked deer and dove into the grass by the side of the road. He dashed off into the trees while they skidded to a stop. They sat for a minute, the dust of the road catching up with them in a cloud, watching his dark form vanish into the darkness behind the trees.

"It doesn't matter if he gets away. I know who he is."

"Now you can call the fire department," Luther said. He shifted into park and turned off the engine. "We've still got the dog, right?"

Dork

"Alison, come and have a look." Todd hardly dared blink, in case the image on his screen morphed into something else, the way things sometimes did on the internet.

She studied the screen over his shoulder, then said, "Those are your phones."

It was the Motorola DynaTAC 8000x, the Sony CM-H33 Mars Bar phone from 1993, and the Ericsson T28 flip-phone from 1999. The bidding for all three together was up to eighty dollars. The bidding deadline was Saturday at midnight. "Such a brazen thing," Alison went on.

"The question is, what do I do?"

"Call the police, dumbhead. They can go after those crooks."

"I am not a dumbhead. I happen to think the police will laugh at me. I happen to think they have other things to do than chase down some punks who are selling my phones on eBay. Besides, your sister is chasing after them, too."

"All right, you don't have to yell. But if you don't do something by Saturday, somebody's going to pick them up for eighty bucks."

"I could always bid."

She threw up her hands and stormed out of the room. Then she came back. "Only a real dork would pay good money for his own stolen property. What are you going to do, buy them *all* back at auction prices? Pay for every last one of them twice? Contact eBay and tell them the phones were stolen. This probably happens all the time. They probably have a whole department for dealing with cases like this. Send them your catalog and let them know about this page, here." She pointed at the screen.

He clenched his teeth. She was right, as usual. But she didn't have to call him a dork.

Broken Heart

Ginger lived twenty miles south, just inside the Chicago city limits, in a condo on the lake, paid naturally on his coin. Most of the signs in this neighborhood were in Spanish. Max Vinyl wouldn't think of parking the T-bird on the street here, nor, for that matter, anywhere in the city. Ginger had offered him the extra space in her underground garage.

He planted himself on her white couch to relax while she worked in the kitchen. The strong odor of fresh garlic sautéing in olive oil, mixed with her old standard orangey perfume that he used to love, teased and tickled his nose. The couch was situated directly across from her smallish picture window with its narrow-angle view out on the lake. Looking east, you couldn't see the sun setting, but it was just as fine to see the late afternoon light transforming itself to that gradually waning misty light of the evening. He gazed at the sailboats far out on the water, all tipped at the same angle.

"You make yourself comfortable over there, Max," his ex-wife called. "I just have to get this sauce going. Then I want to take a closer look at your injuries."

He sipped the Chablis she had poured. Cold and fruity, it puckered him up like lemon juice. It tasted as if she'd left it uncorked for a week. He set it on the coffee table. She hadn't put out any crackers or pretzels. *Okay, take it easy*, he thought. *She'll bring the crackers.*

But how could he take it easy? The entire network had gone down. He'd received an express envelope stuffed with his own briefs reduced to scraps. He'd been blinded and slashed in a pepper spray attack. All unprovoked. All this havoc created by one disgruntled Brazilian stripper with a serious grudge.

His mind kept coming back to Tris's green eyes . . . and that cute dark blond hair, the way it curled around the plastic stem of the headset . . . and those pyjamas all unbuttoned . . . and that tiny bottom, so sweet and light. Never again would he have the pleasure of feeling that bottom on his lap. Sad as it was, no chance of *that* ever happening again.

Ginger came around the couch and sat down, leaving a little space between them. He saw her studying his scratches. Close up, her eyes looked tired and irritated. The skin around her eyes was home to such a complex little world of wrinkles, they couldn't be covered up with mere makeup. When she unbuttoned his shirt, he didn't resist. One of the scratches went right down his neck. She had to follow it to its source.

"Mommy's going to take care of you. There, there, lie down now." She draped his shirt over a chair. When she came back a minute later, she had a vanity bag. "This is where I keep all my potions. Goodness, you did have quite a fight with that cat, didn't you?"

"Mmmmm." The first dollop of cream went to a puncture on his chest. The cream was cold, but her fingers were hot. Not warm, *hot*, as if she had been sautéing them a minute ago instead of some herbs. Ginger's fingers were always hot. She was hot-blooded. Her hot fingers and the icy healing lotion swirled around on his skin, blurring momentarily the sharp edges of those images of all the extraordinary troubles of the day. *The network crash . . . the cut-up fragments of his briefs . . . those bargain-priced roses scattered across Tris's front porch.*

"So, was this a *normal* cat or . . . some kind of escaped mountain lion?" she asked.

"It actually wasn't a cat."

He labored to stay alert. With her hot fingers working the lotion into his scratches, and at the same time her other hand lightly going back and forth over an uninjured part of his chest, it was proving difficult. Was there any reason not to tell Ginger about Tris? Did it matter? He was free to hook up with any woman he pleased. She'd had boyfriends since the divorce, just as he'd had girlfriends, and she had told him about them. Ginger would have liked more money, that was clear enough. It was just as clear she wasn't going to get more. It was like a little game they played, him paying late, her threatening. She wouldn't fuss about Tris.

"Not a cat? Well, how did you go and get so many terrible scratches? On your face and your arms and even your chest?"

"It was actually a bouquet of roses. The thorns on the roses." It came out thickly.

"A bouquet? Max, I don't understand."

He sat up to clear his head. Falling asleep on Ginger's couch was no way to start the evening. Besides, he was so hungry his stomach was rumbling. Between covering incomings and worrying about the network crash he'd forgotten to eat lunch.

"I fell in an awkward way, you see. On the roses." He told her then about the receptionist, Tris, breaking up with him, his attempt to reconcile by bringing the huge bouquet of roses, and the pepper spray attack. Ginger had stopped applying the cream to the scratches on his face, so that he could tell the story. Her mouth formed a giant unbelieving O as she listened.

"That sounds like one mighty ungrateful woman," Ginger said. "Just imagine. A man brings her a bouquet of ten dozen roses, she attacks him with pepper spray."

Like some *rapist*, he thought. That was who you used pepper spray on. No one knew better than Ginger that he was no rapist, for Chrissake. That was what was so wrong about Tris's attack; it was so all out of proportion. That she should yell at him maybe, OK. But pepper spray? She was sick.

"How many times in your life does a man bring you ten dozen roses?" Ginger said.

"Not many."

"And you really don't know what brought this on? What did she say? I mean, there must have been *something* that ticked her off."

"Yes, only I honestly don't know what it was." He wasn't about to tell Ginger that Tris had turned out to be an environmentalist nut who had felt personally betrayed when she found out he wasn't some goody-two-shoes recycler. It wasn't clear whose side Ginger would come down on. He was happy to have her back on his side for tonight, at least.

After applying her magic cooling ointment she put his shirt back on and buttoned it up for him. They sat at her table and ate and, as he talked and she talked, he thought back to when they had been married. For tonight, at least, Ginger's mindless chatter didn't bother him so much the way it used to.

How Furey had laughed as they prepared the divorce. *"She talks too much,"* Furey had said, mimicking him. "I wonder what the judge is going to say to that. Did you ever think what it would do to the divorce rate if that *were* grounds for divorce, Max?" Ha, ha, ha, Furey could laugh, bachelor that he was. No man could ever step into another man's shoes. After a day like this, Max would have gladly stepped into *any* other man's shoes.

But that was the problem. She talked too damn much. Ginger went on and on so incessantly that after a while it became impossible to think, impossible to organize your own thinking. She invaded your brain with her chatter and it multiplied like a fast-spreading virus, crowding out every thought that was your own. You became a zombie that said things like, "Yes, Ginger. Okay, Baby. Yes, Sugar." You were mentally enslaved.

Later they were in bed. "I hope we didn't open up any of those wounds," Ginger said. She still liked to have one cigarette in bed after sex, it seemed, along with a tiny glass of expensive brandy that she set out for herself beforehand. Furey hadn't considered her one-cigarette-a-night habit grounds for divorce, either, even though it always left Max congested.

"I'm fine," Max said. "It was fine."

"Now don't start getting pensive on me. I want you to relax. You're not here to make life-decisions."

"Well, what am I here for?"

"You're here because your girlfriend dropped you. You're walking around with a broken heart, poor man."

He looked at her. "You really think so? I mean, you can really see it?"

"Call it bruised. Severely bruised. Sure, a woman sees these things. You must've really fallen for this girl. You men always think you're so cool and tough. But I really don't see how you could get too worked up about a girl that attacks you with pepper spray. I suppose she's the one who did that job on your briefs, too."

"Sick, isn't it? I've had one hell of a week."

"I'll say. I mean, I'll admit it, I was angry. But I never did anything to get revenge. What would be the point?"

"You've got more perspective. After all, I was your fourth husband."

"My third, Max, honestly. But I'm also ten years older. I could see it wasn't going to work between us, after those first couple of years. So why fight it?"

"You fought well enough in court, I'll say that for you."

She batted her eyelashes. "A girl has to live, Max. You wanted out, you owed me something for the chance I took on you."

"I accept that."

"You don't want me standing on some street corner, do you? Goodness gracious."

"Of course not."

"Only thing is, Max, we have to work on your punctuality. I mean with the payments."

"I know, Baby."

"Mommy has to pay her monthly condo assessments, you know. Mommy has to eat."

When she said *Mommy*, it was as if she was tickling him. It made him feel snug and warm all over.

That orangey perfume took him back to sweaty summer nights in high school. Back to a girl who had come long before Ginger. Even better than her name or her face, he remembered pressing against her on the dance floor at a Homecoming dance. Her sheer dress, and the slip she wore underneath. They had gone outside to cool off and to neck. That orangey perfume had clung to him for days afterwards. It had become unalterably associated with that first primitive groping and dancing, dancing and longing. That perfume had been burned into his memory. The girl must have bathed in it. That first yawning hormonal hunger. Under the strobing disco lights, in the sweaty dance hall, dancing to Diana Ross's "Love Hangover" . . .

And then, fifteen years later, Ginger wearing that same perfume, as if sent to him by destiny, as if destiny itself had programmed those fifteen-year-old olfactory impressions to be stirred up again in his brain, those bewitching smell memories from his high school days. A switch left on in his brain. The orangey perfume released hormones into his system. He didn't need scientific research to tell him how it worked. He had a sensitive nose anyway. Different woman, same perfume. The floodgates opened in his veins the moment he smelled that perfume. The erection followed, a superhero hard-on. With Ginger wearing that perfume he had lost his head. How else could you explain marrying a twice-divorced forty-two-year-old when you yourself were thirty-two?

He had never revealed to her that it was her perfume that had driven him, like a man possessed, into her arms. He had only first realized it himself when the phenomenon had started its metamorphosis. Her chatter had worn down his nerves by the end of the first year. Asking her to be quiet for a while and let him think had never worked. He had timed her. She could be silent for upwards of fifteen, even twenty seconds. But she could not stand the silences. The next conversational elements would be forming: A question, *a propos* of nothing. A comment. A new topic. And the horses would be out of the gates.

He had started looking for escape. Alcohol had dimmed his awareness of her and made her easier to ignore, but alcohol had drawbacks. Car collectors had no business drinking; how did you get the car home? Anyway, he hated the feeling of losing control over his muscles. It made him queasy. He wasn't comfortable drinking so much that it dimmed his awareness of her, because it dimmed his awareness of everything else as well.

He had tried spending far more time at work than a newly married man should. This had helped until Ginger started showing up at TSR. She would get bored sitting at home. No one to talk to. So she would come to work and start chatting with all his employees. They had loved her. The company had been smaller then, more like a family. Nothing made him crazier. Somehow she had figured out this would get him to turn off his computer and stop for the day.

He had even taken up golf one summer before he realized there was a far simpler way.

The first woman Ginger had caught him with, in their own bed, in the house on the lake, was the older sister of one of the programmers at TSR. She had lived right in Waukegan and was a waitress at the Olive Garden, which was where he had met her. Sheila Slade. He had liked Sheila Slade's dimples and her dark brown eyes and the erect way she walked. With those dark eyes she probably had some old Spanish conquistador in her family tree.

When Ginger had walked into the bedroom that afternoon, having sensed something wrong in the house, they had already finished having sex twice like absolute animals. They had gone at each other as if neither had had sex for the last year. They were lying on their sides, facing each other, dozing. He had heard Ginger coming up the stairs, calling ahead, "Max? Max, is that you? Honey, are you ill?" His heart had been going like a triphammer as he heard her steps approaching. Sheila Slade, sleep-deprived due to double shifts at her waitressing job, had been rudely jolted out of deep REM sleep by the sound of Ginger shrieking.

He had really liked Sheila Slade, so it had not been difficult confessing to Ginger that he was in love with her and had decided to run away with her. He had made a point of taking Ginger to the Olive Garden to make sure that she saw his lover again, ignoring the fact that Sheila had refused to speak to him again. Many times he had tried to arrange another afternoon siesta with her. Finally Sheila Slade had quit her job and moved to Texas to make him stop calling.

Next, he had taken up with a girl he had known in college who happened to settle in Waukegan. They had run into each other at the Subway sandwich shop on Main Street. It had been like one of those old TV scenes:

"Max? Max Vinyl?"

"Oh my God. Donna Knox."

"Donna Panagakis now, Max. Divorced. Lost the man but kept the name. But how are you? What are you doing here?"

"Got my own business. Right here in Waukegan. What about you?"

It had been an easy matter to get Donna Panagakis over to the house. He remembered peeling off her top in front of his cathedral window, waves crashing on the beach a hundred feet away, the afternoon sunlight glinting off ten thousand wavelets. When Ginger had waltzed in they had been having sex on the shag carpeting in front of the window.

Donna Panagakis had not been pleased. He didn't remember all the positively evil names she had called him in front of Ginger, while putting on her clothes again, dressing slowly and deliberately, so as to deliver the longest, most high-pitched, most utterly hysterical female invective imaginable. Somehow the tone of her voice had stuck in his mind. She had accused him of hiding the fact that he was married, this he remembered. Which of course he had been forced to do. How else were you supposed to get a nice girl like Donna Panagakis to go home with you?

There had followed Serious Discussions with Ginger, which had ultimately led to the desired outcome, and now, years later, well and truly divorced, but jilted and left heartbroken and also under attack from his Brazilian jungle woman, here he was in Ginger's bed again. He sighed, reliving these dreary experiences. The perfume that had become an allergen in the confines of his marriage now surrounded and suffocated and excited him once again. Had he really just had sex with his ex-wife? How low could a man go?

How fine it would be to see Sheila Slade again. He would have to look her up in Texas, see if she would consider coming back, now that he really was single. How could he have forgotten about her? *Beautiful Spanish-eyed Sheila Slade . . .*

"I must confess," Ginger said now. "I did ask them to serve on you this week."

He sat up in bed. "You did what?"

"You're four months behind, Max. It didn't just slip your mind. You stopped paying my alimony. I can't accept that. I have rights."

"I know you do, of course you do. It's just that with these Koreans in town and so much going on at the moment I wouldn't want to be served. You know, it would look kind of . . . low class."

"I know what you mean. It's just that . . . well, you know Ricardo. I can't go to Ricardo and tell him that I talked to you and you promised to give me a big check next week. It just doesn't work like that with Ricardo. He doesn't trust you the way I do."

"I know, I know."

"I've got another idea, Max. Try this on for size. I don't know how your account is doing at the moment. But why don't you write me one check for your arrears," she smiled, "for the last four months. We put tomorrow's date on the check. I go and deposit it tomorrow. And next week you write me a check for July, just for one month. And I cash that next week whenever I get it. And then each month, once a month, you send me a check, just like a good boy?"

He felt his head bobbing in agreement. Why not, in fact? Then at least he would have Ginger off his case. His account was brimming. That wasn't the problem; he just didn't like doling it out to Ginger. But a formidable mountain of money was also on the way from the Koreans. So why not?

He slipped out of bed and felt in his jacket pocket for his checkbook. To write it he got back in bed, under the covers. It felt damned sexy to be writing a check stark naked. Ginger stayed put. He let her watch him, felt her eyes revisiting his scratches, now healing with the healing power of the lotion applied by her hot fingers. He signed the check, tore it out of the checkbook and handed it to her.

She read the amount, a smile plastered on her lips. Four months' worth of payments in one check. A happy day for Ginger. But the smile turned to a frown. "For goodness sake, Max, did you really have to write, 'for sexual favors'?"

Natural Causes

Greta Vinyl lay in the clinic bed, eyes wide open, staring at the ceiling, breathing hard, the air catching on something in her dry throat so that it whistled slightly. Her mouth stayed open. Her lips were dry. When he looked in her mouth he saw her tongue had dried, too. Her tongue looked like a piece of dried apricot. Each breath she took coated it over with a new layer of dryness. He touched her lips with the handkerchief he had wetted at the sink. At least he could prevent the lips from cracking.

"Your eyes opened, darling. But you can't see me, can you?"

He held her hand with his other hand, still brushing her lips with the handkerchief, bent close over her. But her fingers didn't press back. Her eyes were open, but blank. Yet they had opened, strangely enough, after many days closed.

"What do you see, darling? Do you see the other side?"

In a brochure he had read that it could happen like this. The eyes opened, the breathing became raspy, the body temperature went up and down like a yo-yo.

Of course, she didn't answer.

With his finger he spread a dot of Vaseline on her lips, just in case. Just in case she still had any pain, any discomfort. He couldn't reach in and pull out the tumor, like you pulled a weed. Not even the surgeons had been able to do that. You couldn't do anything really, except talk to her, be there with her. She looked more beautiful with her eyes open. The eyes he had looked into for more than fifty years.

"You look peaceful, Greta," he said softly. He sank back into his chair, wondering why he had said *peaceful* when what he had meant to say was *beautiful*. For she was beautiful. The image he carried in his mind was beautiful, the girl he had fallen in love with decades before – so young and quick on her feet, her hair so soft and shiny, her eyes so big and searching, her full lips so hungry for his kisses, her laugh like river water passing over rocks. It was a long way from that to the state she was in now, eyes open yet unable to answer him, unable even to lick her lips. The mind substituted one image for another so effortlessly. And yet it wasn't that he craved youthful beauty or soft skin, God forbid. It was just that who she was in his mind was the sum total of *all* the images he had ever registered of her: all the talks, all the loving, all the living and all the laughing, but also all the crying your brains out when your only daughter has died, that too, and all the arguments and recriminations that came after it.

He had something in his hand and realized he hadn't capped the Vaseline yet. He set the tube on the table. Now where had he put the cap? It wasn't on her bedside table. He stood and turned and let his eyes roam over the white sheet under which her legs lay. White on white, hard to see. But the cap wasn't in the covers. A small white, rounded, screw-on cap. He bent to look on the floor. Maybe he had let it fall and it had rolled under the bed. The greenish hospital linoleum, cleaned every day with a bucket of Lysol and warm water.

A nurse came smiling into the room. A little knock, and they slid right in the room, these nurses, their eyes checking around. This one was from Nigeria.

"Hello, Gordon. How's she doing?"

"Hello, Gladys. She's . . . it's wonderful. She opened her eyes. It was about half an hour ago."

The nurse was on the other side of the bed now, bent over Greta. Her smile had changed to a concentrated look. She got out a stethoscope and put it to Greta's chest. Her eyes flicked up to meet his gaze.

"Well, she's gone now, Gordon."

"She's . . .?"

"She's finally resting now."

"You mean she's dead?"

"I'm getting no heartbeat. No breathing."

He took in Greta's staring eyes, her bony unmoving form, her gaping mouth. He hadn't noticed when the raspy breathing stopped. How could he not have noticed?

Greta dead. He got up and went to her. Those staring eyes. No more raspy breath. No more of that unbearable dryness.

It must have just happened. One minute ago, he thought. She had taken her last breath while he searched for the Vaseline cap. Now she was on her way somewhere, or maybe she was already there, wherever it was people went to when their heart and their breathing and their dreams and memories ended, and also all their conflicts.

"You know, she wanted to go," the Nigerian nurse said. She had her arm around his shoulders. She was guiding him to a chair. "She told me she was ready."

"It's for the best," he agreed.

But you're alone now.

"You just sit right down here. I'm going to make you a cup of tea."

Well, you've been alone for months, haven't you?

Yes and no. At least you had someone to talk to, even if she didn't answer. Couldn't answer.

You could at least talk. You could pretend to hope for an answer.

And there were times when she answered. With a squeeze of the hand.

Or you imagined that she was answering. What she would answer.

But now you're alone, yes, truly, you old sod.

"Gordon, you like some sugar in your tea?"

All this . . . apparatus will be taken away. Her body cremated. A funeral.

You have to get moving, organize things.

"There you are, Gordon. Can I leave you here a moment while I go see about some things? You're happy to be alone with her a minute, aren't you?"

"I'll be right here, yes."

She organized everything for you a year ago. You have the card, with the number to call. You already paid for the funeral, the cremation, the refreshments.

Typical Greta. She took care of everything. She made you pay a year in advance so that you wouldn't have to think about it now, the moment it happened.

You don't want to have to run around taking care of things like that, she said.

Her voice . . . there it was.

Yes, go on, Greta, go on!

You'll have enough to do, you know – just letting everyone know. Get others to help you. Call up a few people and ask them to call all the others for you. People do that, when someone dies. Don't try to do it all yourself.

That night he made five calls.

Tent

"I don't sleep with boys I've only known for ten hours," Annie said. "I wanted you to know that about me." The moon lit up the side of Bob Olson's yellow tent like a modern art painting. He had driven her back up to TSR to pick up her car, but then they had ended up in his tent.

"You invited yourself. Let's just make that detail clear."

"I did not invite myself. I merely suggested that it might be advisable to move your tent down closer to the water."

"Thanks for the help, by the way."

"Not a problem. Are you really planning to sleep here?"

In the dimness she thought she saw him shrug. Maybe he didn't care where he slept. For a while she just sat breathing and thinking and listening to the noises outside. An owl hooted. Strange to hear one so close to the lake. The crickets and cicadas and other summer insects kept up a high-pitched whine that was always there in the background. The rhythmic sound of wavelets lapping against the shore, not more than a hundred feet away, calmed her frayed nerves.

"Tomorrow I have to get those phones back," she said, half thinking aloud.

"What phones?"

She looked at him. She realized she hadn't told him a thing about what she was doing here. She explained about the GPS, and the two bruisers who had beaten up the busboy at the Domino, then stolen Todd's cell phone collection, and her following them up here and figuring out they worked here, and then starting work here herself. Bob raised himself on one elbow.

"You amaze me. Here I thought maybe I was a little crazy. Well, who's the crazy one here, the guy with the tent and the lost Thinkpad? Or the girl who actually goes and starts working a nine-to-five job in the hope of recovering a collection of cell phones . . . man alive."

"It's partly the phones, but it's also her safety. I can't stand the thought of those guys breaking into my sister's place and trashing it. She's lucky she wasn't there."

"OK, but what're you planning to do once you find them? I mean, come on. Two guys against you. You don't really think . . ."

She waited, but he let the question trail off. "I don't know. I guess I just thought I would tell them what lowdown scum they are, something like that."

Clearly she hadn't given it enough thought. If the guys were capable of beating up that busboy in a public place, and then breaking into Alison's apartment in broad daylight, they would be no less shy about hurting her. Maybe she should just concentrate on the phones. That was something definable.

"Yeah, but . . . I mean, don't you have anything better to do?" Bob Olson asked.

She stared at him. This question caught her by surprise. Maybe because of who it was coming from. She didn't even know Olson, and here he was putting her right in that corner she was normally so good at keeping herself out of.

Her mother would say she could be doing something more . . . productive. She could be contacting her friends at Great Lakes Naval Base, networking, seeing if there were any opportunities there. She could fly helicopters, fix radar, train incoming recruits. Or she could go and find a job in the private sector – a real job, something that would challenge her brain. Thanks to army payouts she didn't need the money. She wouldn't need money for a long time, especially living the way she was living.

But how can you go back to work when you don't know what you want to do?

"Something better, like for example?"

"You're a returning war vet, right?" Bob Olson had his glasses back on now. "So what were you doing before you went to Iraq?"

She thought back. Odd to think how hard it was to retrieve that information from her brain, on demand. Then, all at once, there it was . . . and how completely bizarre. "I was a teacher. Primary school. Third grade."

"You went from teaching math and reading to eight year olds to flying attack helicopters?"

"That's about right. So draw me a line between those two points, and now extend the line. What's the next stop in my life?"

He laughed. "Hell if I know."

He was a good looking man, now that she looked at him across the dim light of the tent. There were men who looked good with no hair. She decided Olson, with his big round eyes, was one of them. It brought her back to another time, another place, a place, like this, of sand and heat and combat. She saw Michael's eyes again, dark as coals, his eyes blazing with passion as they made love in her room. She hadn't felt that passion in such a long time. Then, in her mind, Michael's eyes were closed again. She couldn't see them anymore. She tried to see them, but they wouldn't open, wouldn't let her in.

Olson was sitting there with a guitar across his lap, the long end of it sticking right into the tent wall. She hadn't seen the guitar. It must have been hidden in his sleeping bag. His fingers played a few notes, moving over the strings. He was just experimenting with some combinations, warming up. His fingers knew their way up and down the strings. He was good. She noticed now what long, slender fingers Olson had.

"Been playing for a long time?"

She thought she recognized the beginning of a song, but then the notes went in a different direction, as if he might be considering another idea. He repeated the same line, and then once again, a bass line and a melody on the higher strings at the same time. It sounded familiar, but she couldn't say what song it was.

"Ten years, give or take a few," Olson said. He hummed along with the song. He could intersperse chords with a complicated line of notes. Sometimes his humming would coalesce into a word or a string of words, then revert to an accompanying sound that came from somewhere deep in his chest. She found herself mesmerized, and when he started singing she hardly knew exactly when the song had begun or what it was about. He sang with a strange accent, softly, half under his breath, and she didn't understand half the words. Something to do with an Irish fighter.

It was flattering, frankly, to be sitting in a tent serenaded by a man. It was romantic. Was Olson interested in her? Or was he just releasing the stress he felt because of the lost laptop? Probably he sat in his tent every weekend at one of those campgrounds and played his guitar for someone. The fact was he wasn't kicking her out, and he was singing a pretty song, and there was something about Olson that you had to admire. She decided to sit and listen and just let it happen and not worry.

When she had come home from the military, having nobody to go home to, and no plan and nowhere else to go, she had gone to live in her parents' house. They lived in a suburb filled with wide, tree-shaded streets and big houses, only six or seven houses to a block. The really dumb thing was she had also made no plan for her mind, coming home. Her mind had still been stuck in a strange zone of army acronyms and violence and heavy equipment and male camaraderie and constant boredom, all extended, in her worst moments, to a feeling bordering on insanity.

At night, suddenly back home and lying in bed in her old childhood bedroom, she had stared for a long time out the window at the front yard, the trees, the houses across the street. Ten minutes could go by before a car passed. Most nights an elderly neighbor she had always known as Mrs. Adolfson appeared around ten-thirty, her giant Schnauzer straining at the leash. Apart from her, no one seemed to walk on the street at all, ever. Annie would watch as lights flicked off in the houses across the street, one after another. People lived in there, but you didn't see them.

The quiet of this tranquil suburban place weighed on her. It was too quiet. Like a tremendous weight settling on every cell of her body, there, under the covers, pinning her, paralyzing her. She had trouble breathing under that weight. She couldn't move. All she could control now was her eyes. She opened and closed them, blinked more quickly, but the room was just as inky dark either way. She couldn't get up, couldn't move, couldn't see, couldn't breathe. The weight pinned her to the bed.

That was when the crying had started. What was happening to her? She was afraid. It only happened in bed. She started to dread sleeping. She started sleeping on the floor beside her bed, rolled up in her covers on the carpeting. But that same massive weight always found her, no matter where she lay, trying to sleep.

You couldn't move a muscle, you couldn't see a thing; silence and darkness swallowed you up. Going to bed was like getting into a coffin and shutting the lid. She went to bed later and later, sometimes staying up till first light, then sleeping till lunchtime. Even then the terrible weight found her. Sleep became an agony. She would wake in a sweat, pinned to the bed, still in her clothes, tears filling her eyes.

"When are you going to look up your old friends?" her mother had asked.

"Soon."

"See what people are up to. You could go and stay with your sister in the city. Not that I want you out of here."

"I know, Mom."

"It's just that you're grieving too long, Annie. You're too young to go on and on like this. Nobody gets anything from it. Not Michael. Not you. Not anyone else."

"I'm way beyond grieving, Mom. Don't you think I know? I can't help it. Do you think I want to feel this way?"

She had started driving around the suburbs and the city, just to get out of the house and drive around, see what all there was in this city, maybe to get a feeling for it, in the hope of finding a place for herself in it. It was as if she were new to the city, even though she had grown up here. She would get on a street, at the wheel of her little silver Honda, and just keep heading north, all the way up close to the Wisconsin state line, or just keep heading east, all the way to the Lake Michigan shoreline. Over three hundred miles a day. After a week of driving, she bought a special giant street map to hang on her wall at home. Most streets were laid out in a grid, north-south streets intersecting with east-west ones, clear from the Wisconsin line all the way to where the corn fields started south of the southern suburbs.

She passed a hundred different strip malls, each with its ice cream shop, its fast food, its photocopies and business cards, its muffler repair, its tandoori. Her brain swam at the sight of more tanning salons, convenience stores, liquor stores, trophy and engraving stores, coin and stamp collecting shops, bridal salons, video rental stores, juice and coffee and yogurt shops, jewelry stores, tire worlds, supermarkets for electronics, for furniture, for bathroom fixtures, picture frames, sewing and craft supplies, cut flowers, candy, books, baby clothes, antiques, cell phones, office supplies or toys.

On every larger corner, where vast mall parking lots opened up like a North American pampa, you would find a Wal-Mart or a K-Mart or a Target or a Home Depot. If you drove north on La Grange road you passed a Baker's Square Restaurant, a Denny's, an Olive Garden, a McDonald's, a Burger King, a Starbuck's and a Wendy's. Two miles farther on you passed the exact same seven restaurants.

The names of the streets changed. You were two miles north of where you had been. You were five minutes older than before. But the signs and logos and colors were just the same as that spot two miles back. It was as if you had not moved. Time had stood still. You drove another two miles north, and another, and another, and you saw the same images repeating anywhere you went, north, east, south or west as far as you went, like an infinite mathematical series.

The country had changed while she was away. Or the country had changed more gradually, without her noticing, and *she* had changed. Maybe she just hadn't noticed these things before. Now she was home again and surveying all she had supposedly fought for.

Suddenly the road would take you through a forest, either on one side or on both sides of the street. She loved the massive oak trees that grew in these patches of forest, like a reminder of a forgotten past. The original endless forest had obviously been cut down to make space for the highways and the malls and the vast parking lots that covered the land. These stretches of forest preserve stood like a last barrier, as if holding back the avalanche of chain restaurants and mall parking. It would be over as quick as it started, and you'd be back in the midst of restaurants and gas stations and factories, almost as if the forest hadn't been real.

A look at the city map showed that a nearly continuous strip of forest ran from north to south through the western edge of the city, skirting the Des Plaines River, and she started planning her drives so she would crisscross it at different points. Sometimes from her car she even caught a glimpse of the river.

One day she stopped by the side of the road, ignoring the honks of the drivers forced to go around her, to walk into the forest on her own two feet and stand in the shadow of one of these oaks. She remembered them from her childhood, but only living in an arid land for four years had taught her to really see them. The ordinary oak tree – that gnarly white-gray bark, twisted in on itself, wrinkled and knotted and furiously dead-ending before curling around to encase more of the steel-hard, nail-bending interior trunk. Or those massive, inwardly-curling, infinitely-forking branches that seemed to alternate equally between skyward and earthward ambitions.

From the road, driving past, the forest had been a blurry jumbled picture of bare trees and branches and dead leaves. Once she stood in it, motionless, it opened up magically before her in three dimensions. Standing water everywhere, half-rotted logs and remnants of fallen trees, layers of mud covered in dead leaves from past years. Fallen branches all over the ground and sticking up to trip you as you walked through, inviting you to come and explore. No restaurants, no people, no path – just a thin swath of wonderful wilderness right in the shadow of the airport.

She had taken over the vacant cabin, broken in, then painted the exterior dark green and planted a flagpole out front with an American flag. If anyone ever challenged her, she would point out her efforts at sprucing up the place. The electricity worked fine, and she figured someone would notice sooner or later that some juice was running. Then again, the small fridge, plus a reading lamp and stove that got used once every two or three days for a half hour, with what little she cooked, wouldn't exactly make the dials spin. After two full months it still hadn't gotten anyone's attention.

Inside, the cabin had been completely empty except for a card table, two sturdy wooden chairs that reminded her of something from her old high school, and a big, old clothes cabinet with space for hanging things up as well as six drawers.

She had opened all the windows, scrubbed every surface from top to bottom with cleanser and disinfectant. Toilet and shower both worked. She ran the water in the sink for twenty minutes, then took a drink. When she had not developed any rash or fever after three days, she decided it was safe to drink.

From here she had announced herself to old friends, through a series of emails, and she had found, with increasing astonishment, that while some part of her felt warm and happy at seeing these people again from her past, she had herself changed so much from the Annie Ogden she had once been, she hardly knew what to talk about. Talking about the war, and about life in the war zone, was not easy and in most cases not possible. This was only possible with other veterans.

With civilians who had stayed behind and had nothing to do with the war, it was like their lives had stayed in the same narrow orbits of jobs, relationships, parents, friends. It wasn't that they didn't know what they were talking about. Whether they were outraged by the war, or happy to see America kicking some ass, it didn't matter. It was more that they had not been touched by it, not even remotely. They got passionate talking about their relationships and jobs, the economy, politics. The war was a theoretical concept to them. It shocked her to find out that it bored people.

She didn't know if five minutes had passed or half an hour, sitting in this dimness while Olson played and sang. Maybe she was half-asleep. A loud rumbling, like the sound of an engine, suddenly jolted her back to reality. It was so loud it could have been ten feet from the tent. For a second she felt disoriented, even though she had not really been asleep. *Her helicopter warming up . . . time to suit up.* Then she snapped out of it. *You are back in America, in Illinois, in a northern suburb called Waukegan, in a tent on the beach with a man named Olson.*

The loud engine noise was still there. Not a helicopter engine, but not a car, either, something much bigger than a car. A diesel engine. What could make a sound like that on the beach? Was a bulldozer about to run them over?

Olson had put down his guitar. He stuck his head out the tent fly.

"Do you see anything?"

"Wait a minute. There's a boat coming out of a boathouse. Like a barge."

"What boat? What time is it?"

"One o'clock."

"Let me see." Olson maneuvered so that she could look out, too. She had to be careful not to kneel on his guitar. "Geez, look at that car. And what about those computers and stuff all piled up in a heap. What the hell is going on?"

"Where could they be going with all that stuff in the middle of the night?"

The barge was easing out of its slip, not fifty yards from where the tent was pitched. One small green light could be seen on its side, a small white light on the pilot house. The windows of the pilot house were dark, so it was impossible to see the faces of the person or people driving the boat.

"Rendez-vous on the lake, I guess."

"Excuse me?"

"I don't know, Annie. What do you think they're doing heaped with computers at one in the morning?"

"And a car."

"That can only mean one of two things. Either they're dumping this stuff in the lake, or they're offloading it on another boat."

"Those would seem to be the most likely explanations, yes."

"And you can think of another one?"

"Well, they could be bringing it to another location."

"What, like in Michigan?"

"Why not? Or Wisconsin? Wisconsin is only a few miles north of here."

"So what? It's not like they're crossing the iron curtain or something, if they go to Wisconsin. Why would you haul a bunch of old computers over the state line on a barge? You could just put them on a truck and get there a lot quicker and easier."

They watched the barge churn its way out into the lake for another minute before they ducked back into the tent. The barge could not be doing more than ten miles an hour.

"How many PCs you think there were on that barge?"

"They were piled pretty high," Olson said. "A barge like that probably has some space under the waterline, too. Three or four feet, I'd say."

"Yeah, that's another thing. Like, whenever you move to a different apartment you always have to dig out the original box with the original packing materials. That's how you move PCs and printers and stuff around, isn't it? So they don't get jostled and broken?"

"Good point."

"What we just saw looked more like a garbage heap. Everything just piled up on top of everything. Imagine the condition of the stuff at the bottom of the pile."

The sound of the rough motor had almost disappeared into the distance now. "Pretty clear. That stuff isn't going anywhere else. They must be dumping it in the lake."

"That can't be legal, can it?"

"I guess that's why they do it in the middle of the night."

She thought back to what Manny Rodriguez had said. Refurbish . . . recycle . . . export. Had he lied to her? If they were dumping computer trash in the lake, the whole setup was based on a lie. And no one did anything about it. They made money picking up the old computers. They made money reselling it on their website. The stuff they couldn't resell lay on the bottom of Lake Michigan, where the residual chemicals would leach into the water over decades.

"Yeah, in the middle of the night there's not much happening out on the lake. Do you really think that's what they're doing?"

"I can't get over the way the computer parts were all heaped up. Broken stuff that nobody's ever going to use anymore. Yeah, that's got to be it."

"Well, we can't let them go on with that, can we?" she said.

"What do you mean?"

"That's my lake out there. That's your lake."

"Drinking water for the city of Chicago comes from there, as you might have guessed. Pumping station a couple of miles out. Learned that today in my book. What's so funny?"

She stopped laughing. "I was just thinking. If they're really dumping toxic computer trash out there, they couldn't have picked a dumber place. We're, like, two miles from the biggest Navy base anywhere between the two coasts. I'm going to have to get on the horn with my buddies over there and see about an interdiction mission."

Bob sighed. "What if they had my Thinkpad on that barge?"

"All would be lost."

His brow bunched up with worry. "You don't really think . . . ?"

"Get serious, Bob. That slimy lawyer, Furey, has your Thinkpad. They're dumping trash out in the lake, not the good stuff. They're not stupid."

She lay for quite a while, listening for the motor of the barge, hearing only the seagulls and the other birds. It was creepy how quickly the lake swallowed up the sound. Before the barge had pulled out, the vibrations of its motor had made the earth shake under them.

Olson broke the silence. "So how are you going to get those phones back tomorrow? You still haven't told me."

"I'm going to do exactly what we did tonight."

"What, walk into their place and take them?"

"Have you got a better idea?"

ANCIENT RHYTHMS

The water moved the sand. The wind pushed the water, and the water pushed the sand against the land, under the water. It had been so before she lived, and before the ones before her had lived, and before them, for as long as her kind had existed.

It pushed the sand against the land in the same way, because the Earth's turning and the winds from northeast to southwest had not changed in all of time. Those things did not change, even if the water itself changed in elemental ways, rising in the great long glacier-gouged bowl that contained it, filled by the rivers and streams that flowed into it.

She cruised along the ripples in the sand that were created by the water disturbing the sand. The ripples extended out many miles from the dry land, under the water. She knew the entrances to all the rivers and streams all along hundreds of miles of shore, the Mud River and the Kalamazoo and the Chicago and the Calumet. She stayed far out from the dry land because the food was plentiful along the entire shelf, in the sand ripples, in the sand and under the sand, if she dredged it with her snout.

The ships that lay on the bottom had pulled men down and held them under the water until they were dead. Men could not live under the water just as her kind could not live out of it. There were the wrecks she had always known, all her years, ever since her earliest memory. Every five or ten years she came upon a new wreck, never smelt before. The men's eyes bulged and their hair swayed with the movement of the current. She nibbled on the men but the taste was foul, like eating garbage. She ate the flesh of the men despite the foulness because it was food and because her chief and only occupation was food and because any food was food and because she would have ceased to exist already in time long past if she had ever stopped because of the taste of it.

The big wrecks were concentrated in the northern end of the great water. Here in the southern end, where it was bigger but also much shallower, there were smaller wrecks, sometimes with only two or three men or with no men at all. She cruised around or through these billowing transparent obstacles on the bottom. They never resembled boats, the wrecks; it was more like a bent and broken collection of wooden planks, standing at queer angles on the bottom, one end planted in the sand, the whole crazy construction swaying in the current. The current pushed the sand and made it pile up around the wrecks where they were stuck in the sand. Around the wrecks she found special ripples where the sand had piled up, and many tasty critters living there.

There was one wreck, different from all other wrecks, she could neither go through nor go over. A new wreck, this one got bigger each time she went by. Years ago it had not existed. Now it went right up to the surface of the water, like the dry land, where the only water to move in was the water that flowed in the narrow rivers. To go around this wreck meant cruising some distance around, like a land form. It contained no men but many spicy smells, especially on the southwest side, where the water drifted off the wreck carrying the smells. She avoided that side. There was nothing there for her, no critters and no food, in spite of the sand piling up against the side of it, the sand that drifted against it with the movement of the water. The sand piled up on itself, starting at the bottom and all the way up the wreck, and it filled the all the cracks and holes, always working, always filling, one grain at a time, because the sand was carried by the water and the water was always moving.

Forest Ranger

A knock on the door roused Annie Ogden out of a vivid dream. She lay for a minute on her cot, trying to remember the dream and waiting to see if the knock would come again. Looked like morning already, judging by the degree of light in the cabin. She had driven back long after midnight, having spent two or three hours in Bob Olson's tent in Waukegan. Had she dreamed about spending that time with him? What was this feeling of longing deep in her gut? She had felt it last night. This feeling should not be there. Olson wasn't her type.

"Open up in there. I know you're in there." A man's voice. Shouting. The knocking came again, more insistently.

"Good morning. Who's there?" she called through the door. She pulled on a pair of jeans and a t-shirt.

"Cook County Forest Preserve," the man said. "Name's Scott Dempsey. Dammit, I want to know why my key won't unlock this door."

She opened the door. The man in her doorway stood tall and a bit bent in the shoulders. He stood there staring as if he had never seen blond hair before. His skin was weathered and sun-darkened, like a man who spent a lot of time out of doors. His dark kinky hair, on the long side, possibly dyed, looked like something out of a time capsule. He could have been something under forty or something over fifty. Something told her it was the latter. His uniform looked official enough, as did the huge ring of keys hanging from his belt. A radio squawked something. He quickly reached down and switched it off.

So this was the day she had been waiting for.

"Come on in. Coffee?"

Scott Dempsey stayed rooted to the threshold, arms dangling at his sides, eyes glued to her. She left him standing there, padded barefoot over to the stove, and filled a saucepan with water.

"Well, aren't you going to come in? I've got two chairs."

"Let me guess. You're that silver Honda I keep seeing in the east lot?"

A quarter mile walking through the woods brought you to a parking lot, where there was an access road to the Forest Preserve. "Sure am," she said.

"I've seen it a few times. And I saw the flag out front, here." He turned to stare at the American flag she had put up. Then he turned back. He still hadn't moved off the threshold. "Didn't think much of it. Flag goes in, they don't send out a bulletin, you know. What the hell are you doing, here, anyway?"

"My name is Annie Ogden," she said. "Like Ogden Avenue? I thought these woods here needed a caretaker. I don't need much space or anything. This cabin was just right. If you want, I'll pay rent. I don't mind."

He took a step inside. Evidently a person who was able to speak English and willing to pay rent could win his trust. "So you just . . . decided? Like that? To move in? Without asking anyone?"

"I looked for you," she said. "I looked and looked for people, all up and down the woods. You know, you're the first official person I've ever seen out here."

"How long have you been squatting, if you don't mind my asking?"

"Couple of months."

"Two months?" His eyebrows bunched together in a look of disbelief.

"Maybe a little longer. I'm not really keeping track. I mean, we can call it the first of April if that's important to you. I got home around the twentieth of March, so I guess it must've been early April when I found this place. There was quite a bit of flooding."

The ranger smiled for the first time. "That's an understatement. This whole end of the preserve was under water."

"Except for this cabin. Does the river do that every year?"

"Most every year. Some years more than others. It's part of the natural order, here, even if it's inconvenient for city folks."

"This cabin was high and dry."

"I suppose. I didn't come back to this end till a couple of weeks ago. It never occurred to me we would have someone slogging through the swamp to come in here and squat."

She got up to check the water. "I wish you would stop calling it 'squatting.' I mean, I did clean the place up, fix a broken window, paint the whole exterior, and put up the flag."

"Well, you're getting free rent, aren't you?"

"Yes, but I think a squatter is someone who wouldn't do any work. They break into a place and barricade the door. They don't fix it up. I came in and made this a home." She handed him a mug of coffee. "I hope you like it black. I do have sugar."

"Oh, yes. Well, whatever improvements you made, I suppose the forest preserve should thank you. But you can't stay here."

"I can't?"

"No, you can't. Certainly not."

"Okay. You make the rules. But just out of curiosity, why not?"

"Because this is not your private residence. It's a ranger station."

"A ranger station?" It did sound a bit strange, since this forest lay sandwiched between O'Hare airport and a subdivision that probably contained ten thousand homes with driveways, garages, swimming pools and satellite dishes. If ever there were a fire in this forest, it would be called in by ten airline pilots in as many minutes.

"Yes, that's exactly what it is. It's where we keep our equipment. See, right here in this cabinet." He opened her pantry cabinet. There were two boxes of spaghetti, ten or twelve cans of corn and peas and tomatoes, a bag of white beans, a box of salt, two new rolls of paper towels, a box of sanitary napkins, and other items. "Well, now where is it?"

"Scott, that cabinet was empty. I swear it was."

Scott Dempsey looked thoughtful. He closed the cabinet carefully. "Maybe I moved the stuff up to the north station last fall. Come to think of it, I probably did."

She took a sip of coffee, studying him as he looked around at her home setup. He ran a hand through his kinky hair and registered her things, one after another: her unmade bed, in which just twenty minutes before she had been sleeping; the big Chicagoland map on the wall above her bed; the two-burner stove with a saucepan cooling on it.

"Does it really bother anyone?" she asked.

"It bothers me, yes. I am extremely bothered."

"Because . . .?"

"Well, for one thing it's against regulations for someone to be living here. I see all this, here." He gestured to include her furniture, her books, her laptop. "I'm thinking I'm in a shitload of trouble already."

"I suppose you're upset because I've been here a while without your picking up on it."

"That, too," he agreed.

"But look, Scott. To me that just spells a manpower problem. That's not your fault. The fact that I could be here for a couple of months without you catching me means the resources are spread too thin. You're supposed to cover far too big an area."

"That's true enough."

"How many rangers do we have covering these woods?"

"I'm not allowed to say."

"All right, I don't care. But we agree there aren't enough of them to really do all the stuff they're supposed to be doing. How about you make me your deputy?"

"Deputy?"

"Yeah. Like another pair of eyes for you here at this end of the woods."

He looked at her, and for a minute she thought he was going to agree. But when he finally spoke, she realized he had just been trying to think of a good way to say no. "The county is not paying for another pair of eyes, and the county does not have any insurance on another pair of eyes, and if there's one thing I'm sure about, it's that if I let you stay here they're going to fire me on the spot."

She could not argue with that. She said nothing, just sipped her coffee. By his watch she saw that it was still only six-thirty in the morning. About time for her run.

"You still didn't say why you picked this humdinger of an address," Scott Dempsey said over the rim of his mug. He seemed to be more comfortable, now, safe in his chair and a mug of steaming coffee in his hand.

"You really want to know?"

"Yes, I do."

She sighed. "Iraq. Three tours. Four years of my life. I got back, I craved something different than an ordinary apartment or house, with people, a street outside, a neighborhood. Craving isn't even the right word. It was stronger. It kind of felt like I was in withdrawal, something like that. I was sick. And I was getting sicker and sicker until the day I came here. I came running through the swamp one day, through this forest with all these gorgeous oaks and birches and birds and animals, all half under water, and I found this little cabin on the hill, and right away I knew I'd found my new place. I knew it the minute I laid eyes on it. I didn't feel sick anymore. Right away I felt better."

Dempsey stared at her wide-eyed, his head bobbing up and down, his lips pressed tight together. His mouth worked as if he was trying to say something. She waited. Finally his eyes betrayed him. She saw his eyes watering. His voice came out different, as if it was a struggle for him to speak, his throat all constricted. He stabbed a thumb in his own chest. "Vietnam, 1972, Da Nang," he said. He said it as if the meaning would be clear to anyone. It was enough to understand that something terrible had happened to him there.

His lips moved to add more, but nothing came out. His voice had left him. He took a hanky out of his pocket and wiped his eyes. He blew his nose into the hanky with a loud trumpeting. When he folded it up and put it away again, his eyes were red. He gulped two or three times, then said, "You're doing one hell of a job over there. I know it. And for what! What the hell is it for? Why'd they have to sell you out over there?" His fist slammed down on the table. She saw it coming down, but the bang still gave her a start. He was sobbing. He had totally lost it.

She stood when he stood, not knowing what might be coming next. When he blundered out of the cabin, she let him go. He wandered over to the riverbank, fifty feet away, down the hill, and stood a while. She left the door open the whole time, for the sunlight, to let him know he could come back when he was ready.

Was she going to be like Dempsey in a few years, stuck in a kind of war trauma in her own mind? The guy was a basket case. Maybe he was only fit for a job like this out in the woods, with his keys and his radio, hardly ever running into people.

While she made her bed she confronted the thought, for the first time, that she might have to leave. She couldn't go back to her parents' house. All she could do was get a newspaper like any ordinary person, start circling ads, start looking at apartments. Maybe now it would be okay. She pictured

Todd and Alison's apartment – one bedroom, a living room, a kitchen. Brick house on a leafy side street in the city, plenty of traffic and sirens and noise to keep her company. It would be a lot less perfect than this forest by the Des Plaines River with all the low-flying jumbo jets. But if they were going to kick her out, maybe she would have to try something like that. Just not too near where Alison and Todd lived.

She had finished her coffee by the time Dempsey wandered back over. "I apologize for that slight emotional outburst."

"You don't have to explain."

"I know," Dempsey said. "You've been there. Three tours, Jesus, I want to hear about that. But you know what really gets me about this war?"

"The carnage?"

He shook his head. "You go to war, you're going to have dead people and maimed people. No, what gets me is the media muzzle."

"What do you mean?"

"The blank unquestioning patriotic reporting we get in the newspapers, on TV, on the internet. If you want to cover the war, if you want to *embed*, as they call it, you can only report what they let you report."

She thought back to stuff she had read in the papers. "But that's always been the case in every war. You can't have the *New York Times* identifying targets or intel sources."

Dempsey wagged his finger. "The press is supposed to challenge the government's position, even in wartime. Any journalist who questioned this war became the enemy. All the newspapers and all the networks bought this garbage hook, line and sinker. This war is a crock. People dying over there for no good reason. And the only people who have the resources to uncover that truth and tell that story have agreed with the government's terms. You know what that's called?"

"What?"

"It's called propaganda. Now you know what pisses me off. And that's a big difference between your war and the one I fought in. I have to get back to work."

Now she knew he was a psycho case. But she said, "No problem. Me too."

"You work?"

"Yeah. After I take my run, that is."

"Listen, why don't we do like this? You give me a key so I can get in if I need to, like when you're not here. Of course, I'll try to knock first. But it is Forest Preserve property, after all. If the shit hits the fan, we've never met. If they call me out on the carpet we pretend you just arrived. I'll kick you out so hard you won't know what hit you. And you make damn sure you don't become a liability insurance case for the Cook County Forest Preserve."

"What about the electric bill? I'm using a little juice here, with my fridge and my computer and the light."

He rubbed his chin. "The ranger has to turn on the light once in while, too. I didn't see a TV or anything, right? I'm guessing such a teensy bit of electricity wouldn't get noticed in a hundred years."

"I can live with that deal. Okay if I have the key for you tomorrow?"

"Tomorrow or Monday, suit yourself. Why don't you just give me a call when it's good for me to come and pick it up?"

They traded cell numbers. Five minutes later, she locked up the cabin and set off on a forty-minute run. Most of that time she had to keep reminding herself to slow down and stop sprinting, dammit, just stop *sprinting*.

Offer

"Is this James Townsend?"

"Yes. Who's calling? How did you get this number?"

"You don't know me, Mr. Townsend. My name is Oscar Furey. I'm an attorney in Chicago. You represent Mrs. Deborah Sterling, I believe."

"I don't give information as to who I represent, sir," said Townsend. "What exactly is the purpose of this call?"

"In connection with an unrelated case I obtained information which could be valuable to your client. I suggest that we meet."

"What kind of information? Are you proposing to sell me information? What firm did you say you work for?"

Four hours later the two men sat in a booth in a Baker's Square Restaurant. It was four o'clock in the afternoon. Oscar Furey put the Thinkpad on the table.

"This computer until recently belonged to Mr. Alden Sterling," Oscar Furey said. He waited while the screen lighted up. "There are many documents related to his business that may be of interest to you. But with special regard to the custody fight . . ."

"What the hell do you know about the custody fight?" demanded Townsend. Furey eyed the computer. "Mother of God. You don't have Alden's correspondence in there, do you?"

"As I said, you will find something much more interesting than ordinary correspondence." Furey clicked through to a certain directory and opened a spreadsheet file.

Townsend turned his gaze away. "I must say, Mr. Furey. This is highly improper. I'm not sure I can go on."

"Let's be frank, Mr. Townsend. From the little I've seen in this machine, Mrs. Sterling wants to get the best possible deal for herself. You'd be abdicating your duty to your client not to look. Mr. Sterling is a wealthy man. And I imagine your client is tired of messing around with this custody question. Am I right?"

"Alden Sterling is clean as a whistle," Townsend said. "I don't know what you could possibly . . ."

"Every man has secrets. We all have harmless little secrets, we're all only human. The worst that could happen with most folks is a little embarrassment. Alden Sterling has a bigger secret, Mr. Townsend. I daresay, if you play your cards right, your case will be closed within fourteen days."

"Show me what's so sensational. I've known both Alden and Deborah for more than twenty years. We live in a small town, Mr. Townsend. Well, are you going to fill me in?"

Oscar Furey enlarged the document that was open on the screen. The figures were clearly readable. In the left column were dates, always the first of the month. In the right column was an amount. The amounts were always 1000 up to a certain date, and thereafter always 2500. There were no column headings. The table had no title. The document was named C.

"Mr. Furey, it's Thursday afternoon and I could be watching the Cubs. How did you get hold of that computer, anyway?"

"Don't you find it interesting that Alden Sterling is paying two thousand five hundred dollars a month to someone named C, even though he's still married to Mrs. Sterling? That's thirty thousand dollars a year. We're not talking about some little gratuity, here, Mr. Townsend. By the way, have you noticed that the payments went from a thousand a month to twenty-five hundred a month a couple of years ago? Look at that date, Mr. Townsend."

"Dear God," Townsend breathed. "The same month he served the papers."

"Exactly. And going back five years before that."

"But what does this prove? Who could it be? What is it for?"

"From the email correspondence with her, Mr. Townsend, everything becomes a lot clearer, I can assure you."

"Did you say 'her'?"

"I did."

Townsend sat in his seat somewhat deflated, white in the face, shaking his head. The waitress came to refill their coffee, but Townsend didn't see her.

Oscar Furey asked for the check. He closed the file and turned off the Thinkpad. He knew that look. He had seen it many times in the face of a courtroom opponent. It was the look of a man whose most fundamental assumptions had just been trashed. The look of a man who would have to start over again with his case. But the good news for Townsend was that he could make short work of it, thanks to this computer.

"How much did you have in mind?"

"A quarter million in cash."

Townsend rolled his eyes. His face had taken on a tinge of green. "Are you out of your mind? My client has no money."

"Not yet, she doesn't." Oscar Furey stood. He tapped the side of the laptop and reminded Townsend of his two main points. "She can write her own ticket with this. Sterling will pay big-time to keep this secret safe. And no more messy custody questions."

"I'll have to discuss it with my client. I have no idea what she'll say."

"You have my number."

WAR

Max Vinyl sat in his office checking his emails. He read the answer from Tris.

Dear Max,
Thanks for the video. I loved that car and now you are going to pay. Your illegal disdain for the environment, by the way, utterly nauseates me. I also had the pleasure of watching my brother's beach cottage burn to the ground last night. We saw your man Brainard set the fire and run away. Well, you know what they say, an eye for an eye. Click on the link below. My car got drowned. Your cars are going to get roasted. Then maybe we'll be even. Don't even think about trying to mess with our setup, Max. I wouldn't want you to get hurt. Well, only a little. You know what I mean.
Bye forever

So she had gotten his mail with the link to the video of her Mitsubishi sinking in eighty feet of water. The mail was unsigned. He clicked now on her link. It looked like a webcam. He saw a red Ferrari Testarossa, his Testarossa. It had to be his, because parked behind it he could see his yellow Corvette.

While he watched, the cam moved steadily to the left, giving a view of his '57 Chevy and his red Fleetwood Cadillac, and behind them the mahogany-panelled interior walls of his barn. It was real, for Chrissake. How had she done that? How had she gotten through his security and set up a webcam inside his car barn? Where did the light come from?

But of course . . . he had been at Ginger's for the night.

He clicked on the picture. It enlarged to fill the screen. Then he saw the 55-gallon drums placed near the bumper of several of the cars. The symbol for gasoline and the word "Gasoline" clearly stamped on the sides. The wires running from the drums to somewhere near the webcam. Was this really happening to him? Was she planning to firebomb his car collection? He realized he had broken out in a cold sweat. Drops of sweat were pricking at the scabs on his face. This could not possibly be for real.

He picked up his cell phone and dialed Oscar Furey's number. "Oscar, I've got a question."

"Ask me when I get there. I'm fifteen minutes from your door."

The next email was from Ginger.

Max, the message on my machine last night was from your Uncle Gordon. Greta died. The service will probably be Saturday afternoon. I know how depressed you're going to be. Call me.

Love,
Ginger

Now this. How could she go and die when things were looking up with her treatment?

What Uncle Gordon would be going through! Max picked up the phone, then thought the better of it. Uncle Gordon would probably be sleeping now, after whatever nightmare he had just experienced. He could stop over after work.

If the service were on Saturday . . . well, the Koreans would be in and out on Saturday, in at ten, out by eleven. They wouldn't plan a funeral for the morning, would they? Saturday afternoon shouldn't be a problem. Anyway, if need be Manny could cover for him with those crazy Koreans.

Uncle Gordon had only gone along with the scheme because he needed to finance the supplementary care for Greta. He had never liked it. Their special deal was not exactly something his uncle could hand off to a junior associate.

Hell, TSR would do without the environmental filings from now on. Do without the certification. There was no law requiring it. It wasn't as if customers were beating down the door asking for it. He had needed it for its marketing value in these growth years. But now the business was established. He could probably leave the current certificate hanging for years before anyone would notice it was out of date.

Max was still in the middle of these musings when Furey walked in holding the Thinkpad under his arm. He put it on the desk. He described his meeting with the lawyer, Townsend.

"Go for it," Max Vinyl said. "What do you need from me?"

"A copy," Furey said. "If they go for this deal, which they surely will, they're going to take the computer with them. I'll have to hand it over on the spot. We'll lose all the other stuff that's on there, forever. I still haven't had time to go through all of it, as you can imagine. Plus we won't have a safety copy."

"So copy the hard drive."

"That's what I thought. You've got the equipment for a job like that."

Max Vinyl thought a moment. It wouldn't be smart to let the Thinkpad too far out of sight, especially with that young man still camped on the beach in his tent. "I'll give it to Manny. He can do it."

"Good."

"Oscar, there's something you're not telling me." Max gave the lawyer a long look. He had known him for ten years. Oscar never fidgeted. Furey nodded and dropped the pencil on the desk.

"Wasn't going to mention it. I had a burglar in my condo last night. They didn't take anything. I didn't think too much of it."

"But?" He wanted the whole story.

"Nothing. It just seemed like a coincidence. This computer, and a cat burglar, nothing missing. You know how I feel about coincidences."

"What happened exactly?"

"There were two of them working together. I went out for a few minutes to pick something up at the store. It was pretty late, like eleven. When I came back I heard something, and I knew there was someone in my bedroom. Then the buzzer starts going off, someone in the lobby buzzing me like crazy."

"What did you do?"

"And then of course there's no one on the line. I was totally wigging out. I went and locked myself in the bathroom. The prowler must've left while I was in there. I was so freaked I didn't come out for half an hour."

"These home invasions can be dangerous."

"I know. I just thought it was weird that nothing was missing. Usually these people are after small valuables they can turn into quick cash, right?"

"Because you surprised them." Max Vinyl waved the topic away. "What about this lawyer? When do you expect to hear back?"

"Could be tonight, tomorrow, any day."

"We'll have the copy ready by tomorrow. Now listen, Oscar, I've got another question. Have a look at this." He clicked on the thumbnail photo on the screen that showed his classic cars wired to a firebomb. He gave a brief version of the events that had led up to it. "My question is, am I covered by insurance in the event of a fire up there?"

Furey uncrossed his legs and leaned forward. "A fire, yes. A firebomb, you can forget about it, Max. Arson is not covered in your policy. Are you notifying the police?"

"That's the other thing. Let's assume we have a disgruntled employee, here."

Furey nodded. "You're looking at a sexual harassment suit, big time."

"I understand that. I know I have to be careful. Thing is, she's the one harassing *me*. Isn't there such a thing as employer harassment?"

Furey laughed. "That suit wouldn't even make it into the docket."

"Well, what can I do? Give me options, Oscar."

"Dialogue comes to mind. She strikes me as a woman who didn't get enough attention. Instead of filing suit against you, like most people would, she sends funny packages, she takes down the computer system, she threatens to firebomb your cars."

"Sick, a sick woman! I still can't believe it. She also totaled my Gullwing for me, just by the way."

"On purpose?"

"Pretty sure."

"Yet she hasn't demanded any money, correct?" Max Vinyl shook his head glumly. "It might sound radical, but I'd try talking, Max. She doesn't want money. It isn't going to stop, from the looks of it. You've got to take action, here, instead of just reacting. Send her an email, set up a meeting."

"That's the last thing I feel like doing."

"Did she give you a deadline on the cars?"

"She just says they're going to get roasted."

"Write to her, Max. The cars might not be the end of it. Think of your house. Think of the company, the Koreans. She wants satisfaction. You've got to get her to stop the rampage."

Max Vinyl sighed. Furey was right, as usual. What had he gotten himself into? *Next time, don't hire such a goddamn tree-hugger.* He clicked "answer" and started to write.

SERVER ROOM

On break, Annie met up with Roberto and Murray out back. Murray sucked on a joint. Roberto looked as if he hadn't eaten.

"I haven't seen the server room here," Annie said. "What about a tour? After all that fuss yesteday . . . "

"When?"

"How about now?"

Roberto led her back inside and across triage to the door at the back. He put in the 5-digit security code in such a way that she could see it. The door clicked open. A hallway led to another door at the back. It opened with the same code.

"How often is that code changed?"

"Like, never."

They entered a room with plain concrete walls and indoor-outdoor carpeting. Overhead ran special ventilation ducts and electrical conduit. In the center of the room stood computer racks with twenty or thirty slim black computers on them. Everwhere you looked you saw little red and green blinking lights, no doubt signifying something to the computer jocks. A cool whirring, like an air conditioner or a fan, was the only sound.

"You've got twenty-four parallel servers over there, with automatic power down, multiple backups, firewalls, protection better than some banks and hospitals I've had the pleasure of cleaning up after."

"What's with the ceiling?"

"The ceiling? What do you mean?"

She realized that as a programmer he had probably never given the ceiling a second thought. It was a flat ceiling with square elements in an aluminum frame. It was strange that the ceiling here was so low, when right in the next room it was as high as a stadium. From the outside the warehouse looked like a big box.

She set up a small stepladder that was standing in one corner, climbed to the top step and pushed one of the ceiling elements up into the space above. Using the bright light on her phone, she stuck her head into the space and looked around.

A vast empty space rose above the ceiling of the server room. It must have been another thirty feet up to the W-shaped roof above. The slanted surfaces of the roof above were made of opaque plexiglass or very dirty glass. In triage and the shipping room and in testing, that W-shaped roof gave natural light to the space below.

Where the shipping room ended and the server room started, the vertical wall extended all the way up to the warehouse ceiling. They must have put in the low ceiling in the server room to control the temperature and humidity better. The entire space above the server room was isolated from the rest of the warehouse just like the server room itself was.

A hand clamped down on her calf. "Do you mind telling me what in God's name you are doing in our server room? Up the goddamn ceiling of our server room?"

"You scared me, Mr. Rodriguez." She came down the ladder, leaving the hole in the ceiling.

"I want answers, now!" With his other hand, Rodriguez had Roberto by the scruff of the neck.

"It's my fault, Mr. Rodriguez. We were on break and I asked Roberto if he could give me a tour. That's all."

"A tour?" His voice was thick with suspicion.

"We had similar server architecture in our battle group in Baghdad. After the problem we had yesterday, I thought it'd be interesting to have a look. Thought maybe next time I could help with the repairs."

"If you're so interested in servers, what the hell're you doing on that ladder?"

She smirked. "Rats. It's either rats or maybe a possum or some other small animal. We were standing there and we heard them. Right, Roberto?"

"Yeah, like little scratching noises."

Rodriguez had let Roberto go.

"Better get a man up there, soon," Annie said. "I remember once a rat got into a Com Ed junction box down on the South Side, started gnawing on a wire. Next thing you know the whole South Side was blacked out. Remember? This was like five years ago. Not much left of the rat. Rats definitely do *not* conduct electricity."

"Out of here, both of you. Roberto, you ought to know we see everything on closed circuit video down here."

"Yeah, sure, I know. Didn't know it was off limits for the receptionist."

"Now it is," Rodriguez said. "I can't have people going up ladders all over the place. Let me have a look."

He stuck his head in the hole, muttered something she couldn't hear, and replaced the ceiling element. Annie followed Rodriguez back up front. The whole time he was muttering things to himself that she couldn't quite pick up. At the reception desk he spoke up.

"Wait a minute, Annie. Got something for you." He went into his office, came out again. He had a charcoal laptop in his hands. She saw the words IBM Thinkpad. "I've got to go down to the loading dock for an hour. I can't be everywhere at once in this goddamn place. This is important. A man named Oscar Furey is going to come and pick this up."

"I met him yesterday," Annie said. "When are we expecting him?"

"He's on his way now. Could be half an hour. But I can't wait. We've got three trucks coming in at the same time. I've got to get down to the loading dock, pronto."

"Should I have him sign for it?"

Rodriguez hesitated, then shook his head. "This isn't the army. But don't let it out of your sight, hear?"

She counted to ten after Rodriguez had gone through the door into triage. Then she wrote a text to Olson. With luck he would be sitting in his tent reading a book and not on one of his trips to the mall. The laptop was under the reception desk at her feet. She looked around innocently, trying to think of a plan in case Olson didn't answer. Just when she was getting ready to pick up her phone and try him again, it vibrated. Olson was on his way over from the beach. ETA three minutes.

She killed time by answering the phone, trying to slow her heartbeat down from its flat-out galloping. Another irate caller who had been sent the wrong item. Calmly she read off the service line number and informed the woman that the call would cost ninety cents per minute. She cut off the call as the door opened.

"Bob," she said. "This is a surprise."

He came right around the desk, bent down and put his hand on her back. She actually thought he was going to kiss her. His face came right down next to hers, so that she could smell his minty breath. Her face went hot when she realized there wasn't going to be a kiss. At the same time, with his left hand, he eased his backpack down under the desk by her feet. The big compartment was already unzipped. Smoothly they switched the laptops. Then Olson straightened up, adjusting his backpack.

"Was just driving by and thought I'd stop and say hi. Got to run."

"Take care."

She heard the motor start, and gravel crunching as Olson drove off. She texted: *Come back and get me at 5 pm.* She pressed the send button, then immediately wrote another text. *I'm going to need your help.* Her face was getting hot from all this texting. What in the world was she doing? Well, she had gotten him his laptop and she would probably never see him again anyway. She had just sent the second text when she heard the gravel outside crunching again.

Oscar Furey came in, still wearing his sunglasses. "Ah, good afternoon, Annie."

"Hello, Oscar."

"Look, I'm really sorry about last night. I suddenly had this massive stomach problem. I get these things. I had to get home to my own toilet really quickly. I felt bad about leaving you there without saying goodbye. Did you get home okay?"

"Oscar, don't worry." She stood up and handed him the Thinkpad. "Mr. Rodriguez asked me to hold this for you. Our old friend," she smiled.

"Ah, yes," Furey said, taking the laptop. The Oakleys came down again. "Precisely what I came for. So long, Annie."

"Bye now."

C

Deborah Snyder sat at her dining room table with a glass of Chardonnay, a candle lit, the TV off. She stilled her thoughts. Twenty minutes left before Trip would tumble in the door from soccer practice. Now was her chance to focus.

Who was C.? Alden had paid this person – this woman – one thousand a month for five years. Then suddenly, while they were still living together, at the time he served the divorce papers on her, he had raised the amount to two thousand five hundred a month. Thirty thousand dollars a year. It was astonishing to think that there was such a person in Alden's life. Just astonishing. Another woman. Or was it another man and he just made it seem like he was a she?

At this point, anything's possible.

Alden had never been a cheapskate with her; God knows he had been generous. At the same time, he had always been careful with money. What else would you expect of an accountant?

He had given Trip exactly one hundred dollars to spend in Hawaii. He wanted to teach him the value of money. Typical Alden. He had made Trip write down every expense in a little notebook, and made sure he didn't forget a single one, even a 25-cent pack of bubble gum. It had to balance at the end of the week. He'd nearly hit the roof when the change in Trip's pocket hadn't matched the amount that was supposed to be left over according to the expense log. Alden had accused him of stealing. Trip had probably just brought some of his own money with him from home. It would never occur to Alden that Trip would make a mess of it on purpose just to annoy him.

No, Alden Sterling never spent money without first giving it a lot of thought, even small amounts. And to think of thirty thousand dollars – like a paycheck! And then there was the cold constancy of it – every month on the first of the month. It was just like Alden, of course, to be systematic, never to miss a payment, to record every payment, and to put everything in rows and columns. Enough to make you goddamn dizzy.

Had the payments been made by check? Maybe a friend down at the bank could help her with more information. Cash payments would show up in his withdrawals, wouldn't they, with that amount of money? With cash he would have had to deliver it personally. Where had he gone once a month, always around the first of the month? She could recall no such pattern. All the time he spent at his office was a complete cipher, to her, anyway. He could have flown to Kansas City. As long as he was home for dinner, she would only know about it if he felt like telling her.

But this increase from one thousand to twenty-five hundred a month coming in the same month that he served the divorce papers on her – that could not be a coincidence, could it?

Who was C.? If only she had that computer. His email held the answer. Somewhere in that computer was the name. She tried to think of all the C's she knew – Charles Dranby, the fireman; Carleton Yorgenson, the builder who had done renovation work on their house and on Alden's office at the time of his expansion; or maybe John Crandall, Vice President of the local Citibank branch. All men. All unlikely candidates for a monthly payment from Alden Sterling going back the last seven years.

Seven years . . . what could have changed seven years ago to make Alden start paying this money? Did he have a parallel life? When Trip had been five years old? She searched her brain back . . . to seven years ago. It was a blank. Same house, same car, same husband, same moustache. She searched her memory. Nothing came up. Nothing.

She could call him, ask him directly, *Who is C, Alden? Who's getting all this dough?*

She had better ask Townsend first. Townsend would not be a happy camper if she screwed up his case.

Or she could follow him.

If he were leading a parallel life – another woman, another child – he would have to go there. There's the idea! She didn't have to ask anyone's permission to sneak around and watch where he went. She drained her glass and went to the kitchen. She checked her watch. Trip was late again. Time to start thinking about dinner anyway. She got a TV dinner out of the freezer, left it on the counter, and wrote him a note.

Alden would still be at work. The question was how to watch him without him noticing. He knew her green Volvo as if it were his own car. In fact, he considered it his car. She sat in the car, in her own garage, thinking it through. Anywhere a green Volvo appeared, Alden's eyes would be drawn to it like a magnet, checking to see if she was at the wheel. Not only that, everyone else in town knew her car, too. Everyone would see in two seconds flat that she was going around spying on Alden. This was not going to work. Someone else would have to follow him, but how?

She got out of the car and went back into the kitchen. She had her idea while putting the TV dinner back in the freezer.

She picked up the phone. "Reed, it's me. I need a big favor. Have you got a minute right now, or do you want to call me back?"

Lawyers

"Bob, that you?"

His boss sounded different. But then the last time he had heard him speaking it had been more like the towering rage of a mother bear separated from her cubs. Alden had been a changed man yesterday morning, shoving McCoy so roughly in the office, like some sort of mountain man. Strange feelings had gone through him as he witnessed that.

On the one hand he had felt pure fear, not knowing yet what it was all about and seeing the wild side of Alden. On the other hand, from the moment he realized what must have happened, a kind of admiration had begun to take shape in him. If there was one thing about Alden that he had trouble with, it was his almost inhuman equanimity. Clients forgot to enclose important documentation with their tax returns; clients lied; the IRS agents did something stupid; things happened all the time and Alden still never got the slightest bit ruffled. "People are human," he would say. "They make mistakes. What's the point of getting angry when people make an honest mistake?"

Yesterday was a day he would always remember, the day Alden discovered his laptop was missing. It was the first time he had ever seen the man upset.

"I'm sitting in my car in the parking lot of a Denny's Restaurant in Waukegan, up near the Wisconsin line."

"You got my laptop back?"

"Sure did, Alden. I got it."

"Hey! Good job. I want you here first thing tomorrow morning, with the laptop. Or, wait a minute, do you think I could get it from you tonight? Any way you could do that?"

"We can do that, Alden, only . . . there's something you've got to know. You know, about your Thinkpad . . . let's see, where should I start? The recycling company, see, they saw it was a new computer, so they had a peep inside."

"You think they read my files?"

He was feeling his way, here, working on instinct. "I know they did, Alden. First thing they did, when they separated the Thinkpad out from all the trash we gave them, they gave it to their lawyer."

"A lawyer?" Alden's voice broke.

"Yes, and he had it for about thirty-six hours in all before bringing it back to the recycling company. That's when we were able to snatch it. I've got it now."

The silence at the other end of the line stretched on. He had known the laptop was essential equipment for Alden. That was why he had gone ape when he'd discovered it missing. That was why he'd sent Bob running all over the northern end of the state trying to find it again.

"Do you want me to bring it by, Alden?" he asked.

"Wait. You said 'we'. Who is 'we'?"

"My friend and I who got your laptop back. It's this woman who works for TSR, the recycling company. She helped me."

"Who the dickens is this lawyer? What can you tell me about the lawyer?"

"Name is Oscar Furey. Has an office in the city. Small firm, only a couple of lawyers. Probably on retainer to TSR, far as I could find out."

"House lawyer?"

"Something like that."

"Bob, I'm concerned about the lawyer."

He kept the phone to his ear, listening, waiting, trying to parse Alden's words and read his thoughts. Sure, it wasn't pleasant to think that some lawyer who was a complete stranger might have gone through the files on your computer. But it wasn't the end of the world, either. It wasn't as if Alden had done anything dishonest or had anything to hide, beyond ordinary client confidentiality.

"Here's what we're going to do. You hold on to the laptop. Have you got it in a safe place?"

"Sure do."

"Good. Keep it very safe. Don't come back to work tomorrow. Just keep that laptop safe. I've got to talk to someone. I'll let you know what I want you to do."

"I understand." He said it without meaning it. Not come to work tomorrow? This was the very last thing he had expected.

"Good work, partner. I'll call you tomorrow. Oh, and Bob?"

"Yes?"

"You wouldn't happen to know the name of the principal of this company TSR, would you? The owner or the CEO?"

"It's a guy named Max Vinyl. By the way, did you mean that about not coming to work tomorrow?"

There was a slight hesitation. Then Alden said, "Damned right I did."

"That's fine, only you know there's a lot of work piling up. We're getting behind." He named a couple of clients they had made promises to, with deadlines this week.

"I talked to them today," Alden said. "Your job is to keep that laptop safe, and keep it away from me. At least for a day or so longer. It's enough for me just to know it's safe."

"Alden, you're not making sense. You sent me on a mad dash to get it back. Now you don't want it anywhere near you."

"Because of that lawyer, don't you see? Let me put it this way. They had their lawyer snooping around in my files. I want to talk to my lawyer about that, see what he says I should do. I'll try to get an answer from him tomorrow. Sometimes it's better to talk to your lawyer before you even take another step, Bob. You learn that with time."

He didn't know what to say to that. He wanted to say that he thought it was strange, and it worried him. But that wasn't what you said to the guy who called you partner. So he said, "I'll keep a good eye on it, then. I'll be waiting for your call."

In spite of Alden Sterling's assurances, it still felt damned strange.

Handcuff

By six o'clock Annie sat with Olson in her car with a big thermos of black coffee and a box of donut holes, parked more or less across the street from Ike Mullin's apartment house in Waukegan. It was a four-story wooden structure that might have been painted green or brown or even white twenty years ago.

"It's that brown Lincoln down the street, you say?" Olson asked.

She nodded and finished chewing. "This sort of thing takes patience."

She felt a certain satisfaction in the fact that Olson had gotten his boss's laptop back. She had played a role in that and called in the favor. Olson hadn't put up much resistance when she asked him to help her get the phones back.

"So tell me something. Why are you moving Heaven and Earth to recover this guy's laptop while that other guy from your office, the one who pulled the prank in the first place, he didn't even care?"

Olson looked away from the entrance to the house to look at her. "That's like asking the difference between homemade and store-bought. I guess I'm just made different from him."

"What is it you admire about your boss so much?"

Olson ran a hand over his scalp and looked out through the top of the windshield. A bus went by with a roar and disappeared down the street before he answered. "He believes in me, is one thing. And I think he depends on me. You know, like when someone's counting on you, and you know you just can't let them down."

"As a soldier I had some experience with that."

"Bet you did."

"But that was life and death situations. That was about survival. With people dying every day, you were constantly reminded how crucial it was to follow the rules, do what you were trained to do. The ones who cut corners paid for it."

"With me and him it's like that," Olson said. "Obviously it's not life and death. But it means a lot to me to live up to his expectations."

"Even if they're unrealistic? I mean, look at what we've gone through to get that laptop back. No boss could realistically *expect* you to do what we've done."

"You're right. I would never have gotten it back without you, Annie."

"Fine, but you see what I mean? Was it reasonable of him to banish you from your office and send you on this wild goose chase?"

She liked the way Olson worked his mouth in and out, thinking. "What you're trying to say is what kind of a nut would do that for his boss. Am I right?"

He was right. She nodded.

"Well, what I haven't told you is we've had some discussions. Alden thinks there's a certain amount of risk to the firm if there's just him acting like a king at the top of the hierarchy. You know, heart attacks, stuff like that. He's actually working on a partnership agreement."

"Ah."

"Besides, Alden was practically out of his mind at that moment. He had just figured out his laptop was gone. He was reacting without thinking. You've got to understand, Annie. It wasn't about being reasonable."

"Just the same. I mean, it is only a computer. I wonder why it's so precious to him."

"I told you why. Secret stuff about local companies, people, their tax audits, correspondence, very private information."

"It all seems kind of dry, don't you think? Here's this lawyer guy, Furey, running up and down the highway between Waukegan and Chicago twice in two days with the laptop, holding meetings with the TSR boss. I'll bet they found something super interesting in that computer."

Olson waved. "Whatever. We got it back. That's all I really care about."

Maybe he was right. Tax secrets might just be racy enough to generate meetings with lawyers and suspicious behavior. Olson's boss was not likely to be threatening national security. Still she had the feeling something didn't add up.

"Hey, look."

The two men were coming out of the green house. The tall, heavy blond one with the eyebrow bolt, and the short musclebound Asian one. They were empty-handed. She felt her adrenaline start to run. If the phones weren't in the brown Lincoln, and they weren't at TSR, then they really almost had to be here. The men walked up the street fifty yards and got into the Lincoln, then pulled out and drove away.

"Now what? Don't tell me you're really going in there?"

"Damn straight." She pulled out her phone. "You see them coming, you call me right away. Then you get behind the wheel and start the engine."

"Jesus, Annie."

She crossed the street and went in the front door. Inside she found a directory with old-fashioned little black buttons. Instead of ringing the bell, she went straight up the stairs two at a time to the third floor. The stairs creaked loudly with every step. On the third floor she walked to the end of the hall till she stood in front of 3K. She knocked on the door. No sound came from inside. She knocked again. No answer. She had seen the men leave, but you never knew if they had a friend still inside.

She tried the doorknob. It was locked. She checked under the doormat. No key. She studied the door. It was a laminated wooden door, smooth surface, chipped in places, light composite wood, cheap and flimsy. She jiggled the knob again. Good – it rattled, which meant there was some play between the metal surfaces in the latching mechanism.

She backed up against the railing. The hallway was only maybe six feet wide, but it would suffice. She took two deep breaths and focused on the wood just next to the doorknob. On her next exhalation she turned her hips ninety degrees, lifted her right leg, and slammed the heel of her tennis shoe into the wooden surface. She threw all her weight into it. Something ruptured, and after a split second she knew it wasn't her knee. The door was open, hanging askew on one hinge, the whole area around the doorknob splintered. She pushed the door aside and went in. If the neighbors got interested, she wouldn't have much time.

She didn't need much. In the living room, under a big table stacked with magazines and newspapers, she found four large tote bags filled with Todd's phones. She checked the kitchen, the bedroom, the other bedroom, looking for stray phones. Mostly there were a lot of beer cans lying around everywhere. *Men and beer.* Unwashed plates on the kitchen table, a large, greasy pyrex half-filled with lasagna, still warm to the touch. Now these hoodlums had their GPS back, and Todd would have his phones back.

She heard a noise. Was someone coming up the stairs? Voices. Loud men's voices. It could be the two men. What in the world were they doing back so soon? They must have forgotten something. Her phone vibrated. She clicked it off, hoping Olson would get the message. She put the bags back under the table in the living room where they had been before, and ran back into the kitchen.

"Holy shit, Tranny, lookit this."

She couldn't see them from her hiding place. She heard the squeak as they pushed the broken door in. She heard the big heavy one panting. He would be scanning the living room now.

"What's goin' on here?" the other one said.

"Them phones been moved," Ike said. "Shut yer face a minute, let's listen."

She was trained in being quiet and could stay motionless for long periods. She was careful not to shift her weight in case the kitchen floor creaked like the rest of the apartment. She heard them moving into the living room, step by step.

"You check the bedrooms," one whispered.

Three seconds later Ike was in the kitchen directly in front of her, still breathing heavily, his massive sweaty dirty red tank-top back to her. From her position behind the door she felt the heat radiating from his body. It was now or never. One thing you learned in the army was the principle of striking first. She who hesitated got killed. In the next instant he would feel her eyes upon him, the way people did. Then he would mash her against the wall, like a centipede.

She clobbered him with the heavy pyrex with all her strength. She wasn't taking any chances. Ike caught it full on the back of the head. He never saw her. He went down like a collapsing building, the huge bolt and the wing nuts clattering on the linoleum floor, his face at her feet.

"Ike?"

She heard Tranny coming. She crouched behind the kitchen door and calculated her timing with his approaching footfalls. The first thing he would see would be Ike's body lying on the floor. He'd be asking himself what had happened. His eyes would be locked on Ike, who had saliva running from his open mouth in a pool on the floor and looked like he could be dead. Tranny would come running in to help his partner.

The kitchen door had a big frosted window in the middle. With her right foot she drove it into Tranny's face, leaning in with her whole body behind it. She caught him just as he came charging headlong into the kitchen. The glass shattered. Shards flew everywhere and covered the floor. She stepped out from behind the door, a frying pan she had grabbed off the stove in her right hand. Tranny sat dazed on the living room floor, bleeding from cuts across his face and arms.

He still had strength left in him. From the sitting position he lunged at her with one bloody arm. His left hand clamped on her ankle with a grip so tight that it made her toes tingle. The other arm hung limp at his side and seemed to be useless. She battered his good wrist with the frying pan, no holding back. With the first blow she felt his grip loosen, but still he held on, tugging on her leg. A thick purple vein bulged in his wrist. She aimed the second blow for that vein. The pan came down hard. She heard a loud grunt and realized she had made that noise. This time something shattered in his wrist. She felt it give and knew the bone had broken in pieces. Tranny fell backwards on the living room floor, screaming and favoring his wrist. They must have heard him all over the house, in the next house, and out in the street. He rolled on his back on the living room floor, his face and his arms bloody, cradling his broken wrist with his useless hand and screaming.

When she glanced behind her, the big man still lay on his stomach in the exact same position as before. He was either dead or out cold, his eyes shut tight. Seeing how his face was jammed right up hard against one leg of the kitchen table gave her an idea. She dug in her pocket and pulled out a thin white plastic handcuff. In ten seconds she had it threaded through the bolt in his eyebrow, around the wing nuts a couple of times, and around the table leg and snapped shut. That ought to slow the bastard down. All the skills you learned in combat school didn't vanish that quickly, it appeared.

Yielding to a spontaneous urge, she brought the pyrex with lasagna out of the kitchen and stood over the writhing Asian man for a moment until he opened his eyes. When he saw her, he tried sitting up, ready to go at her again. His arms didn't seem to be cooperating.

"Fuck with us again at your own risk, loser." She mashed the lasagna into his face and pushed him back down on the floor, using the weight of the pyrex and ready to stomp on his broken wrist if she had to. He went back down easy, gurgling for air.

Olson appeared in the doorway to the apartment, his face chalky white. "Is he going to be okay?" He pointed at Tranny, who was squirming on the floor and trying to get the pyrex off his face without the use of his hands. The arm she hadn't broken for him was all slick with blood. Glass and blood covered the floor. The man in the kitchen still hadn't moved.

"The hell with him. Grab those," she said, and pointed at two bags full of phones. She followed him with the other two. "Let's get out of here."

She had walked in blood and was leaving bloody footprints across the floor. It didn't matter. Those two neanderthals could spend the next ten years looking, if they liked, and still never find her, footprints or no footprints. She knew this. They took the stairs down two at a time and hurried across the street to the car. Olson was jittery and had trouble getting the key in the ignition. As they pulled out of the space at last, she saw the Asian one appear in an upstairs window. He cradled his left wrist in his other hand, the wrist all swollen up and the skin shiny in the sunlight. She stared back.

Conestoga Carving

"Get this thing offa me!" Ike lay on the kitchen floor, unable to move, head throbbing. He was hog-tied to the kitchen table.

"I'm trying, man. It won't cut. These scissors are too damn dull. I need something sharper, something to cut the damn thing with. You want I should get a saw?"

"You don't put a saw within ten feet of my face. Who the hell was it, anyway?"

"Some girl, I swear. Short girl, blond hair, dark glasses."

"Yeah, but who?"

"I don't know, man. She didn't show no ID. She took the phones. God damn, will you look at this fucked-up wrist?" Tranny's wrist had swelled up to the size of a gourd. "Hurts like hell, too."

"Can't you get this thing off me? I'm gonna puke my brains out if I have to stay down here on the floor."

"Fuck these scissors. It's all wound around in this hole in the table leg, see. I can't just slip it off the end of the table leg."

"How is the leg connected to the table?"

"Good idea, man. Okay, I'm having a look. Looks like it screws in. You want I should unscrew it from the table?"

"Well, maybe as a first step."

With his good hand, Tranny applied torque to the table leg. He was on his hands and knees on the kitchen floor. He could only work with one hand. He lifted the table off the floor by getting his shoulder under it. In a minute he had the leg off.

"Good," Ike said, and sat up. For the moment he kept the table leg in his hand, to keep it from swinging around and bumping everything. The other end was attached to his eyebrow bolt.

"What about you just unscrew the nuts? Then you can slide it off up there."

This damned hottie, whoever she was, had wound the plastic handcuff so tightly around the wing nuts that the outer one wouldn't budge. At least Ike's fingers couldn't make it budge, not with his head pounding this way.

After a minute of both of them fumbling with the wing nuts, and still no success, Ike struggled to his feet and headed for the bathroom. A new wave of pure throbbing pain spread outward in his head, like water filling a sponge. He had to hold onto the enamel of the sink to keep from collapsing. After a count of five he steadied himself and stared into the bathroom mirror. The white plastic of the fastener was truly wound tightly around the wing nuts and through a hole in the table leg. He studied it until his eyes blurred, the pain once again swelling in his cranium.

When he opened his eyes again, he opened the medicine chest. Time for priorities. Among half a dozen empties he found a bottle of Demerol with some pills left. He put three on his tongue, took a swig of water out of the tap, and closed his eyes again to wait for the pain to start going away, while still holding fast to the edge of the sink.

Half a minute later he opened his eyes and studied the problem again in the mirror. Two years in this apartment, and he had never looked at that table, much less one of the legs. Now he had one of the table legs fastened to the bolt in his eyebrow, and the question was how to get the damned thing off.

Who would have thought there would be a hole in the end of the table leg, through which some bimbo could thread one of these uncuttable plastic handcuffs? He got up close to the mirror to study the hole. The end of the table leg was flattened out, more like a board than your usual tapered spindle. In the flattened-out end there was a cut-out part. Now that he looked at it closely, he noticed there was actually a design in the way it was cut out. It wasn't just a plain hole; it was more like there was a scene carved in the wood. If he was not mistaken, it looked like one of those covered wagons they used in the old west. A covered wagon and a bunch of horses all hitched to it were carved right into the wood. The cut-out part above the wagon and the horses was actually supposed to be the sky. The girl had strung the plastic handcuff three or four times tightly around and through this aperture.

"Hey man, c'mere. Got something to show you," Ike said. When Tranny arrived in the bathroom doorway, he handed him the Demerols.

"I can sure use a coupla these," Tranny said.

"You ever notice this design in our table?" Ike pointed at the covered wagon and the horses. Tranny, blood still dripping from several deep gashes on his face and arms, stared.

"What're you talking about, man?"

"This table leg. See, there's like a picture carved into it. Horses and a covered wagon. Like a piece of art."

Tranny made a face. "Man, let's get the hell out of here and go after that bitch. She got our GPS, remember?"

"You mean our phones."

"That's what I said, asshole. You keep correcting me all the time, I'm gonna finish the job that girl started on you."

Ike observed the way the table leg swung freely in front of him, tapping lightly against the side of the sink, like a giant rhythm stick. It wasn't heavy. For the moment it didn't really bother him. He had never noticed there were scenes with covered wagons in the legs of that table. Probably all four legs had the covered wagon scene. Or maybe each leg had a different scene. He would have to look. The way it hung down didn't bother him at all. At any rate not nearly as much as the colossal throbbing in his skull.

He kept the table leg in his hand going down the stairs. Holding the bottom end in his hand gave him an odd feeling of stability with this ripping headache.

"Hurry, get in the car," Ike said. "You gotta drive. I'm not seeing straight with this contraption hangin' down in front of me."

"Shit, man, I think my wrist is broken. You drive."

They settled on Ike driving. "I don't like the looka that wrist, kid," he said. Tranny held the wrist in his lap, a towel on his lap to soak up the blood from his good arm. His wrist was green and soft and swollen, like a giant zucchini.

"They got a headstart, but I saw out the window what they drove away in," Tranny said. "Silver Honda, late model. Blond girl with sunglasses. Guy in the driver's seat, shaved head. Headed for the highway, for sure. They weren't from here. Never seen them around before."

"City?"

"Yeah. Damn, we got any beer left?" He opened the paper bag at his feet and pulled out a can of Coors. "Oh man, my prayers are answered. Want one?"

"No, man, I'm already seeing double from the wallop she gave me. Who was this bitch, anyway? Some kinda amazon?"

"No, short little bitch." Tranny drained half the can. "Ah, feels better already."

"But not a cop. She didn't show no badge or anything."

"Man, cops don't go breaking into your place, ripping the door down off the hinges, stealing stuff and beating the shit out of you without saying a word. That was some weird fucking Mafia shit back there."

"Since when does the Mafia use a girl working alone? Tell me that."

"Who the fuck cares, man? That bitch got our phones."

"Not to mention conking me on the head."

"You know what this tells me? Those phones are fucking worth something. You were right we had to come back for 'em."

"Maybe you're right about that."

"Must be worth damn good money. That's the only reason anyone would wanna come and beat the shit out of us to get 'em back."

They got on the highway headed south. First they had lost the GPS, Ike thought. Then they had obtained the goddamned phone collection. Now they had lost the phones, too. It wasn't right.

"Tell me something, Tranny boy," he said after they had been driving a while. "Your old Aunt, in between all the shooting, when she said yer name, it sounded sorta like '*Mmm*'."

When he glanced across, Tranny was staring at him. "Man, I got a busted wrist and cuts all over my face and my arms. What the fuck difference does it make?"

"I'm just sayin' if you write it '*Ng*', how the hell do you get round to sayin' '*Mmm*'?"

"Let's talk about your name for a change, man. Like for instance we could call you Batface."

He fingered the table leg hanging down, clanking against the steering wheel. "You think it looks funny?"

"Hell no, not at all, batface."

"Buddy, I just want to know how I should say it. I feel kinda shitty about it. Seems like I been saying it wrong ever since I knew you."

"Everybody says it wrong. I say it wrong myself just so people can spell it right. You know, like that day we went to get our driver's license renewed? Who even gives a shit, Ike?"

"Hell, I think it's important. A man's name. You don't mess around with yer name, buddy. Hey, you see that Honda anywhere? Tell me if you see it, cause I've got my hands full just trying to stay on the road, here."

"More I think about it, more I think she came for that," Tranny said. "To steal them phones. Why else would she take them with her?"

"Right," Ike agreed. "Now, let's think. Who even knows about them phones?"

"Okay, first you got the guy we took 'em from, plus the waitress."

"Right."

"Then you got my Auntie Lee. Then you got your pal, Lance."

"Don't forget the boss," Ike said as he changed lanes. They were heading south into the city. The first skyscrapers loomed up ahead.

"You think he would do a thing like this to us?"

Ike thought about it. "He knows where I live, don't he?"

Tranny shook his head. "It's got to be the guy we took 'em from. He's the only one mad enough. I say we go to his house."

"Boy, will I kick the shit out of him," Ike said, touching the tender spot on his scalp.

For a while they sat in the car out in front of the red brick apartment house where they had stolen the phones in the first place. They ate Italian beef sandwiches and drank cold beer. The building stood quiet in the early evening haze. Occasionally someone went out or in. But the hot waitress named Alison Paine did not show up. Ike kept an eye on the third floor, watching for movements in the window. But to all appearances, they weren't home.

All at once Ike was startled by a loud knocking at his window. He had been dozing. A huge wave of pain . . . his head again. A man leaned down at the window, standing in the street, looking steamed about something. Ike punched Tranny in the arm to wake him, then rolled down the window halfway.

"Hey, bolt-face, you're the assholes that swiped my phones," said the man. "I'm guessing you're here to give them back now, is that it? You got your GPS back. Now what about my phones? Deal's a deal."

"Watch who yer calling what," Ike said, sitting straighter in his seat. He kept one hand on the door handle, ready to clobber the dude with the car door. Cars were going by. Jerk the door open at the right moment, and you could shove him right out into moving traffic. That would be the end of him. On the other hand, it would be messy, and in broad daylight with witnesses. Worst of all, no escape route. Bad idea for men on parole. "We don't got those phones anymore anyway. Got robbed this afternoon. Look at my friend's wrist, what that bitch done to him."

"You're trying to tell me you didn't bring the phones you stole?" The man wasn't listening. He was yelling at the top of his lungs now. "First you come and break into my apartment. Then you steal my phones. Then you get your GPS back but you don't return my collection. Now you come back. You planning to steal something else now? What is it with you illiterate slobs, anyway?" The guy had gone off like a frigging grenade. People walking down the sidewalk on the other side of the street were stopping to stare.

"Man, we don't have to put up with this shit," Tranny said. He groaned. His wrist had bumped against something.

"We're getting out of here," Ike said. He started the engine. In a loud voice out the window, for the benefit of the crowd that had stopped to listen, he shouted, "You're crazy, man. I don't know what you're talking about. Get the hell out of the way."

He pulled out of the parking place and drove away. In the rearview mirror he saw the man standing in the middle of the street, still shaking his fist and hollering something at them.

They drove north, heading aimlessly through the city.

"I don't know about you, but I got a feeling he didn't steal the phones," Tranny said after a while.

"Yeah, it wasn't him. You gotta admit that was pretty fuckin' weird back there. Like he was telling the truth."

"Yeah, the way he came right up to the car."

"And you know what that means."

"What?"

"That means it was the boss, man. He had us beat up. He stole our phones."

"I can't believe it."

"I can't believe it, either. But it's the only explanation that makes sense."

"You really think he would do that to us?"

Ike shook his head, considering. "Seems like money is all that matters to that damn bastard."

"You know what? He probably thought they belong to him because we stole them on company time. That's why he refused to take 'em from us. He thought they were his the whole time."

"Greedy bastard. He coulda said so. Hell, we woulda given 'em to him."

"Question is, what're we gonna say to the boss about it?"

They looked at each other. "Hell if I know," Ike said.

"Whaddya mean, you don't know? We're talking about thousands a dollars he stole from us."

"And, just by the way, it *wasn't* on company time," Ike said. "No two ways about it."

"Yeah, they was our phones. We offered him a good deal. He just didn't wanna accept it. He wanted it all for himself."

"Guess that's how you get ahead in business, get to be rich like him."

Tranny shook his head. "I just can't figure out who this blond bitch could be that did us like that."

"Must be someone that works for him, that's all I can think. I betcha anything she's on his payroll."

"Yeah, just like us."

"Man, if I get my hands on her."

"Me too, man. Just lookit me."

SEVEN YEARS

"Thanks for picking me up, Reed," said Deborah Sterling. "I wouldn't have been able to drive there under my own power."

"You do remember her, don't you?" Reed Hunt drove the unmarked car with one hand on the wheel, not looking at the road at all. He stared the whole time at her, as if his wheels would magically follow by themselves all the turns in the road. It made her nervous. She watched the road for him, feeling his eyes on her.

"Yeah, sure. I remember. All those old stories."

"I tailed him, like you said. I was in one of our unmarked cars. Not this one, a different one. So, around eight o'clock he goes back out. I guess he's probably had his dinner. He drives down the street, and he heads straight for her house, out on Plainfield, you know, where she lives?"

"Absolutely. Where her step-dad got hit by a car that night."

"Right. So he parks there and goes inside, and then I'm thinking, this is kind of weird. I was like, what is Alden doing at Cary Williams's house? I wasn't sure what you wanted me to do."

"Go on." Although she knew now. It was so perfectly clear. C.

"So I decided to go and knock on the door."

"God, Reed, no."

"I thought maybe I could see something that might help you, even just peeking in the door. Don't thank me, no problem. So anyway she opens the door, and there's Cary. And her little girl, Clarissa, that's her name, she's like wrapped around Cary's leg, hugging her, you know, in her pyjamas and everything."

"I knew she had a little girl. I didn't know her name." So then C could be Cary, or it could be Clarissa. Or it could be both.

"So, yeah, that's basically it. We just stand there chatting for a minute. I told her she shouldn't be opening the door like that, especially not with her little girl right there. I gave her a story about a couple of escaped convicts, armed and dangerous, warning the public and all that."

"And Alden?"

"He's there. I didn't see him just then, and she didn't invite me in, but I saw him go in her house, and his car was still parked around back. Maybe he heard me when I came to the door, maybe not."

He parked the car and turned off the engine. Fifty yards up the street on the right hand side stood the old Williams place. With Cary and Clarissa Williams inside. And Alden.

"How old is Clarissa?"

"Well, yeah, I actually did ask her. She told me herself. She's seven."

"Right."

"Why, Deborah? Is that important?"

"Reed, of course it is. Did you get a good look at her? What's the little girl look like?" After the fact, she realized that what she really should have asked was *who* the girl looked like. When she wasn't actually interviewing someone for an article, the questions always came out so imprecise.

"Hell, Deborah. Like any little girl in pyjamas, I guess. I didn't notice anything special."

"You were wonderful, Reed. Wonderful. You solved my problem."

"Really?"

"Yes, really."

"Are you going to tell me what's going on?"

"When I'm sure about it, yes."

"How about dinner some night, Deborah?"

She sighed, but in a very controlled way, so he wouldn't notice. She opened the door and put one foot out of the car. "I don't think so, Reed."

"Think about it."

"I will."

"You want me to wait here?"

"Yes."

She picked her way carefully up the sidewalk, trying to avoid stepping on the mulberries that lay on the sidewalk. How could you avoid them when they lay all over the sidewalk? Mulberry trees stood at fifteen foot intervals along the fence next to the sidewalk. The fruit was good to eat, but seedy, so most of the mulberries around town rotted in people's lawns or on sidewalks. What a nuisance. She gave up and mashed them under her shoes as she walked.

In the grass next to the walk leading up to the Williams front door, she wiped the soles of her shoes clean. A few seconds after she rang the doorbell the door swung open.

In the doorway stood Cary Williams, her hair all permed in a curly hairdo that came down to her shoulders. She had on faded jeans and a t-shirt, sandals on her feet. Cary's eyes went wide. The door started to close.

"Wait," Deborah shouted, and pushed the door back open, stepping inside.

"I've got nothing to say to you. I've done nothing wrong," Cary Williams said, shrinking back into the front hall. Behind her was a stairway going up. Over to the right a wide doorway opened onto the living room. One lamp was on over a chair, as if someone had been sitting there reading.

"Of course you haven't. You don't owe me anything," Deborah said.

"Well, we agree about that, so you can just leave." Cary Williams was breathing so hard Deborah wondered if she was going to pass out.

"I didn't come to bother you, Cary. I came to find my husband."

"Your husband! What do you mean, calling him your husband?"

"I'll be damned. You know something? You're right." She stared the other woman down for a few long seconds. Her hair was so ugly, done up in that fifty-dollar permanent wave. But what could you do with hair like that anyway? She decided to go ahead and say it. "You probably get more money every month than I do."

Cary Williams's eyes widened. Her mouth opened and wouldn't close again. At last she said, "What the hell d'you know about my money?"

"Seven years is a long time to be collecting from a married man."

Cary's eyes rolled up in her head, and she was staring at the ceiling now. Her hands revolved around each other, never finding purchase. Her hands couldn't stay still. Her eyelashes batted. Deborah realized she was right on track.

"A hell of a long time," she pressed on.

"And who else was going to step in?" asked Cary Williams. "He made me a widow. I was left with nothing. Just my little baby that wasn't even born yet."

"He made you a widow? What do you mean?"

Cary Williams focused on her for the first time again. "I saw it happen."

"What? You saw what happen?"

At that moment Alden appeared at the top of the stairs. Or rather, since her view of the top half of him was blocked by the downstairs hall ceiling, first Alden's shoes, then his knees, then, still gliding down the stairs, as he bent to see who Cary was talking to, his face. He stopped where he stood, halfway down the stairs. That was when their eyes met. Even at this distance she saw from his eyes that he was already defeated. He looked so much older. There was more gray in his hair. His moustache had gone white. Such a lot of wrinkles in his forehead. The color drained from his face. She could see it from fifteen feet away. It was as if all the blood was running straight out of his body. His moustache twitched.

What in God's name had Cary Williams seen? Since when had she been married in the first place? She had never been married in her life, so she couldn't be a widow either. Yet something about her story rang horribly true.

"So he is here."

Cary Williams shifted her feet and put one hand on her hip. "He was reading a story to Clarissa, if you don't mind. If you had any decency at all, you would leave now."

Deborah nodded, eyeing her husband who was walking up behind Cary. "It's a beautiful name, Alden. How did you settle on 'Clarissa'?"

"Get out, Deborah. What gives you the right to barge in here?"

"I knocked like anybody else."

"She barged in," Cary Williams said. "I tried to keep her out."

"I came looking for my husband. A woman has the right to come looking for her husband."

"Oh, this is rich. This is very rich," Alden said.

"Aldy, make her stop saying that."

"Two years tied up in divorce court and people are not still married," Alden said.

"Really? I'll have to ask my lawyer," Deborah said. "The way I understood it, we're married until we've both signed a paper. Now, I haven't signed and you haven't signed, last I knew."

"Get out, Deborah. You have no right to be here. I want you out."

"What were you reading to Clarissa, Alden? Do you come over every night and read to your daughter?"

"She's not my daughter!"

"She's not?" Deborah was confused.

"What are you saying? What are you saying? Tell the truth." Cary Williams was screaming hysterically now, beating him with her fists.

"Well, she is and she isn't."

Deborah stared. What was the meaning of it? Clarissa was his daughter for Cary's benefit, and she wasn't for Deborah's? He couldn't really have it both ways. She didn't understand. A good journalist learned to keep her mouth shut. She kept quiet.

"Aldy, she's going to hear you." Cary Williams tried to cover Alden's mouth with her hands, but she went right on moaning and making quite a bit of noise herself. Any minute now Deborah expected a little seven-year-old female version of Alden to appear at the top of the stairs.

She stood rooted to her spot and watched the two of them carry on. Cary Williams's face was covered with tears, her eyes pressed shut. She held tight to Alden's jacket and would have fallen down without her hold on him. His moustache worked, his eyes locked on Deborah.

"I adopted her. It was the least I could do. So she's mine in that way. It's not biological. Satisfied now? Do you have to know every last blasted detail? Put your tape recorder away now. You're not writing for the paper. You already stole my computer, what more do you want from me?"

"What? I don't have your computer. But it's lovely that Trip has a sister, Alden. Why haven't you introduced us all to each other?"

"Oh, Deborah." He waved her away with a look of disgust. "I can always tell when you're lying. Always. *Always.*"

Small steps, now. Things were falling into place in her mind. What did the computer even have to do with it? Small steps backward, now, keeping her eye on her husband, Alden, and the girl who had lost her stepfather in a hit-and-run accident seven years ago, and the girl's daughter. She did not want to hear more. There was a rottenness at the bottom of it. She felt behind her for the door, the door handle. She didn't want to know. This was Trip's father, for God's sake. All those rumors about Cary and her stepfather, years ago – *how had Alden made her a widow?* Had Alden murdered Charles Williams?

In one movement she turned, unlatched the door, escaped. The night air rushed into her lungs like oxygen into a fire. She went down the porch steps carefully, one well-aimed step after another, focusing on the boards under her feet. A comforting thought kept trying to emerge in her brain, just beyond her ability to grasp it. Then it came, bright and clear as a cinema marquis in her mind's eye. Trip. The message flashing in front of her eyes.

No way can you lose him now.

SISTERS

Olson drove for an hour due west out Route 64, which took them into the heart of Sycamore. Annie sat cross-legged in the seat next to him. It had taken her some time to calm down after the fighting. She kept checking the back seat, where the four shopping bags with phones stood, and the Thinkpad wedged in between them.

In downtown Sycamore each three-story red brick building stood shoulder-to-shoulder between two other ones, the whole length of South Main Street. It looked like every building had been built in the 1930s and each one carefully supported the one next to it.

"You come from here?"

"Born and raised. See, right there?" He pointed across her lap out the window. She caught a glimpse of the word *Sterling* on a sign attached to the red brick wall. "That's where I work. Alden's probably still inside right now."

"Are you going to show me your apartment?"

"I say we go to my place, lock up the laptop and the phones, then go and have a nice dinner."

Olson had a one-bedroom on the second floor of a building on North Main Street. They brought the phones straight into his bedroom and put them on the floor beneath the window. His bedroom looked out on Main Street. The place smelled like a museum. He opened the window to let in fresh air, then locked the laptop in the top drawer of a filing cabinet in his living room.

On the wall over the couch hung a large framed photo of a boy, clearly Olson, taken a few years before, but with wild, messy dark hair, and a girl.

"How old were you?"

"Nineteen. I was in college then. That's my sister, Lily. She was two years older than me."

"Was?"

"Hit by a car. Up in Madison. Drunk driver, a student at the university. She and her boyfriend were walking back along the road. They were out of gas. Her boyfriend was hurt badly, but he recovered."

He was still gazing at the picture of his sister. She waited till he looked down at her. "I'm so sorry, Bob." She hugged him then. Losing a sister . . . she couldn't even imagine it. She didn't even want to think about it. Had Alison wondered what it would be like to lose *her* when Annie had gone off to Iraq? She had never thought about it.

"That was lots of years ago, now. Hard on my parents, as you can imagine. Hey, let's go get some dinner. Are you as hungry as I am?"

An hour later she was sitting at a table in a steak restaurant with Olson, eating a good meal for what seemed the first time in days.

"I thought of something," Olson said. "Those guys are going to be pretty riled up after what you did to them, right?"

"No argument there."

"Plus you stole the phones back from them. That's the way they'll see it. Who do you think they're going to go after?"

She put her fork down and stared. She hadn't thought of this. "Alison. They're going to go straight back to her. Oh God, what have I done?"

"Wait a minute, wait a minute, Annie. Maybe I'm wrong. I mean, they saw us, right? They would have no reason to connect us with your sister, right?"

"Plus they got their GPS back. That's what started it all."

"Right. I wouldn't worry too much about it."

The thought had made her feel a little sick, all of a sudden. If all her efforts only made those two thugs go back to Alison and harm her, it would drive her completely mad.

"On the other hand," Olson said, "they're not going to be causing any trouble for a few days anyway, by the look of those injuries you inflicted. Jesus, Annie."

She smiled. He was right. "Well, it shows you don't fool around with me."

"I might want to keep you around for my own personal protection."

"I'm not for hire. Not for just anybody."

"So are you going to tell her?" Olson said. "Maybe it's better if she doesn't know anything about it. Because then if . . ."

"If those guys catch up with her again, she'll be blissfully ignorant."

"Something like that."

"But I want to give Todd his phones back."

Olson lifted one eyebrow. "Let's say those guys break in again and find all the phones back in their rightful place."

"They would make a connection between me and Alison. You convinced me. It can wait a few days."

"So did she write to you over there?"

It took her a few seconds before she knew what he meant. Why was he so interested in her relationship with her sister? "Yeah, we wrote. But, you know, her emails would be full of news about our parents, about her new apartment, her new job. She would send me some article that appeared under Todd's byline in the *Tribune* and tell me all about the research he had to do for it, things like that. At the end of an email she might write something like, *Miss you, kid, love and kisses.* Know what I mean?"

"Nothing too deep."

"There was always competition between us. Ever since we were little. But the day I went off to Iraq it was like something she couldn't compete with, for once. Totally out of her realm. I think she didn't know for a long time who I was anymore. So she didn't have any sense of how to compete with me. Maybe even now she doesn't know it. I'm not sure."

"Sounds like that might be a healthy thing, though."

"I guess maybe we're still feeling our way, a little. When I went to war, I changed the rules. I changed the paradigm. Also I changed. I spent the last four years in the military, you know? When I saw how those guys trashed her apartment, it awakened something from my military training in me. Like I had to protect her, and only I knew how."

Bob chewed, listening. He was a good listener. She felt like she could go on talking for hours, and his gaze would still be locked on her, taking it all in.

"Here I am telling you how ambivalent I am about my sister. I'm sorry. You must miss your sister. Did it take a long time for you to deal with her death?" Annie couldn't get the image out of her mind.

"I used to think you made your own luck," he said. "In other words, I thought there was no such thing as luck. When Lily died I had to reconsider. She didn't deserve her fate."

"I'm sorry. I didn't want to ruin our dinner."

"So why is it that you kept going back?"

"To Baghdad?"

"Yeah. Weren't you asking for it, maybe just a little?"

Her face went hot. The way he looked at her, his big round eyes not letting go, made it seem as if he could see some secret deep inside her, some secret she didn't even know herself. Some sisters had a secret language that only the two of them could understand. Some sisters had a premonition every time something went wrong in their sister's life, even if they were half a world away. And some sisters just drifted apart and then back together again, their closeness dictated by the circumstances of their lives, intermittently knowing each other more or less, caring about each other a little more or a little less, as the years went by.

"Before my military career I was like this *passive* person."

"Passive? You?"

She saw him studying her and she looked down at her plate. In her mind, an image replayed suddenly of the big man in the red muscle-shirt falling to the floor after she had clobbered him with the pyrex. What if he had turned around? What if she had missed, and hit him on the shoulder? Well, she hadn't missed. He had been too stupid or zonked or whatever to turn around. She had singlehandedly knocked him out cold. Passive she was not, no sir.

"My sister was better in everything she ever put her hand to. The first time I ever got out from under her was in the military. But that's just something I see now. It's not something I worked out in advance, and thought, *I can solve this problem if I join the army.* It wasn't ever about comparing myself to her. It was about comparing myself to me. It was about doing something with myself that's meaningful. I guess maybe I knew that by the time I went back for my third tour. I guess maybe I wanted to prolong it. I don't know if that makes any sense."

Olson was nodding. After half a minute he said, "That's powerful stuff. So do you feel closer to your sister now that you've taken care of those two guys?"

She thought about it. Relieved, yes. And satisfied, in a way. But did she feel closer? "I'm not really sure, to tell you the truth."

"And you've landed a job at TSR."

She shook her head. "Today was my last day."

"What? Have you told anyone?"

"You're the first to know. I'll give them a call in the morning."

"But why?"

"You act like that was some serious job or something. We got the phones back. We got your laptop back. I only went to work for TSR to teach those bastards a lesson. You didn't see the effect all this had on my sister. I mean, they were in her apartment. Plus I thought maybe I could find Todd's phones and get them back. And just think, three days ago I was moping around with nothing to do."

Olson smiled in recognition. "Those sure were some bad dudes."

"You're a man. Explain something to me. Why is it some men comprehend no other language but force?"

Olson put up his hands in retreat. "Annie, you're talking about things you know more about than me. I'm just glad you said *some* men."

She nodded. "You want to hear about *some* men? Or should I say *one* man that my sister and I had the pleasure of getting to know? When we were little, in the summer, we had swimming lessons every afternoon at the Dupage Bath and Tennis Club. Alison was like 12, I was 10. We were supposed to walk home along the street, where there were houses along the whole route. Places where a girl could run for help. And we always did walk along the street except for this one day."

"Oh, shit," Olson said.

"No, don't worry. This story has a happy ending."

"Really?"

"Well, you know, I mean, what is *happy*? Relatively speaking, I guess. Anyway, it was much shorter just to walk through the forest. The forest wasn't all thick and overgrown, or anything. Even in the middle of the summer you could see fifty yards ahead of you, through the trees. It was Alison who was always pushing for taking this shortcut, not me. She was my older sister, and she always knew better. So just this once we decided to do it. I follow her into the trees right across from the entrance to the club. I remember how scared I felt. It was like we were doing something Mom and Dad told us never to do. We knew it wasn't safe. But you know how kids are."

"Sure," Olson said.

"So there we are, jumping over fallen logs, pushing branches back to help each other get by, wading through the long grass. I remember this clearing and the sun shining in it. I remember wondering if there were snakes in this grass. And then all of a sudden, the grass in front of me explodes with movement. I jump back, my heart nearly bursting out of my chest, but it's only a rabbit scampering away in a zigzag pattern. We probably disturbed some rabbit babies or something."

"Was this in the springtime, then?"

She thought about it. "We were going to our swimming lessons, so it must've been summer vacation. I guess maybe early June, something like that? Anyway, so running right through the middle of this forest is this street called Madison Street. After a few minutes we come to the split-rail fence by the side of this road. *Come on*, Alison says, and she's bending down and squeezing between the upper and the middle rail. This road is the main danger in the forest. A boy named Ricky Moore was hit by a car and killed on Madison Street, so we know how dangerous it is. *We can cross*, she tells me. *Hurry, there aren't any cars coming.* So we run across.

"A car is coming around the bend just as we squeeze through the fence on the other side of the road. I specifically remember not looking, so that they won't see my face and tell my parents. I can hear the car slowing and stopping as I'm trying to get through this split-rail fence. I don't look at the car. I don't want to look. They shouldn't be stopping, there's no reason for a car to stop here, there's just us two. I don't know why they're stopping, but I know I haven't done anything. Only taking the shortcut through the forest. My jeans are caught on this thick splinter of wood sticking out of the middle rail. I'm there the whole time yanking on my leg, but the jeans won't give, and the splinter won't break. I can hear Alison yelling at me.

Come on, come on! she's yelling. Alison is watching the whole thing from twenty feet away. There's this man standing there. *Well well, what have we here?* he says. This man is standing right next to me, on the road-side of the fence, and he's smiling. His hand is reaching toward my leg. *Just wait, I'll help you*, he says. I'll never forget this guy as long as I live, Bob."

"I'll bet you won't," Olson said. "Jesus, what did he look like?"

"He has this dark crewcut. I remember the beads of sweat in between the bristly hairs on his scalp. He has this white t-shirt, sunglasses, big muscles, big teeth as he smiles. He reaches his big heavy tree-branch arm over the fence just as my leg finally comes free. And I'm thinking, we don't *know* this man. He shouldn't be stopping here. He shouldn't be touching me. That is not the smile of a good person. Alison is screaming, *Run, run!* His hand just touches my back, it grazes me, but now I'm free, and I'm dashing away from the fence, into the forest, toward Alison, just like that scared rabbit from before. *Run, Annie!* she's yelling, and we both take off through this forest, headed for home.

"And, but this sick man has actually leapt over the fence and is running after us. We were young, I'm ten years old, I don't know what he wants with us, but I know in my bones that he's bad. He's a monster. He's a predator, and we're the prey. And of course he's faster. I can hear his *crunch, crunch, crunch* catching up to me, getting closer and closer. Alison is still ahead of me, glancing over her shoulder with every step. She's faster than me, she's twelve, she would get away, but she waits for me. There are all these whipping branches to get through and rotten logs to jump over, and so what happens next is I fall down. My feet get tangled up and then I'm flat on my face in the leaves and sticks and mud."

"My God, Annie. Are you sure you want to tell me this?" Olson said.

"The bastard actually must've tripped me. And then I have this heavy adult man actually sitting on top of me, sitting on my back, I'm lying on my stomach in the mud and he's boxing my ears with his hard hands. It feels like he's hitting me with bricks. *Bad, bad girl! You don't run from me! You don't run away when I tell you to stop!* But then Alison comes right back. She's screaming. It's like this nightmare. But down deep she really keeps her cool, because the next thing I know she's poking a stick in this man's face, going straight for his eyes, taunting him. He jumps off me and goes for her, yelling, but he can't catch her. She runs away into this thicket of brambles."

"And you, Annie? What happened to you?"

"I'm still lying on the ground. It's like I've been pressed into the mud. I can still feel it. I can't move. It's like I'm petrified. Even now I can still smell the mud and leaves and forest rot from my face pressed into the mud there. I can smell that mud as if it happened yesterday."

"So what happened? Did you get away?"

There's a siren. The monster is trying to hack his way into the brambles where Alison has hidden when suddenly we hear a police siren, really loud and close. You can see the flashing red and blue lights through the trees. It's coming from Madison Street. We aren't that far from the road. His car is parked there, maybe three hundred yards away. Alison goes on screaming, she never stops screaming, she keeps hollering louder and louder, from deep in the brambles. Finally the man turns without another word and runs back in the direction of his car."

She hadn't thought about this incident in many years. All the details came back to her as if it had happened yesterday: the smell of the mud, the weight of the heavy man sitting on her back, the beads of sweat on his scalp between the bristles of his crewcut. She shuddered to think of the courage it had taken for Alison to come up close and taunt him with her stick.

"We stayed there for a while, crying, sitting in the leaves and the mud. We wondered if the police were going to come and take us home. I remember thinking the policeman must be there to arrest us because we had come through the forest. We talked for a long time about what to say to Mom and Dad. When the policeman didn't come, we finally got up and limped the rest of the way home. Our house was maybe another ten minutes from the spot where this happened."

Olson stared at her, just listening. She had stopped and started so many times, he was waiting to see if she had finished. They had finished dinner and eaten heavily, but she felt completely drained after reliving the story of the predator of their childhood.

"That was one hell of an experience you and your sister had," Olson said at last. "She saved your life. It's safe to say she saved your life, isn't it?"

"I try not to go back there too often. But I guess it probably made an impression on me. On both of us. To think that guy's still out there somewhere, maybe still going after young girls. What goes through these people's heads, anyway?"

"They're scum. What goes through people's heads who are scum?"

"Something does."

Olson nodded agreement. "Take the guy who was driving the car that hit my sister and her boyfriend. He lost his license and paid a one thousand dollar fine. Do you think he sent his condolences to me and my parents?"

She looked at Olson, waiting.

"His lawyer made him sue us."

"What? He sued you? Why would he sue you?"

"Their car was sitting by the side of the road, out of gas. It endangered him and his passengers, so he sued my sister's boyfriend and, since my sister was already dead, us."

"That's totally perverted."

"He didn't win his lawsuit, either. I mean, this guy was a drunk driver, after all. But the point is as far as we know he didn't even feel sorry for the pain he caused us, for the havoc that he caused in our lives. He never expressed anything like that to us, even though I lost a sister and my parents lost a daughter. For this guy all that mattered was to minimize the damage to his own record. The way he did that was by going on the offensive."

She thought about what Oscar Furey had said in the bar the night before. His job was to write the contracts so airtight nobody could sue TSR, Inc. That was what lawyers did. Not sort out the right from the wrong – just write the damned contracts so they're airtight.

"Speaking of lawyers, what do you think was so special about that Thinkpad?"

Olson lowered his voice and glanced around before answering. "For Mr. Sterling?"

"For the guys at TSR. Why didn't they want to give it back?"

"You keep going on about that."

"It keeps bugging me." They were practically talking in whispers.

"I don't know. I guess a new machine like that, they could resell it. Worth some money."

"But that can't be all of it, can it? Why did the lawyer have to get involved? Lawyers cost a lot of money. The lawyer only has to work for a few hours, there's the cost of the computer right there."

"You think they're selling the information that's on the computer?"

She shrugged. "What else could it be?"

Olson went serious, thinking about the possibilities. The expression on his face told her he was thinking about the information that would be on Mr. Sterling's computer. "I see how they could maybe do things there," he said slowly. "But that would involve a lot of work on their part. Imagine if they wanted to blackmail somebody, or extort money. They would have to do some serious research to fully understand the background, even just to know where to begin. That's assuming they would find anything in the first place. I don't suppose the files are exactly named 'Read this file if you want to blackmail me.' And if they were able to find something after all that, then they would still have to start sending letters, making contacts, making threats, I don't know what all."

"I suppose that's where the lawyer comes in. He would know how to do research like that, and he would know the legality of any sort of situation."

"Do you really think they're capable of things like that?"

She shrugged. "If the money were good enough, why not? I don't see why they would send the laptop to a lawyer, otherwise."

"I've thought about it a lot and I can't really see where that lawyer comes in, either. Mr. Sterling deals with lawyers all the time. Unless . . ." Olson stared off into the distance. He had gone pale. He put down his glass and stared at her.

"Unless what?"

"I know he's in the middle of a divorce. But that can't be it, can it?"

"Who knows? The point is, what's on your computer is your personal information. If someone else gets hold of your laptop, they shouldn't look at your personal documents. I'll bet this happens more often than we think at TSR. That's exactly why the lawyer got involved. That's their system. The lawyer helps him decide how far he can go with whatever they find on a computer, based on the legal aspects of it."

"That does make sense."

"And you know what that means. Lawyers cost money. That can only mean he's making money off of the information on machines like your boss's laptop."

"That's completely outrageous."

"What do you mean?"

"That someone would do something like that. Sneak around in your files until they find something that's so sensitive you'll pay money to get them to keep quiet about it."

"It's just a theory."

"The more I think about it, the more I think you may be on to something. That could be where the real money is. I just can't think what they could possibly have on Alden Sterling, that's all."

She watched Olson finish his bite. She had already finished. An idea was forming in her mind. "Bob, I've been thinking about this guy, Max Vinyl, at TSR."

"What about him?"

"He's running the show over there. These other people are just taking orders. It's not just what he did with your boss's laptop. He shouldn't be allowed to go on trashing the lake. Just think, if he sends six Dumpsters out there three or four nights a week, that's . . . that's like a thousand Dumpsters a year. I'm over on the other side of the world and people are getting their legs blown off, their arms blown off, and we're going through all that so that these bastards can dump boatloads of toxic junk in the lake? I don't think so. I don't know about you, but that seems very wrong."

"So now you want to go and beat him up, too?"

The cool thing about Olson was that he just sat and waited, not smug or arrogant, just neutral, interested, until she was ready. She said, "Actually, I've got something better in mind."

She watched his face as she told him the plan. He had a way of hiding behind those eyes of his. Or no, it wasn't just the eyes. He had a way of keeping his reaction to himself while he thought about how he wanted to react. He was patient. Olson's eyes were a darker shade of blue than hers, a shade closer to gray, but the color of his eyes stood out with that shaved scalp.

Later, back in his living room, looking again at the enlarged photo of Olson with hair, with his sister, she said, "You had such nice hair in that picture. When did you decide to shave your head?"

"I'm thirty-two," he said. "My hair is going white. Bugs the hell out of me. Come here, Annie. I want to show you some photos."

She laughed. "You didn't think of dying it?"

He was sitting on the couch with a photo album on his lap. "My bluebird collection. Have you ever seen a bluebird?" When she shook her head, he said, "Behold."

For the next hour she looked at photographs of bluebirds, cardinals, red-winged blackbirds, barn swallows, bats, great horned owls, red-tailed hawks and many other Illinois birds. He had the glossies in transparent sleeves four to a page in more than thirty albums. He made her turn the pages. "We'd never get through if I did it," he said. As he told her the story of a particular photo of an owl spreading its wings to leave the nest, taken as the sun rose, and Olson having spent the last six hours totally motionless up in a tree in the middle of the forest in the dead of night, she realized she was picking up an almost boyish happiness in his voice.

Later, she made two calls. The first was to Alison to see how she was doing. She picked up on her mobile.

"We're spending the night out at Mom's, Annie. Todd caught those guys sitting in their car in front of our place."

"What? When?"

"Late this afternoon, just before we left the city. They didn't have the phones anymore. They thought maybe he had stolen them back. That's why they came back to our place. He convinced them they were wrong and they drove away in a huff."

It took all her willpower not to tell her side of the story. "How weird. You don't think they were lying?"

"Todd said they looked like they were in bad shape, too. The one guy had a black eye. The other one was all bloody and messed up. I honestly don't think they're going to bother us anymore."

The other call went to an old friend who worked at the Great Lakes Navy base in Glencoe.

"That's totally out of the question, Annie," he said, when she described what she had in mind. But a half hour later he called back. Everything was already arranged.

In Olson's bedroom she said, "Play me that song again. The one you played last night. That ballad." *The Irish fighter.* As he played she watched his fingers on the strings. They moved over the strings as if with a mind of their own. The movement of his fingertips over the strings made the melody of the song open up like a flower. His soft baritone voice brought back that peaceful feeling of the night before. She felt that same hunger deep in her gut, and she knew it hadn't been a dream. And later, when she was making love to a man for the first time in more than nineteen months, and she felt Bob Olson's fingers caressing her body and his lips on her neck, she still had a picture in her mind of his fingers moving over the strings of his guitar, and she still heard the echo of his voice singing that special song.

ABACUS

The text from Alden had come during the night before, proposing breakfast this morning at six-thirty. *With or without?* he had texted back. *Without,* came the answer. He had left the laptop locked in his filing cabinet and left the house at 6:15, ready for breakfast and a few answers. Annie left the house with him.

"You're going to run for a whole hour without stopping?"

"Absolutely. See you later."

The breakfast place Alden had picked was not the one where the townspeople generally went. He had picked a restaurant on the outskirts of Dekalb, eight miles to the south, where everyone would be a stranger. Very strange, Bob thought as he wound around the crowded parking lot, looking for a space.

Inside, he found his boss already sitting at a table. The menu lay on the table in front of him. Steam rose from his coffee. They shook hands.

"I could tell you some stories," Bob said.

"I'll bet you could. I want to hear all about it, too. But not just now, if you don't mind. Today is Friday, and it's crucial that we move today on this."

"Alden, what's going on?"

Alden's moustache moved. "I got you in here this morning in order expressly to keep you in the loop. We're going to be partners, and I don't want to have secrets from you."

Bob held up one hand. "You started up the firm, and you were in business for years before I came along. It goes without saying that I won't ever know everything about every account. There's something to be said for compartmentalization, too. What I don't get is why these bastards got so interested in your laptop. What in the world did they think they were going to get out of a bunch of old tax returns?"

Alden was shaking his head. "Exactly, Bob. Our work is of no interest to anybody. That wasn't at all what they were after."

"Wait a minute. You mean someone got hold of your laptop on *purpose*?"

"My divorce," Alden said, "or, more specifically, who gets custody of my son, is a question that has been held up in court for the last two years. My wife arranged for my laptop to fall into the hands of that lawyer. Now she's going to use certain information from the laptop to try and influence the judge to rule in her favor on the custody question."

"My God," Bob said. It felt like he had a giant rock lodged in his stomach.

A waitress came up to the table, pen in hand. They ordered, then neither one talked. Bob tried to reconstruct the events that had led to Alden's laptop going astray. Something didn't add up. Something bothered him at the edge of his consciousness. He took a drink of milk. Suddenly he knew what it was.

"Alden, if McCoy's intention was to help your wife by stealing your laptop, why wouldn't he just steal it and bring it to her? Why put it on the trash pile? Why go to the trouble of letting this recycling company take it away? Seems like it kind of took the long way around, getting back to her."

Alden wagged his finger. "You don't have much experience with the law, Bob. We've got to get you into a few more legal situations, get your feet wet. It's all about how you get your hands on the evidence, in these things. *How* it happens can make or break the case. If it's done the wrong way, illegally, the evidence can't be used. McCoy must've finessed it with the recycling company to make sure they were expecting it. It's the only explanation. See, what they've done is quite simply to sell it to her. McCoy got a piece of that action."

"But that's got to be illegal. It's unbelievable."

"Of course. But it's a hell of a lot more deniable the way he did it. Nevertheless, that's how I have to go after him."

"This blows me away, Alden. I had no idea he could be so treacherous, or that . . . well, that your custody situation was so ticklish." He felt nervous getting into personal territory. But Alden seemed to want to go there.

"This was the part you didn't know anything about, till now. It's my private life. To be honest . . . well, it's a bit of a godawful mess." The food came, and they stopped talking until the waitress left again. Alden picked up his fork, but he didn't take a bite. "I guess what I'm trying to tell you is I'm not perfect, Bob."

"Of course," Bob said. The omelette and hash browns sat on the plate in front of him, but he didn't feel like eating.

"The way I figure it, when you meet your maker, he adds up all the good deeds you've done in your life. All the charity, and the giving, and the kindness. Like he's got a big abacus. And then he weighs all that against your bad deeds. You know, errors in judgment, nasty thoughts you might've had, times when you were dishonest."

"Alden, you're fine."

"I know I am. I know it. God knows it. But you know, Bob, when your ex-wife gets hold of your computer, frankly it's a little like she's the one holding the abacus."

He looked at his boss. The white moustache twitched once. Alden's eyes flicked up and met his, then looked down again. It was early, and Alden was sharp as ever, but he looked tired just the same. It was then that he understood that there *was* something in that Thinkpad that Alden had wanted to hide. Something he was afraid of. Something that was going to cost him the thing he desired most in the world, custody of his son.

Suddenly, with a shiver, Bob realized he couldn't look him in the eye anymore.

"So how do we fight a thing like that?"

Alden chewed for a while, then cleaned his lips and his moustache with his napkin. He reached across and touched Bob on the shoulder, and he showed just a hint of a smile. He still spoke softly, just in case anyone else in the dining room had any interest in the conversation. "With a good lawyer, Bob. The only way. Fight fire with fire."

Bounced

Ginger sat waiting for Max in his office on Friday morning when he arrived. In his chair. In a red leather miniskirt, a red and white-striped sleeveless blouse, and red pumps. Truth be told, she looked stunning for a forty-seven year old. If only she didn't have to slather on so much of that orangey perfume! His office would stink of it all morning. He made no effort to hide his annoyance.

"Do you mind?" He came around the desk, wondering if he had remembered to lock his desk the night before, especially the drawer where he had stuffed the briefs. She stood up. "How did you get in here?"

"Well, good morning to you, too."

"Good morning, Baby. For your information, I happen to have a few things on my mind."

"You're not the only one, Max. It so happens that your check bounced."

"What? But that's impossible." He could see from her grim look that she wasn't buying it.

"I should've listened to Ricardo."

"No, Baby, I don't know what went wrong, here. Honestly."

"I know what went wrong, Max. It's very simple. You don't have any money in that account, that's what. Now, if you want me to go away, I want cash."

"Aren't you even going to ask how my scratches are doing?"

"I'm going to add some scratches of my own if I don't get my money. And make it snappy."

"Twelve thousand in cash? Just like that?"

"I should charge a thousand extra for having to drive all the way here and pick it up. Not to mention my embarrassment at the bank. They were laughing at me. In addition to having to wait four months for my money. Goodness, Max, enough is enough. Ricardo wants to go back to the judge since you low-balled the value of the company two years ago. If I have to sit here and argue with you about it, so help me, I'll be back to him first thing on Monday."

A quick knock came on the door. Rodriguez stopped when he saw Ginger. His look went from one to the other. "Sorry for barging in, Max. I've got to talk to you about this information you asked me to prepare for the Koreans."

"Not now, Manny."

"Fine. Just let me know when it's my turn."

"What's eating him?" Ginger said when Rodriguez had stormed out.

"Never mind. Let's go get you some cash, then."

He stood and led her to the door. The last thing he wanted today was to spend time arguing with Ginger in his own office. Rodriguez was right. They had more important things on the agenda.

"Where are we going?"

He led her through reception, through triage and out to the loading dock. Maurice sat at the desk reading the paper and smoking a cigarette.

"Morning folks," Maurice said as they walked by.

In the safe room, Max twirled the dial. Before going to the second number he looked over his shoulder. "Don't look, Baby. This combination is privileged information."

"It's probably 36 – 22 – 35 if I know my Max."

This statement from his ex-wife caused a reflex in his knees. He bumped his head painfully on the safe handle, then turned to gape at her. "How in Christ's name did you know?"

"Only you would use my measurements for your combination, Baby."

"Going to have to change it now," he muttered.

"Those aren't my measurements anymore, anyway. Don't even ask, Max. You're not buying my dresses these days, last I knew."

He carefully removed twelve thousand in hundreds. There was such an enormous pile of cash in the safe, it looked like the armored company hadn't stopped by in several days. Rodriguez had better move on that.

Back in his office, he counted out the bills on his desk and stuffed the money in an envelope. "Let's forget about the bounced check," he said. "I wanted to turn over a new leaf. I really don't know how it happened. I didn't mean to cause you trouble."

She buried the envelope in her purse. "You never mean to, Max. It's just that it never changes. The day you turn over a new leaf will be the day you meet your maker. I understand that. Why do you think I let you go?"

Now she was slandering him. He couldn't stand for that. "I'm the one who let *you* go. It's not important to me, but let's get the facts straight."

"That's your version. I could've fought a lot harder. Why don't you ask your lawyer, if you don't believe me."

She stood up to leave. What a way to start the day! First, having to raid the safe to pay her off. And now she was trying to revise the history books and make it *her* divorce. But then, when you thought about it, it wasn't surprising that a person on her third trip through the divorce courts, and an older woman, at that, would want to own the process.

"I wouldn't wish a ten-year age difference on anyone," he added. A cheap shot. So what? A wrinkle briefly materialized in her forehead.

"Oh? Does that rule apply for you and your adolescent receptionists, as well? See you tomorrow, Max."

"Tomorrow?"

"The funeral service for Greta. You wouldn't forget. Honestly."

"She's twenty-nine," he corrected. Well, eight years' difference was acceptable, wasn't it? Ginger laughed. She was out the door. Probably off to see Ricardo to schedule a new court date. As if he didn't have enough to worry about.

He sat back in his chair, wishing he could take back that whole conversation. What had made him blurt out Tris's age? Why did Ginger have to know every infinitesimal detail about him, anyway? It was insane. All the more so, because with Tris it was over. Tris herself was now nothing more than a brief chapter in the life of Max Vinyl. What did it matter what anyone thought, least of all Ginger?

His phone rang. Speak of the devil. He saw from the number on the display that it was Tris. He sighed and pressed to connect.

"Hi Tris. Thanks for calling."

"I got your mail, Max. I was so surprised that you wanted to talk. It's so unlike you."

He felt a strong urge to say his lawyer had told him to do it. But Tris would probably take it the wrong way. He said, "You win. I got your message. I'm sorry about your car and everything. It was kind of a knee-jerk reaction."

"And my brother's beach cottage? Was that your knee jerking, there, too?"

"You lost me, Tris." Here he wasn't about to admit to anything. Brainard had gotten away without the slightest problem. That had sent the desired message.

"Play the innocent. What is the point of this conversation exactly?"

"Are you sure I can't buy you a new car, just like the old one?"

"That won't be necessary."

"To make up for my foolish mistake."

"No, Max."

"You won't let me make amends?"

"Not that way. You owe big time. Much more than a new car."

"Like for instance?"

"You tried to kill me, Max. Your man, Brainard. How would you feel if someone tried to kill you?"

"Funny you should ask. That's exactly how I felt a couple of days ago after your unprovoked pepper spray attack. I felt like I was going to die, Tris. Right on your doorstep. And that was just my eyes. Which by the way are still completely bloodshot. But what about the way I felt inside? You used me. You wanted to hurt me and hurt this company. You wanted to hurt everyone that works here."

"Is that what's bothering you?"

"No, actually, that's not the main thing." He looked at the picture of the cream-colored Bentley Roadster on his wall. Those huge wheels. That red leather interior. He had been dreaming of buying that car for five years now, adding it to his collection. Yet at this moment it felt like the first time he had ever seen it. "The main thing is that I'm really sorry it's over."

"Well, I'm glad we got that cleared up."

He didn't know how to go on from here. As far as he was concerned, nothing was cleared up. But she was waiting for him to talk. "So, about the booby trap on my car collection?"

"Yes?"

"Call it off, Tris."

"I don't think so."

"Why not?"

"I told you before."

"When?"

"In your office. I guess you weren't listening."

"Okay, well, I'm listening now."

"Are you sure?"

"Christ, Tris. Just tell me. You hurt me a lot, you know."

"You hurt me, too, Max."

"But how? What in Christ did I do?"

"I went to work for a recycling company. I thought you were the greatest. Then you turned out to be a scuzball who dumps computers in the lake. Here I am in bed with a man who doesn't see anything wrong with that. You're poisoning the water. You're poison. You poisoned me."

"I don't believe this. That's sick, Tris. You know what? You mentioned you were doing some therapy. You obviously have a lot of pent-up rage."

"You see, you don't want to hear it. You won't listen."

"I am listening. I just think it's kind of warped."

"Are you going to stop?"

"Stop what?"

"Stop dumping, stupid. What were we just talking about?"

"We can discuss that, if you want."

"Not good enough. Say goodbye to your cars."

"Tris, do you know how many years I spent collecting those cars?"

"Not as many years as it's going to take for the lake to recover."

"Listen, Tris. Up until now we've kept the police out of it, even when you took down my entire network with your hack. I can't very well keep the police out of it if you firebomb my cars. Is that what you want?"

"Do you think we kept the police out of it when my brother's beach cottage was torched two nights ago? We saw Brainard running away from the place. I'm surprised they haven't contacted you yet."

"You must be mistaken. What does he have to do with your brother's beach cottage? What does your brother's beach cottage have to do with anything?"

"It burned down, Max, remember? We were talking about burning things."

"Your brother's cottage burned down?"

"Good try, Max. We got a picture of Brainard running from the scene."

He doubted they had snapped a picture. Otherwise she would've already sent it to him. He went on, "Well, I'm talking about things you're threatening to burn. A little computer hack is one thing, Tris. Firebombing my cars is, like, terrorist stuff."

"You sound desperate, Max."

"I am desperate. Because you're not listening."

"Funny, why do I have the same feeling? Goodbye, Max."

"Wait!"

But she had hung up. He sighed. Why had his sales skills gone and deserted him, just when he needed them most? Was Tris really capable of torching his car collection? Seventeen classic cars, collected over so many years, so lovingly preserved. And what if it didn't stop with that? Was she going to blow up his house? Was she going to get in touch with Song Young Park and queer the deal? With a sick feeling, Max realized Song had probably slipped his business card into Tris's thong, back at the Skinny Whip. Everyone had. The way his luck was going these days, she had probably already been on the phone to him. The woman had to be stopped. But first he had to defend his own property.

Brainard, he thought, now that she mentioned him. Brainard knew his way around explosives. That's the ticket, he thought. Send Brainard to disarm the booby trap.

PRAIRIE FIRE

"You live here?" Bob asked. They had driven to her cabin in the forest preserve.

"Temporarily, yes. You like it?"

"It's public property." He went in her front door. She watched him inspecting her camp cot, the reading lamp, the two-burner stove, the table and chairs. "Ever heard of Ralph Emerson?"

"Rings a bell." For a minute they had to be quiet. All talking was drowned out by a low-flying plane.

She led him back outside. "In there, that's just for sleeping, you know. Out here is where it's really grand." She locked the door and took his hand, leading him down to the riverbank. They walked along the Des Plaines River for the next forty minutes, heading north.

She pointed out a pair of wood ducks in the water, almost hidden by reeds. At another point they saw a small green turtle swimming in the water, most of the time only the tip of its nose breaking the surface. Dragonflies, bumblebees and other buzzing, zooming insects crisscrossed the water in the bright June sunshine. "Remind me to bring my camera next time," Olson said. Those dimples gave him such a boyish look. Every ninety seconds another jumbo jet thundered in overhead, so low it seemed as though it might drop out if the sky onto them. The planes didn't seem to bother the animals or the insects.

"I've got to hand it to you," Olson said when they got back to the cabin. "You've found a little corner of heaven, here."

"Come on. I'll make coffee."

While the water boiled they stood staring at the street map of Chicago and suburbs she had pinned up on the wall above the bed.

"You see this street," Olson's finger traced Ogden Avenue, running into the city from the southwest. "I looked it up. Did you know it used to be called the Old Southwest Plank Road? For obvious reasons. Before that it was a trail used by Indians coming in from the southwest."

"Obvious to you."

"Oh." He pushed his glasses up. "Well it seems there were elections coming up, and the politicians wanted to make it easier for the voters to get to the polls. They put down planks in the road to solve the mud problem. Made it a lot easier for buggies to get to the polling place."

"Sounds like Chicago, all right. Anything to try and tip an election. When did this happen?"

"1848."

"Bob, how do you know all this stuff?"

He looked at her through his glasses, obviously thinking of how he wanted to answer. "When I go out with a girl, I've got to know a little about her family, you know? Aren't you a descendent of William Butler Ogden?"

"Dumb question, but who's that?"

"First mayor of the city of Chicago, from 1837 onward. They named the Old Plank Road after him in 1872, five years before he died. Ever since then it's been called Ogden Avenue."

"Oh. I guess I'll have to ask my Dad."

"You should do that. But be advised that the desecration of the land started back then, with those plank roads." He traced another road, north of the city. She had to stand on the cot to read it. "Green Bay Road," Bob said. "Another Indian trail. It follows a ridge. On either side there were swamps a lot of the time. The ridge is the moraine. The Indians kept to the ridge, up above the swamps. So when the Indians were driven out, the roadbeds were already there. They just had to be paved."

"So you're saying my ancestors were the original desecrators of the land?"

Bob shrugged. "There's black sheep in every family, Annie. Anyway it goes a bit far to compare laying roads through the swamp with dumping icky computers in the lake."

"That reminds me of a question. Let's say you move into a deserted cabin, like this. You fix it up, paint the walls, put up a flag. The cabin belongs to someone else, but you fix it up. Is that squatting?"

He stared for a minute, waiting to see if she was finished. Then he said, "I'll have to get back to you on that, Annie. Can I go on?"

"Go on with what?"

"The whole city was built on swampland, see, over the years. I was thinking about this when you were talking about Max Vinyl polluting the lake. Low, marshy land. The lake always flooded. The rivers that flow into the lake flooded all the time. You have some rivers that flow naturally into the lake, like the Chicago River and the Calumet. But this river right out here –" he motioned to the outside. "Your Des Plaines River, even though we're only fifteen miles from the lake, here, flows the other way. The Des Plaines flows west, into the Illinois River, which flows into the Mississippi."

"Wait a minute. I thought the Chicago River flowed *out* of the lake."

"Does now. Ever since they reversed the flow of it in the year 1900."

"Reversed the flow?"

"Think sewage. Now you're talking desecration. You had unbelievable population growth and a river that didn't move. No current. And no filtration plants or other modern technology. Anyway, but the really interesting thing is–"

"That's actually pretty interesting, Bob."

"I know, but listen to this. I mean, why do you think the Indians would bother to come and live in this wretched swamp land? Why did they have trails through it in the first place, if it was so swampy?"

"Let me guess. The berries were in season in the swamp? They liked blueberries?"

"Very funny, Annie. You're making fun of me. Try: running from the fire."

"Fire?"

"Prairie fires. West of Chicago is where the prairie begins. Central Illinois, Iowa, Nebraska, Wyoming. Dry grasses, wildflowers, wide open country, fewer forests. In the late summer, there would be thunderstorms, just like we get them now in late summer, only the prairie was so dry back then, it wasn't irrigated like we do now with our cornfields, lightning strikes in the time of the Indians probably tended to set the prairie on fire."

"Oh, my God."

"Yeah, with their tents and villages and babies and grandmothers and everything. So when they saw the smoke on the horizon, they knew there was fire danger. They probably knew they had to run east till they reached the swamp."

"You're putting me on."

"I'm not. Well, it's just a theory. But they certainly must have known the fire went out when it reached the swampland. The ground was too wet. Everything was wet. Still is. This is where the prairie meets the swamp. This swamp, right here, where you live. The Des Plaines River."

Kneeling on her bed, she cupped his face in her hands. For a moment he had had her picturing Indian families from three hundred years ago roving across the land, a dangerous pall of smoke darkening the sky at their backs. She held him there for a minute. He didn't look away. He looked right back into her eyes.

"Okay, prairie man, let's get that shirt off." She wrestled him down onto the bed. The only resistance he put up was to hold her off while he took off his glasses. She got the shirt over his head, then bunched it up in her hand and threw it on the floor, all the while kissing him. At one point he disengaged.

"You mind closing the door, squatter?"

SEXY

"Furey, we've got a problem."

"That you, Mr. Townsend? Tell me."

"Yes, goddamn it. I got the computer back to my office last night and my people tell me there's nothing on it. I looked myself. It's empty. Zero."

"What do you mean, nothing on it? We started it up together. I showed you."

"Furey, I wasn't born yesterday. Now I handed over one hundred thousand dollars in cash to you, and I have a meeting in one hour with my client that I am going to have to cancel. There is not a single goddamn Word or Excel file or email on this computer."

"I don't understand." Furey searched his brain for possible explanations. Was Townsend so inept that he didn't know how to open files? Impossible. Then there was Rodriguez to consider. Maybe when he had copied the data, he had erased it? But how could that leave no trace at all?

"You can understand my annoyance," Townsend said.

"I'm sitting here trying to think what could've happened," Furey said.

"So help me, Furey, I had a bad feeling about this from the beginning. I don't want trouble, but I know how to make trouble if I have to."

"Mr. Townsend, I'm sure there is an explanation. Bear with me while I make a couple of calls. I will call you back as soon as I can get my hands on some information."

As soon as the line was dead, Furey punched the number of Max Vinyl.

"What is it, Oscar?"

"It's that lawyer I talked to. Something crummy with the data. He's got nothing on the laptop, no files."

"He paid?"

"I've got the cash, yeah."

"Then solve his problem. What do you need from me?"

"Manny copied the data. I think maybe something went wrong. All Townsend needs is the data in usable form."

"I'll put you through to Manny. Keep me informed, Oscar."

Oscar Furey tapped a beat to the company telephone music until Rodriguez came on the line. "Impossible," Rodriguez said when Furey had explained his theory. "After I copied the data I went back in and had a look at the Thinkpad once more. Standard procedure. The data was there."

"Well, it's not there now. You must've erased it."

"I didn't erase the fucking data."

"Well, it's not on the Thinkpad, and we've collected his money. We've got to get that data to him somehow."

"But that's ridiculous. What a hemorrhoid. I've got hours of work to do to prepare something for the Koreans tomorrow. Max has got me doing incomings all day. As if I have time for this."

"Manny, something plain went screwy. There's no earthly reason why he would need us to provide the data twice. You should've heard this guy on the phone."

"Dumb question. Does he know how to operate a computer?"

"Spare me, Manny. Just help me get the data to him. Let's figure out what happened afterwards."

Rodriguez sighed. "We'll put the data on another laptop. How soon do you need it?"

"Manny, you're driving me crazy. Call me when it's done. This guy is absolutely livid, and I've got to bring it to him. I'm getting in my car now. I'll be there in an hour."

"No, I'll call you when it's done." When he had ended the call, Rodriguez opened his locked filing cabinet and took out the external hard drive onto which he had copied the Thinkpad hard drive and all its contents. On the way out of his office he bumped into Max Vinyl.

"Where's that receptionist that started a few days ago?" Max asked.

"Called up this morning. Said it wasn't going to work out. She quit."

"Bitch. I hope you're holding her salary."

"She won't get a penny."

"Unbelievable."

"We're just letting the phone ring. There's a message that comes on. Tell me something, Max. Do we really need a receptionist?"

"You read my mind."

Rodriguez went to testing. The first worker he laid eyes on was the tall, bony programmer named Roberto. He handed over the external drive.

"Find a decent laptop and load this data. Put it on my cost center."

"You need it when?"

"I'm going to watch you do it."

Roberto stared a moment, then took the drive and with the other hand punched some instructions onto his computer. On the second try a green light blinked on his screen. "Bingo. Found a Toshiba Satellite from last year. Should be coming down the belt in a couple of minutes. What's on this drive, here? Anything special?"

"Nothing special at all."

"Just urgent."

"Urgent is right."

They stood watching the conveyor belt. "Here it comes, see it down there?" Roberto said. Rodriguez race-walked over to the laptop, grabbed it off the belt and jogged back to Roberto's workstation. "Go to work, doc."

Roberto unwrapped the Toshiba from its shrink-wrap and handed the bar-coded ticket to Rodriguez for his signature. Roberto then attached a cable to the USB port on the laptop and on the external drive. Next he turned on the power.

"And you are watching me because . . .?" he asked while waiting for it to boot.

"Your backside and mine."

"Uh oh. Got an error message, here."

"Show me that. What's it mean?"

"Not sure yet. I'm guessing this laptop's got a broken hard drive. Let me just . . . try this." He punched some more keys and watched the screen. The verdict didn't take long. "Nope. Laptop is good. So either the data is corrupted or it's the external drive. Let's get another laptop, just to be sure."

Three minutes later a Hewlett-Packard laptop came down the belt. Roberto repeated the process of hooking up the external drive to the laptop and powering on.

"Bad news. The laptops are good, but the data won't read. See for yourself."

Rodriguez was not a computer programmer. He stared at the error message on the screen. Same as the one before. All he could tell was that it wasn't one of those standard ones you saw every day. "What does it mean?" he asked, trying to keep the irritation out of his voice. "Can you fix it? Can you get me that data? I need that data."

"We can exclude the laptops at this point," Roberto said. "Which means it's either some problem with the data itself, or the external drive you copied it onto."

"Shit. But I looked at it after it copied. It loaded the data and gave me a confirmation. Then I looked at it."

"These external drives are kind of fragile, for the purpose they are used for. It could've actually become defective after you copied the data onto it. You know, some little piece inside cracks. It happens."

"Can you test it?"

"Sure. That's our next step." Roberto plugged the external drive into his workstation and opened another program. He punched buttons and studied the screen for a full minute. It looked like he was doing some sort of scan. "There's your problem. The external drive has a broken sector. Says it right here. The data is compromised."

"How compromised? What does that mean? Tell me you can get that data out."

"There's another guy that works here who's actually pretty good with that kind of shit. I could do it, too, but we'd be here all night."

"Who is it? Is he here?"

"Murray. He's got the day off."

"I'm going to go and call him. You get started. Then he can take over."

"It doesn't work like—"

"Just do it," Rodriguez snapped, and headed back in the direction of his office. First he had to call Murray and try to get him to come in on his day off. Then he had to warn Furey it was going to take longer. Then he had to update Max. What a fucking madhouse. As he walked through reception on his way to his office, the little bell chimed, and Furey walked in.

"Well, have you got it?" Furey's upbeat look changed to a snarl when he saw Rodriguez's expression. "You can't be serious. What now?"

"The disc jockeys in there are trying to get the data out of the external drive that I copied everything onto. The external drive is defective. So this is turning into a real extra gigantic pain in the butt."

"Just tell me you used a brand new external drive, Manny. Not some refurbished piece of shit. Not for this job."

He stared Furey down. The arrogance of lawyers. As if he was going to get in his car and drive all the way to Wal-Mart and spend money on new equipment when they were awash in it here. "Straight out of inventory, Oscar. Our stock is good quality."

Furey swore.

"You need to tell your client," Rodriguez went on, starting to enjoy himself, "that we are working on the problem but it could take a little longer than expected."

"What does that mean? Give me something concrete."

"In all probability tomorrow. That's if they can get the data out at all."

"What? What are you telling me?"

The bell above the door chimed. A man wearing a New York Yankees baseball cap walked in with an oversized envelope in his hand.

"Hi guys. Midwest Courier," he said. "I got an envelope for Mr. Max Vinyl, here. Signature of recipient required."

"I can sign for that," said Rodriguez.

"Are you Max Vinyl?"

"General Manager. I'll see that he gets it."

The courier held the envelope to one side. "Be much obliged if he could sign for it himself."

"Let me see it." The courier held it near enough for him to read the return address. Oscar Furey read it over his shoulder. It was from an attorney in Sycamore, Illinois. But not Townsend's firm, Oscar Furey noted.

"Can't be a court summons, delivered by private courier like this," Manny said.

"No one serving on him anyway," Furey said.

"I don't know what it is," said the courier. "I only know I get twenty dollars extra if the recipient signs personally."

"Give me that," Furey said. He snatched the envelope away from the courier and signed. "I'm Max Vinyl's attorney. It's headed for my desk anyway."

The courier shouted, "Fuck you, and your mother crosswise." He slammed the door so hard the walls shook.

Furey went into Max Vinyl's office and laid the envelope on the desk. "Just arrived by courier," he said. "I signed for it."

"Why in Christ would you do a stupid thing like that?" Max went to work on the envelope. He checked the address of the sender. Lawyer. How surprising. At least it wasn't Ginger's lawyer. He had paid her, anyway. "By the way, did you bring my hundred grand?"

Furey took a manila envelope out of his attaché case and poured out the contents onto the desk, ten bundles of cash wrapped neatly with paper bands. One hundred bills in each bundle. His eyes swept over the cash, counting the bundles, then turned to the letter he had removed from the courier envelope. His smile evaporated as he read further. After a minute he dropped the letter on the pile of cash in disgust.

"Oh, this is priceless. This has got to be a first. Oscar, would you please explain how this asswipe found out what we were doing before we even got started doing it?"

Furey read the letter. It was from an attorney representing Alden Sterling, the owner of the Thinkpad. He was threatening to contact the State's attorney of the State of Illinois. He wanted the State's Attorney to indict Max Vinyl on the grounds that Sterling's private and confidential computer data on a laptop recovered by TSR was being used to cause insult and injury to Sterling in exchange for personal gain. The attorney planned to file his complaint with the State's Attorney next Tuesday at 12 o'clock noon. At the same time, he would file suit in civil court, claiming damages of two million dollars.

The filings could only be avoided if two conditions were met: 1) the laptop was returned in good working order, all files intact; 2) Max Vinyl signed a sworn and notarized affidavit to the effect that no third party had seen any of the files or other contents of said laptop. The lawyer further reserved the right to file suit if at any time in the next five years if evidence surfaced indicating that a third party or third parties had seen any of the files or contents of said laptop.

"I wouldn't worry about the State's Attorney," Oscar Furey said. "You can see it yourself. Very overblown. They have to file the civil suit because there is no way in hell they would ever get even five minutes' attention from the State's Attorney. Believe me, Max. They've got bigger fish to fry than us."

"You sure about that?"

"I wouldn't use a word like sure. Reasonably convinced, yes."

"Not good enough, Oscar. What's your advice?"

"Frankly, we've got a bigger problem right now with the wife."

"The wife?" For a moment Max was confused. The word brought Ginger to mind. But she wasn't his wife now. Which Furey knew better than anyone, since Furey had represented him in the divorce.

"Sterling's wife," Oscar Furey said. "The one who forked over this money. They're having trouble getting the data out of the laptop we gave them."

"I know about that. Manny made a backup."

"Manny just told me the backup is broken. They're going to have a hell of a time getting the data out of it."

"Don't worry about that, Oscar. Those guys down there know what they're doing. That's their job."

"Problem is, we've got his money." He waved at the cash on the table. "I've got to call and let him know what's going on. He could get obnoxious."

"Here, use my phone. Let him get obnoxious. Tell him shit happens, you're working on it. Sometimes people just have to wait, damn it. Why can't everybody just be patient, for Chrissake? Why is everyone freaking out around here?"

A knock came on the door. Max went to the door and went out, since Furey was already on the phone. Ike Mullin und Tranny Ng stood in reception.

The sight of them left him speechless. Ike now sported what appeared to be a wooden table leg swinging back and forth in front of his face. It was attached to that ungodly bolt that pierced his eyebrow. Ike held the end of the table leg jauntily in one hand, as if people went around like that all the time, and he had a black eye. Tranny had cuts and dried blood all over his face and arms. It looked like Tranny's wounds hadn't been cleaned, and his left wrist looked swollen and bent the wrong way.

"You guys look like you ran into more than just bad traffic," Max said. "You want to see me? Could you wait in the canteen and come back in fifteen minutes?"

"We've got all evening, boss," Ike said.

He went back into his office. Furey sat there, head in his hands. His face had gone pale. "Bad idea to call from this phone. Now they're on their way here."

"Who cares? It's simple. Just get the data for them," Max said. "Why do you bother me with this shit? Manny's working on it, isn't he?"

"Yes, he's working on it."

"Good. What I want to know from you, Oscar, is what happens if this State's Attorney gets interested in TSR. What then?"

Furey took off his glasses, rubbed his forehead with both hands, and expelled a huge sigh. Then he straightened up. "Listen, these are the guys who come down and haul away your computers and your filing cabinets and interview all your employees. He's got to have probable cause to get them interested. Let's assume he thinks he's got that. Otherwise he wouldn't have gone to the trouble. Thing is, they like media attention, too. Don't forget the State's Attorney is an elected official. So the case has got to be sexy."

"Are we sexy?"

"I'm sexy as hell. You're a fucking disaster." A look went between them. Max was in no mood for banter. "Just kidding, Max. By the way, can I just tell you that I admire the way you stay so cool and collected even when you're under pressure."

"Well I'm not feeling cool and collected right now. I'm feeling like things are spinning out of control, here."

"I was being sarcastic, Max. You look like a train wreck. I've never seen you like this. How long before your eyes are back to normal? You look like some kind of voodoo doctor or something."

"Thanks, Oscar. Anyway, so you're saying we wouldn't be sexy enough to get the State's Attorney interested?"

"That's my judgment, yes. Which is good. Because basically, if you get them on your case, then you're really toast. If there's anything worth finding, they're going to find it. Those guys, think of them like bloodhounds. They're like the cops, only they're like cops that all went to Harvard. On steroids. They never run out of money, and they never give up."

"Okay, *basta*, you're making me nervous. Listen, I've got to have a meeting with my guys. Go in Manny's office or somewhere and think about our strategy for this Sterling guy. I want to know more about the civil suit. I don't like it. Think about how we get that bastard off our backs. I'll be done with them in twenty minutes."

He stood and walked Furey to the door. "I've got to warn Manny that Townsend is coming, anyway," Furey said.

TIMOTHY

Ike and Tranny were waiting in the reception area. Max waved them in. Too late, he remembered the bundles of cash still lying all across his desk. The two men were bug-eyed at the sight of it. He decided to leave it there. If he stashed it somewhere in front of them, it would look as though he didn't trust them. He had trouble even getting them to sit down.

"What happened to you guys, anyway?"

"You know them cell phones we showed you coupla days ago?" Ike said, his eyes darting from the money to him, and back to the money again. "They come into my place to steal 'em. We surprised 'em coming out." The lone woman attacker had become a band of seasoned fighters.

"You let them get away?"

"We chased 'em in the car, but they gave us the slip," Tranny said. "Say, how much dough is that, there?"

"It's a hundred thousand," Max said. Then he lied, but only to bring it down a little closer to their level. "A whole week's receipts on the way to the bank. You know I got a lot of mouths to feed, here, boys. Ike, what in Christ is that piece of wood hanging down in front of your face?"

"You never mind about that."

"I never seen a hundred grand all in one place in my life," Tranny said.

"Okay, now listen," Max said. Time to get down to business.

"No, you listen, boss," Ike said. "We brought them phones to you and offered to sell them through the company website, remember?"

"Yes, I remember." He was so surprised at Ike's tone that he let himself be interrupted.

"You said you didn't want 'em. Didn't want to see 'em again, right?"

Max smiled. "Because they were stolen. We can't resell stolen merchandise, can we?"

"Yeah, that's what you said," Tranny said.

"We went through all the names of the people that knew we had them phones," Ike said. "They wasn't many people. Just a couple of other people we tried to sell 'em to, plus the guy we took 'em from, and you."

Max waited. Nothing more came. "I'm sorry, I don't quite follow."

"Of all the people that knew we had them phones, you're the only one that knows where I live, see?"

It dawned on him. They thought he had had them beaten up and stolen their phones. He laughed. "You don't really think I had anything to do with . . ."

"You're the only one."

"But that's crazy, boys. I told you I don't want those phones. What would I go and do with them?"

"Sell 'em. Just like we was trying to do. Only you're better at selling than us." Ike looked again at the money lying on the desk, as if it were proof that Max was a top salesman.

"Guys, guys, think about this. Just because I know your address doesn't mean I stole your phones. Would I steal from you? For God's sake, I pay your salary. Why would I go and steal from you? Would I hurt you, my own employees? I send you out every night with that barge, I trust you boys to do the job for me. I count on you. Would I send someone to beat you up? Think about this for a second. It doesn't make sense."

Ike looked at Tranny. "You thinking what I'm thinking?"

"Hold on now, what're you talking about?"

They all stood at the same instant. In one quick movement Ike bent and, with one brawny arm, scooped all the cash over to his side. "We'll be taking this as payback for our injuries," Ike said. Max dove into the fray, but didn't even come close to the money. Ike swatted him back with one hand while picking up money with the other. The bundles didn't all fit in one pocket, so he held a pile of bundles in one hand and stuffed two bundles at a time in each pocket with the other. Tranny grabbed the last two bundles with his good hand.

"Don't try to follow us," Tranny said. "We're steamed about what you done. Just look at my wrist, man."

"You can't just steal my money!"

"Oh yeah? Says who?" Tranny said.

"I need you guys," Max said. "Who's going to take the barge out tonight?"

"I quit," Ike said, and headed for the door.

"Me, too," said Tranny.

Max dialed security before the door was even closed. He doubted security would be able to react before they got off the property. He checked under his desk to see if any of the money had fallen on the floor. No such luck. They had gotten all of it. What a priceless turn of events. A hundred thousand gone, just like that, and to whom? To those greasy slobs with their pierced faces and beery breath. What a day! He ran into reception and looked out the door. The brown Lincoln was throwing gravel as it fishtailed out of the parking lot. They turned south on the main road. No sign of security.

He speed dialed Brainard on his phone.

"Yeah, boss."

"Where are you now? Could you drop everything and do me a favor?"

"I guess it's important. Otherwise you wouldn't be calling. Actually I got a question for you, myself."

"It'll have to wait. I just had Ike and Tranny in my office here. There was money lying on the desk. They got irritated about something and took off with all my money."

"When?"

"Just now, three minutes ago. Said they quit and stole all the money."

"How much, boss?"

"A hundred thousand. It's wrapped up in bundles, ten bundles, hundred bills in each bundle. Think you can get it back for me?"

"Piece a cake."

"Good. Five thousand dollar reward, Brainard. They were headed south out of the parking lot. Check their house first."

"I'm on it, boss."

"Bring the money here when you get it. And remember that other job I've got for you tonight, too, Brainard. You got my e-mail, didn't you?"

There was a pause. He waited, but no answer came.

"Brainard?"

"You can count on me, boss."

"Move on it."

* * *

Furey had a nose for trouble. He sensed when trouble was brewing, just as he could smell opportunity. In the case of this laptop, trouble and opportunity had come in one tidy package. Back in Max's office he said, "Basically we can admit that we had possession of the laptop, through legitimate means, and we can deny having used it for any nefarious purpose."

"Which will however fall apart as soon as that information on the laptop is used in the custody trial."

Furey nodded. "Or we have the option of denying that we have any record of ever being in possession of the laptop."

"Some people here must've seen it. It would have to be deleted from the records. All manageable, I guess."

"The third option," Furey said, "is to produce the laptop and give it back to them."

Max Vinyl sat for a moment digesting this idea. "I like it. But how does it work? We've already given the laptop to that other lawyer."

Furey shrugged. "Let's assume the one he got really doesn't have the data on it, like he says. We still have the data."

"Theoretically."

"They're working on it. If we can get that data onto another Thinkpad that looks similar enough, we can pass it off as the original. Yes, the information is still going to come out at the custody trial. But they would then have to prove that we sold it. The other lawyer can't mention us, or the laptop. That would not be permissible evidence because of the methods used to obtain it. We can rely on him to deny all knowledge of it. Otherwise the judge will throw out the case."

"So they can't prove where it came from."

"Exactly. Impossible. So all we have to do is get the data onto a Thinkpad and make it look three months old."

"Have you informed Manny?"

"Yes. He has Thinkpads in stock. He's looking for just the right one. They've got all the information on how Sterling's machine was configured, so it should be possible to get the same operating system, the same browser, and so on. They should be able to make an exact replica, so Sterling himself can't tell the difference. The problem now is just getting that data out of the external drive."

"But that sounds good."

"Best of all, it will make the State's Attorney even less interested in investigating TSR. We act sorry and penitent. Honest mistake, the kind of thing that can happen in this business. You sign the affadavit. They get the laptop back that we claim is his, with all his data on it; and they would have a hell of a time proving it *isn't* his, if they could get anybody to listen in the first place. In the end it all starts to look like an overreaction on Sterling's part. And the State's Attorney certainly won't want to get involved in somebody's custody battle out in the sticks somewhere."

"You came up with all this in just thirty minutes."

Furey smiled. "They don't fool around at DePaul law school, haven't you heard? We can even make it sound like I got the wrong one out of inventory. Some dumbass thing like that."

Max picked up his phone and dialed Rodriguez's extension. He heard the call being forwarded. The general manager picked up.

"How're you coming with the data?"

"Our man just got here, just got started. We're going to have a long night."

"Okay. Oscar told you we need the data on a Thinkpad, too, right?"

"Yes." Now the Mexican sounded testy. But he often sounded testy.

"And you've got one that replicates the one recovered from Sterling, operating system, browser and all that?" He heard Rodriguez hyperventilating at the other end. Just in time, he moved the phone away from his ear.

"Do you have any idea what we are going through down here? You think you're ordering salad dressing here? We're going to spend hours extracting that data, do you understand, *hours*!"

"Manny, Manny . . ."

The line was dead.

"Come on," he said to Furey. "Let's go down and see what they're doing."

They went out of his office but were stopped in reception. Two men in suits stood there, one an older man, the younger one a giant who had to be at least a whole foot taller. The small space was filled with a terrible smell. It reeked of manure or strong piss, or some sort of horrible pungent combination of the two. Although both men were dressed in business attire, the air was blurry with this ferment.

"Christ, what is that rank odor?" Max glared from one man to the other. He didn't care who they were. People couldn't just walk in and stink the place up. Furey stepped in front of him.

"Mr. Townsend, glad you could make it. Can I introduce Max Vinyl, owner of TSR, Incorporated." They shook.

"We're sorry about your data, Mr. Townsend," Max said. "You will get your data. They're working on it right now."

"This is my son, Timothy," Townsend said. Timothy shook their hands without a word. The smell came from him. Max's eyes watered.

"Man, you need to get that suit cleaned," he said.

"Shut your trap," Timothy said.

"Oh, I see," Max said. "Very sophisticated, what you're doing here. Very professional. Come and stink my place up. Do you realize I happen to have a very sensitive nose? You smell like a public toilet. Your odor is turning my stomach."

"I said shut up."

"The data is what we came to get," Townsend said. "Like I told Mr. Furey on the phone. That or the money back. Right now."

"We all have to wait," Max said. "Let them do their work. These days people are always in such a goddamn hurry. We have a problem, we're being open with you, we're getting it fixed. I've got guys working overtime down there trying to fix this problem. Sometimes folks just have to wait, you know? Sometimes there are situations that are out of our control, and this is one of them."

"Then give us the money. We'll wait as long as it takes."

"The money is already in the bank, Mr. Townsend. You don't think we keep a hundred thousand in cash lying around on a

Friday night, do you? We obviously wouldn't be able to get at that amount of cash before Monday morning, anyway. Oscar, how long's it going to be with that data?"

"They said it could take all night."

"All night?" Townsend echoed. A look went between him and his son. Timothy came a step closer to Max. The big guy had clean skin, nicely combed hair, a beautiful suit – only the space around him shimmered with bad air. You could almost see the microbes flying in clouds around him.

"I suggest we all go get a nice steak dinner," Max said. "I'll pick up the tab. All night is obviously worst-case. They're only saying that because they're trained not to make promises they can't keep. With any luck, when we come back, the laptop will be ready to go, and you can go on your way."

"I already ate," Timothy said.

"You keep your distance, big guy. I asked you nicely. You should do something about that fertilizer odor." Timothy had gotten so close that Max was forced to take a step back, toward the reception desk. The smell was making him dizzy. He felt sick to his stomach. He put out one hand on the corner of the desk to steady himself. Timothy edged closer.

"Let's get Manny up here. He can give his update personally." Max turned and went behind the reception desk and picked up the phone. "Manny, Mr. Townsend is here, the fellow who needs the Thinkpad data. Could you spare five minutes and come up front here and give him a report firsthand?"

"Why don't we just go to him?" Townsend said. "I'd like to see what the trouble is with my own eyes. Frankly, I don't believe a word anyone here is telling me."

Timothy turned, questioning. Max tried to squeeze by and get out from behind the reception desk, but Timothy's belly blocked him. "Do you mind?" he demanded. Timothy didn't move.

The door to triage banged open, and Rodriguez came in, his chin sticking out, his brow furrowed with stress. Max made the introductions from where he stood. "Manny Rodriguez, our general manager, meet Mr. Townsend. Mr. Townsend purchased the Thinkpad that's causing the problems."

"Take us down to wherever you've come from," Townsend said. "Show me, don't tell me."

"Against regulations," Rodriguez said. "Basically what we've got is a hardware defect. The data from the Thinkpad is saved on an external drive for safety, but the external drive is defective. So our boys down there are recovering the data sector by sector. It's painstaking work. It's going to take a while."

"Why didn't the Thinkpad he gave me have any files on it?" Townsend asked.

"A mystery to us as well. Possibly the wrong Thinkpad was retrieved from inventory for delivery to you. That could explain it."

"Yes, but then where is the right Thinkpad?"

Rodriguez shrugged.

"Have you checked all the other ones in your inventory to see if one of them is the right one? And if you have the data on this broken external drive, and if it's the data from the right Thinkpad, why is it so difficult to find the right Thinkpad?"

Rodriguez threw up his hands. "If I knew the answers, Mr. Townsend, we wouldn't be standing here. It's Friday night, you know? We obviously didn't go looking for problems, here."

"Mr. Townsend, we're doing everything humanly possible," Max chimed in. "Look around you. You see human beings. We aren't perfect, we make mistakes. Reasonable people like yourself understand that people make mistakes. It's simple. We're not running away with your money. We're right here. This is my company. We're not going anywhere."

"You will shut up," Timothy said. Max sat back down. He had no choice. Timothy's knees were bumped up against his knees.

"I will not be told what to do in my own company," Max said hotly. "Get out of the way. We've got things to do, here."

He straight-armed the big guy and gave a push. It was like punching a big sofa cushion. Timothy took half a step back, corrected, and bulled forward against him. Max fell back onto the chair and rolled backwards a foot or two. The chair stopped suddenly, as its castors caught on something. His head knocked hard against the wall. He saw stars. That smell made him feel like retching.

"You and I are attorneys," Oscar Furey said to Townsend. "Surely we can do without this roughness."

"Produce the money or the data," Townsend said. "We didn't come looking for problems. I paid in good faith. Let's have it."

"Will somebody get this giant reeking turd off me?" Max cried. "Ouch! Let go of me."

Timothy had grabbed Max's hair in one hand and yanked his head to one side. Now Timothy's face was coming down to meet his, closer and closer. Max closed his eyes. His scalp burned from having his hair pulled. The stench was overpowering. So now it was the kiss of death. He felt himself losing sphincter control. He held it a little longer, his eyes shut tight, everything shut tight. He heard yelling and realized he was the one yelling.

"I told you to shut up," Timothy yelled back. "This'll make you keep your goddamn mouth shut."

Timothy hawked.

With a new flash of pain in his scalp Max felt his head jerked backward. He opened his eyes just in time to see a huge gob of spit leave Timothy's mouth. The spit dropped from Timothy's aiming lips and headed southward. Max closed his eyes tight, just in time to keep it from landing directly in his eye. Timothy's iron grip on his hair made it impossible for him to move in any direction and get out of the way of it. His cheek was all soupy with Timothy's spit. He clamped his lips and eyes shut, but there was nothing he could do about the spit draining into his left nostril.

Timothy held him captive in the chair with his knees, the chair tight up against the wall. With this fire in his scalp, Max could not move his head. He tried to move slightly, just to make the gob of spit roll off. But for every movement he made, Timothy countered, holding him tightly by the hair, trying just as hard to keep the liquid balanced, almost as if he was playing some sort of game. Its cool wetness itched and prickled and wetted his skin so revoltingly he thought he would go insane.

"Now you'll keep your mouth shut. Otherwise eat my spit," Timothy said.

"Listen up, all of you," Rodriguez yelled over the fray. "We're making an exception to the policy. Everybody follow me." He turned and led them through the door into triage. Max felt his head being yanked up. The roots of his hair started pulling free from his scalp, or maybe it was just his imagination. It felt like he was being scalped. Suddenly Timothy let go. Max stood, eyes still clamped shut, balancing and teetering on tiptoe, one hand clutching blindly at the corner of the reception desk. He wiped his face hard on his jacket sleeve.

When he opened his eyes Timothy stood three paces away, a small bluish pistol in his hand.

"Follow them," Timothy said. "I like shooting, so don't try any funny stuff."

Max decided to keep quiet. He would look for his chance to escape. They entered triage and walked past workers at their workstations. These morons stared open-mouthed as their boss walked by with a gun trained on him.

Well, you don't see that every day.

Wasn't anybody going to call security? Where was the training, here, the *training*?

"Goober-face," Timothy said. "I've got eleven bullets and a second clip, so get your shit-ass moving."

Max plodded ahead, one step after another.

Rodriguez had stopped up ahead at a workstation where two workers were hunched over the screen, one of them occasionally clicking commands.

"These two gentlemen are getting your data out of that hard drive," he said. "See, that's the hard drive where the Thinkpad data were saved, for safety. That's another Thinkpad that they're putting the data on. And that other one is a new safety copy."

"What went wrong here?" Townsend asked, looking closely at the screen along with the two workers.

"Basically a hardware defect," Roberto said. "It stored all the files and emails and shit, but getting it all out of there is hairy."

"How long till you're done?"

"What do you think, Murray?"

"Definitely going to take all night." Murray flipped his ponytail back over his shoulder without looking away from the screen.

"All night!" Townsend echoed. He gazed wildly around the room, at the high ceiling, the conveyor belts, the other workstations. "What if I told you I only need the bastard's email tonight? Not the Word files, not the Excel files, those can all come later. What about just the email?"

"That would simplify my life immensely," Murray said, looking at Townsend for the first time.

"How long for just the emails?"

"Half an hour, hour maybe," Murray said. "Depends on the browser."

"Do it," Townsend said. "Get me the emails, and make it so I can read them properly, you hear? I mean with the date they were sent, who they were from, all the formatting. The rest you can send me on Monday morning. Then we can get the hell out of this dump."

Murray looked to Rodriguez for confirmation.

"Do what the client says," Rodriguez said.

"I think we could be most helpful by waiting up front," Oscar Furey said.

"Quiet, Furey," Townsend said. "We're staying right here."

At that moment there was an Earth-shaking crash. The concrete floor under their feet vibrated sickeningly. The sound had clearly come from outside, but the walls vibrated, the ceiling rang, and the ground under their feet shook. It sounded as if something massive had collided with the building. Everyone stared at the ceiling for signs of the building collapsing, then at each other, waiting to see what would happen next. But there was nothing to see.

"What the hell was that?" Rodriguez spoke first. He started to walk back in the direction of the offices, but was stopped by Timothy waving his gun.

"Nobody's going anywhere. If you run, I shoot."

"What in Christ . . .?" Max had just seen the blue banner. He pointed at it and glared at Rodriguez. Instead of proclaiming that they paid 25% above minimum wage, it read:

Tris. TRS. Without. I.

"Where in the world did that come from?" Rodriguez said.

"Been there since Wednesday," said one of the programmers.

"Wednesday!" said Max.

A second crash came, just as loud. To Max it sounded as if someone had dropped a huge box of milk bottles from ten stories up. Somewhere he distinctly heard glass shattering – *but this warehouse doesn't have windows.* The cement floor rattled through his loafers right into the soles of his feet. He felt his scrotum contract. Max saw something flicker on Murray's computer screen.

"Jesus, don't do this to me," Murray said. Then the flicker went away, and he kept working.

"What the hell is going on, Furey? Is this place safe?" Townsend asked.

"Everybody quiet! A helicopter!" Rodriguez cried.

Max listened. Sure enough, over the general hum of forty or fifty computers in the room he heard the distant thwack-thwack-thwack of a helicopter. Could the State's Attorney act so fast? Were SWAT troops repelling out of helicopters onto the roof of TSR? That only happened in the movies, didn't it? How in Christ had Tris managed to hang a new banner forty feet above the warehouse floor with her own message on it, anyway?

Or was it the Koreans arriving unannounced? Now that would be timing. If the Koreans could arrive now with their big guns, this situation would be under control in a minute or two.

Rodriguez must have had the same idea. When he noticed Timothy looking the other way, he took off. Rodriguez ran flat out in the direction of the server room, at the back of triage. He had cover from the many workstations in between. He was at least five or six paces into his escape before Timothy turned and noticed. Timothy raised his gun, took a step in Rodriguez's direction, and started firing.

It looked like the only chance Max was going to get. With Timothy using Rodriguez for target practice, maybe he could make it to the side door, and out. Max ran in the opposite direction and headed for the side door, not looking back, staying close to the workstations and keeping his head down. He heard shots but kept running, not knowing if Timothy was shooting at Rodriguez or him. He reached the door and fell against the push bar.

At that instant a burning fire shot through his right thigh. Out the door he went, carried at least partly by momentum, throwing himself to one side, onto the soft grass. The humid air enveloped him and seemed to cushion his fall. He stayed a second on hands and knees in the grass, feeling the fire sweep through his thigh. He dragged himself up, impelled by the idea that the shooter might be coming out after him. He could stand.

A bright light caught his eye out over the lake. He struggled to his feet, found he could walk, despite the paralyzing fiery pain in his leg, and hobbled in the direction of the light.

"Can't believe that bastard shot me," he said to no one in particular. He looked back over his shoulder. No one coming. Well, he could walk. If this was what it felt like to get shot, he would survive for sure. But the situation had certainly deteriorated rapidly, with this country lawyer and his putrid son.

The bright light over the lake materialized as a helicopter. Flying low, it was closing at high speed. So there *was* a helicopter. Christ, what a big thing. The Koreans! They were back with their helicopter. Something gigantic dangled from it. He couldn't make much out in the dark. As it came closer he saw it actually looked like . . . well, a giant *testicle*. The testicle approached, headed directly for him, and there was no getting out of its way, the helicopter flew so fast and so low.

A spotlight from the chopper blinded him as it flew over, casting every blade of grass around him in bright light and shadow. The roar of its spinning rotor deafened you. The violent wind drowned out logic.

Suddenly he was sopping wet, his hair dripping. Water dumped on his head as the chopper passed. It wasn't raining. Anyway, this was no stray drop. For a moment he was practically drowning in it. He was inundated with water, so much so that it made him forget the fire in his leg.

He wiped his eyes on one sleeve and kept walking, staring back over his shoulder as the helicopter flew toward the warehouse.

He stopped and turned to watch as it hovered over the warehouse. The testicle hung at the end of a long cable, maybe fifty feet over the roof of the warehouse. All at once it changed shape, right before his eyes, up in the air. It went from being a big round bulging thing to a long, flattened-out misshapen form. In the backlighting from the helicopter, a massive spray of water filled the air. Water cascaded down.

The testicle turned out to be an enormous bag of water, like the kind they used on forest fires. The helicopter had dumped water on the roof of his warehouse.

Maybe it wasn't the Koreans after all. After all, no bodyguards had appeared.

But why dump water on the roof? Was there a fire? There was no fire, only Timothy and a few pistol shots. Had the smoke from the shooting set off an alarm? Who had called the fire department? Why dump water if there was no fire? It was like a nightmare, and getting worse with each passing minute, only it was all so shockingly real. The chopper now rose higher in the air and turned its light back in his direction, still dangling the empty bag at the end of the cable.

"What the hell is going on here?" He opened his phone and speed-dialed Rodriguez. It rang three times and went dead. Rodriguez had cut him off.

The helicopter flew directly over him and out over the lake again, staying low. A couple hundred yards out, it appeared to stop and hover over the water. It came down a bit. After half a minute, it rose up again with a roar of extra power and turned in his direction again. The bag was full of water.

"This cannot be happening to me!" he shouted into the wind.

"What's with the whirlybird, boss?"

Max turned, startled. He had been watching the helicopter dip into the lake. Ike sat at the wheel of a forklift with Tranny riding shotgun. With the noise from the helicopter he hadn't heard them coming. Ike still had that ludicrous table leg dangling from the bolt in his eyebrow.

For a second Max didn't recognize the large metal boxlike object they had on the forklift. Then, with a shock, he identified it as his safe. For Chrissake, how had they gotten it out of the locked office? They must have used the forklift to batter in through the wall, then ripped it out with a chain. That thing had to weigh two thousand pounds. It also had at least two hundred thousand dollars in it, the last two or three day's receipts, possibly more. They were stealing his safe. Where did they think they were taking it? The barge sat placidly in its slip in the boathouse fifty yards behind him, heavy in the water with Dumpsters that were piled high with computer gear. He watched as the chopper dumped another load of water on the warehouse roof.

"Man, that is quite a sight!" Tranny said.

"Where the hell are you going with my safe? Weren't you satisfied with the hundred grand you already stole?"

"We decided to make one last barge run," Ike said. He looked at Tranny and seemed to decide something. "And you're coming with us."

Back in the direction of the warehouse, Max saw the side door open. A figure came out. The man was too massive to be anyone but Timothy. Max saw the way he stood, looking this way and that, silhouetted in the light from the helicopter, holding the gun up with one hand like a gunslinger in a Western movie. Then Timothy started walking towards them.

"Let's go," Max said, limping and leading the way to the barge.

Ike drove right onto the barge with the forklift while Tranny started up the engine. The barge was out of the boathouse and fifty yards down the channel by the time Timothy ran up, followed by Townsend. His shots plinked harmlessly off the metal sides of the cabin, or maybe off the safe. Then the window in the pilot's cabin exploded. Glass flew everywhere. The three men huddled in the cabin, shards raining down around them on the steel floor. The engine rumbled underfoot. A minute later they were out of range.

"Who's that asshole that's shooting at us?" Ike asked.

"The money you stole," Max said, "came from him."

"Yeah, but what's he so mad about?"

"He didn't get his computer. The money was for a computer, but we had a problem. He got impatient."

"I'll say." Ike pointed at Max's bloody leg.

"Yeah, he shot me. Feels like someone hammered a red-hot spike into my leg."

The helicopter flew directly overhead again in the direction of the warehouse, loaded with more water. Max pulled out his phone and speed-dialed Furey. "Oscar, what in Christ is happening in there?"

"Max, we've got six inches of water on the floor in the whole place. I'm standing in reception with water up to my ankles. Everyone's heading out to high ground, out to the parking lot. All the computers died a few minutes ago. I think you had a short circuit."

"I don't believe this shit. Where did this helicopter come from? Where's Manny?"

"Came out of the server room on a fucking wave, Max. All the water in the whole place is coming from there. The ceiling above the server room caved in. Manny said they dropped boulders on the roof over the servers, then water through the hole. The rocks fell on the servers, then the water. The servers are history. Manny got shot in the chest."

"I'm hit in the leg."

"Where did you run off to, anyway?"

"I had to get away from that oaf that's trying to kill me. They want to destroy us, Oscar. They're trashing the whole place."

"Max, I can only hear half of what you're saying. The ambulance just left. Manny was still conscious. The paramedics said he was going to make it. Townsend and his boy are the least of our problems, now. Manny's going to report the shooting, but he's going to drop the charges if they keep quiet about the money and the data. We worked that out with Townsend before the ambulance left. Townsend wants to keep his son out of jail."

"At least there's that."

"So long, Max."

Max's phone vibrated again as soon as he had cut off. At first he thought he had pressed a wrong button. But a new call was coming in, right out here on the lake. He didn't recognize the number. "Hello?"

"Max, that you?"

"Yes, speaking." The accented voice was familiar.

"Song. We're flying out of Chicago tomorrow night. Two of my board members arrived from Korea. They want to come and take a look with me. Ten o'clock still okay?"

First the rocks fell on the servers, then the water.

If Furey's assessment was right, it would be weeks before the business was up and running again.

"Ah, Song, I'm afraid something has come up with tomorrow."

"Why, what's the matter?"

It was the last thing he was able to say. Before Max knew what was happening, Ike grabbed the phone out of his hand and tossed it out of the shattered window. Max watched in horror as his cell phone splashed into the black water of Lake Michigan.

"You ain't gonna sit there talking on the phone the whole time. This ain't your private luxury office out here. That's for what you done to me and Tranny," Ike said. He stood at the wheel, a can of beer in his hand. The table leg that dangled from his face clanked lightly against the wheel. Ike looked serious. He looked angry. What in Christ did *he* have to be angry about? Tranny stood behind him, a beer in one hand, the GPS in the other.

"You just threw my phone in the water," Max yelled. "First you steal my money, then my safe, and now my goddamn phone."

Ike laughed. Then Tranny started laughing. They were laughing at him.

"What are you laughing at?"

"The money, man," Tranny said. "We gave Brainard ten grand each to go away. Worked like a charm."

"Yeah, ten thousand," Tranny said.

Max realized he hadn't heard back from Brainard since sending him after the thieves. Not even a message on his phone. That could only mean he was gone. Which would mean he wasn't going to disarm the booby trap. Too much cash, too much temptation, in the end. Which meant these two weasels had ended up with forty thousand each, plus whatever was in the safe.

"What makes you think you can just steal my money like this?"

"By the way, boss. How much have we got in that safe, anyway?"

"I'll bet you'd like to know. How do you think you're going to get into it in the first place?"

"Soon as we've dumped all your shit one last time, we thought we'd run down to a place I know. I know a guy that's gonna get us into this safe. Helps to have friends, right, boss?"

Both men laughed at him again. It was extremely unpleasant to have these two beer-guzzling misfits laughing in his face. But not nearly as nasty as the smelly oaf with his blue pistol.

First the rocks fell on the servers, then the water.

What was he going to do with the Koreans? If the visit tomorrow didn't work out, they were going to sit on their money a while longer. You never knew with these foreigners. Getting cut off in the middle of a conversation could not have helped. Maybe they would advance him some of the money to rebuild. If not, he would have to start over. The very idea was exhausting.

"So what're you going to do with all that money?" Making conversation might distract them. He had to come up with a plan.

"We're gonna go into the phone business," Ike said. "You know, used cell phones people want to get rid of. Set ourselves up a website, sell phones off the internet."

"Phones don't take up that much space," Tranny added. "People always want to upgrade their phones. Lotta phones lying around."

A number of potential problems entered his head, but he kept quiet. He didn't owe it to them to touch up their business plan. Let them find out the hard way. Tomorrow was a new day. Tomorrow he could start working on getting his money back.

"That reminds me," Ike said. "Anyone on your staff that's a short blond female with dark sunglasses, maybe knows a few karate moves?"

Max mentioned the new receptionist. "Sounds like her, anyway. But she quit already, anyway. Why do you ask?"

No answer came, just a mysterious look that went between Ike and Tranny. Max decided he wasn't going to try and get to the bottom of that one. The floorboards vibrated noisily under his feet, and the smell of diesel mixed with cigarette smoke irritated his nose. His face ached. His eyes stung. His leg throbbed where the bullet must have gone through or was still lodged. The smell memory of fermented dung and piss had been burned onto his brain. The gob of spit on his face had nearly driven him right over the edge, and his scalp still burned from Timothy pulling his hair. His senses were frazzled to the limit. And here he was, headed out to sea with two men who had stolen first his cash and now his safe.

Maybe it hadn't been such a good idea to get on the barge with them.

Wet Drop

Annie put her headphones back on and gave the pilot a thumbs up. "One last load and we're out of here."

The pilot nodded. They were headed back over the warehouse. "Eight thousand gallons per dump. Forty thousand flushes. This must be one naughty dude to make you so annoyed, Annie."

"Just a question of respect."

The helicopter made its last delivery. Fifty feet below, the water sloshed in through the large jagged holes in the warehouse roof and from there into the dark cavernous space that now housed twenty-four underwater servers. She couldn't see the computers from up here. But the water had gone in. It was the right end of the warehouse. There were sure to be some alewives swimming around in triage right now, direct from Lake Michigan. They would smell to high heaven by tomorrow noon. Her pilot friend brought the helicopter back up and around, and they swung out over the lake again.

"This training run is history. You better hope nobody made our sorry asses back there."

She smiled. "How could they with all the mud I glopped on over your numbers? You're still up for that wet drop out at my boat, right?"

"Give me a position and we'll head for it. Mickey, get ready with the winch." A sailor colleague camped behind them gave the thumbs up.

"Todd, can you guys see us from your position?" Annie asked on her phone.

"Hell if I know. I don't think so. I don't see anything out here except an occasional jetliner. What am I looking for?"

"We'd be pretty low on the horizon for you. Only 200 feet off the water, about two miles offshore. What's your position?"

"We're sitting at the GPS point, about three hundred yards to the east of it. No lights, all blacked out. Alison's tossing her cookies over the side as we speak."

"Really? Why?"

"I don't know. It's like, *Woman Throws Up on Glassy Calm Lake Cruise*. You want to talk to her?"

"I don't think so. Listen, Todd, they're about half an hour from your position. We're coming your way now. By the way, Max Vinyl is on the barge with our two bruisers."

"What? Why? Wait till I tell the guys from the Nine O'clock News crew. This is tremendous. Too much to hope for. How did you manage it?"

"Beats me. Todd, can you put Olson on the line?"

"Okay, here he is."

"This is Bob."

"Ready to see me get lowered out of a helicopter, military style?"

"Long as you're not planning to beat anyone up. By the way, I've got the lowdown on 'squatting'."

"See you in a few, Olson."

Barge Fight

"Okay, we're there. Time to unload," Tranny said. He was studying the GPS. It was flashing green.

"Time to say goodbye, boss," Ike said. He turned away from the wheel, the table leg clanking against his belt buckle, and took a step toward Max.

Max sat on a chair in the back of the tiny cabin. He was damp, either from exertion or from having been drenched when the helicopter flew over. His leg was throbbing, and, he figured, still bleeding. Ike had a strange, evil look on his face. He looked very much as if he was planning to kill him. *Well, not without a fight,* he thought. Max rose from the chair and, in one fluid movement, grabbed it up in his hands and held it in front of him like a lion tamer. The expression on Ike's face changed. His mouth twisted up in an ugly scowl.

"So that's the way you want to play it!"

The chair was a filthy cheap orange plastic thing with spindly metal legs that ended in little disks. Like blunted daggers. *You get one chance,* Max thought. Nothing to lose.

He let Ike make the first grab. Ike got a hand on one metal leg, but his fingers slipped off in the struggle. He missed entirely with the other hand. For a second Ike was off balance. With that beer belly he wasn't so light on his feet in the first place. And he had to be distracted by that piece of wood swinging around the whole time in front of his face.

Max aimed one chair leg straight for the eye socket on Ike's good side. He punched in hard, no holding back. The little metal disk drove straight into Ike's right eye, hard, and stuck there. Blood spurted like a fountain. Christ, a direct hit! Ike crumpled back against the steering wheel, screaming in agony and fountaining red blood like a slaughtered animal. The chair fell bouncing and clattering to the steel floor.

"Now you gonna get it," Tranny shouted.

Max was already out the door. Maybe Tranny would trip over the orange chair. Not that he had any idea where to go. They were out on the lake and it was ten o'clock at night. They had to be ten miles out. On this huge black lake the barge now seemed rather tiny. He had no place to go.

He stepped around the nearest Dumpster and squeezed through the narrow space between his safe and the steel lip of the boat deck, the Asian a few steps behind him. Max's leg throbbed, but it supported him. Tranny had the use of only one hand but was quick on his feet. Even with one arm, Tranny could probably lift him up in the air and strangle him at the same time. The guy was that brawny. The barge engine still rumbled somewhere deep under the floor, but they were not moving in the water. Tranny chased him all the way around the Dumpster.

Max's eye fell on a disk drive on top of the pile in the Dumpster. He grabbed it and threw. Its sharp metal edge missed Tranny's face by inches. He looked for something else to throw. He glanced up just in time to see an object hurtling towards him through the air. So two could play this game. There wasn't even time to duck. He took it full in the chest, an old keyboard, surprisingly heavy thing. It felt like it weighed ten pounds. He tried to lean back to soften the impact. Where was the railing on this tub? He lost his balance.

That was when he felt himself falling backwards, the keyboard nestled in his arms. There was no railing.

This is going to hurt.

He fell backwards through the air, juggling the keyboard in his hands like an idiot, felt his back touch the water. Then the water closed over him. It felt soft and cool and rubbery as jelly. He was in the water, *son of a bitch!* The water rushed around his ears and closed over him. Strong smells of fish, algae, mud, lakewater . . .

He floundered, still going down in the water, fighting it with his arms. Would this nightmare never end? He had fallen off the barge into deep water in Lake Michigan at ten o'clock at night. For a few moments he clawed against the thick water without even knowing which way was up.

Don't panic.

He kicked with his shoes. He broke the surface at last, thrashing around, thrust the keyboard aside, battling for survival, sucking air, treading water.

"Help!"

This was no longer a fair fight. The water wasn't cold, but still, he was in eighty feet of water, in the pitch dark, ten miles out. Strange, he felt warmer in the water than he had on the boat.

Keep your head above water.

How long could a man tread water? What kind of fish swam around out here, anyway? There didn't seem to be any waves. He worked his loafers off, thinking, *it's the shoes, or I'm fish food.* Treading water was surprisingly easy, as long as you could forget about the bottom being eighty feet down, or the fact that you were ten miles from shore.

Like standing on the roof of an eight-story building. That far down.

The barge idled in the water only twenty feet away. Diesel fumes burned his nostrils. Shouldn't he try to get back aboard? Tranny stood at the crane controls, working the levers.

What, and have them stomp on his hands? Kick him in the face, break his arms, throw him back over the side? They had his cash. They had his safe. They had his barge, for Chrissake.

They had plenty of reasons for killing him and none at all for saving him.

The crane swiveled, and a Dumpster rose out of its bay. Right, so they meant to bury him under a load of old Gateways, Compaqs and Dells. He dog-paddled away from the barge. Farther out, the water didn't have that oily film. With a strong rhythmic movement of his arms, coordinated with a deep kick of the legs, he found he could easily stay above water. Out here a little farther from the barge the air was fresher and not laden with that diesel stench.

Off to his right, somewhere out in the blackness, a bright light flashed, like a strobe. Then three or four lights flicked on, one after another. Bright bastards, enough to blind you. Spotlights of some kind. Had to be another boat. He couldn't see anything but the lights, but whatever it was, it hadn't just risen out of the depths. That had to be a boat out there. A boat meant rescue.

"Help! Help me!" he yelled. But the water swallowed up his puny voice. Yelling was pointless at this distance, but he yelled just the same. The Dumpster swiveled out over the water, over him. He backpedaled a few feet farther out in plenty of time before the old PCs and printers and disc drives started sliding into the water. They were too slow to get him that way. The first pieces splashed two or three at a time into the water directly in front of him. Then a whole gargantuan mass of gear slid out all at once, all stuck together, momentarily gouging a massive crater in the water where it hit. The water cascaded back in on the crater, filling it instantly. The whole immense pile of PCs and printers and monitors sank in a commotion of bubbles. The crane swiveled around again, put the first Dumpster back and attached to another one.

Ike appeared on the side of the barge, some cloth wrapped around his head, covering his bloody eye, the table leg still swinging crazily from side to side in front of his face. "You gonna be *dead* now, boss!" he yelled. Ike hefted a big boxy

PC from the Dumpster nearest his position, raised it high in the air, balanced it in his right hand, and shot-putted it in Max's direction. It landed in a tower of water only a yard or two in front of him. The water from its splash rained down on his head.

Ike was already hurling some other big piece of equipment. Frigging laser printer. This time it was going to be a direct hit. Max had no time to dive to one side or the other. The thing was sailing through the air in an arc with his name on it. Treading water, you couldn't just dodge to one side. Your options were limited. Instinct made him duck under the water, down deep, working his hands like fins. The water caught the printer directly above him, and it settled down in the water, bumping him on the way down. Its weight rested on his back for a couple of seconds under the surface, pushing him down with it until, shifting the position of his shoulders, it slid off and went harmlessly to the bottom. *Christ!* Cautiously he stuck his head out of the water. Another heavy monitor hit the water just to his left. They were coming too close for comfort. Meanwhile, another Dumpster swiveled out over the water and all its contents slid out.

Max saw the two men talking to each other. Ike kept lobbing loose items at him while Tranny emptied the Dumpsters. A few minutes later there was nothing left on the boat but his safe and the forklift. The strange lights off to his right had not moved. His only hope was that another boat lay moored there. These psychopaths surely meant to leave him here. He saw them gunning the motor, turning the boat. They were going back to shore, leaving him to drown in Lake Michigan, ten miles out. Marooned out in the lake, not even a life preserver. He wouldn't make it till morning. Marooned, just like in those movies he hated the most. Only this time he was the star of the show, and the show was real life. His life!

And what else could he expect? They weren't about to haul him back aboard and hand him a beer. He wasn't about to get back aboard with them, either. He had been mighty

443

lucky to stab Ike in the eye like that. It had saved his life, if only to permit him to leave this world in a less violent way, slipping under the surface after a few hours of treading water in the dark. Well, they would pay a price for their treachery. At least they would take a few scars with them.

Still treading water, he watched them driving away. Despite the rage he felt, he couldn't tear his gaze away. That was the boat that had brought him ten miles out, and it was leaving without him. He would have left them flailing in the water, too. Hell, he would have turned the barge around and run them down. The idea didn't seem to have occurred to Ike and Tranny. He had done Ike some serious damage to the eye, sure. But the bottom line was they had the boat, and they were going to get home, whereas he was out in the middle of the black infinite lake, which seemed all the more infinite because he was just keeping his nose above water.

All at once a horrible grinding, screeching noise met his ears. The sound came only once, briefly, then all went eerily quiet. The throaty rumbling of the old barge had stopped. The barge was still only two hundred feet away. It had been like the sound of metal colliding with metal, yet muffled underwater. As if the propeller had hit something and stopped mid-revolution. The barge seemed to be drifting now.

Off to the right, the bright lights seemed to be coming closer. He heard the other boat's engine now. He waved his arms, but he was so low on the surface – probably about as easy to spot as a floating log – they probably couldn't see him at all. Back on the barge, Ike and Tranny were leaning over the side staring into the water, trying to figure out what had happened. If he was not mistaken, they had run aground. But on what? He had chosen this spot years before because it was 80 feet deep, clear to the bottom. He dog-paddled slowly in the direction of the barge, not wanting to get too close to the killers, but close enough to be rescued when the other boat came near.

Fifty feet from the barge his right foot touched something. He recoiled in shock. But the thing his foot had touched stayed put, right where it was. It wobbled a little underfoot, but it was hard to the touch of his stocking-covered toes. No sharks in Lake Michigan anyway, he reminded himself. A huge rock of some kind, like an underwater ledge. With his other foot he was still busily kicking, trying to stay above the surface. He reached again with his left foot now and made contact with the rock, propelling himself closer with his arms.

A minute later, he could stand up on it. What an incredible discovery. He took a step and ran into something else that was hard. He felt around underwater, first with his feet, then with his hands. He was standing on something flat, hard and solid in water up to his waist, and it wasn't even wobbly. No wonder they had run aground. The water poured off him now. It felt good to rest, Christ, after treading water for the last twenty minutes. What about that, ten miles out in Lake Michigan!

He reached down in the water again, feeling around with his hands. Something nicked him. He stood up and looked at his hand. Was that a bite? Had he just been bitten? His finger was bleeding. One more injury to add to the list. He had cut himself. He picked up the sharp thing underwater with his other hand this time, careful about sharp edges. Pulled it up carefully the rest of the way with both hands. Heavy fucking rock. He had a hell of a time dragging it above the surface. Just when he was about to give up and drop it, he got it just high enough above the surface to see what it was. Disgusting green algae drained out of the watery hole. A few jagged edges of glass still stuck in the plastic rim.

With a shiver of horror, he threw the old monitor back in the water. That thing should be on the bottom. What in Christ was it doing right here, just below the surface, for him to gash his finger on?

The other boat was pulling in close in behind him, four huge lights bright enough to blind him. Camera lights. Men stood on the rear deck with TV cameras with little red lights in front, filming something. *Filming him.*

"Cut that out," he yelled. "Who gave you permission?"

"Ahoy," said a man from the boat. "Channel Nine News, doing a story on secret dumping in the lake. Are you Max Vinyl, owner of TSR or Tri-State Recovery Incorporated, and is that your boat over there?"

"No comment," he said. His finger was running with blood. He stuck it under the water so that the camera wouldn't pick it up.

His eye caught a movement in the water in front of him, between him and the boat. Had he imagined it? He put a hand up to shield his eyes from the lights. Was it a wave from this boat? A trick of the light?

No, there actually was something in the water. Something moving. The movement had caught his eye. Something big. He saw it writhing and wriggling along the surface of the water, something alive, something from the lake. It knew he was standing here. It was coming straight at him.

He screamed.

It had to be six or eight feet long, a giant fish, an eel of some kind. A long dark bony backbone, zigzagging in an undulating fishy way through the water, heading straight for him. Where had the thing come from? He couldn't run away. It was attacking him. It steered right into the space between his legs before he could move a muscle. The thing was there, moving under him. Its body bumped hard against the inside of his knee. Then against both thighs. An enormous heavy muscled jerking thing. It writhed through the water right between his legs. It went on and on, the fish was so long, disappearing into the water behind him. The last part of its tail whipped hard against the inside of his leg, so hard he lost his balance. He felt himself falling to the left.

He was underwater again, eyes open. Underwater with this giant fish somewhere nearby. It was going to drag him under.

It was going to take him with it. He felt something pulling at him in the water. The fish had territorial instincts. It was guarding its territory. It was pulling him in, pulling him down. Panicky, his head broke the surface again, and he sucked in air. The lights were in his eyes. Men were shouting.

"You all right?" a man in the lights was shouting. Another man held out a gaffe for him to grab on to. A second gaffe was hooked in his belt, pulling him backwards. Max was up to his chin again, panicky, just trying to breathe now, sliding through the water as they pulled him in, looking around in every direction for the giant fish. The fish was nowhere to be seen. But it was surely coming back for another pass.

"It's attacking me!"

"What is?"

"Help me!"

"One more question," another man said. "What were you standing on? We're in eighty feet of water, here. Is that what I think it is?"

"Quick, before it comes back!" Max shouted.

"I see it," said another man on the boat. "There."

"Sturgeon."

"The size a that thing!"

"It's over there, now."

"He won't hurt you, Max. Just an old sturgeon. You want a ride to shore?"

With two strong men on the boat pulling at him and lifting him, he got aboard. Someone put a blanket over his shoulders and brought him in the small cabin. There he sat, a few seconds or a few minutes later, on a bench with a cushion, dripping wet, shivering under a blanket. His mind had gone blank. He had to keep warm. That was all he could think, now. Someone put a warm mug into his hand. Who would've thought you could get so cold in the middle of the summer? His leg ached. He wished it would fall off. He wished he could just shed it, like a lizard losing its tail. Did any of these people even realize there was a bullet in his leg? His face stung. Being in the water so long had re-opened all his scratches. He brought the mug to his lips. Warm bullion. He shivered. Assorted images flashed across the screen in his brain, like a movie, only out of order.

Blood spurting from Ike's eye . . . bright klieg lights flicking on, one after another . . . the phone disappearing into the water – plink! – with hardly a splash . . .

Am I going to die?

A man stood behind him, one hand on the wheel, talking into a radio. "Go easy around that point and watch your draft," the man said. "This barge went aground in eighty feet of water."

"Did you say eight-zero feet, over?" A voice came through the radio.

"Who are you?" Max asked. "Who are you talking to?"

The man with the radio looked down. "That's the Coast Guard. Just giving them a position."

"That safe is mine."

"Confirm eight-zero," the man said. "There's a man-made mountain of garbage just below the surface of the water, some of it metal. Barge ran aground on it. Probably chewed up the props, over."

"Is the barge loaded, over?"

"The barge is empty. Correction, looks like one big object on the barge, maybe a safe." The man glanced down at him. "But no, riding high, riding high. No apparent structural damage, over."

"That's a new one on me, over."

"Tell him the safe is mine."

"Two men on board the barge awaiting rescue, possible injuries, from the look of it, over."

"Two men, possible injuries. Over and out."

Car Heaven

Brainard parked his motorcycle in the driveway and walked up to the barn. The webcam needed power, and wouldn't be running on batteries. So the first thing was to cut off power to the barn. The boss had said the alarm was off. So no silent alarms, no police arriving with blue lights and five cars.

If he was telling the truth.

He took his time. He walked slowly around the entire barn. It was dark, and he had to look closely, but he found what he was looking for. Behind the barn, on the forest side, a junction box sticking up out of the ground. It was dark green, painted to blend in with the lawn and the shrubbery. Very tasteful. With his tools he worked at the lock. These things weren't especially challenging. Not exactly a nuclear reactor he was taking down.

In the box he found a schematic. He'd learned his electronics in prison. In thirty seconds he had cut off power to the barn. Leaving the junction box open, so that when he left he could turn the electricity on again, he went to the door of the barn and opened it with the key Max had given him.

If they had really had a webcam in operation, which he doubted, that eye would now be shut tight. More likely it had been a closed loop anyway, made from a few still pictures of the cars. The barn was so dark inside it was like an ocean of blackness.

He went back out to his motorcycle for the big flashlight he carried, an automotive torch. It cast a wider beam than the penlight in his pocket. In the barn he moved step by step till he was some ten feet inside the door. From there he could clearly see the first 55-gallon drum by the yellow Corvette. With his light he followed the wire running from the bottom of the drum back across the floor in front of him and up through the air to a point on the ceiling. He went down a bit with the beam.

Aha. Looky here.

Right next to the fire extinguisher, clamped to the wall – an ax. For the firemen, he thought, for chopping your way out of the barn.

He went and lifted the ax out of its clamps. Feeling a tingle somewhere deep inside, he stood a moment savoring that heft, the feel of the wood handle in his hands. The wood was rough and smelled of new varnish, straight from the factory. Never used. Not like the ax handles of his youth, worn buttery smooth by daily contact with his hands. It was a damned shame to see an ax like this go unused.

He gazed around at all the highly polished cars. Corvettes . . . Cadillacs . . . an old Thunderbird. Even in the near darkness how they shined.

He had trusted Max Vinyl. But now the bond of trust was broken. The boss had betrayed him.

A hundred thousand dollars stuffed in his pockets . . . his ticket to freedom. A new life somewhere. No sense letting those idiots, Ike and Tranny, run off with the boss's money.

And with all these cars, it occurred to him now, the boss could afford to find one of them reduced to scrap. Brainard's last calling card. Not that the boss would ever understand it. The boss had not known him back in his younger days, back in Uncle Von's scrapyard. His torch beam fell on the Jaguar. A long, sleek car with a hood that made up half the length of the car, it looked strange and unnatural. It looked like a mutant design compared to the fine symmetry of the '57 Chevy a few cars down. He studied the curve of the Jaguar's windshield. That car dated from the 1960s. Slow and steady, now, he set the flashlight down on the floor.

His hands shifted into position on the handle of the ax without even being consciously aware of it. The ax swung in the air once, twice, gathering momentum. This easy motion came back from his younger days, like a long-repressed truth, that old familiar motion of arms, shoulders and wrists all working in perfect harmony together, a truth he had learned before Max Vinyl, before prison, before he'd ever killed a man with a gun.

The metal blade hit the windshield dead center, full force. This Jaguar had been built before the days of modern safety glass. The glass shattered into ten thousand shards, so that the air was filled with them, like ten thousand droplets of water.

At the moment of impact the room lit up. It was as if someone had thrown a giant light switch. For an instant Brainard saw everything in the room in sharp relief, every shard of the windshield flying outward from the point of impact, every detail of every car fender, every inch of polished chrome, every dust mote on the painted concrete floor, even every shadow cast on the floor by the light rising over the dust. Up high on the wall, near the entrance, he had just time enough to see the camera. And the small red light that meant it was somehow operational, after all.

Everything went white. A light too intense for human eyes. He saw nothing more. The heat first tickled him, then pressed in on him like a heavy weight. The fire rose up in an expanding froth. He felt the heat of it, and it was much too close. He had time, instinctively, to raise the ax to protect his head. But the ax, this once, couldn't save him. Fire swirled up at him from below, swooping in under his arms and around his neck and down the front of his shirt, and it hurtled down on him from above. He was in the fire. He staggered back a step, but in so doing only moved deeper into the fire, for it was behind him as well. There was no getting away.

The fire burned him. The burning pain filled him like air filling a balloon, filling him beyond the exploding point. But he wouldn't explode, because he wasn't a balloon, he was a man, and he would only . . . *melt.*

He heard screaming.

Is there someone else caught in here with me?

The jet of fire lifted him high in the air, and as it did, suddenly he could see again. The jet held him up there like a man riding the crest of a fountain, high in the air now, far above the churning conflagration, suspended at the top.

The pain faded. All at once he felt no pain at all.

From up here he saw the entire barn, the roof gone. He saw the whole spiky leaping voluptuous body of the fire, and he saw each one of Max Vinyl's highly polished cars burning up, and the fire still devouring the empty space where the Jaguar's windshield had been.

He saw the man in motorcycle leathers lying on the floor, and the ax on the floor at his side. He saw these things burning in a fire that was somehow distinct from the larger fire, and yet at the same time a part of it, feeding it.

SHOREVIEW

"Guess you got cold. How long were you in the water?"

Max opened his eyes and focused. That receptionist. "You. What in Christ are you doing here?"

"Didn't want to miss the show."

"What's your name again?"

"Annie Ogden."

"You quit. What Manny said."

She nodded. "Your men over there scared the shit out of my sister. Totally despicable, totally needless. Did you think I could let that slide? Besides, you ticked me off."

He met her gaze for a moment. "What in Christ are you talking about?"

"Your meatheads. You know, the one with the bolt in his face?"

"Oh, them. What . . . are you working with Tris or something?"

Annie smiled. "Never met the girl. What made you think so?"

He huddled in his blanket for warmth, staring at her. "I ticked you off. You mind telling me how I ticked *you* off?"

"Did you do it to save money, or are you just too lazy to go through the normal recycling red tape?"

His eyes narrowed. "If I knew what in Christ you're talking about."

"Anyway, looks like you're going to be on the evening news tomorrow. Be sure to tell all your friends. That ought to put a stop to it."

"I've been shot, you know. Can't this boat go any faster? I need to get to a hospital."

"If you can throw your computers in our lake, I thought I could throw a little of the lake on your computers. That's fair, don't you think?"

He stared, trying to comprehend.

"That helicopter." A look of horrified recognition came over him. An image flashed across his brain . . . the evil helicopter, that spotlight growing larger as it came closer, flying low directly over him, dousing him with water just before dumping its load on the roof of the warehouse. "You . . . you fly helicopters!"

"Still training, actually. But of course I've got friends."

"You trashed my business," he said. "You . . . I should . . ." His arms were thrashing around under the blanket as if he meant to strangle her. She wasn't worried. It was a pretty good bet Max Vinyl wouldn't know where to start.

Something made her think of Oliver Greenwood, Michael's friend in prison. His cold eyes. If this had been Greenwood standing in front of her, ready to strangle her in his cold rage, she would have run straight to the other end of the boat and dived in the water. But this was only Max Vinyl. Besides, the captain stood directly behind her, in case of trouble.

"Say, look at that." She stood and pointed. The cameraman from Channel Nine turned quickly, aimed his camera and recorded. Everyone on the boat stared. Far away on shore, a mile or two to the north, something massive had gone up in flames. The fire burned brightly, the flames billowing high into the air. "Captain, what would that be?" Annie asked.

"About two miles off Waukegan now. Damned if I know. All those smaller secondary explosions, looks like a fireworks factory. That there's a biggie."

She saw Max staring at the fire with the rest of them, standing now, his scratched-up face a mask of anguish. The blanket fell on the floor at his feet. She looked at the fire and then back to him. What in the world was he thinking? How could you know what went through a man's mind? She thought she saw tears in his eyes.

End

FREDERICK LEE BROOKE

Did you enjoy Doing Max Vinyl? Please **recommend** it to a friend! Write a **review** if you would like to tell others about it.

Only about 18% of computer parts were recycled in 2009 in the U.S. The rest ended up in landfills or incinerators. For the latest **e-waste facts and figures** in the U.S. go to http://www.electronicstakeback.com/wp-content/uploads/Facts_and_Figures

If you have an electronic product to dispose of, bring it to one of these locations in Illinois for **recycling**: http://www.illinoisrecycles.org/byteback_list.html

If you are a **teacher** and you would like to use Doing Max Vinyl with your students, you will find exercises you can use in your classes on www.frederickleebrooke.com.

If you are in a **book club**, you will find discussion questions on Doing Max Vinyl on www.frederickleebrooke.com.

For information about **other books** by Frederick Lee Brooke go to www.frederickleebrooke.com.

Printed in Great Britain
by Amazon.co.uk, Ltd.,
Marston Gate.